Rebecca Griffiths grew up in rural mid-Wales and went on to gain a first class honours degree in English Literature. After a successful business career in London, Dublin and Scotland she returned to mid-Wales where she now lives with her husband, a prolific artist, four vampiric cats black as night, and pet sheep the size of sofas.

Also by Rebecca Griffiths

The Primrose Path

a
place

Rebecca Griffiths

to
lie

sphere

SPHERE

First published in Great Britain in 2018 by Sphere

1 3 5 7 9 10 8 6 4 2

A CIP catalogue record for this book
is available from the British Library.

Hardback ISBN 978-0-7515-6198-2
Trade Paperback ISBN 978-0-7515-6200-2

Typeset in Sabon by M Rules
Printed and bound in Great Britain by
Clays Ltd, Elcograf S.p.A.

Papers used by Sphere are from well-managed forests
and other responsible sources.

MIX
Paper from
responsible sources
FSC® C104740

Sphere
An imprint of
Little, Brown Book Group
Carmelite House
50 Victoria Embankment
London EC4Y 0DZ

An Hachette UK Company
www.hachette.co.uk

www.littlebrown.co.uk

In memory of Eira and Grace – saviours both.

Acknowledgements

Special thanks must go to my agent Jane Gregory and all at Gregory & Company, especially Stephanie Glencross for her continued guidance.

There are many people at Sphere for whose knowledge and dedication I am grateful to – patricularly, of course, Maddie West, my editor, Lucy Dauman and Thalia Proctor.

But most of all my thanks must go to my husband, Steven, for his indominitable belief, love, and creative inspiration. And last but not least, dear Harris.

I'd give all the wealth that years have piled, the slow
result of life's decay,
To be once more a little child for one bright
summer day.

Lewis Carroll

PART ONE

Present Day

She knows she's in trouble the moment she steps into the street. Corralled by looming buildings and confused by the dazzle from fiercely lit shops and headlamps, the danger that is only a heartbeat away has her braced for attack. With her bag secured across her front like a shield, she slips her hand inside to clasp the knife. Her bag, with its sharp edges and thick leather strap, works as a weapon too. She's grateful for it. And with everyone and everything a threat to her safety, she needs all the help she can get. Overtaking an androgynous couple in dark winter clothes, she spins her head to the amplified rush of tyres on wet tarmac and skids on the rain-polished pavement. Taking a moment to steady herself, she watches a dying bird at her feet – its frantic flapping is distressing, until she realises it's nothing more than a collection of dead leaves.

With her thumb caressing the pommel of the knife, she is on the move again. Supposing she doesn't see him coming ... supposing he springs out on her from behind? She shouldn't have left the flat, wouldn't have done had she not run out of food and been desperate for chocolate ... and painkillers. She's had a thumping headache all day and it's too late to do an online shop, not that she can risk strangers coming to her home.

As she negotiates the string of Bayswater streets spun with Christmas lights, the cul-de-sacs of night-time shadows take on terrifying shapes. She passes open-doored cafes, sniffs the bite of cardamom, the pungency of foreign cigarettes. Sensations once enjoyed, but now everything is tarnished and every stranger – once fascinating and captivating – is out to get her. Each laugh, too loud, too close, is spiked with menace, and the rise and fall of men's voices stoke her paranoia.

Around her, a flutter of women made black as jackdaws by a modesty of layers where faces should be. Only their hands are visible, sallow-skinned and weighted with gold; they engulf her in the smell of Chanel and Gucci. She sidesteps them by crashing through a crowd of metal chairs set out on the empty terrace of an Italian pizzeria. He could be among them – panic flares behind her ribs as she presses her broad back against a window – how would she know? The bastard could be anywhere, disguised as anyone … he could have others working for him; everyone is dangerous … everyone is after her. She thinks of the strange telephone calls in the night, the heavy-breather she swears is him, acting out some kind of psychological torture. And why wouldn't he toy with her, harass her, grind her down until she completely loses her mind? Having tracked her to Bayswater, killing her was never going to be enough; he would want to see she'd been properly punished first.

A sharp rapping on the inside of the glass. She staggers forward, lip-reads the anger spouting from the white-shirted waiter who is wielding a pepper mill and telling her to clear off.

'Fuck you,' she shouts, sticking up two fingers.

4

Her outburst appals her. This isn't how she behaves. This is his fault, her fear of him is turning her into someone she doesn't recognise. Stepping backwards, she collides with a rabble of charity fundraisers disguised as Disney characters. A man pounces, jangling a bucket of change, his Mickey Mouse mask inches from her nose.

She screams into the chaos, and the man flinches. 'Sorry, love, didn't mean to frighten ya,' he says before ducking away to re-join his troupe.

Finally, she sees the welcoming sign of her favourite mini-market. Grateful to leave the perils of the street behind, she steps inside and nods hello to the pretty Asian lad behind the till. Their eyes collide and, aware of a slight quiver in her chest, she is the first to look away. Poised for trouble, her left hand still curled around the knife deep inside her bag, she gives the CCTV camera above the counter a quick glance while reaching out with her other hand for a small trolley.

The store is unexpectedly full. She must dodge a mother pushing a toddler in a buggy and an elderly man in a grubby raincoat before she can reach the bank of confectionary. With lighting as bright and artificially jolly as the piped festive cheer circulating above, the handle of the trolley digs into her big, soft body. The young man at the till smiles as she trundles past with fairy cakes, biscuits, cocktail sausages, jumbo bags of Haribo, chocolate and packets of aspirin.

'Ice cream,' she mumbles, licking her lips as she moves along the sub-zero shelves, hunting down her favourite. There, she spots the tubs of Häagen-Dazs behind the frosted glass and tugs open the door to the accompanying blast of cold air. The movement causes two chocolate bars to fall through the mesh of the trolley and slide to the floor. She crouches to save them before they disappear under the freezer and doesn't notice the man slip free from the end of an aisle, heading straight for her, his reflection lost to the open freezer door. She isn't ready for him, realising too late she can't move. His face pressed close to hers – a face she remembers from childhood – there isn't the time to scream. She whips her head in alarm and is momentarily blinded by the too-bright strip lights as terror rumbles: a thunderstorm on her periphery. Scrabbling inside her bag, she yanks out her knife-holding hand. A scuffle. She puts up a brave fight and is surprisingly strong; she doesn't make it easy for him, but flabby and out of condition, she can't sustain it. The man is stronger.

Then she is down. The seam of her collarbone against the cold linoleum. Her attacker, a black cataract balancing on the rim of her vision, looms over her, pinning her into position. She identifies a hot feeling, deep in her abdomen. It rises up through the befuddled haze and sea of voices. Something is wedged in her side: alien, rigid; a knife, she supposes, touching it and finding it tacky with blood.

'*You?*'

The accusation is far louder in her head, the reality is little more than a whimper above Johnny Mathis telling the muddle of shoppers who've gathered round to look, to help, to *face unafraid, the plans that we've made . . .*

Breath against her lips, hotter than the steam of cooling bread, boiling through her teeth, down into her throat. Blowing her open. Stunning her like an electric charge. Conscious of a face held menacingly close to hers, the hazel eyes are the last thing she sees before her head lolls back against the floor with a sickening crack. Lips are on hers again, ungluing her mouth, and she floats to the surface of her shock.

The world turns and settles. And slipping in and out of consciousness come flickering ghosts of her childhood in Witchwood.

... the slow, summer slop of water ... bulrushes slicing her thighs ...

With her pulse pumping in her ears, she hauls her terrified gaze to the ceiling and makes one final plea for someone to save her.

But no one is listening.

... there is sand from the bank under her fingers, the harsh quack of ducks taking off from the lake, their black shapes flung against an apathetic sky ...

Her attacker's hands sheer back and wheel away.

'Please. No,' she begs, blood bubbling at her lips. 'Not like this ... *please* ...' Air hisses from her lungs. 'Not like this.'

Fearing she is about to be struck again, she scrunches her eyelids closed against the expected force. But nothing comes. When she prises her eyes open again, she sees the man lurch away, absorbed by the pulsating ice-blue lights in the street outside.

Present Day

Joanna is woken by the doorbell. It tips her out of her dreams, as does the enthusiastic barking of the family Labrador. She sits up and fumbles for the alarm clock, its green digits glowing in a room still dark. Three o'clock. The time when the warm, healthy body runs at its lowest ebb, and death certificates are signed ... these are her jumbled thoughts as she rolls sideways out of bed, careful not to wake Mike. Until she remembers, stuffing arms into her dressing gown and stumbling downstairs, Mike isn't here; he's in New York attending an end-of-year conference.

She lunges for the door and pulls it wide to find two uniformed police officers filling her porch.

'Mrs Peters?' One of them requires verification.

Joanna doesn't answer. Disorientated, she tugs the cord of her dressing gown tight against the frosty night. Peters isn't a name she goes by, she's only ever referred to as Joanna Jameson – her concert pianist's name.

'Mrs Joanna Peters?' the officer tries again, and she sees the low-slung paring of moon reflected in his polished boots.

'Y-yes, that's me,' she stammers, pushing her curls from her eyes.

'It's about your sister, Caroline,' one of them says, she isn't sure which. 'D'you think we could come inside?'

Owl-light: eerie and ominous; clogging the passageway of her beautiful Hertfordshire home. Joanna flicks on light switches as she walks, conscious only of the plush carpet pile between her toes. Reaching the lounge, they stand together and she plucks words from the gloom: '... *ambulance called ... knife attack ... a twenty-seven-year-old man living in the area ... in police custody ... arrested at the scene ... we're dreadfully sorry, no one could get to her in time ...*'

'*What?* What are you saying? It can't be ... it can't be Carrie.' Joanna's incredulity spins and flaps around the room.

'Is your husband home, Mrs Peters?' The same voice punctures her crowding confusion.

She stares at the floor, shakes her head. 'No,' she says limply. 'Mike's in America. He's not due back till Christmas Eve.'

'Right.' The police officers exchange looks. 'It's just that we will need you to come in and identify your sister's body.'

'*Identify her body?* What, *now?*' Joanna is horrified.

'As soon as you can, Mrs Peters.'

'Isn't there anyone else who can do it?'

'Afraid not, Mrs Peters. You're her next of kin. That's correct, isn't it?'

'Yes. Yes, I suppose it is.' Eyes downcast. 'But not on my own.' Anxiety rising. 'I don't have to come on my own, do I? I'll call Mike ... ask him to get the next flight home. Can it wait until then? A couple of days?'

'Well, it'll have to, if that's what you'd prefer. But is there someone we can call for you in the meantime? You really shouldn't be on your own.'

'No. It's okay.' She reaches out to touch the Christmas tree glinting through the dark, its artificial branches laden

9

with decorations her sons put up in readiness for their father's return. 'I've got my boys . . . my boys are here.'

Joanna looks away. Out through the darkened window-pane on to a strange moon-washed land where a cold wind from childhood blows. Echoes of things long past ring in her ears as she refocuses on the brace of police officers and shivers, fearing at any moment that Freddie and Ethan will wake and come padding downstairs, demanding answers their mother cannot give.

When the police leave, Joanna sits on the bottom stair, rigid with shock. Buttons finds her and drops his heavy head in her lap, nudging her fingers with his wet nose.

'Good boy.' She ruffles his fur and is grateful for the company.

Staring at her feet, which are as blue as the murky edges of dawn beyond the glass panel of the front door, she tries to absorb the horror of what she's been told. Repeating her sister's name over and over until it becomes flat and feeble, bleached of meaning.

Mike. She needs to talk to him. Only five hours behind, he might still be awake; it won't yet be midnight in New York. She dials the number she knows by heart and he picks up after the second ring.

'Hi, babe. How're you doing?'

'Mike, love.' Her face crumples at the sound of his voice. 'Thank God you're there,' she says, and bursts into tears.

Summer 1990

The women of Witchwood carried bundles of arum lilies into the church. Armfuls of them. Large, white trumpet-headed blooms, which were already beginning to rot. The centuries-old stone walls of St Oswald's could generally be relied upon to keep the outside out. But not today. Today, with the congregation swelling by the minute, transporting the freakish heat within the darkened pleats of their clothes, it bordered on unbearable.

Dora Muller, in her mid-fifties with hair as black as it was when she was seventeen, was seated near the front, a great-niece squashed either side of her ampleness. With her money-slot mouth pursed for the occasion, her Delft Blue irises missed nothing and no one. Who were they all? She blinked in disbelief: Derek Hooper had been bedbound for years. These weren't villagers; the inhabitants of this Gloucestershire parish barely amounted to a handful ... her thoughts as she sieved through faces, dabbing perspiration from her dispropor-tionately tiny nose with an embroidered handkerchief. She saw Cecilia Mortmain, the vicar's attractive and considerably younger wife, tucked out of harm's way at the back. A surprise to see her – diagnosed with multiple sclerosis some years ago, and more recently confined to a wheelchair, she wasn't seen around the village all that often any more.

Dora's great-nieces, fidgety in their finery – well, the finest of what they brought with them; no one had envisaged their need to attend a funeral here – swivelled on the pew for news of what was going on behind them. They were greeted by row upon row of impeccably turned-out women in extravagant hats, who fanned their own corpselike foreheads with the Order of Service. Catching their eye, Tilly Petley – co-owner with her husband, Frank, of Witchwood's only shop – bestowed a generous wink. Shy under her unexpected interest, the sisters turned to the front again, but not before they noticed Cecilia Mortmain.

'Who's that pretty lady?' Thirteen-year-old Caroline: surly, complex, her hen-brown hair scooped back in its Alice band.

'*Shhh.*' Dora pressed a finger to her lips.

Luckily the barn-like church interior held greater interest. Caroline extended a hand to touch the smudged gold Cotswold stone. But ashamed of her bitten nails, she jerked her fingers back and burrowed them in the pocket of her dress to twirl the little flat vanes on a silver teaspoon that, fashioned into a windmill, was just one of the things she'd pinched from her great-aunt's holiday cottage.

'That's Mrs Hooper playing, isn't it?' she asked Dora's glistening top lip as the organ wheezed its way through 'I Heard a Voice From Heaven'. Poor Dora. Sweltering inside her big, black corduroy smock, smelling of mothballs.

'Well,' Dora began, and the sisters, trapped within their humble box pew, felt a story coming on. 'Lillian was a pupil of the great Herbert Howells, you know, and she said she summoned her husband, Derek, by tinkling the ivories. So now, I suppose –' Dora wrinkled her powdered nose against the stench of pollen, fearful of sneezing '– she's tinkling them to send him on his way.'

Mrs Hooper was like the Pied Piper of Witchwood and had been summoning the village children with her piano playing for years. Caroline and Joanna were no exception: breezing past Pludd Cottage on their first afternoon, they were instantly captivated. With her back to the congregation, Lillian Hooper, refined and upright, rotated her gaze to the Reverend Timothy Mortmain as if in anticipation of some celestial deliverance. Her hair, the sisters decided early on, was the same colour and as shiny as the new copper boiler their landlord had recently fitted in their Camden flat.

'That's nice.' It was Joanna who answered Dora, her fingers travelling an imaginary keyboard on her plump thighs in the way Mrs Hooper was teaching her. She kept time by swinging her nine-year-old feet in their Daz-white socks that wouldn't even reach the pedals in her mind. Unlike the effortless grace of Mrs Hooper who, bathed in a halo of light, easily manipulated the organ's complicated pedals in her pretty shoes.

'It is romantic, isn't it?' Dora flapped her handkerchief in front of her face. 'But then, what would I know of such things?' She tipped her head to the eaves and pressed her varnished nails to a brooch belonging to her late mother, which was fastened at her neck.

Joanna and Caroline tilted forward over the mass of their great-aunt and exchanged an eye roll, before dropping into a soulful silence designed to convince their guardian of their good intentions.

Dora dipped her head. 'You're such darling girls,' she cooed, and abandoned her brooch to clasp their little hands in each of hers. 'You wait –' she jiggled them up and down '– us three, we're going to have the best time ever.'

Joanna, smiling up at the double chin that belied her daintily featured great-aunt, listened to the promise as the congregation rose to its feet to greet the pallbearers, swaying and sweating under the weight of Derek Hooper's conker-shiny coffin as it made its slow procession up the aisle.

The Boar's Head wasn't the best place to host a wake. Poky and smoke-filled, the main bar, dubbed *saloon* by its regulars, was shabby and sad. But Derek Hooper, in the days he was still able to hobble over here, had loved it, and Liz and Ian Fry, joint licensees for the past two years, were doing their utmost to accommodate the mourners dribbling along the cathedral-like nave of horse chestnuts into the pub.

Fizzing with enthusiasm, Liz Fry's bottle-blonde head bobbed in and out of the kitchen at the side of the bar, encouraging people into the pleasant beer garden. She was right – with tables and benches set under trees spilling in from the woods, there were plenty of shady places to sit.

'We're still in the process of refurbishing,' Caroline heard Liz explain to Dora, who wouldn't ordinarily be seen dead in a pub. 'We've big plans for the place.'

Dora and her nieces did as they were told and helped themselves from the buffet. Holding paper plates with deltas of green serviette, they made their selection from the mini pizzas and chicken drumsticks sprinkled with parsley, and carried their choices outside into the prickling heat. They found a spot under a broad parasol where, beyond the various trunks of trees, the wide bake of yellow wheat fields shimmered under a relentless sun. Dora, her dress stretched taut across her fat knees, pecked at a portion of coronation chicken, her head darting like the sparrows in Mrs Hooper's garden, reluctant to miss a thing.

The prawn cocktail vol-au-vent tasted stale. Taking a bite and deciding she didn't like it, Caroline got up to hide it under a yellow ashtray advertising Double Diamond on a nearby table.

'I saw you.'

A voice close to her ear. She twisted to receive it.

Wow. Cool, laid-back, nicer-looking than any of the sixth-form boys at school in his Levi 501s and Guns N' Roses T-shirt. I love him, she decided in an instant, blushing pink as a heart.

'Who are you then?' the boy quizzed while she stared, troubled by the image of herself – the long, pale face, the high slope of forehead – reflected in the curved mirror-lenses of his sunglasses.

'I-I'm C-C-Caroline . . . Carrie.' She eventually tipped her name out of her mouth.

'*Carrie.* Yeah – like it, sweet.' He shook out his dishev-elled light brown hair that was curling beyond his collar. 'Seen you about, ain't I?'

'Have you?' Boys didn't usually notice Caroline, not boys like this one, anyway, unless it was to bully and taunt.

'Yeah, playing in the woods and that.' His accent dis-patched him back to the Surrey town of Weybridge where he'd been born. 'On your hols then, are ya?'

'S-sort of,' she stammered, worrying the velvet trim at her neckline. 'Our mum . . . she's not very well, so me and

15

Jo ... we're staying at Pillowell Cottage with our great-aunt for the summer.'

'I know her. I do her garden. Right barrel-load of fun, ain't she?'

It was difficult for Caroline to know if this was a question or statement. She shifted uneasily from one sock and sandaled foot to the other.

'Don't suppose you fancy earnin' a bit of pocket money while you're here?' he asked. 'Course, I'll have to square it with me stepmum first, but this time o' year, reckon we could do with an extra pair of hands.'

'Doing what?' Caroline squinted into the green sting of chlorophyll trembling through the trees.

'You're too young to pull pints.' A burst of laughter; not mocking, but not flattering either. 'So, collecting glasses, washing up, that kinda thing.'

'De-an ... De-an ...' someone yelled.

'That's me.' He whipped his head to the call. 'Wanna come with me now? Could ask Liz what she thinks about you working here, then.'

'Now? Y-you want me to come now? Y-yeah, all right.' Caroline gawped at Dean's long-legged leanness, the muscled bronze of his suntanned arms, his invitation taking a moment to filter through.

Joanna, a plate of gala pie and quartered sandwiches in her lap, watched her sister and the older boy disappear through a rainbow-coloured fly screen at the rear of the pub. Keen to follow, to find out what her sister was up to, she was about to abandon her lunch and go after them when she spotted Frank Petley standing close by. Joanna froze under his gaze. Familiar with him from her visits with Caroline to Witchwood's only shop, she didn't like Mr Petley's creepy-eyed stare or the smile that always seemed to loiter at the edge of his mouth. Girdled by hollyhocks bent under the weight of the weather, he was so still, so quiet, Joanna hadn't realised he was there. Frightened by his presence, she changed her mind about following her sister and was about to alert Dora to him, when a squeal from her great-aunt stopped her in her tracks.

'Oh, Gordon. There you are! I've been looking for you.' Dora, forgetting the solemnity of the occasion, inadvertently made Joanna forget Caroline and the boy.

A man in his late twenties sashayed towards them. Reedily tall like the bulrushes growing down by the clear stretch of water the sisters had learnt to call Drake's Pike, he had a puff of blue-black hair and was clean-shaven inside a dark Armani suit. Joanna watched him swap his gold-tipped cocktail cigarette into his sherry-holding hand and plant a kiss on Dora's cheek, exhaling smoke into her wedge of hair.

'How fine you look.' Dora, insouciant to the disapproval of mourners slinking like black cats into the beer garden, called loudly, over-the-top, 'Girls, *girls*! Come and meet Gordon.' And with further squeals of delight she grabbed Joanna's arms and offered her up to him. 'Where's your sister gone?' she queried, but not with any zeal; Gordon Hooper held far greater interest. 'My, you look wonderful. *Wonderful*. Italy certainly agrees with you.' Dora continued to flirt. 'This is Joanna. Imogen's youngest.'

'So, *you're* Joanna, are you?' Gordon spoke slowly. 'Goodness me, how frighteningly like your mother you are.'

'Like my mother?' Joanna beamed up at him. He had

a kind face and she liked how his eyes were as pale as the liquid in his glass.

'Oh, yes,' he said, and sipped his Tio Pepe. 'Your mother and me ... well, we were great friends once. Not that I've seen her for, oh ...' He hesitated. 'At least a decade.'

Gordon's interest was then stolen by a little girl around Joanna's age in an acid-yellow dress who glided with considerable proficiency across the parched ground on roller skates. Turning from Dora and Joanna, he abandoned his cigarette and sherry to greet her.

'*Ellie!*' he cried, throwing his arms in the air. 'How tall you're growing.' And he dived to gather the child in a ball of giggles. 'I won't be able to call you my little babe in the woods for much longer, will I?'

Home from the Continent, where he crafted violins for a living, Gordon Hooper had chosen to keep a low profile during his father's funeral and rejected the vicar's suggestion to read a eulogy. But swirling Ellie Fry around on her wheels, making her brown pigtails swing, her cheeks bloom cherry-pink, he obviously had no qualms about drawing attention to himself now. As lithe and strong as a trapeze artist, Gordon hoisted the child on to his shoulders and, spurred on by Ellie's shrieks of delight, the two of them played as if no one was watching.

To hide her embarrassment at Gordon's flagrant snub, Dora drained her second gin and tonic to the sinister accompaniment of tinkling ice cubes, and left behind a smear of lipstick: a stamp of protest against the glass. Others by now had tuned into the strange spectacle. Inching in from the shadows, they formed a ring around this loose-limbed man and pretty child. Dora watched too, frowning heavily as Ellie's skater dress lifted up for everyone to see the playground scuffs on her dimpled knees, the nasty set of bruises on the insides of her thighs.

The pub's landlord, Ian Fry, was also watching. Keeping guard from a dish of dappled shade, he gripped a tray of empties in his yellow smoker's fingers and focused hard on Ellie and Gordon Hooper – a man, it was clear from his expression, he neither trusted nor liked. Ian's bald, suntanned scalp gleamed like polished pine as he stepped forward into the high, bright sunshine. Joanna saw the muscles ripple in his bullish neck and the trace of a smile quivering on his lips. A smile she wasn't equipped to read.

'Is no one going to stop him?' Dora, tipsy from one too many. 'Love him as I do, this isn't appropriate – today of all days,' she voiced to no one in particular.

But it was Ellie herself who brought the shenanigans to a close, screaming and laughing, tugging at Gordon's dark mop of hair, threatening to be sick.

Present Day

Joanna stares at the shape beneath the white shroud.

'Yes,' she croaks to the hand folding back the sheet in the cream-walled room and revealing the waxy quality of Caroline's face, her naked shoulders. 'Yes,' she sobs, breaking down completely. 'This is my sister. This is Carrie.'

Caroline Jameson lies stretched out under the starched sheet. Joanna studies the peculiar emptiness that has invaded her sister's face. It is as if the horror of her death has been nullified and erased. Caroline's skin, radiant and wrinkle-free, is flushed with a delicate tint of rosiness that softens her in a way life never did. Death, it seems, has transformed the forty-one-year-old Caroline into the girl she once was – the girl she was when she and Joanna had still been friends.

It is as if Joanna's flood defences have crumbled, unleashing years of pent-up sadness and loss. Weeping uncontrollably, she holds Mike so fiercely he must prise her fingers, one by one, away from his arm. Then, helped to a chair and forced to sit, Joanna waits until she is able to walk out into the corridor.

Afterwards, seated alongside her husband in a barren interview room at the police station, she fires off question after question.

'So, you've released this Kyle Norris without charge?'

'That's right, Mrs Peters. The CCTV the shop provided was pretty conclusive,' Detective Sergeant Pike, a man sporting a set of teeth to match his namesake, does his best to clarify.

'*Conclusive*? How so?' Joanna frowns.

'In that it distinctly shows your sister pulling a knife from her bag and attacking *him*.' He elaborates, 'We've several witnesses who corroborate this too. Their statements are clear: Caroline tried to stab him, he grabbed the knife to save himself, but in the struggle between them – and it was quite a struggle – it seems your sister inadvertently stabbed herself.' A pause. 'She was very unlucky.' He takes his time. 'The single stab wound severed an artery. It meant she died before the paramedics could reach her.'

'But – but this is ... is ... ' Joanna can't find the words. '*Madness*.' She twists to Mike, then DS Pike. 'Pulled a knife from her bag, you say – but why would she be carrying a knife?'

'We were hoping you might be able to shed some light on that for us.' The detective picks at a spray of tomato pips on his tie.

Joanna tugs out her bottom lip. 'I'm sorry, but I don't know. Carrie and I fell out. Well, what I mean is, she fell out with me. At Dora's funeral.'

'And Dora was?' the detective wants to know.

'Our great-aunt. On our mother's side. It was the last time Carrie and I saw one another. Ten years ago ... ' *God, is it really that long*? she says to herself. 'And apart from a couple of failed telephone conversations when our mum died two years ago, we've barely spoken.'

'Right, I see. You say your sister fell out with you – can I ask why?'

Joanna swallows. Fiddles with the frayed hem of her scarf.

'Look—' Mike inhales through his nostrils. 'To say Carrie wasn't the easiest of people would be putting it mildly.' Ever protective of his wife, he picks up Joanna's hand and holds it against his chest.

'It's all right, Mike,' Joanna says softly. 'I'll tell him.' And taking back her hand, addresses the detective: 'Things between me and Carrie were never all that good. We had a tricky home life,' she says, as if this explains everything. 'It was okay when we were kids, I suppose. Although,' a quick glance at her husband, 'we weren't ever right after that summer with Dora.' Joanna slides her gaze to the policeman again. 'Some people would say what we experienced in that place should have brought us closer together, but it didn't, it pushed us apart – not that I want to go into all that now.' She pauses. 'I'm surmising, of course I am, because I could never get my sister to talk about it, so I don't even know if it was based on anything rational – but I think Carrie's underlying problem with me was that I reminded her of that summer. But anyway, whatever it was, it just got worse when she hit puberty and then persisted right through her twenties … Carrie was thirty-one when I last saw her – I'm younger, four years younger,' she tells him. 'Our mum's mental state was always pretty fragile, Carrie's was the same. But I don't want you thinking I was the one who gave up on her, I wanted to be there for her, we both did.' Another look at her husband. 'But she didn't want me around. Simple as that.'

'I see.' A sober nod from the detective.

'But what she did, it was so violent.' Joanna has questions

22

of her own. 'Volatile, she might have been, but not violent. This is so unlike her.'

'But a person could change drastically over a decade, don't you think?'

'I suppose,' Joanna says, thoughtful. 'But it still doesn't make sense. Did this Kyle bloke and Carrie know each other?'

'He says not,' Pike replies mildly.

'Poor guy. Was he all right?' Joanna shrinks from her inquiry, fearing the answer. 'He didn't have to go to hospital or anything, did he?'

'He needed medical attention at the scene for a cut to his arm, but no, he didn't require hospital treatment.'

'Poor bugger. He must've been pretty shaken up.' Mike rakes a hand through his thick sandy hair.

'He was rather traumatised, yes.'

'I can imagine.' Mike raises his eyebrows.

'You say Kyle lives in Bayswater?' Joanna asks DS Pike. 'That he moved to the area six months ago.'

'That's right.'

'Could I see him, d'you think? Talk to him?' She wrings her hands in her lap.

'I'm afraid not, Mrs Peters.' The detective shuffles his papers together. 'As terrible as this is for you and your family, the man did nothing wrong.'

'Oh, no. *No.* Of course he didn't. I wasn't for a minute suggesting he had,' Joanna, backpedalling. 'But he might know something, something that'd help me to understand why Carrie did what she did.'

'Leave it, love,' Mike advises. 'We're the last people he'd want to see. We should think ourselves lucky he's not pressing for damages.'

'But how am I going to find out what happened? I've got to find out why she armed herself with a knife – haven't I?'

Joanna gives way to further tears. Sitting on her hands, she half expects someone to dig her in the ribs, to tell her to pull herself together, but no one does.

A door creaks open behind them. 'Sarge?' The brown head of a uniformed officer beckons to his superior.

'Won't be a moment,' Joanna and Mike are informed as Pike rises from his chair and leaves the room.

'Why don't they know anything, *want* to know anything? Don't they want to find out what happened?' Joanna keeps her voice low.

'It's not that they're not interested, Jo-Go.' Mike yawns: jet-lagged after his unexpected need to fly home; he hasn't even had the chance to change out of his suit. 'It's probably got more to do with limited manpower, resources, that kind of thing. Because I'm telling you, if your sister had survived this, well –' he loosens his tie '– she'd be in pretty hot water, wouldn't she?'

'I should have been there for her. I should have tried harder. I was a rotten sister.'

'No, you weren't.' Mike slips an arm around her, cuddles her close. 'Everything we ever did she threw back in our faces. And I don't mean to sound disrespectful, babe, but your sister was her own worst enemy.' He buries his nose in his wife's saffron curls. 'And I'm sorry to say it, but I could see it a mile off, even if you couldn't – Carrie resented you, pure and simple.'

'I suppose.' Her response smothered by his shoulder. 'But she was my sister – I was all she had.'

'Then she should have looked after you better then, shouldn't she?' Mike is firm.

'I know what you're saying, but I should've tried harder to stay in touch. Just because she could be a bit difficult—'

'A *bit difficult*,' Mike splutters, releasing his hold. 'Remember when you were going through your chemotherapy, the way she spoke to you. The way she slammed the phone down on you.' His face is serious. 'That was the most terrible time in your life and she treated you like that? What was it she said – oh, yeah, that's right: "It's all about *you*, isn't it?" – well, yeah, for once it was, and if that wasn't a sure indication of how little she cared, then I don't know what was.' He tips his head to the bald bulb above their heads, blinks back tears. 'I'm sorry, Jo, but I can't forgive her for that, and neither should you. Yes, of course I'm sorry she's died, that she died in such an awful way, but I'm not having you blaming yourself for the way her life worked out – you did nothing wrong, you've nothing to reproach yourself for.'

'I know.' Joanna forces a smile. 'You're right. I know you're right.' She listens to the emptiness of her words. This isn't what she feels, not deep down, but her relationship with Caroline has been a bone of contention between her and Mike throughout their fifteen years of marriage and she hasn't the strength to argue about it now.

'I'm only thinking of you, love.' Mike softens, conscious of the opening door and the re-emergence of DS Pike. 'I just don't want you making yourself ill again, that's all.'

'Sorry to abandon you like that,' the detective apologises and passes Joanna a large plastic box. 'Your sister's things,' he explains. 'They were found on her when she died.'

Joanna squints through wet lashes at the array of objects.

There isn't much, but in the same way Mike does, she looks at them carefully. Aside from a large handbag, there's a decent-looking watch, its leather strap smeared with what can only be blood. A credit card. A ten-pound note along with some coins. A thin gold chain knotted with her sister's brown hairs.

'And, I'm sorry if it's distressing, but I do need to ask ...' The detective holds up a clear plastic bag, its insides streaked with blood. It contains a hefty-looking knife with a German inscription etched along its blade. 'You don't happen to recognise it, do you?'

Joanna sucks back her breath. 'Is that it? Is that the knife ... the knife t-that ... that killed her?'

The detective's expression confirms it is.

'But ... but—' She struggles to unravel what it is she's seeing. 'That was Dora's ... Dora's dagger ...' she splutters, jabbing a finger at its silver cross-guards and swastika logo. 'It belonged to her father ... our great-grandfather. I thought Dora chucked the bloody thing out years ago.' Her revelation splinters the unforgiving light. 'What the hell was Carrie doing with it?'

Summer 1990

Dora had driven into town. She said she needed the super-market and they could entertain themselves for a few hours, couldn't they? It wasn't a question, more a demand, and one the sisters mulled over as they watched their great-aunt reverse her Morris Traveller with its rotting mock-Tudor sides out into the lane and beetle away. They hadn't minded being left behind, far preferring a day playing in the woods with Ellie Fry to crowds and pavements. And besides, they were used to fending for themselves with a mother too weighed down by her own misery to bother with them – things in leafy Witchwood under Dora's care weren't all that different.

The sisters slotted into a certain routine and soon forgot the troubles at home in London – the mother they loved and feared in equal measure, the nastier elements of school. It all dispersed like pollen from forgotten flowers. Even their Camden flat was like a distant memory. Fitted with a frugal mismatch of their landlord's furniture, the mildewed tiles in the bathroom they needed to share with another family, their mother's tights drip-drying above a sink of dirty dishes. Pillowell Cottage, with its opulence and abundant clutter, harboured a surprising amount of space for their fantasies and at least seemed to want them.

Home, with its upset smiles and their mother's hopelessness, was no place to return to.

Washed and dressed in record time, they flung what they could find for lunch into a pair of khaki knapsacks, fastened themselves into matching pink jelly sandals and headed off to find Ellie.

'Your auntie home?' Clean-shaven with an unnerving Plasticine sheen, Frank Petley at Dora's gate blocked their egress. 'I've come to collect paper money,' he said, jingling coins in his trouser pocket.

'Sorry, she had to go out,' Caroline told him, then instantly regretted it – Mr Petley knowing she and Joanna were alone made her uneasy.

'Mind you tell her she owes us in shop.' Frank, devoid of smile. 'Memory like a sieve, that woman. There'll be no more deliveries of *Telegraph* till she settles bill,' he warned in his ripe Yorkshire accent before striding away.

Sweltering already and it wasn't even ten o'clock. Caroline, Joanna and Ellie grappled with ways to kill the time. Hidden in trees and cloaked in a relentless melancholy, Witchwood, with its tall, dark forest, had frightened the sisters to begin with, but left to their own devices they have become enchanted with its fairy-tale beauty.

Not that everything was as it should have been in this idyllic playground. There were maleficent forces at work. But chattering happily the girls were unaware of the eyes in the dense, dark shade, watching them.

The children left the main section of the village behind and ambled along the traffic-free lane, stopping when they reached the crossroads.

'Dare you.' Joanna pointed in the direction of Dead End Lane: a narrowing stretch of tarmac hooded in greenery that led to St Oswald's church and its spooky, high-sided rectory.

'I'm up for it.' Caroline, inspecting her bitten nails, began to gnaw her middle finger.

'We could look round the graveyard?' Ellie suggested brightly, scissoring back and forth on her wheels.

'Did that yesterday.' Caroline scowled, her attention momentarily snatched by a red tractor inching its way along a farm track beyond the trees.

'I don't mind what we do,' Joanna said.

At the end of the lane, the girls straddled the squat church wall, the stones hot against their bare thighs as they traced the tapestry of lichen with outspread fingers. Mindful of the repetitive *coo-coo* of a woodpigeon: a far sweeter sound, the Jameson sisters judged, than the fume-choked song of London pigeons that their mother called vermin. It was difficult to stoke up the spirit of sadness in the champagne sparkle of such a morning, but over the children's backs was the most romantic necropolis for miles. An extraordinary nirvana flaunting gleaming sandstone monuments and pink gravelled paths that criss-crossed beneath the glamorous spread of oaks and sycamores.

'Wanna try my roller skates?' Ellie fiddled with her bunches and swung her feet high into the air to tempt them.

'Me first.' Caroline relinquished her nail-chewing and jumped down from the wall. 'I'm the oldest.' She unlaced the skates and slipped them free of Ellie's feet.

'Best sit down to put them on.' It was clear to Ellie from

Caroline's huffing and puffing that she was about to lose her temper. 'You tried them before?'

'Course I have, stupid – I've been ice-skating; it can't be any harder than that.'

'You look like one of the ugly sisters in *Cinderella*.' Ellie throttled a giggle.

Red-faced from the effort, Caroline balanced on one leg. 'It won't go on,' she snapped at Joanna as if this was her fault, and flung the skate at her.

Joanna took it and spun the plastic wheels, making them rattle and whirl. The sound reminded Caroline of the windmill teaspoon she'd pinched from Dora. Not that the teaspoon was the only thing she'd stolen, and it made her quiver with unease to think of the brass table bell, the snuff box and the little beaded drawstring bag she found in her great-aunt's jewellery box. Trinkets, that along with other things pilfered from the pub and Mrs Hooper's, she'd squirrelled away by the reed-edged lake. But observing Ellie and Joanna's togetherness, their easiness, sensing they were deliberately shutting her out, Caroline understood exactly why she stole things. Things could be relied upon, it was people who let her down. Her thoughts were gloomy ones as she listened to Ellie encouraging her sister to 'Have a go, it's easy when you get the hang of it.' Then watching her kneel down to lace them up, the pair of them laughing, indifferent to her.

The roller skates were a perfect fit. Upright and trundling over the apron of lawn that skirted the churchyard, Joanna, blind to her sister's seething disapproval, appeared to be enjoying herself.

'You can have them if you want – I'm getting a new pair

for my birthday.' Ellie beamed. 'Hey,' she added. 'You two have gotta come to my party next Saturday. It's gonna be brilliant. Daddy's doing me a pin-the-tail-on-the-donkey and everything.'

'You're lucky to have a daddy,' Caroline said, dampening the mood. 'We haven't got a daddy, have we, Jo?'

Joanna shook her head, the baby-blue of her eyes downcast.

'He drowned in the sea. Five years ago. We were on holiday in Wales, he saved me from the waves.' Caroline, her voice proud, wholeheartedly believed it was necessary to share this painful history to make herself sound more interesting.

'Oh, that's horrible.' Ellie looked shocked.

'It's why we're here. Mum's been so sad about it she tried to kill herself. Dora's the only family we've got to stay with while she recovers in the loony bin.' Caroline shared the cruel taunt she suffered in the playground as if it meant nothing.

Ellie reached for Caroline's arm. 'Later, if you want,' she said, squeezing it, 'you can play in the Wendy house Daddy made me?'

'No, thanks, I'll manage.' Uncomfortable with being touched, Caroline stepped away, pretended the Judas tree propped against the churchyard wall was of interest. 'But we'll definitely come to your party,' she said stiffly, kicking through what remained of the pink blossom embedded at its roots.

'I love birthday parties.' Joanna spread her arms to balance as she skated round and round.

'Like you've ever been to any,' Caroline sneered.

'I love these too.' Joanna ignored her sister and looked at her feet. 'You sure I can have them?'

'Course you can – I won't need them, will I?'

'Ellie! You're brilliant.' Joanna laughed her thanks to her new best friend, but clocking her sister's annoyance added, 'I'd better give them back to you for now. We should go and do something else.'

'Yeah, come on.' Caroline lifted her hands, scooped her damp hair from the back of her neck. 'Dead boring watching you on them – I wanna go down Drake's Pike.'

'We could take the boat out,' Ellie said as she re-laced her skates.

The sisters, contemplating the miserable supplies scraped together from Pillowell's kitchen, hoped Liz had thought to pack extras for them.

'Can we go through the tunnel?' Joanna asked.

'Yeah, be cool in there.'

'*If you go down to the woods today ...*' one of them piped, and within seconds all three were singing their version of the vaguely sinister tune, '*... you'd better not go alone ... beneath the trees where nobody sees ...*'

One rolling, two skipping – the children were still being watched as they pushed open the five-bar gate and dissolved into the dark-throated woods. Not only by the menace hiding among the gravestones, or the quizzical-eyed buzzard fixed to a telegraph pole, but a woman doomed to look out on a world she could no longer move within. And had any of them stopped to look up at the imposing rectory – a Georgian manor rising incongruously from the regal layering of blue-green cedars – they'd have seen the Reverend Mortmain's wife, Cecilia, trapped by her multiple sclerosis inside its wisteria-smothered façade. Spectral and seated at a lofty window with only her Rapunzel-long hair for company, even if she had been aware someone was watching the children, she'd have been powerless to rescue them had they found themselves in trouble.

Present Day

More flowers than mourners at Caroline's funeral and even these are thin on the ground. Joanna grips Mike's hand and tries to hold it together as she stares at the pale wood coffin. Unable to join in with the feeble warbling of 'Abide With Me' – her sister's favourite hymn – she hears a sweet and strong soprano from somewhere at the back take the lead. She is grateful for it; grateful things at least go without a hitch. She doesn't flinch once during the service. Not when the Reverend Hugh Mumford fluffs the lines she wrote for him and needs a glug of water from the bottle by his elbow, or when the coffin slides behind the curtain and disappears forever.

Some of her father's relatives are here. Huddling together at the back of the east London crematorium, clutching wreaths they don't know what to do with. Dressed in black, they're like the scavenging crows that crowd the bins in the park on sunny afternoons. Barely recognising them, Joanna has nothing to say and refuses their frosty sympathies, their automatic shoulder squeezes. She recalls their ineptitude, and worse, their condemnation at her mother's failed suicide attempt when she and Caroline were small. Every member of her family, apart from Great-Aunt Dora, turned their backs on them, reluctant to sully their sanitised lives with their troubles. Joanna can't forgive them, not that they've asked for forgiveness, and having them within her sights makes her skin shrink inside her clothes.

She hasn't the faintest idea how they got to hear about Caroline. Yes, she supposes – even though she's been avoiding the newspapers – her sister's violent death would undoubtedly have been reported, but she and Mike haven't told a soul. Her colleagues at the Royal College of Music haven't been informed yet, so even if they had read about Caroline's death in the papers they wouldn't know she was Joanna's sister. But this is how bad news travels – it was the same when their mother died two years ago – because not one of her father's lot congratulates Joanna on her sell-out performances at the Wigmore Hall last month. Not one of them seems to have caught that.

She can't help but be embarrassed by the lack of numbers, the lack of occasion; sitting with Mike in an otherwise empty row at the front of the chapel of rest, Joanna's thankful the boys aren't here to see it. The place provides no more reverence than a village hall, with its pine-clad walls and high glass ceiling. And afterwards, chivvied along by a team of obsequious undertakers, they are ushered out under a stone-hard sky in time to see another cortege move up the long avenue of gravestones. Like a bloody death factory, she thinks, her mind whirling as she watches funeral cars disgorge themselves of mourners who, whiplashed by the tails of their coats, stand shivering in the December wind, waiting their turn.

'Joanna.'

A voice beside her: timid, hesitant, breaking her mood.

She turns to a tall, stylish, white-haired woman, her dark wool coat buttoned to the neck.

'No – it can't be?' Joanna clamps a sodden tissue to her mouth in disbelief.

As slender and upright as ever, Mrs Hooper has barely changed. Impossible to think – Joanna does a swift calculation of the years to have fallen between – Lillian Hooper must be at least eighty.

'How lovely to see you.' Mike gives Mrs Hooper a kiss.

'Are you coping all right?' Mrs Hooper enquires and Joanna sees again her kind, knowing eyes. 'Such a terrible thing to happen, I'm so very sorry about Carrie.'

'It's so good to see you.' Joanna presses her lips to Mrs Hooper's powdered cheek. They stay like this for a long time, Joanna's gratitude crackling like static into Mrs Hooper's hair, its scent of lily-of-the-valley opening the door on to that childhood summer in Witchwood. The two of them singing and playing the piano together, before everything was blighted and a blackness descended on the village.

'It's amazing to see you,' Joanna reiterates when they finally pull apart. 'I can't believe you're here – how many years has it been?' Trembling against the cold, she finds a dry corner of tissue and dabs her nose.

'Ten. Dora's funeral.' Mike does the maths.

'Well remembered . . . and what a fraught day that was.' Mrs Hooper digs Joanna a fresh tissue from her bag.

'That was the last time I saw Carrie,' Joanna says. And fearing she will cry again, focuses on the impossible shine on Mrs Hooper's patent-leather shoes. 'Are you still living in Witchwood?'

'Yes, still there.' A small smile.

'However did you manage the journey?' Mike poses the question Joanna was about to ask, the pair of them noticing that as well as a matching patent-leather handbag, Mrs Hooper is also armed with a stick.

'I'm staying with my sister in Wandsworth – she invites me now and again.'

'And how did you hear about Carrie?' Joanna sniffs, plucks a Labrador hair off Mike's coat.

'Oh, that was Gordon – one of the rare occasions he actually telephoned me.'

How did he find out, Joanna wonders, did he read it in the papers too? 'Is Gordon here?' is all she asks, spinning to look for him.

'No. He couldn't make it. He sends his condolences.'

Joanna dips her head, thinks again how little Mrs Hooper has aged; aside from her snow-white hair she's exactly the same.

'He sent flowers.'

'Yes, it was a big surprise to see them. Please thank him for us.'

'I'm sure he'd love to see you,' Mrs Hooper says. 'He's quite the devoted fan. You won't know it, Jo, but he's been following your career from the off. Buys all your CDs.'

'That's so sweet.' Joanna blushes without knowing why. 'How is he, is he still in Italy?'

'Oh, no. He retired. Couple of years ago. He lives in London now. Not that it means I get to see him any more frequently.'

'Has he got a family, kids?' Mike asks.

'No, dear. There was someone special once. A lifetime

ago. But she was already married. I'm not entirely sure he ever got over her,' Mrs Hooper says forlornly. Then, eyes brightening, an idea forming, 'Why don't you bring your boys to Witchwood? Gordon might actually come and visit me if he knew you were going to be there. You could stay at Pillowell – it's yours now, isn't it?'

'Oh, I don't know.' Joanna shifts her gaze to her husband.

'Yeah, the cottage must be in a hell of a state by now.' Mike, keen to put obstacles in the way, is fully aware of his wife's reluctance to return to Witchwood, and the nightmares she still suffers from because of what she experienced there. 'Jo said it was a bit of a wreck back then and I doubt Carrie's bothered with it.'

'No, I don't think she did. Dora was silly; it would have made much more sense for her to leave the cottage to you two after Carrie'd been given the London flat. Anyway, don't let that put you off, I don't think it's too bad. Tilly Petley keeps an eye, puts the heating on, that sort of thing, and Frank does the garden, any urgent maintenance – Dora fixed it up with them years back. They're still being paid out of her estate so far as I know, along with any utility bills. You remember the Petleys, Jo? They ran the shop. Still do.' Joanna nods that she does. 'With a bit of love, Pillowell would make a wonderful retreat. To be honest, it's all Witchwood is these days – holiday homes for those rich enough. Place is dead come winter. The heart's been sucked right out of it. Although –' Mrs Hooper stares off into the middle distance – 'we all know any heart that village had was snuffed out the summer you and Carrie came to stay with Dora.'

They fall into a reflective silence, their contemplations oscillating through the surprising birdsong.

'I'm sorry, love.' Mike, touching Joanna's hand, is the first to speak. 'I didn't realise how late it was.' He consults his wristwatch. 'I'd better get back to work, we've got the Geneva lot coming in this afternoon.'

'Oh, yes, your presentation. You get off,' Joanna assures him. 'Good luck with it all. I'll see you at home later.'

'Lovely to see you, I hope we can get together again soon.' With another kiss for Mrs Hooper and a quick embrace with his wife, Mike strides away.

'You've got a good man there.'

'I have.' Joanna smiles. 'He's a darling, and such a great father. I'm really very lucky.'

'It was a lovely service, you know,' Mrs Hooper says automatically.

'You think? Dire organist.'

Mrs Hooper agrees and they titter into their necks like a pair of schoolgirls, forgetting for a moment why they are here, who it is they are missing.

'Shame you couldn't have played?' Joanna says.

'Me? Oh no, dear. With these?' Mrs Hooper splays her hands to show the nobbled knuckles of arthritis. 'It's only for my own entertainment nowadays.'

'A shocking thing.' A pink-faced man in a button-popping cardigan of black and white diamonds zooms into their conversation. 'You have my deepest condolences.'

'Oh.' Joanna flings her head to him. 'Thank you.'

'Hi. I'm Jeffrey ... Jeffrey Morris.' The man dressed as Punchinello extends a hand. 'I worked with Miss

Jameson . . . *Caroline* . . . at the Animal Rescue Centre. Your sister was one of our volunteers.'

'Oh, right.' Joanna shakes the slightly damp palm. 'I didn't know.'

'I've been following the story in the papers.' Punchinello looks at her through lowered lids. 'I heard they arrested the man that did it.'

'And promptly released him again,' Joanna explains tersely, her civility wearing ghost-thin. 'The shop had CCTV and there were witnesses – the guy did nothing wrong.'

'*Nothing wrong*?' Jeffrey pulls a preposterous spotted handkerchief from his pocket. 'But he killed her.'

'No. Really. That's not what happened . . . not what happened at all. The poor guy was just defending himself. It was Carrie who attacked him, and in doing so she somehow stabbed herself.' Joanna turns away to hide her tears.

'Oh. Oh, I see.' Punchinello, embarrassed, buries his nose in his handkerchief. 'I'm ever so sorry, it really is a terrible thing, but please,' he adds, before shuffling away, 'do come and see us. We're just off Birdcage Walk, St James's. Your sister was a hugely valued member of the team, and . . . and, of course, there's things she left in her locker you might like to have.'

'There, there.' Mrs Hooper rubs Joanna's arm when Jeffrey Morris ambles away.

'What the hell was she doing carrying a knife?' Joanna sobs. 'None of it makes sense and the police haven't got any answers. I've got to get to the bottom of this.' Her expression determined. 'Mike's not keen but I'm going to Bayswater next week to sort out the flat – thought I could do some digging around then.'

'*Digging around,*' Mrs Hooper echoes. 'Whatever for?'

'Because I want to find out what was going on,' Joanna tells her. 'Carrie was obviously frightened of something ... *someone*. Why else would she have armed herself?'

'Promise me you'll be careful,' Mrs Hooper warns, passing Joanna another Kleenex.

'You're as bad as Mike.' Joanna blows her nose.

'I'm serious, Jo.' And Mrs Hooper looks it. 'You don't know what you're getting yourself into. You've no idea what Carrie was mixed up in.' She puts an arm around Joanna's middle to stop her teeth from chattering. 'Fancy getting a cup of tea somewhere? Get warmed up?'

Joanna, at the end of her reserves, sways her response.

'Come on, then, I know a nice little place just a short taxi ride away.'

Summer 1990

At the Boar's Head, it was Caroline's job to empty ashtrays, clear glasses and wipe tables. Irrespective of her rather odd appearance: the penetrating stare, the slight adolescent frame bulked out in bewildering layers despite the unrelenting heatwave, Liz and Ian Fry liked having her around. Kicked off by a suggestion of Dean's, it wasn't long before she was trusted to serve ploughman's lunches and butterfly-chicken to the hot-faced cyclists and hikers who followed the six-mile footpath from Slinghill.

It was lunchtime and the bar was heaving. Another fine day had attracted a steady stream of people. Thrilled to have yet another opportunity to spend time with Dean, Caroline stood at the bar to watch him. Pink from the shower, his damp curls stamped to the back of his neck, he reached for a shot of Jack Daniel's from the bank of optics and inadvertently furnished her with a glimpse of his toned midriff. Dora said she shouldn't be working here, that it was an unsuitable environment for a budding young woman, but Caroline knew her great-aunt wouldn't object too loudly about the drink-sticky floor and tables ringed from years of glasses because with Joanna learning the piano at Mrs Hooper's and Caroline here, Dora was free to please herself.

'I've been thinking.' Dean, stretching up for a second shot, gave Caroline a wink that made her insides cartwheel. 'You wanna cut a fringe in that hair of yours. Trust me, it would really suit you.'

His unexpected interest in her appearance was nearly enough for Caroline to drop the pile of plates she was carrying.

'Whoa.' Dean gulped back his drink. 'You can't manage all them.' And darting forward, he helped to transfer the dirty crockery into the kitchen.

'I like that song on the jukebox,' she said, loading the dishwasher the way Ian showed her. 'What is it?'

'"Hey You". Pink Floyd.' Dean passed her a fork she'd missed and smiled; handsome and casual, he ran a sun-tanned hand over his head. 'Want me to put it on again?'

Nodding vigorously enough to make her Alice band shift, she saw him lean into the bar to feed coins into the jukebox.

'Me dad's saw 'em live at Earl's Court.' His voice competing with Dave Gilmour's guitar and a melody she was coming to know. 'Bloody awesome.'

A holler went up from a ring of drinkers. Dean, on to it, dried his hands on the seat of his Levi's and swung into action.

'Right, you've asked for it, Danny Matthews.' Caroline heard his call before the kitchen door swung shut.

Reluctant to miss any action she quickly switched on the dishwasher, but something by the sink caught her eye. A gold ring with a bold blue stone that had been left behind in the soap dish. She picked it up. Decided to take it. And with a sharp look over her shoulder, slipped it into the pocket of her dungarees before heading back into the bar.

'Watch this.' Dean winked again as he retrieved something from beneath the till. Pointing the lens and pressing the button, there was a whirring sound and the machine spat out a small square of shiny black card. 'Magic.' Dean projected the word above the music and the roar of protest from the table of rabble-rousers. And it was, because right before her eyes, it revealed the scene she'd just witnessed.

A boisterous punter took a swing at Dean, but a little worse for wear, he fell forward on all fours. Ian leapt from behind the bar like a WWF wrestler and picked the bloke up by the scruff of the neck. 'Any more of that,' he shook him, pushed him down on a chair, 'and you're barred.' Then stepping back, he crossed his muscled arms to watch his son snap out Polaroids. 'Acting the goat, you know the rules,' he informed the room. 'And they're *Liz's rules*,' he stressed. 'Any rowdy behaviour and we take a picture, and you're on the Wall of Shame. For eternity.'

'There you go.' Dean returned the camera to its home on a fresh stash of tea towels and handed Caroline a pile of Polaroids. 'Find room for them with that lot.' He jabbed a thumb at a wall plastered with photographs of drinkers captured mid-slurp, mid-stagger, many of them faded to a strange sunset pink at their edges.

'Is that Drake's Pike?' Caroline pointed to ones of Witchwood in the snow.

'Yeah. The winter before we came.' Dean was close enough for her to feel the heat of his skin through his clothes. To see the unusual flecks of green in his hazel eyes. 'Awesome to think that, ain't it? Snowed in for weeks, apparently. The lake was frozen solid, people was skating on it.'

'Lethal. A youngster from Cinderglade skidded under the ice. They never found him.' Ian dropped the chilling nugget into their conversation.

'Oi, take that damn thing down,' a red-faced drinker shouted.

'No way.' Ian rubbed his broad hands together. 'These are for posterity. You shouldn't piss about if you don't want your picture up here.'

'Yeah, Danny,' Dean joined in. 'It's about time you lot learnt to behave.'

'Have you finished with this one for the day, Liz?' Ian asked his wife when the door at the side of the bar opened.

'I have – Carrie's worked hard, haven't you, love?' Liz hugged Caroline. 'You paid her?' She looked at Ian, who gave the thumbs up. 'Oh, I nearly forgot. I've got something else for you.' And she reached into the kitchen. 'Here,' she said, and passed her a carton of hen's eggs. 'Get that auntie of yours to cook them up for breakfast.'

'No,' Caroline said. 'Dora's got enough – I'm going to give these to Mrs Hooper. She hasn't got anything.'

Liz stole a sidelong glance at her husband, smiled her big, warm smile that made the corners of her eyes crease up. 'What a sensitive young lady you are,' she congratulated her. 'That's a lovely thing to do.'

Present Day

'Look, forget the tea – why don't we go and get a bite to eat, have a drink?' Mrs Hooper suggests on their walk to the taxi rank. 'You say your train isn't for an hour or so, and my sister's not expecting me anytime soon.'

Joanna barely responds.

'It'll give us the chance for a proper catch up, what d'you say?'

The interior of the taxicab they choose smells of pear drops, and the driver's seat has great chunks ripped out of its lining. Must be his stress toy, Joanna thinks, watching Mrs Hooper lean forward to ask if they can be dropped outside Manor Park station.

'Here all right for you, love?' The cabbie draws back his security screen a fraction, and Mrs Hooper confirms it is before handing him a twenty-pound note and waiting for the change.

Despite the overall drabness of this part of town, Joanna notices there are a surprising number of smart-looking bars and bistros.

'That place looks nice. Fancy giving it a try?' Mrs Hooper waves her stick at a pub on the other side of the road.

They opt for a table in the bay window, although, looking around, they have the choice of any; the place is virtually empty. And after the rigmarole of removing coats, gloves and scarves, they sit staring out on the December street prettified with fairy lights.

'I used to come in here with my husband. He worked nearby when we were first married.' Lillian Hooper makes a quick scan of the laminated menu wedged between the cruet. 'Course, it's rather smarter nowadays.' She smiles. 'Back then it was what you'd call a *real London boozer* – bit like my Derek,' she volunteers, once the jaded-looking waitress has taken their order. 'We were happy once.' She twists the thin gold wedding ring, loose behind the knuckle, rhythmically, hypnotically; as if to summon the ghost of him to her. 'Before Ursula died and Derek sent Gordon away to that horrible school … and we came to Witchwood. Because if Derek had been better with money we'd never have needed to move there.'

'I thought you liked Witchwood,' Joanna queries.

'No, not really.' A wry smile. 'The glories of the great outdoors are wasted on me, I prefer the noise and bustle of city streets.'

'I had no idea.'

'Why would you? The place must have been like an adventure playground to you little ones,' Mrs Hooper says kindly. 'But what I'm trying to say, in my roundabout way, is that I know all about loss.'

Anchored to the spot by the weight of her words, they watch a scattering of pigeons drop down on the rooftops opposite.

'You've had a rotten time of things.' Joanna fiddles with the lid of the vinegar bottle. 'It's why you're so easy to talk to.'

'Well, talk then,' Mrs Hooper urges.

Joanna sips the wine that's been poured for her. Watches shoppers dip in and out of the smattering of shops, their windows decorated with fake snow and glitter to tempt Christmas. 'I'm feeling really guilty about Carrie,' she says eventually. 'We never made it up after that awful row at Dora's funeral. I said some horrible things.' She wipes away fresh tears with a tissue. 'But Carrie was so difficult, so immovable – always pushing me away.'

'She was jealous of you,' Mrs Hooper says matter-of-factly. 'It wasn't necessarily her fault, but it wasn't yours either.'

'Funny.' A weak smile. 'That's what I accused her of the last time we spoke. But I should have gone to see her … it's … too late now.'

As Joanna talks, her memories of the past and all that's been lost dissolve with each mouthful of Merlot.

'Carrie predicted this, you know,' she continues. 'As a teenager, she was convinced she was going to die a violent death. Horrible, isn't it? Why would you think such a thing, let alone say it?' Joanna, serious, fixes Mrs Hooper with the flat of her eye. 'All I could think sitting at the front of that crematorium was: is this all her life amounted to? Next to no friends, no partner – apart from that Jeffrey bloke, the few that bothered to come didn't seem to even know her.'

'Rubberneckers,' Mrs Hooper says bluntly. 'Your sister's probably become a bit of a celebrity in death.'

'D'you think? What a farce that is. What d'you reckon she'd have made of it?'

'She'd have probably laughed; Carrie had quite a sense of humour when it suited her.'

'Did she?' Joanna struggles to conjure a time when this

lighter side of her sister's character was shown to her. 'I suppose we had some fun when we were kids,' she concedes. 'The two of us were great friends once.'

'I know you were – try to hold on to that,' Mrs Hooper says.

'It was after that summer in Witchwood when everything started to go wrong between us. *Uch*, it's such a waste. All this ... ' Joanna flings out an arm. '*I* let it happen. Too wrapped up in my own family, my career – I've been so selfish.'

'You didn't let it happen, you said yourself she pushed you away. Jo,' Mrs Hooper reasons. 'Carrie was pretty challenging, even as a child.'

'I know, but she was still my sister. I should've made allowances for her.'

'You can't keep blaming yourself,' Mrs Hooper soothes. 'You've got to let it go.'

'That's what Mike tells me.' Joanna squashes her tissue into a ball. 'Hang on ... you said you wanted to see a photo of the boys ... I've got a ... in here somewhere,' her voice disappearing into the caverns of her bag. 'Yes. Here we go. Us holidaying in Spain last summer.' She retrieves her purse, tugs out a photograph of her sons. 'Sorry it's a bit dog-eared,' she apologises, handing it over. 'Mike was ever so kind to Carrie, you know? He really tried in the early years.' She talks while Mrs Hooper stares into the faces of the children she has yet to meet. Freddie, as Joanna points out, was only two at Dora's funeral, and Ethan had yet to be born.

'Oh, how nice they look. A shame not to meet them. Didn't they want to come with you and Mike?' Mrs Hooper asks.

'They never met Carrie; it would've been silly to pull them out of school.' Another anchoring pause. 'You knew that Carrie tried to kill herself sixteen years ago, didn't you?' Joanna waits for confirmation as she returns the photograph to her purse. 'Mike was really sweet with her when she came out of hospital, wanting to take care of her, making sure she knew she wasn't on her own. We hadn't been seeing each other for long.' She bounces her hands in her lap. 'It used to upset him when Carrie ... well, she could be pretty nasty to me.' Joanna avoids all mention of her three-month hospital stint, followed by eight months of chemotherapy for a tumour on her spleen six years ago – information about her private life she managed to keep out of the press. There's little point worrying Mrs Hooper, especially as her oncologist gave her the all clear last July and she's totally well again.

Joanna takes another gulp of wine, before replenishing both their glasses.

'You look so like your mother, you know,' Mrs Hooper announces. 'She was such a beautiful woman, and her hair ...' a broad smile of appreciation. 'Like the rosy gold of sunsets. Just like yours.'

'I didn't know you knew Mum?' Joanna, curious, says nothing about her hair falling out during her treatment, her fears it wouldn't grow back.

'Didn't you? She didn't tell you about the time she stayed at Pillowell?'

'No. When was this?'

'Oh, now, let me think – the summer before you were born, if I remember correctly. It annoyed Dora,' Mrs Hooper chuckles, 'the amount of time Imogen spent with us at Pludd

50

Cottage. But it was hardly our fault she preferred our company. Your mum liked listening to me playing the piano; she said it relaxed her.'

'That's nice.' Joanna scrunches her lips, refusing to cry again. 'But where was Dad? I can't imagine Mum going anywhere on her own, she was way too nervy.'

'I'm not sure where Robin was. Perhaps he took Carrie to see his parents. I seem to remember your mother didn't get on with her in-laws particularly well.'

'That's putting it mildly. She refused to have anything to do with them after Dad died.'

'Gordon looked after Imogen. Drove her to town, showed her the sights. The two of them got on remarkably well, as I remember.' Mrs Hooper smiles at the waitress when their lunches arrive. 'Your mother could be very charming when she put her mind to it.'

Joanna doesn't answer as she unravels her cutlery from a serviette, reluctant to discuss her troubled mother any further; some things are best left alone.

Summer 1990

There was a path that cut through the overhanging trees and thigh-high ferns; a path beaten flat by the rougher boys from Slinghill who came down to Drake's Pike to swim. A place where the water was shallow and safe, but only if you steered away from the helter-skelter madness where the River Teal emptied itself into the lake.

With knapsacks strapped tight across their clammy backs, Caroline, Joanna and Ellie felt the slow heat through their thin clothes as they moseyed along in single file. Arrow shafts of sunlight speared the canopy of leaves and an unspoken danger hung in the air like an imminent storm. Subdued by the ethereal stillness, they intermittently turned their heads to the deeper, darker section of woods that unfolded around them like a wing.

'Daddy says to watch for snakes.' Ellie, the crunch of last year's leaves under her wheels, gleefully distributed Ian's warning into the sap-thick air.

'*Snakes*?' Caroline shrieked out of all proportion.

'Oh, yeah. They love this weather.' A sideways glance at Joanna and the two of them swapped secret smiles. 'You could get lost in here,' Ellie persisted with her game.

'But you remember the way, don't you? You've been here

loads of times, right?' Joanna scratched a bite on her leg and looked concerned.

'Course I do,' Ellie was quick to reassure her.

Scattering unseen wildlife, the girls tiptoed around ash piles from recent fires of other visitors. Blissfully unaware of the figure that followed them from churchyard to woods. The someone who scuttled soundlessly back into the shadows, satisfied with the photographs they'd taken of these young girls. This was a setting where the little wind there was moved stealthily through the compressed foliage. Where rabbits and deer came to drink and leave their skittering tracks pushed into the fudge-soft reed bed. It didn't cross the children's minds they could be in any danger.

When the woods finally widened into a sun-filled clearing, a singing blackbird was there to greet them. Through the swaying bulrushes, beyond the signal and flash of the water, was their destination with its little boat moored to the snout of a dilapidated wooden jetty.

'There's a good place to have our lunch.' Caroline gestured to the lower junctures of a weeping willow that swept the skin of the water like dead men's fingers. She led Joanna and Ellie over the moisture-laden ground, stopping when they reached a log as large as a pew in St Oswald's where they could sit down. Stippled on its wetter underside with unidentifiable mushrooms they knew not to touch, the sisters whipped off their sandals, Ellie her skates, and the three of them dangled their insect-bitten shins in the deliciously cool water. Caroline, whose legs were the longest, was in the middle of divvying out the contents of all three knapsacks when a burst of flapping made them look up at the rush of white taking shape on their periphery. Two swans hit the water and skimmed to a halt. They watched the majestic waterfowl glide in perfect synchronisation, gasping in amazement when they folded their pure white wings away.

'What's that?' Ellie snatched Caroline and Joanna's concentration, and pointed to something in the trees.

A shaking of heads; they saw nothing of interest.

'Over there. Wanna go and look?' Ellie asked Joanna, who happily left her seat in the reeds behind.

'I'll stay here and look after our stuff then, shall I?' Her sarcasm wasted, Caroline returned her gaze to the stretch of water: a spangled cloth of diamonds under the dazzle of a big bald sun. Silence fell into Ellie and Joanna's receding chatter, and Caroline found she rather liked the sensation. She focused on the golden rim of horizon, which shimmered thin as a leaf at the edge of the world, and pondered on the magic of such a place, until she remembered the stash of stuff she'd nicked. Jumping down from the log to check it was still where it should be, she squatted on the bank to grope for the hole she'd scooped out with stones, but it was too risky to lift the drawstring bag into the light and she withdrew her hand.

Just in time. At the snapping of twigs a jack snipe – a streak of stripes and pale underbelly – rocketed away. Joanna and Ellie were back at the log, urgent and pestering her to come and see what they had found.

'Bloody hell, it's like the *Marie Celeste*.' Caroline, tugging on her jelly sandals, kicked through a half-eaten picnic on a red tartan blanket. A bottle of Piat D'Or, its rocking indicating those who were *al frescoing* – a term of Dora's – hadn't long scarpered.

'What's the *marry selest*?' Joanna enquired, but was more interested in a Tupperware box of homemade cakes than Caroline's potted history.

'Maybe a boar chased them off,' Ellie suggested. 'We do get them, you know.'

Caroline glared at her ... *snakes, wild boar* ... her thoughts tripping over themselves. 'Something made them run; they were having a right nosh-up by the looks of it. Wanna swig?' she said, bending to retrieve the bottle of wine.

Ellie and Joanna turned their noses up and Caroline flung it to the ground.

'Cor, I love chocolate brownies.' Ellie peered into the transparent container.

'Who d'you think it belongs to?' Joanna crouched to examine the largest apple she'd ever seen.

'Who cares. Finders keepers ... Come on, take them.' Caroline, privy to more than she was letting on about the picnickers. 'They won't be coming back, trust me.'

'Did you ever actually *see* him?' Ellie leant back in the boat, her share of the chocolate brownies eaten.

'Who?' It was Caroline who answered; Joanna was busy munching on an apple the size of the moon.

'Mr Hooper.'

'Only once.' Caroline scowled as she hauled the single oar through the water. 'Mrs Hooper told me to take his tea up.' Aiming for the mouth of the tunnel; it was proving difficult to steer.

'*And*?' Ellie, all ears.

'And nothing.'

'You can't say *nothing* – if something happened, you've gotta say,' Joanna joined in, apple juice wetting her elasticated cuffs.

'Oh, come here,' Caroline grumbled. Securing the oar within its rollock, she yanked up Joanna's sleeves. The puckered material left two bracelets of indented flesh on her sister's chubby wrists and she rubbed them briskly to make them go away.

'Err, *gerroff.*' Joanna wriggled free of Caroline's grip and sucked the sweetness from her fingers.

'Clean on, that was. Get it dirty and you'll only make Dora cross.'

'It's you she gets cross with; making those great big holes in your woollies – don't you ever want to take it off? You must be boiling in that cardigan.'

'No, I don't. And anyway, Dora's always crabby with me for something.' Caroline took up the oar again.

'Don't tell fibs.' Joanna, finished with her apple, lobbed the core into the water with a small plop. 'She's doing her best.'

'*Doing her best*? She's bloody bonkers. She shouldn't be trusted to look after children, she's probably damaging us.'

'I like her. Being here's way better than home.'

'What about that fuddy-duddy music she makes us listen to? You're not saying you like that.'

'*Fuddy-duddy music?*' Ellie was eager to know.

'Yeah, we have to sit on our hands,' Caroline filled her in. 'It's like doing detention.'

'No, it's not.' Joanna shook her head at Ellie. 'She's doing it to make us more ... ' She paused, wanting to share what Dora said, '*Well-rounded human beings.*'

'Huh,' Caroline snorted, '*well-rounded*, all right.' She

poked Joanna's tummy, which strained the stitching of her dress. 'All that weird food she cooks us.'

'Better than Mum. All she does is sandwiches and them microwave chips.' Joanna, indignant, brushed her sister's hand away as if it was a wasp at a picnic. 'I like Dora's cooking.'

'You would, you'd eat anything. D'you wanna know what she made us last night?' Caroline turned to Ellie. 'Roast chicken.'

'Yum. I love roast chicken.' Ellie licked her lips.

'Yeah, but not with homemade onion marmalade – *marmalade*! Who eats marmalade for dinner?'

Ellie didn't answer.

'And she made a fruit salad.'

'For pudding?'

'That's what I asked her, thinking she'd mixed it up. But no, it was to have with the chicken. It's a Dutch thing, she said.'

Ellie giggled.

'I didn't believe her neither, I think she still got it wrong. She's off her rocker, she really is.'

'I like her.' Joanna was determined to have her say. 'And anyway, it's not like we've got a choice – Dora's all we've got.'

'We could stay at Mrs Hooper's? She must be lonely without her husband.'

'Seems happy to me.' Joanna inspected her midriff.

'Yeah, but she's loads more interesting than Dora. Dora's so boring, all she does is eat, sleep, and read. My teachers tell me I need stimulating ... and that's hardly stimulating, is it?'

'Dora is interesting.' Joanna, persistent in her defence of her great-aunt. 'And she's clever. What about that job she had? Mum says she speaks loads of different languages.'

The sisters spent the next few minutes picking over what they knew of Dora's mysterious career at the Foreign Office during the Cold War years. Titillating snippets of espionage and deceit harvested from eavesdropping on the conversations of grown-ups and nosing through three generations'-worth of treasures secreted at Pillowell. Ellie, meanwhile, had stopped listening; she was thinking about how much she loved the lake. Its wrinkled surface cobbled with light looked good enough to drink; but heeding her mother's warning that it wasn't safe, that anything could have crawled into it and died, she never dared.

'I like those.' Ellie, joining in with the sisters again, pointed with a long green reed to Joanna's earrings.

'You should get yours done.' Joanna grinned, pleased the entrance of the tunnel was at last in sight.

'No way.' Ellie screwed up her face. 'Mummy says I can if I want, but I'm scared it'll hurt.'

'It didn't hurt.' Joanna squeezed the plum of her earlobe. 'Well, only a bit. It wasn't bad, was it, Carrie?'

Caroline made no attempt to reassure as she twiddled the knob of gold under her hair with bitten fingers.

'I hate any kind of pain,' Ellie announced in a way she might have expressed a dislike of semolina or Marmite and tugged the sleeves of her T-shirt down to hide the tops of her arms.

'Ever twisted your ankle?' Joanna had already seen the bruises Ellie hadn't wanted her to see.

'No.'

'Not even doing your roller skating?'

'No.' Ellie, thoughtful.

'What about kneeling on a drawing pin, or ... or cutting yourself with scissors?'

'*No* – have you?' A look of dismay.

'Loads of times.' Joanna extended a knee to show what remained of a recent injury.

'Err, that's horrible.' Ellie buried her face in her hands.

'Ever had anyone *die* on you?' Caroline said, her eyes unreadable beneath the hard line of eyebrow. *She reckons she's special, just because she's got a lovely, happy family.* Her resentment rushed at her, and she dropped the oar into the boat to let the current suck them inside the tunnel; the plan she was hatching to show Ellie the world wasn't nice, and no one, however good they were, could get off that lightly, began to sprout wings.

Eerie and magical, the boat glided like a gondola over the satin-skinned water, into the enveloping darkness and dripping sounds. Their voices shrunk into the spooky silence that seemed to swallow them whole, as water droplets from lemon-yellow stalactites hit their necks, icy and shocking, sliding down inside their collars. They floated downstream, back towards Witchwood, much as the boats transporting fleece from the sheep-rich pastures of the Cinderglade Valley had done a hundred years ago.

The tunnel was over a mile long, the light at the end, nothing more than a pin-prick. The children pressed their tacky palms to the limestone crust of tunnel roof. Nefarious and unnavigable. They held their breath to the dark and traced the names of tunnellers chiselled into its rusticated stone pillars and pediments with their fingers – names echoed on the tombstones they'd seen in St Oswald's graveyard.

'Dora showed us this book of old photographs at the church. It's called the *Book of the Dead*. Have you seen it, Ellie?' Joanna's question buffeted the blackness.

'No. I've never heard of it.' Ellie's reply reverberated through the gloom. 'Sounds horrible, what's it like?'

'It's really creepy – isn't it, Carrie?'

'Too right – it's full of dead people,' Caroline was keen to stress. 'Them who died building this tunnel. Well, the ones they could dig out after it collapsed,' she added with relish.

'I didn't like it.' Joanna squirmed.

'That's 'cos you're just a big, fat baby. I think it's great. I've been back loads of times to look at it.' Caroline grinned into the obscurity. 'You must have seen it, Ellie – why haven't you seen it?'

'I dunno. I've never heard of it,' Ellie reaffirmed.

'But you live here!' Caroline was incredulous. 'Don't you even know what's going on in your own village? It's like one of the main attractions, that is.'

'To you, maybe,' Joanna piped up. ''Cos you're sick.'

'No, I'm not. I'm just mature and sophisticated,' Caroline asserted. 'Dora said it's a really important piece of history and should be in a museum or something. So, Ellie, I think it's gonna be up to me to educate you and take you to see it.'

Then – the fringes of Slinghill long behind them, the River Teal snaking its way back to Witchwood – the tunnel ended and they were thrust into the white, bright endorsement of the afternoon. Momentarily blinded, none of them saw Gordon Hooper waiting for them on the bank. Suited as usual, his silk tie, pink as a bullfinch; he threw a sharp black shadow over them before darting away unseen through the trees.

Present Day

The Sunday train is almost empty and is a totally different experience from Joanna's twice-weekly commute between St Albans and the Royal Academy of Music. A woman with chapped cheeks sits across the gangway and Joanna, fishing around in her bag for her mobile, listens to her gabbling vaguely to herself in a lilting, soothing voice.

'You doing all right?' she asks Mike when he finally picks up the phone.

'Hi, babe. Yeah, all well here. You okay?'

'Fine. Nearly there. Hardly anyone on the train.' She stares out at the fast-moving roofs and high-rise buildings that make up the northern suburbs of London. 'Freddie and Ethan okay?'

'They're fine. Watching cartoons with Pauline's two.'

A twinge of insecurity at the casual way her husband drops the name of their attractive and recently divorced neighbour into the conversation. 'Pauline's there then, is she?' Joanna tries to sound indifferent.

'Yeah, she is. D'you want a word?'

'No, no. It's you I want to talk to.'

Still early, the sun barely up – Joanna sees it has yet to burn away the January frost that has settled on everything.

'What you up to today?' she asks, twirling a curl around a finger.

'Paperwork. Mostly.'

'*Mostly?*' she quizzes.

'Pauline wondered if we should take the kids to the aquadrome in Welwyn later.'

'But you said you hated it there.' Joanna, busy envisaging the lovely Pauline in her swimsuit splashing around in the pool with Mike. 'It's what you tell me whenever I suggest going.'

'Yeah, I know that, but—'

'Because Pauline likes it, you want to go?' Joanna interrupts him and prods the flesh around her middle, the baby weight she gained and struggled to shift.

'Why are you being like this? It's your fault if you think you're missing out on things here – I said I'd come with you, didn't I? I wanted to come with you.' She hears his frustrated sigh. 'Pauline said she'd have looked after the boys.'

'Oh, because of course that would've been great fun, wouldn't it?' Joanna darts a look at her only travelling companion, thankful she is still absorbed in her own little world. 'Don't pretend you'd have been happy to give up a Sunday sorting out Carrie's flat.'

'I wouldn't have minded.'

'*Wouldn't have minded?* Oh, come on, Mike, we both know that's a big lie. Why would you have wanted to do anything for her? You hated her.' Joanna knows she's being unreasonable and regrets the unfairness of her words, but they're out now and she can't unsay them.

'I didn't *hate* her.' Mike sounds affronted. 'I just knew how bad she was for you, that's all.'

'But you didn't have to discourage me from keeping in touch with her, did you?' Joanna, while acknowledging she's still in a state of shock about her sister, isn't sure why she's attacking Mike.

'Hang on a minute. I was protecting you.' Mike holds his ground. 'You don't remember, do you? How long it used to take me to put you together again after she'd finished tearing you to shreds.'

'I know, I'm sorry.' Joanna softens – it isn't fair to transfer the shame she has about her only sibling on to Mike. 'I don't want to argue with you about it any more.'

'Neither do I,' he agrees. 'But honestly, Jo, I wish you'd let me come with you. It would've been nice for us to spend some time together. And I'm sorry if you think I'm fussing, but I'm really not happy with you going there on your own. You said yourself you're not entirely convinced Carrie stabbed herself ... Suppose she was in danger from someone, and that someone tries coming after you?'

The train wheezes to a stop, then remains stationary for some time. Stiflingly warm, the heaters belt out artificial air, and wafts of whatever her travelling companion is eating drift over to her.

'Pauline can't hear us talking, can she?' Joanna ducks her husband's concern. She hates the idea their neighbour could be privy to any discord between her and Mike.

'No, she's with the kids.'

'It is kind of her to help out while I'm away, taking the boys to school tomorrow – you will thank her for me, won't you?'

Mike's answer is lost to the barking Buttons.

'Someone at the door.' He tells her what she already senses. 'I'd better go and see who it is.'

'Speak later?' she asks.

'Speak later,' he says, then hangs up.

Joanna checks her mobile for other messages, thinks about replying to an email from one of her music students, but scrolls through her contact list instead. Sees her sister's number and activates the call. Pressing it to her ear she listens to her sister's recorded voice, the slight hesitancy, the little puff of breath, before inviting the caller to leave a message.

'I miss you so much.' She says the things she couldn't say to Caroline when she was alive. 'Why didn't you tell me if you were in trouble? I could have helped. I wanted to be a sister to you but you kept pushing me away.' Joanna blinks through the sharp winter sunshine flooding the carriage and settling in warm bands across her body. 'There've been times when I could've done with you too, y'know. Where did we go wrong? How did we let things get so bad between us?'

With the sway and rock of the train speeding through cuttings again, she dozes off ... until a frantic tugging of her sleeve, and she wakes to the face of her co-traveller alarmingly close to hers.

'Wake up. Wake up.' The grip, tightening, shakes her arm. 'This is King's Cross – they won't let you sleep here.'

The walk from the tube to her sister's old flat is short but, needing to sidestep numerous cross-legged beggars and hawkers pushing leaflets into her hands for things she doesn't want, it takes an age. Joanna has always thought of the London district of Bayswater as a village within a city and, out under a milky sun, the streets around Queensway bustling with colour and life, she is reminded how much she loved coming here. It makes her question if the sleepy little nook of Hertfordshire she and Mike ended up in had in fact been the right move. Often invited by Dora, the visits stopped when she died and Caroline inherited; for reasons Joanna never got to the bottom of, her sister didn't want her anywhere near the place, or anywhere near her.

When she reaches the flower stall that has always been on the corner before the turn into Edinburgh Terrace, she stops to smell the roses as she always did in the days when she used to stay with Dora. With no Dora or Caroline to buy for, she noses through the buckets of sprays with their leafless, thorny stalks, wanting the heady scent of the ones that grew at Pillowell, but they always elude her. Those types of roses don't exist beyond her imagination. Like her memories of warm summer evenings barefoot on Dora's lawn, the air thick with their perfume and the song of the linnet, they were little more than a rumour of the heart. Much like, as things turned out, the postcard-pretty setting of Witchwood, when she thinks of the horrors that were to occur there.

A good-looking man in a pinstripe suit is suddenly at her elbow. He smiles appreciatively at her while he chooses a bunch of flowers. Joanna returns his smile, she can't help it; contrary to Caroline's green-tinged accusation whenever they were out together, she doesn't go looking for this kind of attention, but can't pretend it isn't flattering when it comes. 'If you didn't go round with a scowl on your face,' she used to tell her sister, 'then people might smile at you.'

'Nice, aren't they?' the man says. 'I can't resist them.'

'I'm the same; they're so pretty.' She knows she shouldn't

talk to strangers, let alone strange men, but something in the way he searches her face makes her forget the risks others warn of. 'Are they for someone special?'

'Maybe.' He winks, making her blush.

She moves away from the flower stall and is about to step off the kerb when she spots a black guy with Bob Marley dreadlocks, strumming a guitar. She is wriggling coins from her purse when he shifts forward into another song, plucking the opening chords of a calypso melody ... *yellow bird, you sit all alone like me ...*

The tune, with its strong associations, makes the horizon swim. Dipping her head to hide her tears, Joanna is back there ... back among the tall bulrushes, the cold water up to her middle, teeth chattering wildly as she scrabbled with the noose of weeds ... the dangling disbelief in those first few moments when she hoped someone would tap her on the shoulder and tell her it was all an awful joke.

Rooted to the pavement, she realises, perhaps for the first time, how closely she's lived with this memory. How it has loitered like a blot on the landscape of her mind, the darkness oozing from it, a wound that can never heal. Impossible to contemplate someone as fragile as Caroline coping with such a dreadful experience. Harrowing enough for Joanna to carry around, but at least she's been able to let it all out with Mike. Who did Caroline have? Because it can't have been healthy to bottle that up. Nowadays you'd be given counselling, especially when you consider how young they'd both been, but not once did the sisters speak of what happened in Witchwood, boxing the misery away, much as they did when their father drowned.

Joanna misses the way the busker's smile folds in on

itself, but he doesn't stop playing as others have gathered around, singing and clapping, dropping coins into his guitar case. When her memories release her, she breaks into a run, her holdall banging against her calves.

'Excuse me ... excuse me,' she cries, ripping through the dwindling crowd and into the quiet terrace to hunt for number seventy-three, aware how the man in the pinstripe suit appears to be following her, and is worryingly close on her heels.

Summer 1990

Mid-afternoon and despite the hot, high sun, Pillowell Cottage continued to perpetuate its twilit mood. With its preponderance of tassels and bobbles, the Strawberry Thief wallpaper thieved the light as well as the strawberries and a lamp glowed dully on the sideboard. Shaking out the last melting Wagon Wheel from a family-size packet, Dora jammed it into her mouth whole and threw open the French doors to the summer sounds of her garden, the breeze stirring the pendant quartzes of the chandelier: a gift to her long-dead parents on their wedding day. A flickering from the leaves made her dart her head. She expected the girls to emerge through the side gate and was relieved not to see them. Licking her fingers clean, she squinted at her reflection in the round-faced mirror in the hall. Satisfied there was no trace of chocolate, she reapplied a fresh coat of lipstick. Hot Candy Pink, the sticker informed; a jaunty shade and far too young, but Dora didn't care, she liked it.

Dean was there. Pushing her father's old petrol-powered mower and giving the tunnel of lawn with its awning of trees a smart set of stripes. Leaning back in her Dr Scholl's, she watched him through the quartered kitchen window with her brass opera glasses; saw how he glistened with sweat in the turgid air, his lean, young frame in ripped Levi's, his suntanned arms batting away flies. The boy sure was a dead ringer for that Jim Morrison … She hummed her favourite Doors track and considered his dangerous edge, because Dean Fry – he had it written all over him – was definitely the archetypal Bad Boy. Small wonder Caroline was besotted; Dora might have been too, had her heart not been lost to Gordon Hooper. She glared at herself in the mirror. Get a grip, you fool, you're old enough to be his mother. But – her thoughts as she heaved a sigh into the pain of unrequited love – maybe she wasn't so foolish, maybe Gordon was growing fond of her. Why else did he keep dropping round?

Dora gave her hair a squirt of the Silvikrin kept on the hall table in case of visitors. In case of Gordon. The anticipation of seeing him bubbled in her chest. She held it there, luxuriating in its promise. Could love be possible? Fifty-four wasn't all that old. She squashed her lips between a tissue in the way her mother did in this same mirror. Not that Dora's thoughts were with her mother – her mind, shifting from Gordon, unexpectedly landed on Caroline: a troubled child who doggedly scrutinised her reflection. Dora caught her staring into the chrome curve of the electric kettle earlier, not because she was especially narcissistic, certainly not in the way Dora herself had been aged thirteen, but – she suspected – to hunt her features for clues she might be a harbinger of death.

'Is it because I look like Dad? Is that why Mum wanted to die?' Caroline's question had left Dora floundering. 'I'm not stupid; I know she can't stand to look at me.'

And what was Dora expected to say? Suggest she wear a Mickey Mouse mask so her mother wouldn't have to see her face? Poor kid.

Bereft of her chattering nieces, Dora slumped down on her chaise longue. Strange to feel the lack of them when she could be so awkward around them, but at least when they were off playing with Ellie Fry or at Pludd Cottage, she was free to indulge in whatever took her fancy. Crammed with relics displaying her Dutch ancestry, Dora had hoped to use Pillowell to convey something of their shared cultural heritage, but to her bemusement, only the family photo album was of interest to Joanna and Caroline. Heavy as an anvil, its vellum skin worn by generations of fingers to a murky brown, it was packed with photographs of their shared Dutch–Jewish relations. It at least got the conversation going, although not always in the direction Dora would have liked.

'Flip wanted to marry a Catholic girl.' She relayed the story of her favourite uncle to the sisters who sat side-by-side, eager for tragic tales of the smiling-faced cousins, aunts, uncles and grandparents, captured at weddings and bar mitzvahs. 'But my mother forbade him. His own *sister.*' She dabbed her lips with a handkerchief, as though she might find blood there. 'Threatened to cut him off without a guilder unless he married the nice Jewish girl they found him. So, they all perished. Ruth, Flip, their three little children – carted off to the gas chamber ...'

'How come your lot got out?' Caroline, nonchalantly turning the parchment pages – the dead faces of Dora's loved ones meaning nothing. 'You're Jewish too, aren't you?'

Dora felt the sting of that question afresh. In a cottage clotted in secrets, the story about what her father cooked up with a select group of Nazi officers to ensure him and his family safe passage to England was something she would never divulge.

A thump against the French doors. Jolted out of her reverie, Dora, now sprawled over her velvet-tongued chair, saw a sparrow hawk throw its weight into the opalescent afternoon. Especially fond of the families of finches and tits that fed from her bird tables, Dora hoped the bugger didn't catch anything. Absentmindedly stroking the uphol-stery as if it were a pet, she kicked off her shoes and looked beyond her toes at her garden. Quiet enough to hear a thrush whacking out snails against a stone. The tapping, reminiscent of her old Remington typewriter, spun her back to the brown-walled rooms of the Foreign Office: a setting where her flair for European languages had been applauded and she was held in high esteem. Nowadays, fearing she'd become a figure of fun and that people rid-iculed her behind her back, she regretted giving up her important work after inheriting her parents' money. Her role within the Diplomatic Service meant responsibility and overseas travel; it gave her unquantifiable purpose as a younger woman. Now, lonely and hurtling into middle age, there was little to sustain her, and she seemed to have lost her way in life.

Realising the lawn mower had stopped, Dora sauntered barefoot to her kitchen door to look outside. All afternoon, the heat followed the journey of the sun, and it was with considerable relief she saw it finally slipping below the tops of the trees.

'*Dean*. Are you there?' She flung her head around and called into the ripe smell of cut grass. 'D'you want a drink?'

He appeared on the back step, out of nowhere, blocking the light.

'Come in, come in,' she gasped, unnerved by his sudden-ness. 'Nice glass of Robinson's barley water do you?'

'Ta.' He nodded, sweeping the back of an arm over his perspiring brow.

'The girls like it,' she said, waving him inside, but he didn't budge. 'Lemon flavour,' she announced over the rush of the cold tap. 'There.' She passed him the beaker she had deliberately set aside for him, along with a fiver for the thirty-minute labour.

'Ta,' he said again, yanking his headphones free and tucking the crumpled note into the pocket of his jeans. He downed the barley water in one thirst-quenching gulp. Thirsty herself after her chocolate binge, Dora watched the bounce of his Adam's apple until, returning the empty beaker to her and repositioning his Walkman, Dean sprinted away, seemingly reluctant to linger a moment longer. 'I'll be back in a week or so.' He tossed the guaran-tee over his shoulder.

'Okay, thank you,' she said to his receding torso with its dark triangle of sweat. 'See you then.'

Dean was gone, bobbing in time to the music clamped to his head.

'Not sure I like him.'

A voice from her hallway severed her contemplations. She bent her large body to receive it. No one ever used her front door. Panic fizzed over her scalp. But identifying Gordon – his smart-suited self, obfuscated by shadow – it dropped away again.

'Gordon!' A squeal of joy and she swayed towards him. 'How lovely of you to come and see me.'

'Are the girls here?' he asked immediately, bending to

bestow the obligatory kiss Dora presented herself for. 'I've something special for them.' A rustling as he lifted a substantial carrier bag.

'Oh, *presents*?' As excited as if the bulging bag had been for her. 'You naughty boy, you shouldn't have.' She patted her sticky wall of hair, pleased she'd had the foresight to apply fresh lipstick. 'They shouldn't be long.' She glanced at her watch, its delicate strap sunk deep into the fleshiness of her wrist. 'Such good girls, always off amusing themselves – I barely see them.'

'I could come back later?' he offered.

'No. *No*.' Dora, determined to keep him. 'Come in, I'll fix us a drink – I could murder a gin and tonic.'

Gordon Hooper's car was there again. The black BMW he secured in a lock-up at Gloucester station when he was away in Tuscany. The Jameson sisters and Ellie Fry circled it in a way they would if a new child had turned up unexpectedly at school, saw themselves reflected in its wax-polished sides, the curved chrome of bumpers. They peered through its windows at the plush leather seats with their bright red piping, identified road maps of Europe, a folded newspaper, two violin cases, stray items of clothing suspended from coat hangers.

'Wasn't he supposed to be going back to Italy?' Caroline adjusted her Alice band in the car's wing-mirror. 'He's always hanging around here.'

'Mrs Hooper says he changed his mind,' Joanna informed them. 'He's staying the whole summer now.'

'You're joking.' Caroline touched the car roof. Stove-hot under the unrelenting sun, she jerked back her hand.

'He wants to look after her, 'cos he's kind.'

'That's nice.' Ellie squatted to tighten the laces on her roller skates.

'Is it?' Caroline, fists on hips.

'I dunno why you've got such a downer on him.' Joanna, linking arms with Ellie the moment she was upright again. 'I like him,' she said dreamily. 'He reminds me of Daddy.'

'You don't remember Daddy.' Caroline, teeth bared. 'You're too young.'

'No, I'm not. I remember what he smelled like and Gordon smells the same.' Joanna, defiant, not blinking.

'You don't know what you're talking about,' Caroline, scornful, as the finger of memory poked her in the back and forced her down the well-trodden path to times with her father ... the paper bags of sherbet pips he'd dig from the pockets of his coat that smelled of typewriter ink and London trains when she cuddled him ... home from the pub at the end of their street on Sunday evenings, sucking humbugs to disguise the smell of ale, the two of them humming along to *Sing Something Simple* on the radio. Robin Jameson was born on Valentine's Day, wore checked sports jackets with leather elbow patches, and his hair was glossy with Brylcreem. He was thirty-two when he drowned. And was she worth dying for? Caroline doubted it, and supposed her pretty little sister would have been a far worthier sacrifice. Bright and special, it wasn't difficult to see why everyone preferred Joanna; if Caroline was honest she preferred Joanna herself. But it was easier for her, four years Caroline's junior – she wasn't troubled by unwanted changes in her body or bothered about whether Dean Fry liked her or not. No – Caroline regarded her sister – Joanna wasn't the least confused as to where she fitted in.

'Anyway,' Caroline said, back in the now. 'How d'you know what Gordon smells like?'

'I sit on his knee.' Joanna lifted her other arm, used it as a visor.

'*You sit on his knee*? When? I've never seen you.' Caroline was horrified.

'When I go to Mrs Hooper's and she's late back from church.'

'I sit on his knee too,' Ellie said.

'*Yuk!*' Caroline scowled. 'I wouldn't let him anywhere near me – he gives me the bloody creeps.'

'*Carrie!*' Joanna, eyes wide. 'You're not supposed to swear. Mum said.'

'Like she gives a sod.' Caroline skimmed a hand against a foxglove as tall as she was.

'Yes, she does.'

'You can kid yourself if you want, but I know different.'

'Why are you being so horrible? It's not my fault we've been sent here, that Mum did what she did.'

'Did I say it was?' Caroline glared at her. 'Anyway.' She seized hold of Ellie's other arm, loath to be left out. 'For your information, I like it here. I like being far away from everything.'

And they were. This somewhere, which their mother referred to now and again as 'the back of beyond', suited them fine. For there were no abandoned places where they came from; London living meant it was impossible to get away from people. But in Witchwood, with its abundance of secret nooks, you could hide away for days, weeks, if you needed to. And if there was one thing Caroline and Joanna wished for most of all, it was to hide. Life under the scrutiny of neighbours and the concern of teachers since their mother's *cry for help* had been suffocating; all they wanted was to be left alone, to be allowed to be normal. But things were never going to be normal, were they? Not since Robin Jameson left them behind on the beach with his wire-rimmed spectacles tucked into his sandals.

'Don't go using language in front of Dora, she don't like it,' Joanna warned in a tone copied from her teachers, but only because Ellie was beside her – she wouldn't have dared ordinarily.

'Huh, tell me what she does like?'

'She likes Gordon,' Joanna tittered, showing her neat row of milk teeth. 'She's always in a good mood whenever he comes round.'

Caroline grinned blithely, forgetting the taunt from a boy at school who said her front teeth looked like a pair of hankies on a line.

'Mummy says your auntie's got the hots for Gordon,' Ellie said, and the three of them collapsed into a fit of giggles.

'You coming in, Ellie?' Joanna asked once she'd recovered.

'I can't.' Ellie looked down – her scuffed roller skates suddenly interesting. 'Daddy said I'm to stay away from Gordon.'

'*See.*' Caroline swooped on the subtext. 'I'm not the only one who doesn't like him.'

'Oh, don't go, stay,' Joanna pleaded.

'No, I'd better not.'

'We won't tell.'

Ellie sucked on her bottom lip and thought about it. 'No, it'll make Daddy cross.'

'But you said you liked Gordon?'

'I do like him – it's Daddy who doesn't, not me,' Ellie defended herself.

'Why? Are you frightened of him, your father?' Caroline, deliberately provocative. 'Does he hit you?'

Ellie squinted through the sunshine and declined to answer.

The sisters didn't move. With the sun dropping low over their backs they listened to the receding *whoosh, whoosh* of Ellie's wheels. A rattle of rooks from above; a sound virulent enough for the house sparrows caught in the coil of honeysuckle by Pillowell's front door to flee.

'Funny her dad don't like Gordon.' Joanna splintered the spell.

'No, it's not.' Caroline, her eyes glued to Ellie as she skated away through the trembling green. 'Gordon's weird – playing with her like that at Mr Hooper's funeral? It's not normal.'

'Gordon's loads nicer than Ellie's dad is – he's scary.'

'No, he's not; Ian's nice. And anyway, what would you know? You're only a kid.'

'So are you.'

'No, I'm not!' Caroline, indignant. 'Liz says I'm a young woman now.'

They turned their attention to their lengthening shadows, to the breeze pickpocketing the treetops. Dora had lots of callers. It wasn't something they were used to; people rarely visited their mother. Yesterday it was the reverend's turn, eating all Dora's pink wafers and dropping crumbs down his front like the confetti he won't permit in his churchyard. Rushing in on them sitting cosy-close, it

78

stunned the sisters into silence, unsure why he was there, neither of them comfortable with the way he looked them up and down.

'It won't be the vicar again, surely?' Caroline juddered at the memory of Dora putting away his side plate unwashed. The pretty National Gallery serviette, with its voluptuous Rubens' nudes he'd wiped his mouth against, to be used again and again. 'Right dirty old sod, him. Just because he wears a dog collar. I know what the bastard's up to.'

Joanna winced under the weight of Caroline's imprecating. 'You don't like anyone much, do you?'

'Can't trust no one, that's why. You'll learn soon enough, when you grow up.'

Hot and tired – it took energy being introduced to new people all the time. But no matter how lumpy their legs were from nettle stings and insect bites, their clothes soiled from playing outside, they must come forward to be presented; they must make an effort to smile and answer questions politely. A bit of a joke their great-aunt may be – a flash of her giant pink knickers flapping like flamingos on the washing line – but she was a stickler for manners. Hovering in the heat of the porch with the cobwebs and peeling paintwork, the sisters peered into the subfusc of Pillowell's front-facing rooms, half expecting to see the phantoms of Dora's relatives come rustling through in crinoline skirts. Poker-straight Victorian women with faces they'd come to know from the photo album, stepping about the Persian rugs in slippered feet. But there was nothing, and no sign of Gordon or Dora either. They must be in the sitting room round the back.

Accompanied by the lethargic buzz of summer, the sisters unhooked the side gate and squeezed along the path. They stopped to press their noses to the damask roses growing along the south-facing wall, wanting the tickle of petals on their sunburned cheeks. The roses and the lawn were the only things tended to nowadays; long gone – Dora's old photographs of the garden were testament – were the bee-loud borders that, when their great-grandparents holidayed here, were awash with colour. Since Dora inherited in the late seventies, nature had been left to its own devices much as Caroline and Joanna were. Stuffed with verdant shadows, heavy as foliage, Pillowell Cottage and its unruly garden echoed the claustrophobic feel of this corner of Gloucestershire.

Identifying the smell of cut grass, they saw the compost heap had been recently added to.

'Dean's been,' Joanna said when they stepped in through the kitchen door, swapping the outdoor smells for whatever Dora was cooking in the oven for their dinner. They saw his empty beaker turned upside down on the draining board. 'We must've missed him.'

'He could still be here.' Caroline, ever hopeful, scanned the kitchen surfaces for clues. But aside from the chopping board heaped with redundant onion skins, there was only a dead bluebottle, the debris of melting ice cubes and slivers of lemon – necessary accoutrements for Dora's evening gin and tonics – and nothing more of Dean.

'Don't worry.' Joanna, seeing her sister's sagging expression, wanted to lift her mood. 'He told me he's going to ask you out soon.'

'*You what*? He said that!' Caroline, all smiles again.

'When? When did he tell you?' Fizzing with excitement, it didn't occur to her to ask why a lad of eighteen would entrust his romantic intentions to her nine-year-old sister.

'Yesterday, I think. I was helping Liz with the chickens.'

'And, what? He just came out and said it?' Caroline could barely contain herself. 'Why didn't you tell me?'

There wasn't the time to answer. The sisters, aware of the rumble of conversation coming from the sitting room, edged out into the hall to listen.

'Imogen? Well, yes, of course I've *seen* her. In London. Not here. I haven't been able to tempt her back here for ... *ooo*, how many years is it?' It was Dora's vaguely foreign accent the sisters identified first. Blurry from her usual aperitif, it curled up through Richard Clayderman's *Love Collection* she'd set to play on the turntable.

'Ten.' It was Gordon Hooper who provided the answer.

'Really? That long.'

'Yep, that long. Have you ever tried to persuade her to visit Pillowell again? She rather liked Witchwood, as I remember.'

'Of course I have, Gordon. Imogen knows she and the girls are always welcome,' Dora was quick to interject, and Caroline and Joanna imagined a flourish of the black lace fan.

'But you say you see her. What, fairly often?'

'Oh, yes. She comes to Bayswater. Although, when I think about it, she's not been for at least a year, certainly not since Lion died.'

'*Lion?*'

'Imogen's father. My brother.'

A brief pause.

'But you know' – Dora again, her tone wistful – 'the poor thing's not been right since dear Robin drowned. She took it so very, very badly.'

'I'm sure.' Another pause. 'Perhaps she'll come to Witchwood this year. As you've got Carrie and Jo staying with you.'

'Oh, I doubt it, Gordon. We can't possibly understand the state she's in. I've been telephoning the clinic but they say she isn't up to taking calls— Oh, *cooee* – is that you, girls?' Dora's voice interrupted itself. 'Guess who's come to see us.' A fruity chuckle that made the sisters' toes curl inside their jelly sandals. 'He's got something for you.'

'Do we have to?' Caroline hissed, desperate to be alone with the joyous news Joanna had just given her. She wanted to be free to moon about Dean and all they were going to do together. 'Can't we just pretend we didn't hear and sneak up to our room?' Upstairs, the two bedrooms and generous-sized bathroom shoved under the eaves was a space in which she could breathe and daydream. Not down here with Gordon Hooper and his sugared smiles and spooky eyes.

'You do what you want. I want to say hello.' Joanna bounded away with a puppy-like eagerness.

Dallying on the threshold: Joanna bashful, Caroline aggrieved. Dora beckoned them into the room filled with the peppery tang of Gordon's aftershave. Something far more troubling to Caroline than the green light dribbling in from the trees.

'There you are, come on ... come on. No need to be bashful.' Dora let go another spice-filled giggle.

Ellie was right, the sisters thought as they observed the

object of their aunt's affections sipping from a tumbler, a lilac-coloured cigarette between his elegant fingers, blowing bracelets of smoke into the room. She definitely had the hots for him.

'Goodness me!' Dora, louche as a tabby cat on her pink chaise longue, had flung off her Dr Scholl's, and the fan, just as the girls had visualised, fluttered like a blackbird at her throat. 'Look at the state of them, Gordon. Look how filthy they are. *Oh –*' another flirty flurry of the fan – 'you're like a pair of didicoys; whatever would your mother say?' The gin and tonics obviously dispensed with, Dora slurped from a large wine glass that, when she pulled it away, left an arc of red on her upper lip.

And Gordon did look, stealing from one little girl to the other in that unflinching way of his. Joanna looked straight back, happily giving him a willing smile. But Caroline, instinctively throwing the dark of her eyes elsewhere, watched the flapping distress of a huge moth which had alighted on a lamp, its shadow flickering against the wall.

Gordon saw it too, and rose from his seat to scoop it gently in his hands to tip it outside. 'It's wonderful you're able to give them so much freedom. More fun than London, isn't it, girls?' he said, and, sitting down again, handed them the large carrier bag that had been waiting at his ankles.

Dora smiled as he lolled back in one of Pillowell's stout leather club chairs and made a steeple with his hands beneath the fine line of his jaw. She liked the way his large onyx ring, another eye, blinked coldly in the lamplight and, seeing his attention had been seized by her shambles of a garden, twisted away, as he had done, from the chatter, the rustle and rip of wrapping paper, to share in the multiplying midges caught in the last shards of orange sunshine as it was swallowed by the dying day.

'I'm so pleased, they're every bit as lovely as I remember them being before the shop assistant wrapped them.' Gordon dropped his thoughts into the diffused lighting of the room. 'I've a weakness for lovely things,' he said, almost as an apology. Dora thought of Lillian, of her concern about Gordon's fondness for spending more than he earned. About the only thing he'd inherited from his father who, twice bankrupt, had no qualms about plunging his family into a state of near-ruin time and again.

The hobby-horses were indeed beautiful. Mounted on long wooden poles with wheels, their heads of soft chenille felt real to the touch. Caroline, despite being a little too old for her toy, was fascinated with the dramatic palomino sporting a fine leather halter. Joanna, equally spellbound with her black-headed one, waved it through the languid air and made its Christmas-red bell sing.

'Go on, girls,' Dora shrieked her encouragement. 'Give your Uncle Gordon a nice big kiss to say thank you.' Behaving in her usual haughty way, she lurched forward over her comfortable middle and pushed them towards him. Gordon bowed in his seat to receive them: a king to his subjects, Dora thought wistfully, as the girls did as they were told and planted kisses on his surprisingly bristle-free cheeks. Gordon missed the way Caroline scrubbed her mouth with her sleeve, but Dora didn't, and an unexpected fury sprouted inside her.

'Good manners cost nothing,' she barked, ripping open

a packet of Twiglets. 'Say sorry immediately, or you can go to your room.'

'Oh, don't worry, Dora.' Gordon was unperturbed.

Dora nodded through her crunching, but she wasn't happy, fearful Caroline's display of insolence would reflect badly on her. Then, with no preamble, Gordon, who hadn't taken his eyes off Joanna, scooped her up around the middle, hobby-horse and all, and plonked her on his knees with such unexpected boldness, it made Dora gasp.

'*Ahh*, now isn't that nice,' she cooed at her neighbour's grown-up son cuddling her little niece. 'What a lovely picture you two make.' Buzzing with romantic notions learnt from books, experiencing little in reality, it didn't cross Dora's mind that there could be anything darker going on here. But Caroline was on to him. Carrying her toy, her long face fixed in solemn intent, she rescued her defenceless sister from this sinister houseguest.

'Come on, Jo – let's go and play outside.' And she prised Joanna's tubbiness from Gordon's grasp. 'I'm calling my horse Beau Geste.'

'*Ooo*, how clever of you – that's perfect.' Dora clapped her hands in appreciation. 'I loved that book as a kiddie. Who wrote it . . . ? Who wrote it . . . ?' Mind turning, unable to release the name.

'P.C. Wren,' Caroline informed her coolly.

'What a clever girl you are.' Dora, proud. 'Isn't she clever, Gordon?'

'You what?' Gordon, reluctant to release Joanna, lifted his pale eyes to Dora and made her blush.

'Isn't Carrie clever for coming up with that name for her *horsey*?'

'What are you going to call yours?' he asked Joanna, who was cuddling up to him.

'Black Beauty.' Joanna smiled.

'All right, all right.' Dora clapped her hands again, wanting to move things on. 'You two go and play for five minutes, then bath and supper. All right?' A mock frown for the benefit of her male companion, to show she was capable of organising two little girls. 'Are you staying for supper, Gordon? You're very welcome. I've made a goulash, it's simmering in the oven,' Dora offered as Joanna slid from his knees and raced out into the lowering dusk with Caroline.

'What a lovely idea,' he agreed. 'I'll go and fetch my mother.'

And a final look at the sisters – a swirl of giggles on the blue-dark lawn – meant he missed Dora's glazed look of disappointment.

The sound of an imagined sea pervaded Caroline's dreams. Nightmares of her father, his dead-fish eyes slipping below the waves before anyone could reach him. Draped in the mellow glow of moonlight, her face creased from the pillow, she let the smell of washing powder hurl her back to Camden and her mother's eyes that were raw as onions from the years of crying Caroline blamed herself for.

She studied the back of her hand that dangled over the side of the mattress. The more she stared, the more alien it became. Weren't humans odd, she thought, likening her fingers to the trussed-up bellies of pork the butcher along Camden Road squashed into bloodied steel trays. The skin both smooth and puckered and 'perfect for crackling', she'd heard him suggest to her mother in that *I-don't-half-fancy-you* voice of his.

Caroline knew all about what it was to fancy some-one – she fancied Dean Fry. With his rock-star looks and mirror-lens sunglasses. And to think, her fantasies about the two of them kissing and touching were about to come true. It filled her heart to bursting.

Laughter from downstairs forked through the floor-boards. There was no laughter at home, not since Daddy died – her mother was too sad. It was why she needed to have her stomach pumped, they said. Caroline tried not to think about what this meant. Removed from the action as soon as the ambulance arrived, she was left to picture the brutality of rubber tubes and sucking machines. And would their mother be pleased? Would she thank her daughters for intervening and embrace their homecoming by pressing a thousand *sorrys* into their wounds? Sorry they needed to find her like that; sorry if she frightened them; sorry she didn't think they were enough to live for and that for one gilded moment believed there could be an alternative?

The shriek of a fox stabbed the crust of her deliberations. As distressing as an infant's cry, she hadn't known what it was until Mrs Hooper explained. When it sounded again, she eased back the bedcovers and inched on to the land-ing. Chilly under her nightdress, she stood with her toes curled over the top stair, eavesdropping on the scuttling voices below. The popping of corks as wine bottles were opened, then tinkling sounds as it was poured into the long-stemmed glasses Caroline had seen loitering at the back of Dora's cupboards. A frisson of loneliness as she left behind what little of the shadowy scene she could make out through the balustrades.

*

87

When Gordon and Lillian had gone, a rather dishevelled Dora – lipstick and powder long evaporated – decided to leave the washing up until morning. She looked around at the wreckage from an evening's entertaining – it had been an enjoyable enough few hours, but worth the effort? She wasn't sure. Not when she'd envisaged being alone with Gordon once the girls had been packed off to bed. Why he needed to include his mother, she didn't know – perhaps he was shy and couldn't trust himself to be alone with her. The idea made her smile, until she spied the cast iron Le Creuset soaking in the sink, the stubborn tide of burned-on goulash.

Moving into the sitting room for a few moments of freshness before securing the French doors against what was left of the balmy night, she pictured the horses at the bottom of her garden. Beyond the point where her ribbon of lawn met the boundary fence of the farmer's field. And in this phantom-light, she half-fancied seeing them through the dance of mist: their meandering shapes, liquid as ghosts under the thin moon. Such majestic creatures, they were why she saved her fruit and vegetable parings, liking the sensation of their suede-soft noses nuzzling her palms when she fed them.

Switching off the last of her lamps, she turned to the hobby-horses that were now propped against the cold hearth. So kind of Gordon, she thought, simmering with resentment for Caroline, who had sat sideways at the table and sulked all through dinner. Such a naughty girl and so hostile to Gordon; if the child didn't wise up, he might stop calling round. An image of Gordon glided into view and she held him there for a moment, wanting to enjoy him. How cool he was inside his expensive suits, how composed, barely seeming to notice the suffocating heat she struggled with. The man oozed sophistication and possessed an unruffled charm that belonged to a bygone era. It was obvious he nurtured feelings for her – how else to explain the frequency of his visits? And that lingering kiss goodnight. Dora, tingling into the memory, pressed a hand to her heart that was beating far too quickly. A gurgle of a laugh as she made for the hall and, trapped in the stairwell – a space jammed between the tight curve of stairs and the plum-coloured curtain her mother put up to keep out the draughts – Dora took the deep breath necessary to drag her bulk up the wooden hill. Pausing halfway to look at her prized John Everett Millais print of Ophelia's face that, in the watery moonlight, looked as if it floated free. The rogue floorboard creaked as she pushed open the door in to the children's room.

A few seconds passed before a small voice perforated the dark: 'What you doing, Dora?'

'Can't I watch my beautiful nieces sleeping?' The tone accusatory. 'Is that a crime all of a sudden?'

Joanna didn't answer. Yawning, she dropped down on her pillow.

'Is Carrie awake?'

Joanna turned her head, saw her sister's arm flung out to the side. 'No,' she whispered. 'She's dead to the world.'

'Night, night, then … beaks under blankets.' Dora's parting shot fired off as a warning. Relieved not to have to converse with Caroline, she wondered later, hot between her polycotton sheets, why she could smell Gordon's aftershave in the draught as she closed the children's bedroom door.

Present Day

Joanna turns the key of her sister's old flat and feels her pulse return to normal as she opens the door on to the musty, unlived-in smell. A dark shape over her shoulder and she twists in time to see the man she thought was following her. He strides across the sweep of landing, about to head up to the top floor.

'Hello again,' she calls, realising he must be Caroline's neighbour.

'Hi.' The man steps backwards to look at her. 'I thought I recognised you at the flower stall.' He swings his bunch of pink carnations through the air.

'Did you?' Joanna, a touch embarrassed.

'Yeah. You're Carrie's sister, there's photos of you in her flat.'

'*Really?*' Joanna doesn't have pictures of Caroline. Aside from a single photograph of them as children squirrelled away in her sock drawer, there's nothing of her sister in her home.

'You're Jo, aren't you?' The carnations drip water on the black and white floor tiles.

'I am, yes,' she confirms, relinquishing her holdall to the tenebrous embrace of the unlit flat. 'I've come to sort things out.'

'Well, pleased to meet you.' He extends a broad, hairless hand. 'Me and Yvonne, we were so sorry to hear what happened. Sorry, too, not to make it to the funeral – I couldn't get the time off work. We'd have liked to have gone, we sent flowers.'

'That's kind of you, thank you.' Joanna forces a smile. 'Did you know Carrie well?'

'Reasonably, yeah. We used to chat now and again on the stairs. Sometimes she'd invite me in for coffee, which I saw as a real privilege.' He grins. 'Your sister wasn't one for visitors.'

'No, I don't imagine she was.'

'She was nice, though, I liked her – we both liked her, me and my wife. She was very kind to us. Last year, we ... we, erm, it's Yvonne actually, she was pretty unwell. Cancer.' Joanna hears his voice constrict against the emotion. 'And Carrie, well, she was very kind to us, doing our shopping, checking Yvonne was all right when I was out at work.'

'I'm sorry to hear that about your wife. She's okay now though, I hope?'

'She manages. We're taking things one day at a time.'

Joanna bows her head, shares nothing of her own health scare. 'Carrie could be very kind,' she says instead. 'And it's nice to know she had friends – friends like you and your wife – Yvonne, you said?' Another forced smile as she replays the contents of a telephone exchange she had with her sister during her gruelling treatment, which Mike reminded her of recently. 'Did Carrie have many friends?'

'No, I don't think so.' The man stiffens inside his suit. 'As I said, she kept herself pretty much to herself. It was odd, though.' He rubs a hand over his face. 'Me and Yvonne were saying, after we'd heard what happened in the mini-mart that night, we hadn't seen Carrie around for a quite a while.'

'Really – was that unusual?'

'It was a bit.'

'When did you last see her?'

'*Oooh.*' He takes a moment. 'At least a couple of months before she died. And another thing I noticed, looking up from the street – she was keeping her curtains drawn.'

'And you didn't think to find out how she was?' Joanna pushes, even though she knows it's a cheek when she hasn't bothered with Caroline's well-being for years.

'We heard her moving around – but you don't like to interfere.' He waits for Joanna's reassurance. 'But yeah, we thought it was odd, because she was always gadding off somewhere. She'd been losing weight too, probably from all the dog walking.' He laughs; a jerky, brittle sound. 'She was working as a volunteer at that animal rescue place the other side of Hyde Park.'

'Near St James's, that's right,' Joanna confirms.

'I admired her for that. Not many people happy to give their time for free these days. We brought a stray to her not all that long ago, but they wouldn't let her keep it – said a flat wasn't suitable and rehomed the dog elsewhere. A real shame that, it might have been company for her, because she did seem pretty lonely.' He pinches the end of his nose, looks sad for a moment. 'I know she liked visiting art galleries. Was always off to the Tate to look at that painting. She talked me and Yvonne through the symbolism of it once, the Christmas before last when she came to us for lunch . . . She'd bought us a printed tea-towel of it from the gift shop.'

'*Ophelia.*' Joanna smiles. 'Yes, Carrie loved the Pre-Raphaelites. Especially Millais – she used to drag me along to look at that one when we were teenagers.'

'Mmm.' The man holds her gaze. 'It seemed rather peculiar to us. We asked her to sign a petition once, can't remember what for now, and she wrote her name as Ophelia, of all things. Anyway.' He raises his eyebrows. 'You're a pianist, Carrie said. Pretty famous, we heard.'

'Did she— she said that?' Tears prick her eyes.

'She was very proud of you. Talked about you all the time—' He breaks off, responding to something in Joanna's expression. 'I'm sorry, me and my big mouth; my wife's always telling me I talk too much.'

'No. No.' She tugs her hair off her face, refusing to give in to her emotions in front of him. 'I want to hear. I want to know everything. Me and Carrie, we lost touch, you see.'

'Oh, dear. That's a shame.'

'You say you hadn't seen her out and about for a couple of months?' Joanna steers their discussion to her sister again. 'D'you have any idea why? Had she been ill, d'you think?'

'No, I don't think she was ill – well, not ill like that.' The choice of words suggests to Joanna her sister might have been suffering in some other way, but she misses the opportunity to ask him to elaborate. 'Oh, now, hang on, I did see her,' he mutters to himself. 'Once. Coming in from work one evening – it must have been the last time I saw her.' He shifts uncomfortably from foot to foot. 'She would've heard the front door go and came out on to the landing. I barely recognised her, it looked like she'd just got out of bed – still in her dressing gown, hair all over the place. She said, but she was rambling a bit, that she'd been getting silent calls, plagued by them in the night. Said they were stopping her from sleeping.'

'Did she know who they were from?'

A shake of the head. 'They were silent, weren't they? I told her to get on to BT, that they'd have ways to block nuisance numbers. But – but . . .' he hesitates, 'her reaction did seem a bit extreme.' A frown. 'I don't know, I suppose I sensed there was something more serious than a rogue caller bothering her. Getting weird phone calls in the night wouldn't make you so . . . so . . .' He fished around for the right adjective. 'Agitated. And she did seem very agitated. Sweating too, here and here.' He taps his forehead, his top lip. 'And so very insistent . . . wanting to show me her scribbles in a notebook, going on about how she was keeping tabs on him—'

'*Keeping tabs on him?*'

'It's what she said.'

'*Who?* Did she say who?'

'No, she didn't.' He lowers his eyes to Joanna's. 'But whoever he was, she was obviously very afraid of him. In fact, I'd go so far to say she was so afraid, she'd stopped going out.'

Summer 1990

The lane threading its way to Pludd Cottage was festooned with Queen Anne's lace. Coupled with the last of the condensed, white wood sorrel, the sisters imagined the hedgerows were preparing for a wedding. They held hands to cross the strip of tarmac – a habit forged on London's streets and quite unnecessary here, as it was rare to see a car at that end of the village. Pludd Cottage, coddled by trees, was as squat as a pepper pot. The girls needed to stand on tiptoes to reach its fox-head knocker. Peeping over the rambling dog rose into the pretty garden, they listened to 'All My Hope on God is Founded', a favourite hymn of Lillian Hooper's. The piano piece rang out through the open windows and hung in the pollen-heavy air. It gave the impression the cottage had a voice of its own.

The music stopped and the girls watched the front door swing wide. But no sign of Mrs Hooper – it was her little dachshund who greeted them. Dark and smooth as molasses, Lillian had named her Laika after the first dog in space, and the girls loved hearing the heartbreaking story of how the Russians made 'no provisions for poor Laika's return to Earth, which meant she died there'. The dog squeezed under the gate and shimmied towards them. Watching her carve a corridor through a verge of grass and buttercups,

Joanna scooped her up for them both to stroke, wanting to love her for herself as well as her namesake they envisaged spinning in the firmament.

'What a little velveteeny you are.' Joanna copied the nickname Mrs Hooper used and buried her nose in Laika's muscly sleekness. 'You've been in the geraniums again.' She giggled, the dog's smell reminding her of her mother's fingers after she'd deadheaded the tubs on their Camden windowsills.

'You girls coming in?' Lillian Hooper, her lustrous copper hair and beautiful smile, beckoned them inside. 'I've made chocolate brownies.'

A quick scan of the drive told them Mrs Hooper had no visitors. Even Gordon's car was missing today. Where had he gone then? The sisters' thoughts collided, then forked off in different directions as they followed Mrs Hooper's tall, elegant figure into the white-walled nub of her hall.

'Is your cottage as old as Dora's?' Caroline fiddled with the hole she'd made in the sleeve of her cardigan.

'I think so. They were made for the tunnel workers. You've heard about them, I'm sure?'

'Oh, yes.' Caroline nodded. 'Dora showed us that book of old photos at the church for us to see the people who died building it.'

Mrs Hooper didn't answer. Despite knowing it wasn't uncommon practice for the Victorians to photograph their dead, she couldn't bring herself to look at it, and wondered why Dora deemed it appropriate to show these children. Tuned into the afterlife as Lillian was through her palmistry and fortune-telling, Witchwood, with its gruesome history, was filled with enough violent myth and legend; the grisly images she carried in her head needed no further embellishment. Gathering a handful of last year's conkers from a container in her kitchen, the girls watched her distribute them to dust-free windowsills. Brown and wizened, they reminded Caroline of the heads of the hardened drinkers she served lunches to at the pub.

'What are they for?' they chorused, trotting along behind.

'To keep spiders away,' Mrs Hooper told them, deliberately enigmatic.

'Is it magic – like when you read tea leaves and stuff?' Joanna wanted to know.

'A bit. Now,' Mrs Hooper clapped her empty hands, 'who's for a drink and a chocolate brownie?'

Lillian didn't take a cake for herself, instead she poured a measure of her homemade rosehip syrup into two glasses and filled them and the kettle from the tap. The pressure of the cold water soaked her forearm as she contemplated those who came to have their fortunes read. Carrying a ten-pound note pulled back from their meagre housekeeping, they travelled from the plain little town of Slinghill, as desperate for good news as she was for the extra cash. Displaced souls, she thought of them as, in the same way she thought of the Jameson girls. Not that she feared for Joanna, the child sparkled amid the mediocrity – it was Caroline she worried for.

'D'you want me to read your palm later, Carrie?' she suggested, to compensate for her uncharitable thoughts.

'*Please.*' Caroline grinned her tooth-filled grin over the top of her glass. 'I love this flavour.' She took another gulp. 'Dora buys that horrible barley water – I hate it.'

She missed the look Mrs Hooper gave her. Caroline's

eyes, exploring the lemony-fresh kitchen, compared it to Dora's hotbed of bacteria with its food-splashed surfaces and overflowing swing bin ... salmonella, botulism, bubonic plague ... deadly diseases learnt at school; it would be a miracle if they survived the summer.

Mrs Hooper scooped out loose tealeaves and poured boiling water into a dumpy teapot. Caroline pictured Dora's fussy one, its illustrated scenes from *A Midsummer Night's Dream*, the lid sticky from decades of fingers. And when passed a sparkling side plate with a simple square of kitchen towel, she inspected hers for the greasy thumbprints she associated with her aunt's unwashed crockery.

Caroline saw that Mrs Hooper drank her tea black, that she held the cup close to her face and breathed out against the steam; until a clunk of empty teacup on saucer, and Mrs Hooper thrust herself back from the table.

'Right then, little one. Shall we get going with your lesson?'

Bobbing her head, Joanna scooped up the last of the cake crumbs. Plump for her age, with nothing of Caroline's sharp-boned angles, it added to her cuteness.

'You'll be all right, won't you?' Mrs Hooper checked with Caroline. 'Take your cardy off, if you like – you must be ever so warm.'

'No, I'm fine,' Caroline assured, fretting the hole in its sleeve again.

'Help yourself to anything you want,' Mrs Hooper told her brightly, not thinking the child intended to take her at her word – Caroline, remembering something she found in the study on a previous visit, thought she might take it away with her this time. 'But not upstairs, if you don't mind.'

Upstairs.

The word sparked feelings that prickled the length of Caroline's arms. Not that there was anything to fear from the sickroom since it had decanted its patient: the frightening Mr Hooper was deep under the earth in St Oswald's churchyard and couldn't hurt her now. It was like a scene from *Little Red Riding Hood*, not that she hung around to exchange niceties with the patient whose breath smelled worse than the bin lorry that crept around Camden's streets at dawn. Bad enough to think of the sweetish smell and his eyes ferreting her out from the gloom, but the shock of that hand, attached to its cadaverous blue-skinned arm, still made her judder. Knitted with veins, it shot out to grab her legs as she settled his tea tray among the bottles of pills on his bedside cabinet. 'My,' he'd said, in a voice as rusted over as Dora's Morris Traveller. 'What googly eyes you have.' His remark continued to bother her too, and she made sure to check if she was googly in every reflective surface. Was she googly? Was it another sign she was bad? What a thing to tell someone, she thought unhappily; something like that could scar you for life.

Caroline waited until Mrs Hooper had settled herself alongside Joanna on the piano stool before wandering Pludd Cottage's compact downstairs. Again, in contrast to Dora's, this dwelling, with its peacock-patterned carpet, was spotless and shipshape. Without the opulence and dusty-topped antiques that dimmed Pillowell's crowded rooms, the only thing dominating the front room here was a piano.

Reluctant to head out into the heat again, Caroline stood at the window and looked out on the slope of lawn with its clutch of apple trees singing with birds. Unlike Dora's garden, Mrs Hooper's was clearly defined by flowerbeds of sweet Williams and hollyhocks that this part of the country was famous for. She saw the swifts were well ensconced. Noisy and gregarious, drowning out Joanna's lesson, they swept against a sheet of sky so blue it could have come straight out of her box of watercolours. It made her wish she'd brought them with her, there was so much to draw and paint here. But in the chaos that home became after she and Joanna bounced in after a day at school to find their mother comatose on a sofa pebble-dashed in vomit, Caroline had forgotten to pack them.

Before she returned her attention to the room, she noticed a creature no bigger than a Labrador step daintily into view: fascinating, the glassy-gleam of its huge eye, before it leapt to freedom.

'I just saw a deer.' Caroline poked a finger into an ashtray heaped with Gordon's spent cocktail cigarettes; incongruous amid the neatness, they were the only disorderly things she'd seen.

'You what, luvvie?' Mrs Hooper, continuing to direct Joanna to the right keys.

'A deer. In your garden.' Caroline cleaned her finger off on her dungarees.

'Oh, a *muntjac*,' Mrs Hooper furnished her with the foreign-sounding word. 'Flamin' nuisance, chew my apple trees ... It's foxes I love. That's it, one, two, pass your thumb under ...' She returned to Joanna.

Caroline circled the room, picking up anything that caught her fancy, humming idly along to the background melody.

'You've a pretty voice,' Lillian told her.

'What's the tune called?' Caroline flushed bright red under the low-key compliment. Unaccustomed to any kind of praise, she leant down to stroke Laika lolling on a cushion with doggy paw prints.

'"The Little Lark" – there's words, if you want to sing?' Mrs Hooper took the tune from Joanna, played it fluidly from beginning to end.

Caroline shook her head, preferring the crop of photographs she'd found. The large prints in silver frames of Mrs Hooper in floor-grazing dresses, holding bouquets of flowers, the points of her shiny shoes poking out like exclamation marks.

'Why have you got photos of Jo?' Caroline, avoiding snaps of a small, dark Gordon, fired her arrow of a question into the room. Tinged with envy, believing it to be yet another example of favouritism, the arrow was directed squarely at Mrs Hooper's head.

'Sorry, luvvie – what was that?'

Caroline indicated to a black and white picture of a pretty little girl. 'They look a bit old, I know, but they're Jo, aren't they?'

The room fell silent.

'No, luvvie . . . ' Mrs Hooper answered. 'Those are of my daughter . . . Ursula.' She swallowed the emotion quivering at the back of her throat. 'She died long before either of you were born. Although, now you mention it, there are similarities, aren't there?' Mrs Hooper tipped sideways to look at Joanna. Memories of Ursula's funeral rushed at her, and she saw herself raw as a December morning in her mother's black shawl: no one came near her; it was as if the terrible disease that took her child had infected her too.

'You must miss her.' Caroline was concerned she'd said the wrong thing.

'Ursula was a joy, gifted on the piano too, so –' a tap of Joanna's pudgy little knee – 'that's why it's so lovely to have you to teach. You've such a talent.' Mrs Hooper, grateful to steer the conversation into safer waters. 'Right, how about an F major scale while I give your sister a reading.'

'I love your garden,' Caroline said, and sat on a couch the colour of winter clouds.

'Thank you.' Mrs Hooper smiled. 'Have you a garden in London?'

'No.' Caroline manipulated the sleeve of her cardigan again. 'We had one in Primrose Hill – but Mummy had to sell that house after Daddy died.'

Poor little mites, Lillian thought; what sorrow they've known in such tiny lives. How was that fair? She flicked her regret from Caroline to Joanna and back again. But with her mind still hovering with her own dead child, she couldn't express herself further.

'Dora gets Dean to mow the lawn,' Caroline told the sadness held in the folds of skin above Mrs Hooper's eyes.

A snigger from the piano. 'He don't do much of a job.'

'Yes, he does.' Caroline jumped to Dean's defence. 'He does what he can, the place is a tip.' She pictured the constricting corridor of shrubs, the tree-high hedge ... the horses she should have fed the apple cores and carrot tops Dora saved in the colander on her drainer, worrying they'd think she'd forgotten them.

'It's not a tip,' Mrs Hooper said, believing it to be what she should say, rather than feeling it. The juxtaposition between filth and frill in Dora Muller's holiday home had always bothered her. 'She does her best – Pillowell's not the only place she's got to maintain, she's got her flat in Bayswater too, remember.'

The girls fell into a contemplative silence and listened to the song of a blackbird close to the window.

'Anyway.' Mrs Hooper reached for Caroline's hands: tenderly, slowly, as if she were ill. 'You got a boyfriend?'

Joanna, a ripple of giggles. 'No, she don't; she loves Dean.' Bolstered by Mrs Hooper, Joanna was free to tease without fear of reprisals. 'She wants to *marry* him.'

'*Dean?*' Lillian's turn for incredulity. She looked at Caroline's hands and winced at the ravaged nails. 'Oh, dear,' she said more fiercely than intended. 'That Dean's a wrong 'un – you're to keep away from him.'

'A *wrong 'un?*' Caroline, finished with scowling at her sister, tested the word. 'What d'you mean?'

Mrs Hooper frowned as she studied Caroline's palms. 'The police are always after him for something.' *Drug dealing, petty theft ...* she lists to herself, unwilling to share his wrongdoings with the children. 'He's a blooming nuisance, revving his motorbike all hours of the day and night, disturbing the village – this was a sleepy little place before he turned up.'

'It's still sleepy, though, isn't it?' Caroline thought of the continuous noise of London.

'That's as may be, but there's people here who wish he'd go back to where he came from.' Caroline noted, not for the first time, the striations around Mrs Hooper's mouth whenever Dean Fry cropped up in conversation.

'But he's nice to me, and we've loads in common.' Such was Mrs Hooper's disapproval, Caroline was afraid to divulge Dean's intention to ask her out, and prayed Joanna kept her mouth shut. 'His mummy died when he was little too – like Daddy did. He knows what it feels like.'

'When did he tell you this?' Mrs Hooper quizzed.

'At the pub.' Caroline stared at the carpet, tried to put the configuration of bright blue peacocks into some kind of order.

'*The pub*?' Mrs Hooper was appalled. 'Dora lets you go there?'

'I collect glasses and stuff.' Caroline wiped her nose on her hand, assessed the snail trail it left behind on her skin. 'I help Liz with the washing up.'

'Lovely woman, Liz,' Mrs Hooper said vaguely. 'That Dean ... she can't control him. He runs her ragged.'

'He said he liked it better before Liz came along. When it was just him and his dad.'

'Did he now?' Mrs Hooper gripped Caroline's hands: a pair of upturned clams that, closing over, needed to be intermittently prised open. 'You watch yourself with him, okay? Just because he's handsome – well, actually, *especially* because he's handsome.'

The sisters swapped puzzled looks.

'Has Gordon got a girlfriend?' Joanna, stumbling over the notes, wanted to know.

'*Girlfriend*? *Gordon*?' A chuckle. 'No, no girlfriend. Certainly not one he's told his mother about, anyway.'

'Dora wants him to be her boyfriend.' Caroline dropped the titbit into the tightening awkwardness.

Mrs Hooper ignored the comment, saying instead, 'Nothing to see, my love.' And concluding her palmistry session before it properly began, snapped Caroline's hands shut like book covers. 'It happens sometimes, I'll try another day,' she promised, but clearly disturbed by whatever it was she'd seen, turned away to rearrange her face.

At that moment came the unmistakable crunch of tyres on gravel.

'Oh.' Mrs Hooper sprung to her feet. The sisters, identifying the trepidation in her tone, strained their necks to it. 'Gordon's home.'

Laika tipped herself out of her bed and raced away. Claws scrabbling the kitchen floor, barking wildly. Caroline didn't move. A hand curled around the snow globe pinched from Mrs Hooper's study and buried within the thick folds of her cardigan, she squeezed so hard, she feared it might crack clean in two.

Summer 1990

When Ellie called round the following afternoon carrying her roller skates, it took the sisters a moment to get used to her being a couple of inches shorter.

'It's my birthday Saturday,' she bubbled excitedly on Pillowell's doorstep. 'I'm going to be ten years old.'

'We know.' Caroline yawned. 'It's all you've gone on about.'

'Here,' Ellie said, ignoring Caroline and beaming at Joanna. 'These are for you.' And she handed over her old roller skates.

'You're not wearing them now.' Caroline was fearful of being left out. 'We agreed, we're going to the church today to show Ellie the *Book of the Dead* – even though I still can't believe no one told you it was there. You still want to see it, don't you?'

Ellie nodded, but looked unsure.

The girls followed a narrow footpath that eventually widened into a meadow. Wedged between woodland shimmering silver under the bullying heat, the way ahead was littered with dead trees, vast as dinosaurs, stretched out in the tussocky grass. Scattering a cluster of nervous ewes, the cries of lambs almost as big as their mothers, they watched them in the pearly light. They liked the sheep; liked the snags of wool they left behind on the briar and bramble, and equated their muzzles to the downy heads of sow thistle Mrs Hooper identified in the hedgerow.

'D'you like butter?' Ellie plucked a sunny buttercup, held it under Joanna's chin and was in the middle of confirming she did when a rabbit bounded out from a patch of waist-high thistles. Fascinated, they didn't dare move as it rested on its back legs and surveyed its surroundings. Until one of them sneezed. An involuntary sound that triggered the rabbit's quick-flash reaction, and it bolted to safety.

'Oh, look . . .' Skipping along without her wheels, Ellie jabbed the air. 'A bunch of cows.'

'*Herd* of cows,' Caroline corrected.

'Course I've heard of cows.' Ellie, suitably insistent. 'I just said – there's a bunch of them over there.'

Placid and liquid-eyed, the cows stood guard over their dozing offspring, swishing their rope-like tails. The Jameson sisters were wary, and wrinkled their urban noses at the plate-sized dung pats, admitting that apart from the horses, they'd only seen creatures this huge behind bars at Regent's Park Zoo. Ellie was familiar with these farm animals and it was good to have the upper hand for a change. Sensitive to Joanna's wariness towards her sister, she too had a tendency to tiptoe around Caroline, a little afraid of the girl that her mother warned 'had a mood that could spin on a sixpence'.

'It is all right, isn't it?' Joanna queried. 'Dora said to watch out if the cows have got babies with them.'

'It will be if we get a sodding move on.' Caroline, in control again, whisked them through an excited swarm of midges and onwards to the church, its spire spearing the mantle of trees, skewering it to the heavens.

At the sound of a strimmer from the perimeters of the churchyard, the children rotated their heads in unison to see Frank Petley, with large sweat stains drenching the under-arms of his shirt. He was giving the nettles and brambles snaking in from the wild their monthly going over and lifted his goggles to sneak a look in their direction. Not that they acknowledged him, preferring to throw their gazes to the high-sided vicarage, to the top-floor window and Cecilia Mortmain, who was always there. Caroline raised a timid hand to Cecilia, her heart ballooning with joy to have her wave reciprocated. She smiled at the silliness of things, the smallness of things: things that meant the world to a girl who believed herself unlovable. And with a squeeze of pity for the pretty lady who didn't look well, Caroline thought of her sitting alone, watching the world turn from her upstairs room, and half-wondered if she should call round one day and see her.

Beyond its vast storm doors, the church smelled of damp stone, its breath cold from years of failed prayers and soul-searching. This was where God was hiding, they thought independently, and stepped inside. The book Caroline was keen to share with their summertime companion was as heavy as an infant. And, establishing the coast was clear – the tallest and always in charge – she balanced aboard the rickety stool Tilly Petley sat on to turn Mrs Hooper's sheet music. In grave danger of overreaching herself, she wobbled from side to side as she stretched to tug the book from its tomb of greasy hymn books and pigeon droppings. Joanna and Ellie waited, hands clamped like limpets to their mouths, trapping the anxiety that always trembled in their throats when they were with Caroline.

Ellie and Joanna tasted the dust and mouldiness as they watched their leader climb the pulpit and lower the book on the lectern. Looking over her shoulder as pages were turned on a gruesome world none of them fully understood, they listened to Caroline embroidering its history the way Dora had done, repeating the remembered words to explain the fetish the Victorians had with photographing their dead.

'These were the people who died when part of the tunnel collapsed on them,' she informed Ellie, enjoying the way her voice rang out authoritatively as she identified the frilled collars and caps, the neatly combed hair, the silt-blackened nostrils. How some had their eyelids closed in readiness for the stuttering camera lens, while others stared blindly with expressions of wonderment and awe. 'They were scrubbed clean of the rock and mud that suffocated them, then dressed in borrowed finery and photographed to meet their maker.'

All Joanna could think through her sister's drone was how utterly dead they were; these mothers and fathers and children and babies. But what were children and babies doing in the tunnel, she had wanted to ask, but there was no one to ask, and she wanted Caroline to shut up. Death was a place, she thought, a far away, shifting place where these people had gone. It was where her father had gone, and she would go there one day and see him again. It was probably what her mother believed too, except she just wanted to get there more quickly, Joanna supposed, and that's why she took those tablets.

Caroline, in contrast, thought it marvellous that such ordinary people could be transformed into beautiful, sleeping angels after suffering such brutal ends. She hoped someone would dress her up in pretty things when she died, and wondered why no one thought to take pictures of their father after he'd been pulled from the sea.

Equally fascinated, Ellie looked on without a sound. Unflinching and not the least perturbed by the peculiar ensembles of families as dead-eyed as the dolls she played with at home. They were neatly arranged on plush uphol-stery, leaning into one another on tasselled cushions and throws, the likes of which these poor dead souls would never have known when living. Only when Caroline turned the final plate and Ellie saw what lay buried between the last page and its hardback cover, did her stomach tighten.

A Polaroid of Ellie on her roller skates. Taken only two days ago. Joanna recognised her bubble-gum pink leg-warmers and pinpointed it exactly. Startling, unsettling and wrong; the shock made Ellie's heart beat faster. What did it mean? No one spoke; each seemingly as frightened as the others to touch the incongruous square of plastic as they were to break the spell of unexpected pure, white light pouring in through the large plain windows. A light so bright it bleached out shadow. Caroline whipped the Polaroid out, then shut the book; the creak of its cover reverberated through the hush that closed over them like the lid of a coffin.

A scrape of furniture and the door to the vestry opened behind them, making them jump. They'd assumed they were alone, and panicking, thinking they needed to replace the book before there were questions – questions none of them wanted to answer – they dived from the pulpit and charged back down the aisle, and once Caroline had returned the book to its bed of bird droppings with far less drama, raced out into the sunshine. But in their mad rush to get away, Caroline dropped the Polaroid: something she realised as the church door thudded shut, trapping the murmuring voices of a man and a woman there wasn't the time to turn around to see.

'Why was there a photo of me in that book?' Ellie, round-eyed and pale, stared out on a world no one had prepared her for. 'I don't remember it being taken – I don't understand.'

When the children left the church, silence was restored. Setting aside the red tartan blanket he'd been folding, Reverend Timothy Mortmain stepped into the aisle. With muddied turn-ups and twigs in his hair from his yomp through the trees, his soft-soles slapped against the muffled serenity of his domain.

He'd been watching the children from the depths of the woods, and then from the shadows provided by his vestry door. Such a shame the younger two seemed put off by the macabre contents of the book, unlike the older one, who'd been back to the church many times since Dora first showed it to her and her sister. He might not mind the intrusion so much if the younger ones came with her. They really were such pretty little girls.

Present Day

Once inside her sister's old flat, Joanna locks the door and secures the bolts Dora would have fitted years ago. She bends to gather the post from the mat and hears Caroline's neighbour moving around above. Robert, Richard … *Roger*? Roger the Lodger? Joanna isn't good with names. Not that he was ever her sister's lodger; Dora's parents had the house converted and sold off the top and bottom floors. But such a nice man, she wonders if she should have invited him and his wife in for a cup of tea. Maybe Yvonne knows more about what was going on with Caroline than her husband, maybe Caroline confided in her about this man she said she needed to keep tabs on; but it didn't sound as if the poor woman was very well, so perhaps it's better not to pester them.

Turning her attention to the flat's interior, the telephone is the first thing she sees. Its sinister red eye winking through the gloom. She spots the brown leather scabbard with its swastika emblem on the table beside it. Missing its blade, the thing had done more than enough damage; she asked the police to dispose of it even though it was doubtful they would have returned it to her. Sifting through the pile of junk mail and unopened letters, Joanna finds a flier for her recent concert at the Wigmore Hall. Quartered and creased and kept safe from unforeseen draughts by a potted fern. *You kept this?* She picks it up, her lips bunching with emotion. She hadn't really believed the neighbour, but supposes she must have meant something to her sister if she held on to it.

Peering at the thumbnail-size screen on the telephone, she sees there are nine missed calls. Listening to her own messages that she left Caroline, things she should have told her sister when she was alive, Joanna hears others from Jeffrey Morris at the rescue centre, informing Caroline that they'd had 'some bloke in asking after her, that he was wanting to know when she was next in', and imploring her sister to please return his call. Another from Caroline's GP surgery, voicing concern that she hadn't been in to collect her prescriptions. And one from a Sue Fisher, from St Mary's Hospital, Paddington, saying she was a 'wee bit worried' that Caroline had missed another appointment with her at the clinic, and if she could 'please get in touch'.

Joanna jots down the number when it's given, presses it into her mobile.

'St Mary's Psychiatric Clinic, Sue Fisher speaking.' A woman answers almost immediately.

'Oh, yes. Hello.' Joanna transports the voice, via the handset, to the window, picking up a pair of brass opera glasses remembered from Pillowell along the way. 'I'm Caroline Jameson's sister – Joanna Peters?' She tapers her introduction into a question. 'My sister was seeing you. You've left telephone messages for her.'

'Aye, hello,' Sue Fisher replies, and after a brief pause, 'I was very saddened to hear what happened to Caroline, please accept my condolences.'

'Thank you. Yes, it's been awful. Erm, I was wondering, perhaps . . .'

'Would you like to come and see me?' the voice offers.

'See you? Well, um, yes. Yes, I would.' Joanna, flummoxed, hadn't expected the invitation to come this readily. 'That's very kind of you, if you've the time.' Getting an appointment at her surgery in St Albans is near on impossible. But, she supposes, this is different, and Joanna hopes that, unlike doctors, this Sue Fisher will be able to disclose things about Caroline a GP never could.

'I think we need to talk,' The Highlands accent assures, 'I'm sure there'll be much we can discuss.'

'Yes, there's loads I don't understand, and maybe you could help.' Joanna, borderline gleeful. 'Were you Caroline's psychiatrist?'

'No, I was her mental health nurse,' the woman explains. 'Your sister was referred to me by her psychiatrist . . . now, give me a wee second . . .'

Joanna hears Sue Fisher swap the receiver to her other ear, the clunk of an earring against the shellac handset and sounds of pages being turned. Nosing between a gap in the heavy brocade curtains, she surveys the rooftop view of Bayswater that came with this large, two-bed flat. Unaware of the latter state of her sister's mental health, she had no idea Caroline had been receiving psychiatric help: her thoughts as she looks down to the pavement filmed in thin winter rain.

'Tomorrow.' Sue Fisher: definite and final. 'I can do eleven-thirty tomorrow.'

Doing a room by room, Joanna, aware of the hollow sound her heels make as they strike the dark polished floorboards, draws back the curtains and instantly changes the dimension of the flat. Far more spacious than she remembered, with its huge mirrors reflecting the seemingly endless rooms opening on to one another, but she can tell at a glance that Caroline never bothered to modify the place; the bathroom, plain and functional, doesn't even have a shower. The taps squeak and drip, the pipes bang; they are going to have to spend a fair amount renovating if they're to get the good price Mike is banking on. Wandering around, still in her coat, she strokes the chenille head of Caroline's hobby horse. Faded and fraying, it leans against the door of the master bedroom. Seeing a white wisp of her breath, she claps her hands together for warmth. No central heating either. She makes a quick appraisal of the plug-in radiators and electric fires scattered throughout. And despite loving the feel of the place – the subdued tranquillity transfused with the chalky London light pouring in through its large sash windows, the Persian rugs of mulberry, bronze and plum – she wonders if it's going to be possible to stay overnight.

Dragging her gaze from a curtain of cobwebs clinging to the far ceiling, she scans the room, recognises various pieces of furniture from Witchwood, the odd knickknack and curio squeezed in here and there. No sign of the chaise longue and miniature tables with their velvet drapes, but there are plenty of tasselled lamps and oil paintings. Understandable Dora wasn't able to part with anything – enshrined in family history, it would have been too much of a wrench – but Caroline should have sold it off, made a fresh start. A constant reminder of that particular pocket of time wouldn't have been any good for her.

An inspection of the kitchen cupboards and fridge informs Joanna there is nothing to eat. She considers her cupboards at home – the well-stocked larder and freezer – and deduces Caroline can't have bothered cooking herself proper meals. From the state of the microwave and the contents of the swing bin, it looks as if she lived off ready meals, chocolates, cakes and ice cream. Returning to the expansive living room, she scans the shelves of books – Dora's, not Caroline's – written in languages she doesn't understand. Her aunt, a polyglot, was a surprisingly clever woman; Caroline too – she should have finished her A-Levels and gone to art college, because like Dora she had a gift, a gift she squandered. Joanna looks about her in despair; she had no idea how much stuff there was to sort through and questions whether the Salvation Army couldn't be persuaded to take the lot, and she and Mike donate the money to charity.

Talking herself into at least removing the most personal of Caroline's belongings, she makes a start with the escritoire, another item of furniture evoking memories of her great-aunt's summer home. The first thing she lands on is Mrs Hooper's snow globe. Dusty-topped, but otherwise in perfect condition. She swirls it through the air and watches the white flakes settle on the magnified world with its perfect little family. 'You were naughty to take this,' she says to her dead sister as she guides it inside her holdall, folding it into the soft layers between her woollens to keep it safe, intending to return it to Mrs Hooper, although when, she doesn't know. The idea of going back to Witchwood is deeply unsettling, and up to now it's a place she's managed to avoid. But, Joanna supposes, she's going to have to face it

116

at some point, if only to establish the state Pillowell Cottage is in, and whether they can sell that too.

What she finds next, tugging open the top drawer, is a gold ring with a large blue gemstone. Topaz, she guesses, slipping it on to her middle finger, admiring the way it snares the light. Dora's? She supposes it must have been; her aunt owned many beautiful things, all of which were left to Caroline. Deeper inside the drawer, filtering through sticky-tipped biros, toffee wrappers, bank statements and half-empty bottles of Stop'n Grow, the clunk of something heavy. A brooch this time: beautifully ornate with a deep-red stone and something she thinks she recognises. She pins it to the collar of her coat – Caroline's things belong to her now, don't they?

Delving further, she finds a set of keys with a handwritten tag reading: *Pillowell*. What she also finds, pocketing the keys, are several notebooks. Cracking one open, dark thoughts crowd her mind as she attempts to unravel the spill of what she supposes are the warped contents of her sister's dreams, but with the writing largely illegible, she will have to devote considerable time to get to grips with it. A fatter notebook, its cover the same William Morris design that papered the walls of Dora's holiday cottage, contains more ramblings until the writing becomes tighter, the biro marks darker where the nib has been forced so hard it nearly rips the paper. Joanna deciphers dates and times underscored as *SIGHTINGS* that begin in early autumn and go right up to her sister's violent death in late December. A shudder when she pictures the knife Caroline armed herself with, and to push the upsetting feelings away, she flicks through the pages and uncovers the most lucid writing so far. Cohesive sentences describing Witchwood and a faceless couple in a lane at dusk, picnics in the woods ... A memory of the abandoned one they found with Ellie that afternoon near Drake's Pike, but hadn't known what it meant. Is that what Caroline is describing here, she wonders, turning more pages. But just when it seems to reach a crucial reveal, with tantalising promises of *dirty secrets ... filthy lies*, it runs out of steam. The letters making words that would solve the riddle, loop back on themselves in the margins and are lost to her.

She attempts to close the drawer, but something jammed at the back stops her. A large scrapbook. She carries it to the sofa and sits down for a proper look. What Joanna finds is page after page of neatly spaced and carefully glued-in newspaper cuttings and fliers documenting her piano-playing career. A record that begins with a picture of her cut from the *Evening Standard* when she was awarded her music scholarship aged ten. Then the photograph the BBC took when she won her section of the Young Musician of the Year in 1997. Joanna presses a finger to her sixteen-year-old face and gulps back tears. She had no idea Caroline cared enough to do this and thinking she could have meant this much to someone she's not seen for a decade comes as a shock. The meticulous logging of reports and reviews of what appears to be every performance she's given in the UK and Europe would have taken real dedication, she realises; even Joanna doesn't keep a record of all she's done throughout her twenty-year career. And look, there are tickets dating back to the late-nineties from the South Bank, the Wigmore Hall; Caroline must have been coming to her London recitals too – she must have been sitting in the audience.

Deeply moved as she is by this show of sisterly love, this isn't the whole story; it isn't how Joanna feels about her life. The glitz and glamour, the showering with flowers – Caroline, she remembers sadly, had fewer flowers at her funeral – she appreciates how it must have looked to her sibling, who from what she can make out, now she's inside her home, led a pretty lonely and unfulfilled existence. But the reality, like most things, is always a diamond-faceted thing, and Joanna would have gladly tilted the flaws to the light for Caroline to understand the bigger picture. Talked about the sacrifices she's needed to make, the lengthy hours of piano practice she must apply herself to each day – days that, after repeating the same phrase over and over, push her to the brink of insanity. The months of touring, the string of airports, hotels, living out of suitcases, miles from her family. All things she would have happily confided in her sister. Yes, she's been lucky in all she's achieved and is grateful for it, but it has its downside – things are nowhere near as picture perfect as they're being portrayed in these images.

Midway through the chronicling of her prolific musical career, something stops her turning the pages. Sandwiched between Joanna – spot-lit, in long black dresses – is a collection of grainy photographs cut from various newspapers four years ago. Appeals made by the Gloucestershire Constabulary for information on the whereabouts of a Freya Wilburn, aged eight, missing from her home in Cinderglade.

'Why would Caroline have been interested in this?' Joanna says out loud. But her mobile, vociferous from her handbag, forces her to abandon her question and answer it.

Summer 1990

Cecilia Mortmain had cats: two narrow-skulled Siamese that slinked like aristocrats from room to room. A source of constant fluidity on her periphery, they tiptoed along an imaginary path that ran up and over the spine of a settee, the coffee table heaped with library books, and the Turkish rug from a long-ago holiday. Graceful as ballerinas, they were nothing to do with her husband. As with her, he barely noticed their existence, except to complain of hairs.

Beyond her window the sky was a freaky cartoon-blue. She drained the last of her tea and watched a lone cloud drift aimlessly across it. Positioned, as usual, at her high look-out post, Cecilia contemplated the listing tombstones that like St Oswald's perpendicular frontage and soaring spire were smothered in ivy. Saw – along with the smattering of sheep that shouldn't be there, and Frank from the shop thigh-deep in nettles wielding his strimmer – the plot her husband had reserved for her beneath the Judas tree. Refusing to dwell on her own mortality, she dragged her gaze back to her cats. The seal-point and chocolate-point, which, like her, rarely breathed fresh air, circled her legs as sharks do their prey. Until three dark shapes snagged her eye-line and made her look outside again.

Ellie Fry and the Jameson sisters. Cecilia saw them happily skipping inside St Oswald's less than twenty minutes ago. The transformation, when they scurried back outside, alarmed her. Clearly upset by something, she watched their pale faces emerge from the shade of St Oswald's porch. Had her husband done something to them? Timothy said he was heading to church after they'd lunched together. Perhaps it was the elegantly heeled Lillian Hooper? Cecilia hadn't seen her, but from the muffled breath of the organ earlier, she was definitely inside. Tilting forward in her wheelchair, rucking the Burberry rug she needed over her knees despite the soaring temperatures, she saw that Ellie Fry looked close to tears, and her dimpled smile was totally extinguished.

The children separated off: Ellie back to the pub, the sisters to Dora Muller's crumbling holiday home. Then it was her daughter, Amy, Cecilia was looking at. Showing off her fabulous curves in the leather cat-suit Cecilia's sister, Pippa, gave her from her wardrobe. Arm in arm with Dean Fry, they emerged from the dark mouth of the woods just as the Jameson sisters vanished. Dean, louche as ever beneath his mop of girly curls, spun her daughter by her waist, and Cecilia watched them kiss. Seeing her daughter happy made Cecilia happy. She'd had a wretched year that began with her best friend being killed in a hit and run. Then Philip Norris, her boyfriend of two years, dumping her. Although, Cecilia suspected, their split had more to do with Timothy warning him off. Amy had been inconsolable, but look at her now, throwing her head back and laughing. This was Dean's doing, she smiled, hoping her husband – who took against the boy immediately – didn't go spoiling things for Amy again.

Timothy used to kiss me like that, she thought, gazing down on them. But be careful, Amy, your father isn't the man he once was. Her warning steamed the glass. Best not let him catch you. But why not enjoy yourselves – she argued in her head in a way she could no longer do with her husband – when your lives could be snatched away at any moment. She should know: look at what life had handed her. Cecilia nodded to herself, liking the sensation of her petal-pale hair: sinuous and flowing down her back. At least her debilitating condition hadn't robbed her of that. Small pleasures. Timothy had no idea, pestering her to cut it, saying it wasn't proper for a woman in her late-thirties; but she flatly refused, it was all she had left of her original self.

Amy and Dean sprung apart when the wooden doors of the church creaked open. 'In the nick of time,' Cecilia sighed through the dust motes, scattering them like seeds. Dean, hands in pockets, and whistling as if to beckon the world to his feet, withdrew from the frame. Cecilia prayed the fliers in St Oswald's porch would waylay her husband long enough for Amy to slip away unseen also. Interestingly, Timothy's attention had been grabbed by something, but not the parish noticeboard. What absorbed him looked like a square of black-backed card, possibly a Polaroid, but tucked swiftly away into the folds of his vestments, Cecilia couldn't be sure.

Timothy stepped into the sunlight and tugged at his dog collar as he slid a furtive gaze to her window. Hating him to think she was spying on him, Cecilia retreated sharply on her wheels. Not that there was any real need, the gesture was probably automatic; Timothy Mortmain had stopped looking at her years ago. She understood his disillusionment,

122

the debilitating symptoms of her condition impacted on his life too, and although it wasn't her fault, neither was it his. Within seconds, Lillian Hooper appeared, clutching a wad of music manuscript. Beautifully turned-out as always. Cecilia thought she was as classy as that Stefanie Powers in *Hart to Hart*, with her easy attractiveness. A demon of an organist, Timothy couldn't praise her enough, and so kind; Tilly Petley said the woman never had a bad word to say about anyone.

Downstairs the front door slammed. *Amy?* Cecilia twisted from the window. The front door slammed again. This time it was accompanied by raised voices, followed by the thudding of someone charging up three flights of stairs.

Amy burst in. 'You okay, Mum?' Flushed and panting, she adjusted Cecilia's blanket. 'Bit stuffy, shall I open the window?'

'What were you two arguing about?' Cecilia asked.

'Dean.' Amy shrugged. 'Dad knows.'

'I'm not surprised, sweetheart – you're hardly discreet, the pair of you.' Cecilia smiled.

Amy returned it, her prettiness lifting Cecilia's afternoon. 'I don't care. Dad can shout all he likes – I love Dean. I really do.'

Cecilia spread wide her arms and Amy, kneeling, her thighs pressed against the footrests of the wheelchair, lay her head in her lap.

'Best not rub his nose in it, though, eh?' Cecilia stroked her daughter's glossy hair that, fanned over her knees, smelled like the joints she'd smoked at college. 'You know it riles him,' she said, wondering if Dean had given Amy any more of the cannabis she needed to help ease her pain.

'But why can't he just be happy for me?'

'He worries you won't achieve everything you should . . . that you'll throw your future away on him.'

'What d'you think?' Amy lifted her dark irises then dropped her head again.

'I'm thrilled you're having a good time . . . trying new things.' A wry smile as she inhaled the smell that threw her back to a relatively carefree time in her own history.

'*Trying new things.* I'm not *trying*, Mum – this is for real.' Amy fidgeted on Cecilia's thin thighs.

'I know you think that now, sweetheart, but you'll be off to university before you know it, and—'

Their conversation was severed by the arrival of Timothy Mortmain: slightly out of puff, although this had more to do with his temper than the arduous ascent to his wife's bedroom. Imperious in his crow-black vicar's garb, he made the cats scatter; they didn't like the reverend, these intuitive creatures who lived on the tips of their nerves.

'How dare you run off when I'm speaking to you!' he shouted at his daughter from the threshold. Amy sprang upright. 'You're not too old to be put over my knee, my girl.' The vicar wagged a pious finger.

Striding into Cecilia's room to administer a disinterested squeeze of her shoulder through the cable-knit shawl she needed to keep warm, Timothy dipped his head to bump a tacky cheek against his wife's. This was what passed as a greeting between them nowadays, the kisses – along with any intimacy – sadly fizzled out after her diagnosis. Perhaps, or so she wanted to believe, from an irrational fear he had of worsening her pain.

'Oh, Timothy, you're sweating. Why don't you use the

stair lift we paid all that money to have put in? You're always complaining it doesn't get enough use.' She teased him, trying to lift his mood; but he refused to give the merest glimmer of amusement. 'And you've been in the woods again, look at the state of your shoes.'

'Don't fuss, Cecilia,' he said, the huge silver cross around his neck winking insolently in the sharp sunlight. 'Nothing a good polish won't fix.'

'What did you say to those little girls?' Cecilia stared into the recess of her husband's philtrum, to a thatch of bristles that always eluded the razor.

'*Little girls*? What girls?' The words thick with menace.

'Ellie Fry and Dora's nieces?'

'Nothing.' He stepped back too briskly for her to see his expression.

'You must've said *something*, they looked terrified, poor things – came running out of the church.'

'You've been reading too many thrillers,' he accused. 'You think everyone's up to no good. Not enough to do, that's your trouble.'

'Take me somewhere, then. I only get wheeled out for funerals.' Cecilia knew this wasn't true, it was her illness, not Timothy, that dictated whether she left the house. It was why they had the top floor of the rectory converted – because even if she wasn't up to socialising, at least she could look out on the village and still feel part of things. But it made Amy giggle, and lightened the atmosphere.

Although only momentarily. His daughter's laugh reminded the vicar she was there. 'And as for *you*,' he started up again, 'we don't pay for you to go to one of the finest schools in England to throw your life away on that *waster.*' The deep rumble he usually saved for Sunday sermons crackled against the Eau de Nil-painted walls. 'Smoking dope . . . riding around on the back of his motorbike . . . it's disgusting. What must people think?'

'Timothy, *please,*' Cecilia intervened. 'She is eighteen. And Dean's not a waster.' She lowered her voice. 'Don't you remember what we were like when we first got together? The things we used to get up to.'

A grunt from her husband. 'Why don't you come downstairs this evening? Share a meal with me for a change. We could open a bottle of something.'

'Not tonight, Timothy. I'm sorry, but I'm really not up to it.'

'Okay,' he said, sounding defeated. Cecilia read the disappointment in his tone and wished they could have their old life back; that she could be the wife she once was. The man was lonely. Not that he admitted this to her face – he saved it for his poetry, which he then gave her to read. 'Give me a shout if you change your mind.' And with long strides, he left them to it.

The room, churned by his presence, spun and settled into the languid heat of the afternoon.

'Don't cry, love.' Cecilia cupped Amy's face between her hands, drew her close and breathed her in like a rose. 'You two used to be such friends.' Her own eyes glistening with emotion. 'He used to teach you the names of flowers and trees – do you remember? He was besotted with you, wanting to give you a head start so you shone at school; which of course you did.' She wiped a tear from her daughter's cheek with the pad of her thumb. 'D'you remember going with him to the old farm labourers' cottages?'

'Yeah.' A tentative nod. 'The squalor, Mum – you wouldn't believe it.'

'As a young vicar, your dad tried so hard to empathise with his parishioners. Did everything in his power to help them,' Cecilia explained. 'You won't know it, but he wore himself out campaigning for better living conditions for those rural workers.'

'But they never really liked him much, did they?' Amy said.

'Things were better when he had a thriving congregation. Nowadays, those who've remained loyal only do so out of habit, or a belief the sky would cave in. You can see what he's up against – how hard it's been for him to stick it out here? Especially since I got ill.'

'Yes, I'm sorry.'

'Say it to him, Amy. Because it's not really his fault he's so grumpy these days, is it?'

'No, I suppose not.' Her daughter shook her head, then changed her mind. 'But he doesn't have to take it out on me.'

'I know, love, but he gets frustrated. You've heard him, the things he says to me sometimes, but I know he doesn't mean it. He's got a lot on his plate.' Cecilia, counting herself as yet another of her husband's burdens, smiled a smile that didn't reach her eyes. 'I suppose his inability to identify with his parishioners is why he writes poems. He's trying to make sense of it all ... of what's happened to me.'

'Is that why he takes himself off for those long rambles, smoking his pipe?'

'Yes, he said that because God had failed to show Himself inside the church, he owed it to Him to search elsewhere.'

127

Cecilia gave her daughter the reasons Timothy had given her for disappearing for hours on end. And what choice did she have, other than to believe him? Confined to a wheelchair, she could hardly follow him about to see what he was really up to; because she was certain he was up to something, and whatever it was, there was nothing godly about it.

Present Day

Woken by the violent squeal of tyres in the street below, Joanna tries to go back to sleep. She thought she had slept for hours, but her head had barely hit the pillow. Too full of the unresolved questions about Caroline she had hoped she was free of when she climbed into bed. Unblinking, she watches moonlight nudge between the folds in the bedroom curtains. It curdles with the glow of city streets and moulds itself to the withers of Dora's old furniture.

Accepting she isn't going to be able to drift off now, she rolls over. Groping the graveyard of earrings her sister occasionally wore, the framed black and white photographs – of their father, another of Joanna and Mike on their wedding day – standing proudly amid empty bottles of temazepam and zolpidem. She switches on the bedside lamp, swaps the sickly pre-dawn light for the artificial and swings her legs off the bed. Pulling on one of Caroline's cardigans, she slots her feet into her sister's old slippers. Finding the hollows Caroline's toes had made brings a memory of her father's shoes, and not of Caroline at all. Shoes Joanna would push her hands inside to feel where his toes had been, before her mother bagged them up for Oxfam to take away.

Padding to the bathroom, she tugs on the light and is greeted by more of her sister's medication lined up in the cabinet above the basin. The sight of it pushes her back to that damp, cramp Camden flat of her childhood: the stuffiness, the mustiness, the rows of brown pill bottles, their necks plugged with pink cotton wool – pills that if her mother didn't take spelt trouble. Shaking them and finding each of them empty, she drops them into the bin. She snaps shut the mirror-fronted cabinet and catches a glimpse of Dora over her shoulder. The draught of ghostly breath on the nape of her neck. She jumps, ice cold beneath her night-clothes. Joanna experienced something similar to this when Dora first died, but nothing since. Why is she seeing her again after all these years – is her aunt trying to communicate something? An unsettling thought as the real world recedes then shifts forward into the startling sound of the telephone.

'Who the hell rings people at this hour?' she grumbles, listening to it summon her. 'It could be urgent,' she says to no one, in no hurry to answer it.

Joanna sweeps Caroline's thick woollen cardigan around her, finds a hole worn away on the sleeve. Coddling herself, she aims for the hall, letting the swell of a rare gibbous moon lead the way. Slithering free from a fold of cloud, its supine stare is enough to override the stain of streetlamps and allows her to circumvent the sharp-edged furniture, picture frames and vases. Checking what can be seen of the clock above her head to confirm the absurdity of the time, she picks the telephone up on the sixth ring.

'Hello?' she interrogates the handset, pinching sleepy dust from her eyes.

Nothing.

'Who's there, *please*?' Her voice shaking. '*Mike*, is that you, love?'

When no one answers, her mind spins to what the neighbour said about Caroline being beleaguered by silent calls. Could this nuisance be the same person who'd been pestering her sister? Could it be connected to why Caroline was too frightened to leave the flat, so she missed her appointments at the hospital, didn't collect her prescriptions? And – worse – why she armed herself with Dora's knife that night?

'Who's there, please?' she asks the caller, a shiver of fear running the length of her. 'Answer me. Who are you, what do you want?'

Again nothing. But there's definitely someone, she hears them breathing. The sound fights for room alongside her in the dark.

Summer 1990

Asked by Ian Fry to do another stint at the pub, Caroline –
eager to see Dean and hoping today would be the day he
got around to asking her out – was up before Joanna for
a change. Elbow-deep in a basin of tepid water, humming
the tune about a yellow bird that Ellie played them on her
mother's guitar yesterday, Caroline felt the happiest she'd
been for a long time as she slapped a flannel under her arms,
across her back and neck. 'Could grow potatoes there,'
an expression of her father's between fresh applications
of soap, made her scrub harder. The padded linoleum of
Dora's bathroom was sodden, despite the cork bath mat she
stood on. She wiped away condensation with the back of
her arm and scrutinised her face in the mirror. Found she
rather liked the fine spray of freckles that had blossomed on
her cheeks. She wasn't too bad, she decided; better yet if she
kept her mouth closed. At least her nose was straight and
her eyebrows neat, certainly not like the vicar's – those were
like the tails of the foxes Mrs Hooper fed scraps to. But it
didn't matter what she believed about herself any more. A
bright thought skidded into her head: nothing mattered now
she knew Dean loved her, and soon they were going to be
together. Forever.

Running the cold tap, she splashed her face and wondered

if she should cut her fringe as Dean suggested. Reaching this crossroads in her life – no longer the cute little kid her sister still was, but not a fully-fledged woman either – Caroline knew, despite Dean wanting her to be his girlfriend, she wasn't nearly pretty or interesting enough to join the realm of grown-ups proper. Cutting her fringe might help make her look older, she decided, repositioning the red Alice band Dean said complemented her hair – hair that up to then had only ever been referred to as *ordinary brown*. She would do it tonight, when Joanna and Dora were asleep: she would do it to please Dean.

Sounds of Dora moving around downstairs. Dropping things on purpose, as if to communicate how busy she was, how much hard work looking after them both for the summer was. Hunting for the nice lavender talc Dora said she could use, Caroline scraped what passed for a fingernail over the grey tide of scum inside the bath she and Joanna were reluctant to sit in. It fell away in flakes like dry skin, and she rewashed her hands, sniffing to check they didn't smell. Perhaps the talcum powder was on the windowsill, she thought, as she dried herself on a towel. She tugged the chintzy Austrian blind up an inch, careful not to touch the dust-thick pleats, but the state of the windowsill – a grave-yard of candied bluebottles – made her drop it again. God, this place was disgusting. The fancy soaps and luxury toilet paper pulled under the crocheted skirts of a round-faced dolly didn't fool her; Caroline reckoned she'd used cleaner public conveniences.

The hum of the vacuum cleaner propelled her into action, but before she could put on her T-shirt, she must first fasten her bra. Hanging nonchalantly over the wicker laundry bin, she eyed it warily. These two weren't friends. Uncomfortable with it in the same way she was with those thick pads her mother bought her once a month to put in her knickers, she picked up the bra and rubbed the cornflower-blue polyester that chafed the tender skin under her arms. She must wear it, must get used to it, even if she still didn't have quite enough to fill the little fist-sized cups; all the girls at school had them, and she needed to show Dean she was all grown up.

Fully dressed and out on the landing, Caroline still wanted the talc. She wondered if it could be in Dora's room and peeked around her aunt's partially open door. Stepping inside, she was hit by the vinegary smell of unwashed feet and a vague tang of sweat that, mixed through with Dora's signature perfume, made her wrinkle her nose on impact. It was as slovenly as the bathroom. The room was exactly as she expected it to be: half-empty mugs of cold tea, one with a bloated custard cream floating in it; dregs of red wine in smeary glasses; unwashed plates daubed with dried-on unmentionables. Clothes that had obviously been stepped out of, heaped on the floor. A pair of jumbo-sized knickers draped over a chair. It was like the bedrooms of school friends, the few she'd been invited into.

A curtain twitched at the window that wasn't quite closed. The faded material did little to sheath the room from the greenish light pushing in from outside. Tiptoeing over, Caroline looked out on a garden cobwebbed in early mist and dew then, withdrawing into the room again, saw that the jam jar of pretty wild flowers she picked from the woods and thoughtfully arranged for Dora only yesterday had been relegated from the dusty-topped dressing table to the waste paper basket. The indifference of it hurt and, interpreting it as yet another rejection, she rifled through Dora's ornate jewellery box for something to compensate her. A fleeting thought about the small yet beautiful things already pinched from the pub, from Mrs Hooper's, from her aunt's holiday home – a place crammed with so much, she'd convinced herself they'd never be missed. *What's this?* She sifted a substantial pendant attached to a heavy gold chain that, once in her palm, she saw had been fashioned into a ladybird. *Nice.* She smiled, dropping it into her pocket, the weight distorting the shape of her cardigan as she considered the state of the bed. An opulent affair, heaped with pillows, its silk counterpane kicked into a mound at the bottom. Turning away, quietly disgusted, she noticed the convex doors of the huge lacquered wardrobe wouldn't close over the bulge of dresses and coats. Dora's clothes had the luxuriant feel of money, with their deep hems and silk linings, the shoes of hand-stitched leather. Not that anything was appreciated, Caroline thought judgementally, stroking a particularly vivid green blouse.

She glimpsed herself in the sliver of mirror inside the wardrobe door. Pale and slight, it was as if someone else entirely was being reflected back at her, and she rather liked her ghostly pallor and wished Dean could see her. Turning sharply, something else caught her attention: a moonstone, blue with cold and larger than a fish's eye, fastened to the collar of a slinky-sleeved top. A brooch her complacent, lazy aunt had forgotten to remove. She drew it into the limited light for a better look, unpinned it, and dropped it into her pocket, liking the neat little click it made when it joined the fat-backed ladybird. Deciding there could be things she was missing in the bottom of the wardrobe, she crouched for a rummage. Nothing beyond the sea of mismatched footwear and brightly patterned scarves, until something far weightier than a stray shoe thumped against its panelled insides. Holding her breath, fearing she would be heard from downstairs, Caroline dragged it towards her. Hefty as a hammer in a slim leather sheath: a knife. She gasped in awe, tugging it free to inspect the frightening sharpness she needed to hold in both hands to understand its capability.

'What you doing?' Joanna barged into the room.

'Shit. *Jo.*' Caroline jumped, hitting her head on the wardrobe door. 'Don't sneak up on me like that. And keep your voice down,' she said, and rubbed where it hurt.

'I wanna know what you're doing.' Joanna's whispered demand.

'Look.' Caroline beckoned her closer. 'Look at this.'

'Blimey. Where'd you find that?'

'At the bottom of here,' Caroline pointed.

'Lemme hold it.' Joanna jigged from foot to foot.

'No way.' Caroline tested the blade with the pad of her thumb.

'*Nooo.*' Joanna winced and stepped backwards. 'Don't do that, you'll cut yourself.'

'It's sharp enough,' Caroline agreed with a smile. 'What's Dora doing with a knife like this?'

'I dunno. And I don't care.' Joanna persisted with her face pulling. 'Just put it away, Carrie. *Please.* It's dangerous.'

'What's going on up there?' Dora bullied through the floorboards.

'Now you're for it,' Joanna said gloomily, and slipped from the room.

Caroline quickly coaxed the blade back inside its brown leather casing, back under the layers of jumble, still wondering why her aunt would keep such a lethal-looking weapon, and if that black stuff trapped under the cross-guards was blood.

'You two coming down for breakfast?' Dora continued to pester from the bruised lighting of the hall. Her top lip – a white smear of Immac – glowed from the shadows.

'I'm not hungry,' Caroline lied. And with a grumbling tummy, she stood on the landing and peered into the large framed print of the pale, floating Ophelia.

'You're not looking at that *again*,' Joanna groaned as she jostled past and bounced downstairs.

'Mind your own business.' Caroline gave her sister a filthy look. 'She's beautiful. Can't you see it?'

The smell of singed toast wafted up the stairs, but Caroline didn't move, too absorbed by the painting.

'Carrie ... Carrie ...' Dora, spoiling the moment. 'You must be hungry. Your sister is.'

'I'll get something at the pub ... won't give me the trots, neither,' Caroline mumbled, *sotto voce*. And abandoning *Ophelia*, her mind sprinted ahead to Dora's tip of a kitchen. Let her feed Joanna: Joanna who eats everything put in front of her; keen to try new things, keen to please.

'At least have an apple and a glass of milk before you go, I don't want Liz thinking I don't feed you.' Dora, caught in a coil of light at the foot of the stairs, then disappeared into the living room to put a record on.

'Okay,' Caroline agreed, knowing she wouldn't – she hated milk, the film it left behind on her tongue was enough to make her sick.

Dora, without her make-up and tied into what was once a duck-egg blue dressing gown, had woken to yet another sunny day. A damp dishcloth in one hand, she wandered aimlessly around the kitchen trying not to trip over the empty wine bottles, the abandoned shoes, wiping things at random, her eyes gritty behind their lids. Humming along to Beethoven, she watched Joanna through the partially open window. Barefoot with breadboard, following her shadow over the lawn, she scraped her breakfast scraps on to a bird table. Such a kind little thing, Dora mused, brushing blackened toast crumbs off her front. Caroline too, she supposed, although her prickly over-sensitivity – a trait Dora identified in herself – made her difficult to love. Cautious enough around Caroline before ever discovering her left-handedness, when Dora recalled the drill of Latin lessons, and how 'left' meant evil and unlucky, her suspicion ratcheted up a notch, and now she secretly thought of her as *the sinister child*.

Caroline saw Dora tip her head to the creak of floor-boards as she made her way downstairs. Descending into Beethoven's *Violin Concerto* – stentorian and grand – she had stopped biting her nails by the time she reached the threshold of her great-aunt's kitchen, and was looking straight at her.

Why d'you keep a knife in the bottom of your wardrobe?
Has it got something to do with your old job at the Foreign

Office? Questions she didn't have the nerve to ask fizzed like a sherbet fountain on her tongue.

'What's the matter with you?' Dora, clearly unnerved by her presence, cracked open a new box of teabags. 'I do wish you wouldn't stare at me like that.'

'Hello, love.' Ian, big and burly, a duster in hand, turned when the pub door swung wide. A smouldering cigarette drooped from his bottom lip. 'You looking for Liz?' Dropping ash down his front, he buffed the beer pumps, making them shine like his bald pate under the pendant lighting.

A wary little nod as Caroline's eyes wandered the Boar's nicotine-stained interior, the length of dark, oak bar.

'In the kitchen. We had a few stragglers; she's only just finished breakfast.'

Missing her own breakfast, Caroline was near collapse, and happily turned her back on the bar with its wooden floors, chalkboard menus and Union Jack-draped boar's head – a thing so real, she was convinced its eyes tagged her every move.

Liz Fry, her sleeves rolled to the elbows and singing along to Radio 1, was washing out a huge frying pan. 'You're early, love,' she said when she looked up and found Caroline standing in the doorway. 'Everything all right?'

'Oh, yes, fine.' Caroline salivated into what remained of the fried-bacon smells. 'How are you?' Caroline liked Liz; in her eyes, she was as pretty as Doris Day in films her mother sobbed through on Sunday afternoons. A twinge of remorse for pinching the pretty blue ring she found by the sink that day. It obviously belonged to Liz, and Caroline knew she shouldn't have taken it, but at the same time, she couldn't quite bring herself to put it back.

'Me?' Liz hesitated – this clearly wasn't a question she was often asked. 'I'm fine too, thanks for asking.' And she turned the cold tap on so hard, water spurted high as a fountain, soaking the tiled surround. 'You're early, love,' she repeated. 'I've still got downstairs to vacuum.'

'I can help,' Caroline offered, wanting to be useful.

Liz heard this, but sensing something else, spun her head in alarm. 'Bet you've not had breakfast again, have you?'

Caroline swayed her response; the detour through the woods to hide the ladybird pendant and moonstone brooch meant she'd reached the end of her reserves.

'Come on, sit down.' Liz steered her towards the pine-topped table, dragged out a chair. 'I'll sort you something.' She dried her hands and peered inside the fridge, beyond the shelves of party food made in readiness of Ellie's birthday tomorrow. 'Fried eggs do you?' she offered. Wondering, as she closed the fridge and plugged in the kettle, why Dora never appeared to feed the child.

At this small show of kindness Caroline's voice failed, and Liz saw a ripple in her neck as she swallowed, trying to gain control. Wiping the damp frying pan with the tail of her apron, she set it against the Aga. 'You can help me with the chickens after I've cleaned the bar,' she said, her tear-shaped earrings splintering the light.

Caroline grinned into the welcome smells of sizzling lard; it was usually Joanna who helped Liz with her poultry.

'I fetched these first thing; lovely and fresh.' Liz, tapping egg after egg against the lip of her pan, stood aside to watch the whites harden. 'But I'm sure they'll have laid more by

140

the time we get out there.' She cut slices from a densely textured loaf and threw them into the hot fat. 'Sweltering again today, isn't it?' She waved her spatula at Caroline's cardigan. 'You can take that off if you want.'

'No,' Caroline said simply, sweeping it around her like a blanket. 'It's all right.' Shy of the perceived ugliness of her developing body, parting with the cardigan was unimaginable.

'Okay, love.' Liz, sneaking a sidelong glance at the child, understood more than she let on. She sang along with Elton John as memories of her own transition from child to woman butted up against Simon Mayo, who was now giving things away. Such an awkward time, she'd hate to live through it again, and dreaded the inevitable complications when Ellie reached puberty. At the moment her child was safe, she could live untroubled; but it wouldn't be long, children grew up frighteningly fast. Liz struggled to grasp where the last decade had gone. Only moments ago, it seemed as though she was holding her baby girl in her arms, and now she was a thinking, speaking person, with a personality all her own.

'You've got a lovely voice.' Caroline smiled without showing her teeth.

'You what, pet?' Liz, miles away, remembering Ellie as a baby.

'You've a lovely singing voice,' Caroline tried again.

'Thank you, love.'

'Mrs Hooper says I could sing – if only I wasn't so shy.'

'Shyness is no good. Mrs Hooper's right.' Liz turned the radio down a notch.

'Ellie says you're brilliant on the guitar, too.'

'Well . . . ' Liz's laugh: a spoon tinkling against a jam jar.

'I'm a bit rusty nowadays, but I used to play in a band, when I was younger – it's how I met Ian.'

'That's nice,' Caroline said, not knowing what playing in a band meant. 'Did you teach Dean to play the guitar?'

'*Dean*?' Liz raised her large, round eyes from the frying pan. 'No, not Dean,' she said, giving the impression the idea was distasteful, before adding, 'but I'm teaching Ellie – she's getting good.'

'I know – she played us a song about a yellow bird in a banana tree. Ellie's good at everything.'

Liz heard the unwarranted bitterness in Caroline's tone and chose to ignore it. 'Nice hearty meal, you're going to enjoy this,' she said cheerily, distributing eggs and fried bread on two glazed plates.

'Thanks ever so much,' Caroline said, wondering who the second breakfast was for. But before there was the chance to ask, there was a draught of warm air on the back of her neck and Dean bounded in from the bar.

'Ta for brekkie,' he greeted his stepmother, straddling the chair opposite.

Smelling of engine oil and the popcorn sweetness of whatever it was he smoked, Dean was still in his motorbike leathers and Caroline saw how the creases of the stiffened material followed the contours of his body. It kicked off a fantasy – soon to become reality, she reminded herself – about the pair of them riding off into the sunset. She imagined the kisses he would give her. Kisses that in her dreams were tender and firm, drawing her into him like oxygen. Feeling herself colour, she pressed her fingers to her cheek, then remembering the ugly nails she didn't want Dean to see, she shoved her hands under the table.

'I used to bite my nails.' Liz held the plates with the cuff of her apron and with a caution of '*hot*,' positioned them in front of them. 'It's a hard habit to break,' she said, examining her own hands. 'I know they look all right now, but sometimes when I'm stressed ...' She pretended to gnaw them, making Caroline giggle and forget herself for a moment. 'It was Ian who made me stop.' Liz's expression hardened as she continued her story. Caroline tracked her annoyance to Dean, who was smacking the bottom of a bottle of tomato ketchup, the redness shooting over the perfectly tasty breakfast she'd taken such care to cook. 'Bought me Stop'n Grow, I'm sure I've still got some – dig it out if you like?'

'Please,' Caroline said, gathering her cutlery.

After a couple of mouthfuls, Dean, too warm in his leathers, shrugged free of his heavy bike jacket. 'Aw, you've not cut your fringe?' he said, as if only just noticing Caroline. 'And there's me –' his bare arm, tanned below the cut-off sleeve of his Pink Floyd T-shirt, seesawed through the air – 'thinking we was mates, that we understood one another,' he teased and dragged his mouth south to feign disappointment.

Struck dumb, Caroline stared at him; she'd never seen a boy wear a necklace before, and liked the way it shimmered at his throat. How different Dean sounded from when she rang the pub in the dead of night: groping her way downstairs, dialling the number she knew by heart on Dora's toffee-coloured telephone. Nine times out of ten it was Ian who picked up. And nibbling what passed for fingernails in the dark, she would listen to his crossness as he coughed his smoker's cough. But if she was lucky it was Dean: yawning into the receiver, not half as bothered as he should have been about being woken. She knew she shouldn't do it, making silent calls was *malicious* – her mother complained often enough. But she couldn't help it, any more than she could help gawping at him now; she'd risk anything for him, it was something she decided the moment they met.

'Dora's got a big knife hidden at the bottom of her wardrobe,' Caroline announced over the clatter of crockery.

'A *what*?' Liz yelped from her position at the sink.

'A knife ... well, it's more of a dagger, really.' Caroline, pleased to have something to say. 'It's got a long metal blade and this weird writing on it ... foreign ... and one of them famous symbols.' She pushed the sauce bottles aside, traced the shape of an equilateral cross on the table.

'A swastika?' Dean, interested in what this kid had to say. 'Your Dora's got a Nazi dagger? Where the hell did she get that from?'

'She used to work at the Foreign Office, maybe she got it there.'

'Don't you go playing with it, will you?' Liz exhaled her warning, mind racing – that Dora Muller was a bloody liability.

'I wouldn't mind cadging a snout.' Dean restrained a burp with his hand, not sharing his knowledge that Nazi memorabilia carried a hefty price tag in certain quarters, and with the contacts he had, there were plenty he could fence it off to.

'Yes, well, unless you're prepared to go and ask Dora yourself, then you'll have to forget about it, won't you?' Liz snapped at him in a way Caroline hadn't heard her do to anyone, not even the most boisterous of punters. 'You're not to make young Carrie fetch it for you, d'you hear? I'm sure Dora didn't mean her to find it.'

The news kicked in somewhere, it plugged the awkwardness that had dropped between them.

'Ta, Liz. That was delicious.' Dean mopped up the last of his egg with a corner of bread. His stepmother barely responded as she tidied the kitchen, bobbing her white-blonde head in time to the music on her radio. Caroline wondered if she was deliberately ignoring him.

Dean gave a satisfied sigh and retrieved a shallow-hinged tin from the pocket of his leathers. He flipped it open on his well-muscled thigh: cool, nonchalant, rocking on his chair in a way Caroline was always being told off for doing at school. She watched him methodically construct one of his reefers from the necessary paraphernalia. Licking the flap of Rizla paper and smoothing it into position, he guided it between his lips and reached for his lighter.

'Oh, no. Not in here you don't.' Liz interjected sharply. 'Outside with that muck, if you don't mind.'

Dean unstuck the roll-up from his mouth. 'Okay, okay.' He scraped back his chair and was up on his feet, barely making eye contact with his stepmother. 'You should definitely do it.' He gestured to his forehead, his heart-stopping gaze dipping close to Caroline's face, snatching the air from her lungs. 'It'll show off your eyes – and she's got real pretty eyes, ain't she, Amy?'

Amy Mortmain, with her bounce of jet-black hair, slipped unexpectedly in from the bar and swished past Caroline's elbow. Her heels: pitter-patter against the ceramic floor tiles. Close enough to smell the tell-tale remnants of a recent cigarette, she scowled into Dean's compliment while bestowing a small nod of recognition to Liz who, untying her pinnie, swapped her pumps for the larger wellingtons kept alongside Ellie's little red ones by the door. Caroline may be naïve, but she was perceptive; she could tell Liz was as uncomfortable around this other girl as she was with her stepson and wanted to get away.

'Aren't you going to do the vacuuming?' Caroline asked.

'Chickens first, I'll vacuum after.'

'Can I come?' Caroline, doing what she was employed to do, gathered the crockery and carried them to the sink.

'Sure you can.' Liz sounded pleased to have the company. 'Dean will load the dishwasher, won't you, Dean?' she said, before gliding between the plastic strands of the fly screen and into the pub garden.

'Yeah, course.' Dean grimaced and folded his tin away into a pocket. 'See you later,' he chuckled to Caroline as she scurried outside. 'I'm down for the lunchtime shift too – we're gonna have a right larf.'

'You shouldn't encourage her, y'know,' Amy hissed when Caroline and Liz were out of earshot. 'Can't you tell she's nuts about you?'

'You're jealous.' Dean, playful, sidled up and nuzzled into her.

Amy giggled as Dean's bristles tickled her cheek. 'I'm only saying.' She put an arm about his waist, pushed the stub of her thumb into the belt of his jeans in a way she knew he liked. 'I don't think she's all there.'

'Aw, come on. She's only a kid.' Dean skimmed his lips over her neck.

'Yeah, but a kid who's desperate to be a woman, and dangerous because of it.'

Too busy to answer: Dean's hand, a mind of its own, was under her crop-top, caressing her breasts, making Amy arch under him. His love for this girl had pulled his heart as wide as a sail. She didn't know it, but for the first time since his mother died, Dean was happy; happy to let the soft, warm breeze of Amy Mortmain blow him along. And on this sea of bliss, riding the waves that made his insides soar whenever they touched, he couldn't help but extend his joy to others: to his stepmother, to the Boar's regulars, to the orphan-eyed and awkward Caroline Jameson – by paying her attention and flattering her in a way he would never ordinarily have done.

'Don't worry about her,' Dean breathed through his kisses. 'She can't trouble us.'

'Who's that girl?' Caroline asked Liz as she shook out saw-dust for the chickens. All glossy and confident, with curves like the women in films – Caroline hated her on sight.

Liz stood up to brush her jeans, pressed a hand to her per-spiring forehead. 'That's Amy. She's the vicar's daughter.'

'Oh, right.' Caroline knew all she needed to know about the vicar. 'I don't like him much,' she said, and shook his image away. 'He stares at me and Joanna all funny.'

Liz laughed. 'You're a one, you are.'

'Am I?' Caroline fiddled with the straps on her dungarees. 'How d'you mean?'

'You aren't afraid to say it how it is,' Liz answered, rip-ping open a sack of poultry feed. 'And that's refreshing, especially round here.' She passed Caroline a heaped scoop of grain. 'Scatter that – they'll soon come running.'

And sure enough, from beneath the shady fringes of

rhododendrons and wooden henhouses came every variant of fowl. Jerky in feathery jackets, they clucked and hooted into the filmy heat and damp sawdust smell.

'Isn't Jo with you?' Ellie, appearing from nowhere, scattered her mother's plumy friends.

'She's having a piano lesson,' Caroline answered.

'Oh.' Ellie looked at her feet that were waiting for the brand-new roller stakes she'd been promised for her birthday. 'I'll see her later, then.' And spinning round, she skipped away.

Liz decoded the disappointment on Caroline's face. 'It's only because they're closer in age. She's shy with you, that's all – what with you being so grown up. Here, you can help me carry the eggs if you like. Look—' Liz held out her hands. 'We've got all these.'

Caroline smiled into the compensation Liz forced through her eyes. Silvery and alert, she compared this woman to her sluggish, pale-faced mother, and wished she could swap her city life for one here at the pub. A momentary lapse in concentration and she dropped an egg on her foot. The sickening crack and slide of yellow yolk over her toes, and she began crying out of all proportion.

'Aw, now. *Now.*' Liz looped an arm around her. 'You don't need to get so upset over a little thing like that, I'm not angry with you. What a funny little thing you are.' Liz ruffled Caroline's hair. 'Come on, let's get a drink, eh? The sun's getting to you.'

Present Day

Ignoring the check-in screen at the Psychiatric Unit at St Mary's Hospital, Paddington, Joanna gives her name and reason for her visit to a woman at the desk and is told to sit. The waiting room is a rustling calm, punctured by coughs and whispers, but it isn't long before she is led along a corridor and ushered into Nurse Practitioner Sue Fisher's consulting room. Wire-thin, bespectacled, with a wisp of platinum hair, she unravels her legs as she swivels in her chair, but doesn't get up.

'Mrs Peters? Please, sit. *Sit.*' A bony hand waves at the chair beside her. 'Thank you, Helen,' she speaks to the closing door, to the flurry of *l'air du temps* left behind, before wordlessly returning to her computer screen.

The room is beige: the carpet, furniture, wall coverings, Venetian blinds; everything chosen for their neutrality, for their inability to offend. It even smells of nothing now the perfume has dispersed, and the light too, leaking in from outside, knows to behave itself. Unbuttoning her coat, Joanna doesn't remove it as she assesses the array of posters offering the stressed and over-anxious helplines and group therapy sessions, the boxes of syringes, hypodermics and dressings adorning windowsills and shelves. The modesty screen with its taupe examination couch.

The only thing of colour is the pink handwash balanced aboard the basin.

'There.' Caroline's mental health nurse, finished with whatever she needed to do, rolls back on her wheels and gives Joanna her full attention.

'Thank you for taking the trouble to see me.' Joanna unsticks her tongue.

'It's nay trouble.' Sue Fisher: full-time member of the Psychiatric Clinical team, with her 'wee' and her 'aye' and her heathery-Highlands accent. 'You have my deepest sympathies – it's a terrible business.'

'Thank you.' Joanna grips the arms of her chair: about to ride the rollercoaster ride of her sister's life. 'Was Carrie under your care for long?'

'A wee while, aye.'

'Did her GP refer her to you?'

'In a roundabout way.'

'Is that because Carrie was having trouble again?'

Sue Fisher makes a face.

'I was hoping you'd be able to tell me what's been going on.' Joanna wants answers – after all, this is why she's here. 'Her GP wouldn't see me, and I understand they can't divulge details of Carrie's personal and medical history, but I'd hoped you'd be able to give me something. I'm struggling to come to terms with what's happened ... I've got to understand why she was in such a mess.'

'Look.' Nurse Fisher removes her spectacles, buffs them on the hem of her skirt. 'I am bound by a certain degree of patient confidentiality, but I'm sure anything I say – off the record, you understand – will stay between me and you?' She waits for Joanna's agreement as she repositions her glasses. 'And, yes, these are such dreadful circumstances.'

'Thank you.' Joanna brightens. 'Anything that'll help me understand what might have been going on in her head.'

Nurse Fisher takes a breath. 'Caroline's GP referred her to a psychiatrist at the hospital after she tried taking her own life again three years ago.'

'*What?*' Joanna shudders into the bombshell. 'I didn't know that. I know she tried to when she was twenty-five, but you're telling me she tried again?'

Sue Fisher holds her gaze; Joanna having no knowledge of this comes as little surprise. 'Your sister was quickly diagnosed with clinical depression, and after that was transferred to me to provide her long-term care. She and I've been working together to try and help her recover from her illness.'

Joanna plays with the buckle on her handbag, thinks of her sister's severe mood swings that worsened into adolescence. Her debilitating sense of hopelessness spanning weeks into months – episodes when she couldn't be bothered to wash and dress, never mind go out.

'Do you have any idea what caused the two of you to fall out?' Sue Fisher, startlingly blunt, barges in on Joanna's contemplations.

A moment's hesitation. 'Carrie told you that? She told you we fell out.'

'She did, aye.'

'I don't know. I'm not sure it was any one thing. Our relationship was more complicated than that ... *Carrie* was more complicated than that. I don't think I ever properly understood her.'

151

'So, there was no single thing?' the nurse pushes.

'No, I don't think so.' Joanna thinks about the question. 'She was always having a go at me for something, but I suppose that row we had at Dora's funeral was the worst. The way she behaved towards me was pretty shocking.'

'And how did she behave?' Joanna isn't going to be let off that easily.

'By shouting at me in front of everybody, accusing me of being jealous that Dora had left everything to her.'

'And were you?'

'No, I wasn't.' Joanna, adamant. 'I had Mike. My career. Carrie was on her own, incapable of holding down a job – I understood Dora's reasons. She wanted to make sure she'd be all right. I'd have done the same.'

'And how many years is it since you last saw one another?'

'Ten. There were a couple of failed telephone conversations, but nothing recent. Dreadful, isn't it? D'you think it's dreadful?' Joanna, wanting reassurance.

'I know it hurt Caroline that the two of you weren't in touch. She often talked about you, said she missed having you in her life.' The nurse is surprisingly candid. 'But she said she couldn't forgive you for lying to her.' A box of tissues is pushed forward on the desk.

'*Lying to her*?' Joanna flings her head around. 'I never lied to her.'

'When you were little?' the nurse probes.

'I'm sorry, I don't know what you mean?' Joanna takes a tissue, blows her nose.

'When Caroline was thirteen. She seemed to think you lied about a boy she was in love with – that you apparently led her to believe he was interested in her.'

Joanna waits a minute, mind whirling. '*Dean*? You're not telling me she was still going on about him?'

'You remember it, then?'

'Yeah. Vaguely. But we were only kids. I only said it to stop her moping around after him, I didn't mean any harm.'

'Ah, but Caroline obviously didn't see it as harmless.' The nurse checks the notes on her screen, relays them to Joanna. 'She said you underestimated her feelings for him ... that the consequences of your lie were far-reaching.'

'*Far-reaching*? My lie? How? I don't understand.' Joanna is confused.

'I can appreciate all this sounds strange to you, but I'm merely passing on what your sister believed.' Sue Fisher pushes her spectacles up her nose. 'And according to her, you duping her into thinking this boy loved her when he plainly didn't, well, it drove her to do something terrible – something she was ultimately never able to forgive herself for. Or that's what she said ... what she believed.'

'*Duping her ... driving her to do something terrible ...* this is insane, I was only nine. I don't believe I'm hearing this.' Joanna clutched her face in her hands. 'I'm sorry, but come on, surely this is stretching it a bit ... isn't it? We were kids, for God's sake.'

'I understand that, but it shows us how something unintentional and innocuous can sometimes, with certain people, be misconstrued. And particularly so with a lot of the people I deal with on a day-to-day basis.' The nurse speaks slowly. 'We can't underestimate the intensity of feelings in certain adolescents – they can last a lifetime.'

'Obviously.' Curt, Joanna tries to process the revelation that this had been her sister's underlying problem with her all along. 'Honestly, though, talk about getting things out of proportion.'

'Aye, well,' the nurse says. 'But, you see –' she readjusts herself – 'your sister really was very ill. Clinical depression is a terribly destructive condition, as I'm sure you know. And one your sister suffered with for far too long ... You've a history of depression in the family, I believe?' The nurse listens as Joanna fills her in on her mother's mental fragility that, although dying of natural causes two years ago, meant she was never free of the blackness, as she termed it.

'Carrie was frightened she'd be dogged by it all her life, too,' Joanna concludes.

'Well, let me assure you, she was doing really well. It took us a while to establish the right balance of drugs, but the change in her was magical.' A smile. 'I really think the future was finally a country she wanted to dwell in. That's why this is all so sad.' The smile vanishes. 'I know you weren't in touch, but d'you have any idea what happened? Why she should suddenly stop coming to see me, stop collecting her prescription?'

'No. That's why I'm here, I was hoping you'd be able to tell me. It does seem as if she was able to talk to you. And I thank you for that.'

'I liked Caroline.' The nurse fiddles with the rubber tubing of a blood pressure testing kit. 'She was an interesting woman. I also knew she was on her own, that she had no family support.'

Joanna squirms under Sue Fisher's gaze. 'I know, who else did she have?' She raises her hands, the whites of her palms flagging her surrender. 'I should have tried harder ... If I'd known she was still fretting about Dean Fry, that she blamed me for it all ...' She tips back her head to stave off tears.

'She was terribly fragile, and it's often those closest who bear the brunt of things. Far easier for me, I wasn't emotionally involved.' A warmer smile melts into the watery sunshine sliding between the slats of the blind.

'It's kind of you to say.' Joanna's face collapses, preparing to cry. 'She was difficult, flaring up at the slightest thing, taking offence when none was meant ... accusing me of thinking things I wasn't.'

'All usual symptoms of people suffering from your sister's condition, I'm afraid,' the nurse says matter-of-factly.

'But now it's all too late, I can't put it right.' Joanna takes another tissue, dabs her eyes. 'I feel awful about it.'

'You can only do so much, and I'm sure you had your own life to get on with. Caroline told me you're a concert pianist. She was very proud of that.'

Echoes of what her sister's neighbour shared the previous evening, the contents of Caroline's scrapbook, brings more tears. 'But she couldn't forgive me for something I did when I was nine?'

The nurse pulls another face but declines to answer.

'We used to be close, really close.' Joanna continues to twiddle the buckle on her bag, guiding the thick leather strap in and out with her long, pianist's fingers.

'What was your home life like, when you were children?' Sue Fisher enquires.

'How d'you mean?'

'When your sister first came to see me, I suspected she'd suffered severe trauma in childhood – as well as this boy ... this ... ?'

'Dean.'

'Yes, him. But something else, something worse, perhaps? A trigger for what she went on to be. We never did get to the bottom of it. She'd talk, but only so much.'

'I suppose Carrie's problems –' Joanna stares into the crop of glazed family snaps of happy, sun-soaked people on the desk without really seeing them – 'began when our father died. I suppose she told you all about that, didn't she?'

Sue Fisher nods.

'My lasting memory of Carrie,' Joanna continues, 'is of her wearing these big, heavy cardigans, even in the summer. She was too shy to take them off. Thought she was ugly, unworthy. It only occurred to me how sad this was when I had children of my own. Two,' she says quickly, before being asked. 'I've two boys. Eight and twelve.' She takes another tissue. 'Carrie was obsessed with mirrors – she could get quite obsessed about things in general, actually; things and people.' A small laugh she doesn't mean. 'It got worse when she hit puberty, fixating on the configuration of her face, her budding body. Told me she was looking for reasons why Mum couldn't love her.'

'Are you saying your mother blamed Caroline for your father's death?' The nurse, reading between the lines.

'It's what Carrie thought, yes.'

'And you – what did you think?'

'That Mum was mixed-up. She was always tricky like Carrie was tricky, but she became a hundred times worse after Dad died. I suppose, when I think about it, we had a rotten childhood. Granted.' A thin sigh. 'Carrie had a worse time of it than me. At least Mum . . . ' These thoughts aren't ones Joanna wants to admit out loud.

156

'What?'

Joanna swallows. 'At least she didn't hate me. Didn't resent me being alive in the way she resented Carrie.'

Nurse Fisher doesn't move, her eyes sorrowful behind their glasses. 'You say your sister was volatile, difficult – was she ever violent?'

There is a pause. 'No, I don't think so. Not with me.'

'But that night in the mini-mart, that was violent, wasn't it? I heard she was carrying a weapon, that she attacked a man. Why d'you think she felt the need to arm herself like that?'

'Again, I was hoping you'd be able to tell me,' Joanna answers. 'Could it have been a side-effect of the drugs she was on?'

'There's nothing to suggest this. And, of course, by this point, Caroline had been missing her appointments, had stopped taking her medication.'

The sound of the telephone cuts between them. Sue Fisher flaps an apologetic hand before answering it. 'Aye ... aye. Please do.' She speaks into the receiver, then hangs up. Refocusing on Joanna, she asks, 'Did your mother ever hurt Caroline, abuse her?'

'Not physically, no. But mentally, yes, I think she did that.'

The nurse clears her throat. 'There's something else that's been troubling me,' she says. 'Particularly in light of what's happened—'

'What's that?' Joanna reacts to Sue Fisher's ominous tone.

'The last few times I saw Caroline, she'd become quite agitated – almost, dare I say, frightened.'

'Of what?'

'I don't know its significance, but she was complaining about silent calls during the night, asked me to prescribe sleeping tablets, which I did. Reluctantly.'

'Carrie's neighbour said she'd been troubled by them,' Joanna tells her. 'I don't know the significance either, but somebody rang the flat in the early hours – I stayed over last night.'

The nurse nods again.

'I admit it could be a bit unnerving, there on your own – I found it unnerving. But it could just be a fluke, couldn't it?'

'Maybe. But if not, it shows your sister wasn't imagining it. Do you think you should tell the police?'

'I would if I thought they were interested. As far as they're concerned ... well, they're not *concerned*, are they? They think whatever threat Carrie thought she was in was all in her head, particularly as no one was to blame for her death.'

'She thought she was being followed too,' Sue Fisher announces. 'That the flat was being watched. But,' a shrug, 'when I pushed her to elaborate, she clammed up. Whatever it was, it seemed to be at the centre of her fear ... *oh*, what was the name of the place again ... Hang on, let me get it right ... ' Sue Fisher spins on her chair, checks something on her screen. 'Witchwood.'

'*Witchwood*?' Joanna blurts. 'But that was nearly thirty years ago ... the same time as that lie I was supposed to have told about Dean Fry. What did she say?'

'Not much – as I said, she didn't clarify fully.' A rasp of nylon as Sue Fisher plaits her slender legs together. 'Caroline said something about you staying there one summer – is that right? When you were children.'

Children. Summer. The implied innocence of those words, when in reality what actually happened there was far from innocent. Because Witchwood – that quaint little village, that delightful country idyll – turned out to be the most dangerous of places.

Summer 1990

Pludd Cottage and Pillowell were dwellings unequivocally set apart from Witchwood's community. Not that there was much of a community. The village, hugged by the broad-leafed wood it was named after, was little more than a cluster of old farm labourers' cottages arranged around a rectangle of green. Apart from the pub and the Post Office stores, there was little else, and the wind of tarmac from nearby Slinghill tapered to an end when it reached the cross-roads: its choices limited to the church and its vicarage, or the woods itself.

Out under a golden light, Caroline, on her way back from a shift at the pub, was to collect Joanna from Mrs Hooper's. She read the Boar's lop-sided chalkboard boasting of Home Cooked Food and her stomach growled. She hoped there would be something worth eating back at Dora's. Passing hedgerows thick with berries that were yet too green to pick, Caroline was happy in the belief that any day now Dean was going to make his move. Convinced by what Joanna had told her, she believed he was as besotted with her as she was with him. The weight of silver coins Ian gave her was a bonus; she'd work at the pub for free if it meant she could be close to Dean.

Skipping up Pludd Cottage's driveway, Caroline pushed

against the already open door. Music – raucous, ornamented – filled the hall. But not from Mrs Hooper's piano, this was like the stuff Dora set to play under her stylus. Caroline paused to untangle the laughter floating above the swell of strings, and when she had, she charged full-pelt into the front room.

What she found nearly stopped her heart. Joanna and Gordon were dancing. Little feet balancing aboard big feet. Gordon was doing what Caroline's father once did with her. And with a hand pressed to her mouth, she watched the leggy grace of Gordon swirl Joanna over Mrs Hooper's peacocks, making her saffron-coloured bunches swing.

'What are you doing? Where's Mrs Hooper?' she yelled, expecting Gordon to be ashamed and relinquish his grip. But no, he couldn't care less that Caroline had sprung him – if anything, he twirled Joanna faster.

Only when the record wheezed to a stop did the dancing cease; not that either of them acknowledged Caroline. Absorbed in Joanna, Gordon proceeded to position his well-dressed self on his mother's couch and patted his long, lean thighs as if to encourage Laika – impassive in a strip of sunshine – into his lap. But it wasn't his mother's dachshund he was after, it was Joanna, and she dutifully climbed into it to play along with the trotting-pony game.

'I said – *where's Mrs Hooper*?' Caroline leapt to Joanna's defence without fully knowing why. It just seemed wrong: a grown-up man they barely knew cuddling her baby sister. Surging with love and a need to rescue Joanna from this danger, she tugged at Gordon's well-manicured hands, but, stronger, he wasn't surrendering his prize. 'Mrs Hooper's supposed to be giving you a lesson – where is she?' Crying

161

in frustration, Caroline put her arms around her sister's waist to try and wrench her free.

'Stop it, Carrie. Stop it.' Joanna smacked her away. 'I don't know where she is.'

Caroline stepped back, pressed herself against the knobbly woodchip wall and glared at them through the slanting rays of early evening sunshine. It was a shame, she used to like coming here, it used to feel safe – but not any more.

'Come on, Jo,' she insisted as Gordon remained unnervingly silent, his wolf-eyes glazed and dreamy-looking. 'Let's get outta here.'

'It's all right.' Joanna snuggled deeper into Gordon, and Caroline watched them swap glances she couldn't read. 'I've been learning to waltz ... Want us to show you?'

'No, I don't,' she snapped. 'You're coming with me.'

'But what about my lesson?' Joanna whined.

'Yes – what about your lesson?' Gordon turned his gaze to Caroline, registering her at last. 'Mum won't be long – I don't know where she could've got to?' And releasing a hand to look at his watch, Caroline seized her chance and pulled Joanna free.

'Let her go, you pervert,' she shrieked into Gordon's face, tears brimming in fear and vexation. '*Let her go.*'

Gone eleven and Dora, tucked up in bed with a set of earplugs jammed in her ears, was dreaming of Gordon Hooper's beautiful luthier-skilled hands. Oblivious to her thirteen-year-old niece inching downstairs for the kitchen scissors to cut a fringe into her plain brown hair.

Snipping, snipping, Caroline got it as even as she could in the reflection supplied by the night-blackened windowpane, before tugging open the kitchen door and zipping outside. She was off to the Boar's Head – something she often did under the cover of darkness – hoping for a glimpse of Dean. The idea of Dean reminded her of Dora's dagger. He had expressed an interest in it, so she said she'd show him. She dipped back inside to retrieve it from its new hiding place behind the vegetable rack, but her arm collided with a cauliflower and it bounced to the floor with a sickening thump. It rolled heavy as a severed head across the cracked linoleum, and she froze, anticipating her aunt's shout from above, but was relieved to hear nothing.

The night, warm as a living thing, pressed itself against her. And stepping into the lane that was as dark as a nostril, she listened to something rustling within the tunnel of nocturnal trees.

'Who's there?' she pleaded with the blackness, playing with her new flap of fringe. '*Hello?*'

Nothing but the bark of a faraway dog and hoot of a tawny owl as the skipping moonlight pinched out the silhouettes of things she didn't recognise. What she heard was probably the rush of the river, which in this stillness was loud as London traffic. Familiar only with the grumble of tube trains, the petrified squeal of sirens, people shouting and banging in the street, sounds of the countryside were ones she was coming to learn. Caroline tried to envisage what Witchwood would be without people, if nature were allowed to take over as it was doing with Dora's holiday cottage. It wouldn't take long, she decided, identifying her insignificance amid the abundant vegetation.

Reaching the carousels of postcards the Petleys left outside the shop, she caught her reflection in the window, but not clearly enough to see the mess she'd made of her fringe. She ducked into the beer garden through a gap in the rhododendrons as the moon slipped free of its moorings, washing the rear of the pub in a cold vein of light. The shadowy wilderness spooked her, as did the geese Liz let out to roam after last orders. Benches and parasols: innocent objects in daylight which under the cloak of darkness mutated into shapes of a far more sinister nature. Something brushed her cheek: a bat. She stifled a scream as it swerved away, her eyes drawn to the tawny light from an upstairs window. Thrown wide to the curious stars, it pumped heavy rock music into the hush. It was Dean's feet she saw first, the grubby soles of his trainers, propped on the window ledge. Then the amber-end of his roll-up, lolling like a drunkard's eye. She sniffed the now familiar, yet persistently elusive sweetness that was nothing as chemically smelling as cigarettes; not those girly, gold-tipped ones Gordon Hooper was forever puffing on anyway.

Then it was Amy Mortmain's backside she was looking at, squeezed into acid-washed denim, wriggling around on Dean's windowsill. Until Dean appeared, leaning out to screw his expended roll-up against the exterior wall, lobbing it high into the bank of rhododendrons. What happened next made Caroline yelp in disbelief. What was he doing? He was supposed to be in love with her, Joanna said so. It was why she chopped her hair off, took Dora's knife; things he wanted her to do. Her face fell open in dismay as Amy pressed her shapeliness against Dean's muscled torso. The lovers were backlit by a single lamp, which meant she missed nothing, and she watched them kissing through the continuous crash of music. Caroline pressed a hand to her chest and felt the corkscrew that already pierced her heart give another three-quarter turn.

Dean was going to pay for this, she promised herself as she spun round and ran. Leading her on, letting her think it was her he wanted … how dare he! Caroline's pain hardened into something dark and dangerous as she pulled her mouth into an unforgiving line. Then she remembered the knife she was carrying, her hand still curled around its scabbard. She had to dump it, it was too much of a risk to take it back to Pillowell; Dora could catch her with it. Hang on – she turned, saw the corrugated doors of Dean's motorbike shed had been left open. She could hide it in there. A solution finding her that, coupled with the possibility it might land Dean in trouble if it was ever dis-covered, went some way to balm her choking humiliation. But Caroline wasn't stupid enough to leave her own prints on it. If it was found, she didn't want to be the one accused of nicking it. And in the same way she'd seen criminals do in that *Morse* programme on the telly, she gave both the leather casing and the knife a thorough wipe with her cardigan first.

'Jakkes! What in God's name have you done to yourself?' Dora cried when she saw Caroline the following morning. 'Your mother's going to skin me alive.'

'Doubt she'll notice.' Caroline, still reeling from what she saw Dean and Amy doing, believed everything, not only her hair, had been spoiled. Like a fountain, the pain of Dean kissing and touching that girl replenished itself each time she ran the scene over in her mind.

'I'll book you an appointment at my hairdressers,' Dora

said. 'She'll tidy you up.' Behind her, the sun was rising, gathering strength over the trees. In the morning light Dora's own hair looked thin and dry. Caroline appraised it coldly.

'Difficult in this heat, isn't it?' Dora confided.

Caroline nodded.

'Breakfast?'

Another nod.

'What d'you fancy? There's toast, or fruit. Got some of that cherry Ski yoghurt you like ... or what about a bowl of Coco Pops ...?' Whatever remained of Dora's breakfast menu was lost to the rattling throb of the lawn mower. 'Ah, Dean's here, is he?' Dora, knotting the belt of her dressing gown. 'I'd better go and make myself decent, hadn't I?' She giggled, raising her voice a notch to compete with the approaching motor. 'Won't be a jiffy. Help yourself to anything you want ... you're good at that.'

Caroline's insides flip-flopped. The unexpected sight of Dean, or the startling undertone of Dora's instruction? She tapped the pocket of her baggy jeans to check the gold ring with its pretty blue stone was still there, her mind darting to the other things she'd stolen. Were they safe? Had her hidey-hole been discovered? She pushed a hip-bone against the sharp metal side of the sink and peered through the window at Dean: Walkman clamped to his ears, dancing as he lugged the mower over the parched lawn. Fears she'd been rumbled ebbed away, exchanged for the new thoughts she was incubating ... deadly, dangerous thoughts. Casual in stonewashed jeans and U2 T-shirt, Dean looked happy and she hated him for it. What right did he have to be happy after he'd betrayed her so badly?

If she had anything to do with it, he wasn't going to stay happy for long.

Utterly absorbed, Caroline didn't hear her sister push open the kitchen door.

'You *love* him.' Joanna, effervescent, despite the malevolent heat of the morning. 'You want ten thousand of his *babies*.'

'Shut. Up.' Caroline turned on her. 'And you'll stop going on about it with Ellie if you know what's good for you.'

On seeing her sister, Joanna burst out laughing. 'What have you done to your hair? It looks like a dog's bit it.'

'You girls all right?' Dora: a puffball of perfume in a dress as colourfully suggestive as a Georgia O'Keeffe painting. Only gone minutes; Caroline didn't believe she'd had time for a proper wash. 'So.' Their aunt squirted a blob of hand-cream on to her palms. 'All set for Ellie's party, are you, my little *putti*.' She chucked Joanna under the chin.

'It's gonna be brilliant.' Joyful, Joanna twisted from her sister's sulkiness.

'I bet. I love parties.' Dora rubbed her hands together, dispersing the sweetness of magnolia as she anticipated an afternoon to herself. 'What about you, Carrie? Are you looking forward to it too?' The question was hopeful as her mind raced ahead to the big bar of Dairy Milk secreted in the sideboard.

Caroline grunted, peeled her eyes from Dean.

'Wish I was coming,' Dora said.

'No, you don't.' Surly, Caroline lifted a hand to her mouth. 'Not if Gordon's not going to be there.'

'Stop it!' Dora smacked her niece's fingers away before

167

she had the chance to bite them. 'What man's going to want you with ugly nails like that.'

'Like you'd know.' Caroline blinked back tears she didn't want her great-aunt to see.

'Here.' Dora ignored her, opening her purse. 'Both of you; come on.' She rallied them together. 'Once you've had your breakfast, why don't you both nip down the shop, settle my paper bill and fetch me a couple of twits and a Double Decker while you're at it.'

'*Twits*?' Caroline took the tenner. 'Don't you mean Twix?'

'If you say so.' Dora, irritated. 'And anything you girls want.'

'What's the matter, Carrie?' Joanna asked when they were in the lane. 'Don't worry, the hairdresser will sort you out.' Wanting to comfort, she slipped her arm through her sister's.

'I don't care about my hair ... It's Dean – I saw him snoggin' that sodding Amy girl,' Caroline snapped.

'*Uch*, that's gross.' Joanna, disgusted. 'You don't want him to do that to you, do you?' A nervous sideways glance.

'Why not?' Caroline yanked back her arm. 'It's what proper women do.'

'Is it? *Yuk*.'

'It's not fair. You said he was going to ask *me* out. Why would he be with her if he wanted me?'

'I dunno, but it's what he told me.' Joanna persisted with her lie, too afraid to admit otherwise.

Into the awkward gap in their conversation dropped the mocking *coo, coo* of a wood pigeon.

'I didn't think you were serious about him,' Joanna said eventually. 'He's way too old for you.'

168

'No, he's not. We'd be perfect for each other. I don't understand it, he's really nice to me at the pub – telling me I've got pretty eyes and stuff. If he wasn't serious about me, he wouldn't say things like that, would he? He wouldn't have said those things to you?'

Joanna kept quiet as she struggled to keep pace with her sister's longer strides.

'It's not fair,' Caroline prickled again. 'That Amy . . . she could have anyone.'

'She is pretty, isn't she?' Joanna, forgetting herself.

'No, she's not, she's a bloody tart. I hate her.'

'She's all right.'

'That's it, take her side.' Caroline started to cry. 'I've got no one.'

'You've got me.' Joanna, her voice small.

'*You?* What use are you? You're gonna get married and leave me on my own soon as you can.'

'So will you.'

'Yeah? Who to, then?' Caroline, switching from angry mode to feeling-sorry-for-herself mode – Joanna was never sure which was the easiest. 'Who's going to want to be with someone as horrible as me?'

'You're not horrible,' Joanna reassured. 'Not all the time.'

'Shut up, will you,' Caroline shouted, angry again. 'You're supposed to be on my side.'

'I am on your side.'

'No, you're not, you don't care. Why would you? You don't have the first idea what it feels like for me. Everyone *loves* you.'

'No, they don't.' Joanna cowered under the allegation and pulled back her arm.

'Yes, they do.' Caroline was definite. 'Want me to list them?'

In the hush of the traffic-free lane, the girls were mindful their breathing kept strange rhythm with the breeze.

'Why d'you cut your hair?' Joanna's gaze followed the row of tiered cottages curling round the green: painted alternate strawberry, lime and lemon; she pictured them as neatly arranged Opal Fruits.

''Cos Dean said it'd look nice.' Caroline sneaked a look at the pub, felt her face burn with shame.

'Right.' Joanna stifled a laugh with a fist.

'This is serious.' Caroline turned on her. 'I'm going to get him back for everything he's done to me.' Vehement, hateful; something in her tone scared Joanna.

'How are you gonna do that? You gonna get that dog to bite his hair off too?' she asked, weighing up whether to slip an arm back through Caroline's to calm her down.

'Shut up, Jo.' A flicker of a smile. 'You'll see.'

'You're to stay on the bench. Don't wander off.' Caroline gave her instruction to Joanna at the same time the vicar emerged from the shop doorway cuddling a brown loaf to his chest like a pet. 'Want me to get you an ice-lolly?'

Joanna grinned her reply before raising her eyes to the rather peculiar sight of a heron – impassive and hunchbacked in its raincoat of grey feathers – balanced aboard the shop's corrugated roof.

'Morning, girls.' Reverend Mortmain eyed them with interest. 'Your lovely aunt's well, I trust?' He licked his teeth and Caroline saw how his tongue rode the waves of his lower incisors like a surfboard.

It was Joanna who answered him: her willing, clear-eyed self. Caroline wished she wouldn't. Why couldn't she see the evil in people like the Reverend Mortmain and Gordon Hooper? Reluctant to leave her sister's side, Caroline waited until the vicar strode away, for his broad black shape to be gobbled by the trees engulfing Dead End Lane.

Witchwood's shop, with its dingy, threadbare feel, was owned and run by Tilly and Frank Petley. Mirror images of one another, with their side-partings and unflinching stares, the rumour was that these two weren't husband and wife at all, but brother and sister.

'Ooo, it's a terrible thing.' Tilly, talking to herself as usual, gave up arranging the apples bruised sides down and moved on to the tomatoes. The door tinkled as Caroline opened it, but it was the frenzied yapping that fanfared her arrival, severing whatever terrible thing Tilly had been about to reveal.

'Hush now, Mitzy.' Tilly gathered her tiny dog and tipped her head to nuzzle its white fur. 'Hush, baby, hush ... ' And she jiggled it up and down in a way Caroline's mother did to placate Joanna as a baby. Caroline saw the woman's well-muscled arms that, bare from the shoulders down, showed off a mahogany suntan and tattooed pair of love birds caught mid-flight.

'Hello.' Caroline lifted the lid of the freezer and plumped for a Funny Feet ice cream and the chocolate Dora wanted from the ranks of confectionery barricading the till.

'For your auntie, are they?' Tilly winked, before calling through to the back: a muddle of cardboard boxes, plastic

171

crates and yellowing newspapers. 'Frank! Got a customer.' Her voice, splintering the gloom, was as brittle as glass.

Caroline spied an abandoned copy of the *Cinderglade Echo* lying open on the counter, and turned pages showing photographs of agricultural shows, charity events, end-of-school-year concerts, Princess Diana opening a new wing at the hospital in Cinderglade . . . the continuing saga of a local spate of unsolved robberies in and around Witchwood . . .

'Eh-up, lass – that's twenty-five pence if tha wants to read it.' Frank, suddenly at his counter. 'Tha get off to Liz's if tha wants.' The shopkeeper whipped his head to Tilly, who was still clutching her frothy white dog. 'I can manage.'

'Just these, please. And Dora said I'm to settle her news-paper bill.' Caroline gestured to her meagre purchases and dug through her pockets for the ten-pound note she knew was there.

'Not buying paper, then?' The shopkeeper's eyes glinted like teaspoons.

Caroline shook her head.

Without averting his gaze, Frank Petley counted out her change to the chromatic accompaniment of the till. If he didn't keep gawping at her, Caroline supposed, she might be able to nick some stuff from here; but thinking how he was always gawping at her, even when she wasn't in the shop, she added Mr Petley to her ever-growing list of grown-ups not to be trusted.

'Going to Ellie's party?'

Caroline stared at his paunch that strained at the buttons of his faded shop coat and nodded.

'Enjoying your holiday, are you?'

Caroline watched him place her items into a plastic bag.

'Yes, thank you – I don't think I want to go home.'

'Where's home, then?' The mouth screwed out its question.

'London.' Caroline, self-consciously touching her coarse wedge of fringe.

'*London*, eh,' he thundered on in his Yorkshire burr. 'Can't say I've ever bin . . . can't say I've ever had a mind to.'

The chime of the shop bell sliced between them.

'Mornin', Charlie.' Frank's face widened to a sickly grin.

It was her cue. Sidestepping the pair of them, Caroline shot out the door. But where was Joanna? The bench she gave strict instructions not to leave was empty.

'*J-o?*' she called, her cardigan pockets swaying with Dora's treats and the rapidly melting ice cream. '*Jo?*' she tried again, blowing out air to inflate the tiny word.

Then raised voices and, like a magnet, she was pulled towards the commotion coming from the outbuilding where Dean kept his motorbike. Joanna forgotten, Caroline pressed her spine to the undergrowth and craned her neck to see what was going on. The shock of seeing Dean for the second time that morning – wielding an oily rag, his hair laminated by sunlight – thumped in her chest. Was that Ellie with him? Yes, Caroline saw her roller skates, the new pink ones she must have had for her birthday. But what was she doing? Clambering on to the seat of Dean's Suzuki, crossing her arms and wearing a look of determination Caroline hadn't seen before.

'Get down, damn it,' Dean told her. 'You'll scratch the paintwork with those flippin' things.'

'But you promised me a go,' Ellie grizzled.

'I didn't. And I can't,' Dean asserted. 'I'm taking Amy to Slinghill.'

Caroline baulked at the name. And as if on cue, the vicar's daughter strode into view. Zipped into an indigo leather catsuit, she gave Dean a sexy, come-get-me smile.

Fat cow – Caroline, drinking her in – *you really think you're something special, don't you? Pretty?* Caroline's thoughts, blackening at the edges. *Well, you're not pretty, and your bum looks massive in that getup.*

Caroline continued to observe Dean as he retrieved a small plastic pouch from his motorbike pannier. He passed it to Amy.

'Precious stuff.' He winked at his girlfriend in a way he sometimes winked at Caroline in the pub. It made her hate Amy even more. 'I don't mind waiting,' he said. 'If you want to drop it off at home first.'

'You sure?' Amy weighed whatever he'd given her in the flat of her palm. 'Okay, look, give me five . . . ten minutes tops. It'll give me the chance to check in on Mum too.'

'Take your time, I'll get this baby warmed up.' Dean surrendered his girlfriend's backside to pat the shiny-chromed snout of his other love, and Caroline saw Amy scoot away.

'Dean.' Ellie again, she still hadn't got down. 'Now you can take me for a quick go while you wait for Amy to come back, can't you?'

'No way, Ellie – and that's final. Your mum'd string me up . . . *Ellie.*' Caroline caught the frustration in his voice. 'You're not listening – I said, get off. *NOW.*' And grabbing her by the arms, after a short, stiff struggle, Dean hauled Ellie down from his motorbike. He then turned from his stepsister's demands to unbutton and step out of his overalls.

'You're so mean,' Ellie yelled, her face wet with tears. 'It's my birthday,' she sobbed, lifting then dropping the candy-striped skirt of her new skater dress. 'You said I could have a go on my birthday.'

'No, I didn't.' Dean laughed and tugged on his leathers. 'It was you who said, *on your birthday*. I agreed to nuffin.' Shaking out his curls, he positioned his crash helmet over them.

'You're horrible – you're only nice to me when you want something.' Ellie rubbed the tops of her arms where Dean had grabbed her. 'I'm going to tell Mummy on you. You love Amy more than me . . . '

Whatever else she said was lost to the growl of the engine. Caroline lingered long enough to see Ellie roll away in the same direction as the vicar on her pretty pink skates, then further, into the open jaws of the woods.

'Liz told you not to go too far,' Dean hollered after her. 'You're to stay on the lane, d'you hear? You'll get your party dress dirty.' And straddling his sleek-sided Suzuki Marauder, the engine ticking over, he waited for Amy to return.

Caroline found Joanna at Pludd Cottage's gate stroking Laika through the slats. She was chatting to Mrs Hooper as she weeded between her hydrangeas.

'Where've you been? Your ice-lolly's all melted now.' A flash of her usual sharpness; Caroline had difficulty curbing her frustration in front of Mrs Hooper. 'Why'd you run off like that?'

Joanna didn't answer. Up on her feet, she exchanged goodbyes with her piano teacher and joined Caroline in the lane.

'Drop by on your way to the party.' Lillian had seen the state of Caroline's fringe. 'I'll tidy your hair for you.'

Present Day

Avoiding puddles and pedestrians pulling suitcases behind them like recalcitrant children, Joanna picks over her recent conversation with Sue Fisher as she weaves her way along Queensway. Hyde Park, now the rain has stopped, gleams under the bleached look of winter. A rush of runners in obscenely tight Lycra dodge dog walkers and buggy-pushers. An attractive-looking couple, arm in arm, remind her of Mike and her boys, and the gnawing anxiety that she spends too much time away from home rears its head again. A flash of a laughing mouth close to hers. The teeth, like Caroline's, spin Joanna back to her sister and how she had loved this time of year, with its low-hanging sun and the need for scarves and gloves and woollen layers. Joanna wonders, gazing up through a canopy of filigreed branches and inhaling January's melancholy breath, if her sister used to follow the same webbing of paths through the park to the rescue centre she's now taking. The idea Caroline could have been fretting about something Joanna said to her when she was nine is difficult to get her head around. Why didn't she talk to her, clear the air, instead of letting her resentment fester?

'You must have known I only said that about Dean to cheer you up, I didn't mean anything by it. I don't know why you'd hold something so small against me all these years? And that thing your nurse said,' Joanna mumbles to the dead Caroline, 'about it *driving you to do something terrible, something you could ultimately never forgive yourself for* – what the hell was that about?'

A squirrel from within the darkened undergrowth catches her eye, and she forgets her troubled sister for a moment or two. Vaulting from grass to blackened bough, to grass again, the flick of its tail amuses her. She wishes Freddie and Ethan, with their eternal *What? Why? How?* could be here to enjoy the experience. But before there is the chance to dwell on her sons, the slow slop of the Serpentine, when it finds the concrete bank, brings thoughts of Drake's Pike. She stops to watch the bob of moor hens and swans on the water, the geese clustering the path. It makes her jump, the whizzing of plastic wheels on tarmac. Wrenching her head to it, she sees a girl on quad skates: hair pulled back from her face like party streamers, arms akimbo. The sight of her flings Joanna back to Ellie Fry ... her bunches the colour of demerara sugar ... the pink birthday cake ... the ten silver candles ...

What's this girl doing out on her own? Joanna's mind rolls her into the present, to the urgent concern for this unknown and seemingly unaccompanied child. Where are her parents? They should be with her, don't they know it's not safe? *You're not safe*, she wants to shout, to warn, but barely a whimper betrays her.

St James's Animal Shelter, when at last Joanna pushes open the wide glass doors, reeks of damp dog and disinfectant. The reception area is littered with 'cleaning in process' hazard signs and, clutching the directions she was given over the phone, Joanna tiptoes across the wet concrete to the empty registration desk. Looking through to high, mesh-walled kennels spreading off into the distance, she hears the frenzied barking of dogs throwing their weight against the wire, frantic for attention.

Rotating this way and that, looking for someone, anyone, she spots a wall of full-length photographs under the banner of *Our Volunteers*. Stepping closer, Joanna instantly identifies the forty-one-year-old Caroline. It's easy to distinguish the mixed-up, solemn-eyed little girl she once was from this overweight figure with straggly salt and pepper hair. Her sister, trapped in childhood – a childhood which ended that summer in Witchwood. Caroline's inability or unwillingness to grow up is displayed for all to see: the velvet Alice band, the sandals and ankle socks, the baggy dungarees. It's enough to break her heart.

The clunk of a tin bucket and Joanna turns to a teenage girl wearing regulation overalls, the slop of her zigzagging mop perilously close to her feet.

'Hi,' Joanna calls, raising an arm in greeting. 'Is Jeffrey about?'

'*Coo-ee*, Mrs Peters.' Jeffrey appears from nowhere, crisp in striped shirt and what looks suspiciously like a lady's cardigan. 'You found us okay then.' His voice rings, staccato sharp, above the incessant barking. 'Amber.' He waves at mop-girl, who up close is tattooed to her neck and smells of patchouli oil. 'This is Caroline's sister. You remember Caroline?'

A shrug. 'Spose,' is all she's prepared to give, and the three of them stand in awkward silence.

'Okay then, you carry on, Amber.' Jeffrey nods at the saturnine teenager, who slinks away, towing her bucket. 'Something I've come to realise over the years,' he whispers conspiratorially, 'is people who do volunteering work usually have a need to atone. Yes, it's surprisingly common.' He claps his hands theatrically. 'Take Amber, for instance.' Jeffrey steers Joanna through to the office. 'She stabbed her stepfather to death. *Yes,*' he reiterates, sensing her shock. 'Sexually abusing her, he was – admittedly, her *volunteering* here is part of the conditions of her parole and enforced by the court, but you catch my drift?'

Joanna pretends she does and follows him into a tiny office piled floor to ceiling with cardboard files.

'Not that anyone here asks questions, you understand.' He winks. 'And it must be a relief not to have to share intimacies, don't you think? Wonderful, for the mutual love of animals to be enough of a foundation for friendships. After all, who needs the burden of other people's sins? Each of us has areas uncharted by our imaginations, areas too dark to penetrate, don't we?' He pauses, the ominous weight of his hand on her arm. 'And I suspect your sister was only just learning to close the doors on such places in her past, don't you? The last thing she'd have wanted is any of us opening up old wounds.'

The tatty canvas rucksack Jeffrey Morris said he found in Caroline's abandoned locker appears to contain very little. Hardly worth yomping all the way over here for, Joanna thinks, opting for an empty bench along Birdcage Walk: a setting as deprived of birds as it is a cage. Beneath an arch comprising of the shrivelled heads of dangling roses, she pulls the rucksack into her lap, cuddles it in a way she wishes she could have done to Caroline when she was alive, but rarely did. Unbuckling the rusted fastenings, she pulls out various bottles of antidepressants, a tutti-frutti lip balm, an old Nokia mobile that wouldn't look out of place on *Antiques Roadshow*, and a couple of notebooks she stops to flick through.

Stuffing the things back inside, her fingers collide with a hardback library book on the Pre-Raphaelite brotherhood and, posing as a bookmark, a piece of stiffened card. A postcard: expensive, dog-eared, miles from its intended destination. Lifting it free, the image is one Caroline had been fixated on, believing it echoed her own life story. But refreshing herself with its descriptive forms, Joanna finds it conjures up painful memories of her own.

... it drove her mad, Hamlet murdering her father ... her sister's voice, maybe Dora's too, find her out of nowhere ... *then one day, out picking flowers by the river, she fell in and drowned, slowly, singing all the while.*

It was this particular painting and the allegorical message it contains, a framed reproduction of which hung on the landing at Pillowell Cottage, that Dora – along with her classical records and exotic foodstuffs – took great trouble to explain to them as children. Caroline took it all to heart, believing the weeping willow leaning over Ophelia's body signified forsaken love; the floating fritillary, sorrow; the pansies, what it is to love in vain. But it was the garland of violets looped around Ophelia's neck – indicating faithfulness, chastity and death of the young – she had the deepest affiliation with.

I am the true Ophelia ... Her sister's voice again, talking in a way that would repel and frighten. And Joanna sees Caroline as she was, twirling her hair around her finger, making it greasy where it met her neck, a faraway look in her eye ... *that should've been me, I should've been the one to die.*

She turns the postcard over. Sees the date it was written: 11 November, a first-class stamp pressed to its top right-hand corner. Joanna's full married name and Hertfordshire address is written in neat block capitals, safe within the designated lines. But it's the five truncated sentences that make her suck back her breath: *He's here. He's hunted me down. He wants to kill me. You've got to stop him. You've got to help me.*

Summer 1990

Alone in her room at the top of the vicarage, Cecilia Mortmain needed to think about what she was going to wear that afternoon. Whether to have her hair up or down. Trying it out in the mirror, her reflection on her dressing table given as a triptych in its three-hinged panels, she drew it back off her face. Up, she decided, less trouble out of the way, and she could snazzy herself up with those emerald earrings her sister, Pippa, gave her for Christmas.

Her body jerked. A bird – big, black, out of nowhere – smacked itself against the window. A bad omen. She gasped, reading its message. Not that her cats noticed; continuing to frisk her through her pyjama bottoms, they didn't look up. Cecilia let her hair fall and refocused on her reflection, wanting her sister's face – which if she stared for long enough she could sometimes find. But there was nothing of Pippa's mellowness, only Cecilia's own despondency. Today of all days, she scolded herself, she should be feeling happy with the prospect of an afternoon at the pub celebrating Ellie Fry's birthday.

The cats, hunting out her thoughts, leapt on to the dressing table to lick her wrists with dry, barbed tongues. Carnivorous-breathed, they poured themselves over her hands, responding to her touch in a way her husband no longer did. Fetching whatever remained of her marriage out for a polishing, she manoeuvred her wheelchair to the window in the hope of seeing Timothy coming home. She'd caught sight of his tall, dark shape whisking into the woods earlier that morning, but there had been no sign of him since.

'Hi, Amy.' Cecilia's thoughts severed as her daughter bounded in. 'Enjoy your trip out with Dean?'

'It was great, thanks.' Amy gripped the handlebars of her mother's chair and wheeled her into the centre of the room. 'You feeling all right today? How's the pain?' She rubbed her arms as if feeling her mother's discomfort vicariously.

'Under control for now.' Cecilia dispensed a weak smile. 'Dean give you any more of that stuff?'

'Yeah, he did. I nipped back here with it before we went out. I came to check on you, but you were having a lie-down, and I didn't want to disturb you.'

'You're a good girl – it's the only thing that touches it.'

'Far better than those drugs the doctor gives you, they're destroying your stomach. I'll get on and make another batch of those cakes while you and Dad are out this afternoon, if you like?'

'Aren't you coming to the party?'

'No, not my thing. And Dean's not sure if he's going to be there. Anyway, more to the point,' Amy, taking charge, 'have you thought about what you're going to wear?'

'Certainly not a leather catsuit.' Cecilia, admiring her daughter. 'You look amazing in it, by the way.'

'Thanks, Mum. It was really kind of Pippa to let me have it, it's the ideal thing to wear on the bike. Must have been super-expensive.' Amy smiled a secret smile and smoothed the supple indigo leather down over her hips. 'Dean loves me in it.'

'I bet he does,' Cecilia chuckled. 'I've got photos of Pippa wearing it. I'll dig them out. *Ha –*' a quick laugh – 'she was a bit of a raver in her day. Was always leading me astray.'

'I can just see the two of you out and about in Cheltenham, bet you were right girls on the town.'

Another laugh into her memories before Cecilia refocused on her daughter. 'Anyway, it's great you're getting plenty of wear out of it – Pippa and I certainly haven't the figures for clothes like that any more.'

'You're daft, Mum. You'd look lovely in a plastic bag.' Amy kissed her mother's cheek. 'Come on – what's it to be?'

'You choose; you're so good with clothes.' Cecilia waved a feeble hand. 'D'you know where your father was off to this morning? He came back from the shop as usual, but then the phone rang and he rushed straight out again.'

'No idea, I've been with Dean till now – I assumed he was at church.'

'Early on, maybe, but then he disappeared on one of his walks, and I've not seen him since.'

'Perhaps he took himself off for a ramble, looking for divine inspiration.' Amy fumbled through the wardrobe's contents.

'He was hardly dressed for a yomp to the lake ... I don't know how many more times I have to tell him not to wear his church shoes.' Cecilia, fitful and stiff from her wheelchair. 'Wherever he's got to, he'd better hurry up, we're due at the pub in less than an hour.'

'D'you want me to go and see if I can find him?' Amy offered, plumping for a red top of her mother's, then changing her mind.

'No, don't worry. I'm sure he'll be back in time.' Cecilia shook her head at the plum-coloured dress her daughter now showed her. 'I saw Ellie too, earlier this morning. Coming along the lane at a fair old lick on her wheels.' A smile. 'She went into the woods not long after your father, come to think of it. Not that I've seen anything of her since either.' The smile slid away. 'Mind you, I could have easily missed her – I did go and have a sleep, didn't I?' Cecilia muttered as she assessed the papery quality of her hands. 'Ellie had such a pretty dress on.' She looked up. 'Liz always decks her out in lovely clothes, doesn't she? Must have been a new dress, special for her party; I've never seen it before ... Were her skates a present from Liz and Ian too?'

Amy nodded.

'Beautiful pink leather. Must have cost them a fortune.'

'I think they wanted to spoil her, as it's a special one.'

Cecilia, smiling to herself, wasn't listening. 'D'you remember those skates we bought you?'

'I've still got them.' Amy had chosen a linen dress as pale as her mother's hair. 'How about this?' She swished it around on its hanger, making it dance in a way her mother no longer could. 'You look gorgeous in this.'

Cecilia looked down at her legs, at her flaccid, useless body. '*Gorgeous* – my lovely girl,' she corrected, 'is hardly a word one could apply to me, now is it?'

In a Laura Ashley dress the colour of a flower-filled meadow, Liz Fry circled the table she'd laid in readiness for Ellie's birthday tea. Pleased with how wonderful it all looked, she went to fetch the camera from the bar to capture it in a Polaroid before the kids descended.

'Oh, wow.' Dean, still in his leathers, stopped wiping the tables to admire his stepmother. 'You look great, Liz. Has Dad seen you?'

'Thanks.' She managed a smile as she searched between clean tea towels and boxes of crisps. 'No, I've not seen him all morning. He's been up to his eyes sorting out party games. You going to smarten yourself up a bit?' She frowned, although not at him for a change, but at her inability to locate the Polaroid camera.

'D'you need me, then? 'Cos I was thinking, once I've tidied up here—'

'*Dean?*' Liz cut him off. 'You seen the camera?'

'The what?' Dean didn't look up from his wiping.

'The camera. It's missing.'

'Don't look at me,' he said, immediately on the defensive. 'I always put it back.'

'Bugger.' A transitory thought of the beautiful gold ring with its blue topaz Ian gave her last Christmas which she mistakenly left by the sink. Could the person who stole that have taken the camera too? It wasn't a comfortable feeling to think they had a thief in the village. 'I wanted to take a picture of the birthday cake.'

'Shall I find Dad, ask if he's seen it?' Dean offered.

'No, don't worry him; he's busy. It's bound to turn up.'

Mrs Hooper wasn't half as rude as Dora had been about Caroline's hideous fringe, but Joanna could tell she thought it. Pulling faces behind her back as she tried to style it into some kind of shape.

'Pain to be beautiful,' she said whenever Caroline wriggled to get away.

187

She was without her cardigan for once – Caroline swore Dora had hidden it. The sisters had decided on the same outfits they wore for Derek Hooper's funeral. Almost matching, their dresses – Joanna's a pale apple green, Caroline's a custard yellow – had necklines trimmed in cream velvet ribbon and short sleeves that showed off their sun-freckled arms.

The car park at the Boar's Head was jam-packed. Slightly intimidated, Caroline and Joanna hung back to watch parents of Ellie's schoolmates drop them off – a quick comb of hair, a handkerchief for the administration of last-minute spit washes, a reminder to collect the present for the birthday girl from the back seat – until Liz saw them and waved them over. She looked the loveliest either of them had ever seen, in her pretty patterned dress and matching lipstick.

'Don't be shy, come on.' She scooped them against her hips, the slide of her dress against their bare arms: a gorgeous, perfumed, mother hen. And with a stroke of their hair, a little shove between their shoulder blades, Liz propelled them through a swing door of stuffed oxblood leather, and into a dark-panelled room neither recognised. They looked around, wide-eyed at the party streamers, the pink balloons, the goodie bags. The huge drawing of an animal with disproportionate ears Ian called *Pin-the-Tail-on-the-Donkey*. The table was heart-stopping too. Aside from the sequinned cloth, it offered up a spread of everything from egg and cress-covered rolls to bowls of crisps, and weenie sausages on sticks. And as a centrepiece, what must have been the largest pink birthday cake in the world.

'It's got ten candles,' Joanna gasped, counting them up.

'No shit,' Caroline snapped, but not at Joanna – she was worried about bumping into Dean, fearing his mockery at the mess she'd made of her hair. But he had it coming, the humiliation of seeing him smooching with Amy after what he'd promised, curdling to a hard-edged anger as she girdled the room.

'That sounds fun.' Joanna grinned when she heard Ian placate a grizzling child with news that a clown was on his way. 'D'you hear that, Carrie? *A clown.*'

Caroline had to give it to her sister: despite her own grumpiness, Joanna's optimism would not be dampened. And finding it from somewhere, she clasped her chubby hand in hers.

The minutes rolled on. More children spilled into the room. Decked out in party clothes, they milled about, looking for somewhere to dump the presents their parents chose and wrapped for them. But nowhere was appropriate. The sisters appreciated this without even looking. Clutching theirs, the wrapping paper sticky in their anxious fingers, they were reluctant to hand them over to anyone but Ellie. A small boy with a set of knees as scuffed as the toes of his sandals grew tired of waiting for the birthday girl, and reached for a golden-topped sausage roll. He put his greasy hand out for more, but Caroline smacked it away like a fly.

'Where's Ellie?' someone asked. The observation triggered a low mumble that swelled through the room.

'I'm not sure.' Ian's corrugated forehead beaded with sweat. 'You girls seen her?' He bent forward, whispered his whisky-breath into Joanna and Caroline's hair. 'The three of you go everywhere together.'

They shook their heads, watched him raise a hand to Ellie's party guests as if to stop traffic.

'Don't worry, folks,' he announced, his peanut-shaped head glistening with fresh perspiration. 'She can't have gone far. I'll go and find out where she is.' And he pitched from the room.

Trailing behind him, still carrying their presents, it was a relief for the sisters to distance themselves from the unblinking stares of Ellie's school mates. They were back in the main bar, busy with regulars and a selection of villagers invited to celebrate Ellie's special day – Dora, Mrs Hooper and Gordon not among them. No sign of the vicar and his pretty wheelchair-bound wife either, which was strange because Caroline knew they'd been invited.

'Everything all right in there?' Liz was slicing lemons.

'Great. Yeah. Fab spread you've done, love ... but, erm ...' Ian hesitated. 'You seen Ellie? She's not in her bedroom. I can't find her anywhere.'

'Isn't she back yet?' Liz flicked her eyes to the clock above the bar.

'Back from where?' Ian, mid-reach for a shot of whisky, downed it in one.

'She wanted to try out her new roller skates.'

'That was hours ago.' Ian reached for a second. Swallowed it. And with a neat little click, laid the glass on the counter. 'She must've come home for something to eat? She can't have been out all day?'

'I'm sorry, Ian.' Liz dried her hands on a cloth. 'I skipped lunch myself; I've been rushed off my feet – sorting the food, the table ...'

'But you must have *seen* her.' Ian rubbed his earth-encrusted hands over his face and the girls wondered if he'd been digging the garden. 'I've been sorting the games, restocking the bar.'

'No, I haven't – you know what she's like on those things. She can't have gone far, I told her not to leave the lane.' The girls detected the merest fissure of anxiety in Liz's voice.

'I saw her,' Caroline announced and, encouraged by the light in Liz's eyes, added, 'When I went to the shop for Dora.'

'What time was this?' Ian seized her firmly, spun her to face him.

'Early. Half-nine.' Caroline squirmed free of Ian and stepped away to stand with Joanna, their backs pressed to the Wall of Shame. 'Ellie was with Dean in his motorbike shed. He was being really rough with her and shouting.'

'*Dean?*' Liz leapt on the name. A flash of the little round bruises she saw on her daughter's body from time to time – bruises Ellie dismissed as bumps from playing on her roller skates. '*Rough with her*? D'you hear that, Ian?' she shrieked. 'Haven't I always said it?'

'But he wouldn't hurt Ellie,' Ian reasoned, visibly distressed by the suggestion being made.

'You wouldn't say that if you'd seen him,' Caroline said, ignoring the questioning look Joanna was giving her.

'What d'you mean?' Liz, alarmed.

Caroline caught a slice of her reflection in the metallic sides of the till and gulped back tears that sprouted too easily. 'He was being really horrible. Grabbing Ellie's arms and shouting. I saw him shaking her too. He made her cry.' She looked down, stared at her toes through the translucent pink of her jelly sandals.

'Don't you go getting upset, love. It isn't your fault.'

Liz stepped from behind the bar, put a consoling arm around Caroline.

The contact, the feeling she could matter to another human being, made fat tears gather at the edge of Caroline's large, dark eyes.

'Did you hear what Dean was shouting at Ellie about?'

'Something to do with his motorbike, I think.' Caroline, missing her cardigan, wiped her nose on her wrist.

'You're not telling me he took her out on *that*,' Liz yelped. 'I've told him it isn't safe.'

'No.' Caroline shook her head. 'Ellie skated off. Ever so fast.'

'Did you see where she went?' Liz, desperate to bring things back to her glaringly absent child.

'Down Dead End Lane. Into the woods.' Caroline's story gathered strength around her. For the first time grown-ups were listening to what she had to say, she was of interest. Liking the attention, liking how they were poised for whatever she was to say next, spurred her on.

'And Dean?' Liz crouched beside her. 'D'you see where he went?' she coaxed.

'Yes. Off on his motorbike.' Caroline looked up through her wonky fringe and pushed the pain and embarrassment about Dean's broken promise into his stepmother's troubled expression.

'Which way?' Liz persisted.

Caroline knew Liz had no time for her stepson and wanted to please her by giving her what she thought she wanted to hear. 'Same way as Ellie did,' she said, forsaking her bitten nails to point in the direction of the woods with her wet finger ends.

Liz turned to Ian, who looked anxious. 'Go and find that no-good son of yours. Find out why he was shouting at my daughter!' Liz raised her voice for the first time; loud enough to make those nearest the bar flinch. 'I'm going to look for Ellie – come on, girls, you can help me.'

'Okay,' Ian agreed. 'Things can take care of themselves here for a minute. But please don't worry, love, she'll turn up; you know what she's like ... she's always wandering off. Kid lives in a dream half the time.' He reached out to reassure his wife, but she stiffened and pulled away.

'Just go and ask your son.' Liz gave him a look that knocked him back.

Ian slapped a grimy hand to his shiny head. 'Right, yes. I'll go and find him right away.'

'God, Carrie – that's horrible what Dean did to Ellie.' Joanna at Caroline's elbow, as they zoomed off in the direction Liz piloted them. 'Did he hurt her bad?'

'Yeah, he did.'

'Why didn't you tell me?'

Caroline shrugged.

'But this morning you said you wanted Dean to kiss you and stuff.' Joanna grimaced. 'Why would you want him to do that if he could be so horrible to Ellie?'

''Cos I hadn't seen him being horrible to her then, had I? Stupid.'

'Did you really hear them shouting?' Joanna, close to tears.

'Course I did. You heard what I said.'

'Yeah, but I never heard nothing.'

'You weren't there, though, were you?' Caroline shot a sidelong glance at her sister. 'You'd buggered off to Mrs Hooper's.'

'He's gonna be in such trouble,' Joanna whispered and slipped a tentative hand into her sister's.

'Good.' A ghost of a smile. 'He should be punished for what he did to me.'

They followed Liz. Clipping along on unaccustomed heels into the kitchen, she swapped her peep-toe shoes for the rubber boots kept by the door.

'Perhaps she was so busy playing, she forgot her party,' she said, half to herself, as she swept aside the fly screen and rushed out into the blistering sunshine.

Forgotten her party? It was all Ellie had gone on about, the sisters thought, staring at their friend's abandoned little red wellingtons.

'Come on, girls.' Liz darted off towards her poultry patch. 'She might be with the chickens. She's like you, Jo, she loves my hens.' An automatic smile. '*Ellie . . . Ellie . . .*' she shouted, then turned to the girls, a look of desperation in her eyes. 'She has to be somewhere, she can't have gone far.'

But Ellie was nowhere. And exhausting the beer garden and lane, calling her name as far as the crossroads, the gates of the church, the opening to the woods, the three of them returned to the pub to find Ian pacing the kitchen: a caged animal.

'I don't know where that son of mine is. I can't find him anywhere.' He wrung his hands in distress.

'Is his bike there?' Liz asked.

'In the outhouse. Warm to the touch. He's definitely been out on it today.'

'I saw him in the bar about half-three,' Liz said, suddenly remembering. 'I was looking for the camera – I've forgotten what he said, but it didn't sound like he was coming to the party.'

'I don't know what to do.' Ian looked on the verge of tears.

'I know what I'm doing.' Liz reached for the telephone.

'What?'

'I'm ringing the bloody police.'

On their walk back from the pub, the sisters, doggedly clutching Ellie's presents, saw that Pludd Cottage's drive was empty. Watching from the lane, they also saw Mrs Hooper's slender shadow moving around inside, and that the back door had been flung wide on to her beautiful, bird-filled garden. But despite there being no sign of Gordon, it still wasn't enough to tempt Caroline to rap the brass fox knocker. To explain about Ellie being missing and her birthday party ending before it began was too hard.

Then Mrs Hooper's sausage dog, determined as a freight train, beetled over the bleached-out lawn and squeezed under the gate. Fearing she could come to harm in the lane, the girls took a small detour to say hello. They knelt to appreciate the satin-smooth of Laika's huge hanging ears, and stroking the little dog made the upsetting thoughts of Ellie and the reprehensible Dean Fry melt away, temporarily giving them back their smiles.

Horses. Their shifting shapes stamped against the brindled light of evening. They meandered to the fence at the bottom of Pillowell's garden. Alone, Joanna was aware of the advance of shadows – an invading army, crowding from the corners to take possession of the light – and tilted her neck to watch slow-moving clouds, pink as candyfloss.

Feeding the horses on her own this evening, she held her hand flat in a way she'd been shown. Up close these creatures smelled of warm digestive biscuits, their broad muzzles with their velvet nap insistent and vaguely disconcerting. Something moved within the frail webbing of mist that was adhering itself to the trees.

It made her jump. The empty colander swinging at her side.

Dean Fry.

His face, waxy as the moon, rose before her, and she saw a pile of spliff-ends – not that she identified them as this – littering the base of a tree.

'What you doing here?' Joanna, startled by his presence.

'*What?*' he snapped, unusually brusque. Joanna thought he looked funny, drunk perhaps, like her mother sometimes was when they came home from school.

'What time is it?' he asked gruffly.

'Dunno, but there's people looking for you.' Joanna took a step back to distance herself, saw his messy hair was strewn with bracken and bark.

'*People?* What people?' A flash of fear as he scanned in all directions. Then, grabbing his leather jacket, he was gone.

Present Day

Joanna wants to utilise every moment before she catches the train home. Still playing detective, she picks out the 24-Seven store across the road from the description given by the police. A brief lapse in concentration and a Lambretta buzzes past as she steps out in front of a double-decker bus. Dumbstruck, she stares after it. Then, adjusting herself, she aims for the pelican crossing a little further along. Passing racks of souvenirs set out to tempt the tourist, she grimaces at the tacky black-cab key rings, the Queen Elizabeth fridge magnets. On a superficial level, the district of Bayswater has barely changed in all the years she's known it, but scratch the surface and it becomes clear this London postcode has evolved into one of the city's most bustling and cosmopolitan. Of course, nowadays everything is subdivided into flats and boarding houses, and if not, then converted into hotels. How else are people supposed to afford to live here? Had Dora not left Caroline a cushion of money and a mortgage-free flat, there's no way she could have done.

Picking up speed, she smells the aroma of food spilling on to the street and slides a sidelong glance at the condensation-streaked window of a Cantonese takeaway. It makes her smile. The tawny-lit interior, garnished with glistening roast ducks as leathery-looking – or so her sister used to say – as their father's old slippers. Mrs Hooper was right – even if it was only something Joanna glimpsed occasionally, Caroline did have a sense of humour. It was the darker side of her personality, her mood swings and debilitating negativity, that made their relationship so hard to navigate. Well, that and the stupid lie Joanna told, that for some reason Caroline never forgave her for.

Sudden tears as she steps inside the mini-market. They make the captions on the rows of trashy magazines wobble: *15 Mins from Death, Knifed to Death by Own Son, Raped and Killed by Dad.* 'Real Life Stories', the blur of black-ened taglines claim. Aren't they just, she thinks miserably, imagining herself to be standing only yards from where her sister bled to death.

The young Asian man at the till gives Joanna a shy smile. Watching him assemble her purchases into a neat pile, she works out ways to ask if he knew her sister. Was the night Caroline died the first time she shopped here? Did the two of them ever exchange more than a please and thank-you? Coins from her purse tumble over the counter and bounce to the floor. As fluid as water, he bends to scoop them up with his slender fingers, returning them to her one by one.

'I don't know if you were here that night, but I'm–I'm Caroline Jameson's sister,' she falters, unsure where to start. The change in his expression is enough to tell her he knows exactly who Caroline was.

'I told the police everything what happened,' he says, snapping shut the till.

'It's okay,' she reassures, pressing a hand to his fine-boned wrist. 'I'm not here to cause trouble, I just wanted to talk to someone who was there. I need to find out what happened.

I'm struggling to piece things together, you see. And the police . . . ' Tears sprout again, and she fishes a tissue from her pocket.

'I was here.' His voice trembles against the piped music that fills the otherwise empty store. 'It was terrible. Terrible.' He leans his back against the shelves of cigarettes and alcohol as if needing the support. 'It happened so quick. I saw her come in—'

'Oh, so you recognised her then? Carrie.' Joanna, immediately encouraged, interrupts his narrative like a rock thrown into a stream.

The young man nods. 'Yeah, she used to shop here a lot. We never said nuffin much to each other, but she was definitely one of me regulars. Late-night shopper mostly; always on her own. She looked kinda sad. I s'ppose I felt sorry for her.' Joanna sees his knuckles whiten as he grips the edge of the counter. 'I could tell she liked sweet things.' He throws out a tight ball of a laugh that bounces against the horror of what went on here a month or so ago. 'It was like she was always shopping for some kid's birthday party or summit. Chocolates, ice cream, cakes, jellies, sweets, crisps . . . them cooked chipolata things. Dead weird for a grown woman. Not that she was old, was she? Yeah, she looked old,' he adds, 'the way she dressed, her hair, but that was because she didn't bother with herself much, innit? But up close, I was surprised, she was much younger-looking.' Realising his observation may be inappropriate, he pulls himself up, and shoots a look at Joanna. 'Sorry, I didn't mean to be rude or nuffin—'

'No, I know.' She helps him out, feeling his awkwardness. 'It's good to build a picture, it's what I wanted. Me and

Carrie, we'd lost touch, it's why I'm here – I'm trying to . . . I don't know, make sense of it all?' She stares at the floor, her gaze travelling with a split in the linoleum as it disappears under the cooler cabinet. 'Did she look stressed or troubled to you that night? Can you remember?'

He waits before answering. Seemingly feeling the importance of Joanna's question, his mouth moves as if to assemble the right words before he dispenses them. 'It was bizarre,' he starts, then moistens his lips. 'I hadn't seen her for weeks, honestly.' He looks her in the eye. 'She'd not been in here for ages, and I noticed 'cos like I said, she was in dead regular, like. Anyway, it weren't like she was ever chilled or nuffin when she come in before: always chewin' her nails and shit, but she was definitely different that night. Really edgy and wired, like. Checking over her shoulder all the time, like she was frightened someone was followin' her.' He throws his head to the ceiling tiles, takes a breath. 'But it was her who pulled the knife on him. Had it in her bag ready, she did. Went for him like some mad woman. I told the police . . . I told them she really meant business, innit?' Joanna shows she does know. 'And that was some piece of kit, man. Where do a woman like her get a knife like that? Well dangerous.' He shakes his head in sorrowful bemusement.

'You saw it all then? You saw what happened?' Joanna tips out the question she isn't sure she wants the answer to.

'Yeah.' He purses his lips, tussling with the memory. 'Over in a flash, it was. Weren't time to do nuffin. But people tried to help, giving her mouth-to-mouth and stuff. There was so much blood. So much blood,' he says, his eyes landing on Joanna again. 'Someone called an ambulance, but there weren't nuffin no one could do. That bloke she tried to stab, he was lucky, y'know – she nearly had him. Dead determined, she was. All fierce, like. I'd never seen nuffin like it.' He shoves his hands deep into his trouser pockets. 'I'll never forget it. Never. Police had the shop shut for over a week ... all that scene of crime tape ... like *CSI* stuff, innit.' His look is wretched. 'I weren't even sure if I wanted to work here again after that.'

'I don't think I'd have done either. I'm so sorry you had to witness it,' Joanna says, feeling strangely numb.

'Yeah, gotta earn a livin' though, and this is me uncle's place, yeah? So ain't really got no choice in the matter, like.'

'Look.' She moves aside to allow a woman to pay for a box of Maltesers and a puzzle book. 'You've been so helpful, thank you. I'm sorry I made you rake though it all again.'

She steps backwards, out through the automatic doors; a befuddled daze beneath the streetlights quivering against the encroachment of night. Then it hits her. And images of what went on in there fire at her like missiles she can't avoid. Blood, he said, so much blood ... and they tried to help her, but no one could do anything. She slumps against the trunk of a plane tree, stares up through the jigsaw-patterned boughs. Rigid amid the abuse of car horns and the burn of diesel, her mouth full of the questions she still wants answering.

Then a voice. Shouting through the crowd. She swings around to pinpoint it but is blocked by a photograph of her own face. Captured on one of her publicity fliers, it flaps in the wind and shows off her clear complexion, her Pre-Raphaelite twist of hair. *The spit of your mother.* Joanna filters the lopsided compliment she is frequently given and wonders what it must have been like for Caroline to see her younger sister adorning lampposts and billboards from here to the Wigmore Hall. Joanna, 'the favoured one', with hair their mother loved to brush at bedtime. She chews the inside of her mouth and pushes the unwanted images of her only sibling deep into the folds of her heart. The regularity with which Caroline was rejected as a child is why Joanna works so hard to be impartial with her sons; observing her own mother's contempt – something that was in direct contrast to the barefaced favouritism she exhibited towards Joanna – must have broken her sister's spirit.

'*Miss?*'

That voice again. Closer this time. Startling her out of her retrospection.

'Yes?' she replies, looking into the face of the young man from the mini-mart again.

'I forgot something . . . it might be important,' he gushes, a little out of breath. 'Your sister . . . she shouted something when she pulled the knife on that bloke. I'm not sure, but it sounded like . . . oh, I dunno, I might've got it wrong.'

'What?' Joanna, mouth open, ready to catch it when it comes. 'What did she shout?'

'*Dean* . . . I'm pretty sure she said Dean.'

PART TWO

But our cold maids do dead men's fingers call them.
There on the pendant boughs her coronet weeds
Clamb'ring to hang, an envious sliver broke,
When down her weedy trophies and herself
Fell in the weeping brook.

Queen Gertrude on Ophelia.
Shakespeare, Hamlet, Act IV, Scene VII

Summer 1990

After a Sunday afternoon spent with Mrs Hooper, the sisters drifted into Dora's kitchen through the back door. Subdued, their thoughts with the still missing Ellie, who, failing to return home at all last night, meant the roads around Witchwood were teeming with patrol cars and TV vans sporting huge satellite dishes. They stared at the empty wine bottles, the debris of lemon for the ritual evening's G&T, and frowned. Who was their aunt entertaining now, and why wasn't she out looking for their friend? Caroline and Joanna tried to join in with the rest of the village, but the vicar told them to go away, said it was 'adults only'.

A rumble of voices from deep inside the cottage. They identified Dora's, but not the others. Wanting to find out, Caroline left Joanna with a packet of Hula Hoops and a can of pop from the fridge and crept along the shadow-filled hall to peek around the sitting-room door that, slightly ajar, allowed her to remain hidden.

A chink of sunlight, thin as a blade, sliced between a brace of male police officers. And tuning into the snippets of their dialogue, Caroline quickly grasped the subject of their discussion.

'... a roller skate was discovered this morning.' The

younger of the two-uniformed officer's attention was momentarily seized by a surge of sparrows from nearby shrubbery. Caroline saw how his eyes followed their journey across the garden.

'And you think it belongs to Ellie Fry?' Dora mopped beads of sweat that had bloomed on her forehead with an embroidered handkerchief.

'Her parents have confirmed it to be so, yes.'

'Where – where d'you find it?'

'In the woods.' The policeman removed his helmet, held it in front of him like a begging bowl.

'*In the woods?*' Dora yelped. 'But Carrie and Jo play in there.'

'Carrie and Jo?' The other, the scribe: eclipsed by his bobble-top helmet. Notebook ready, he dragged a fist across the empty page as if to clear the way ahead. 'Who are they?' he asked, pen poised.

'My great-nieces.' Dora brandished her wine glass while Caroline, still hidden from view, swung her head from one to the other as if watching a game of table tennis. 'Their mother's not well; I'm looking after them for the summer.'

The policeman flicked back a few pages in his notebook. 'Ah, Carrie – is that *Caroline* –' he referred to his notes again – 'Caroline Jameson?' He waited for Dora's confirmation. 'Ellie's mother mentioned that Caroline had some information regarding her daughter.'

'*Information* – what information?'

'That's what we'd like to establish. Could we possibly speak to her, do you think?'

'I'm sorry, the girls are with my neighbour, Mrs Hooper. Marvellous arrangement ...' Dora broke off and lowered her eyelids as if to analyse the quality of the silence before speaking again. 'Lillian gives Jo piano lessons.'

'Right.' A nod, as this was jotted down. 'And how old are your great-nieces?'

Dora supplied the necessary ages and waited for them to be recorded in cheap blue biro. 'But what's all this about? Are you saying Ellie's been *abducted*?'

The word whirled about the room like a Catherine wheel. Caroline took a step back and shuddered. What's happened to Ellie? Where was she? The idea she might have come to harm was sharpening into a spike. What was also sharpening were the things she told Liz about Dean hitting Ellie and racing off after her on his bike – as it now looked like she was going to have to tell the police these things too. Warm and airless in the hall, the conversation made Caroline feel woozy. She needed to sit, to feel the cool of the kitchen linoleum under her feet, but she couldn't move, daren't move, fearful of missing something crucial.

'Please understand, Miss Muller,' the police officer reminded Dora as he scanned the room, appreciating – or so Caroline thought, moving back into position to spy on them again – the Delft ceramic mantel clock, the vitrines sagging under the weight of silver curios, the oil paintings of Dutch tavern scenes and watercolours that left hardly the space for a hand between the frames, 'we're here to ask *you* questions – we're not at liberty to discuss the specifics of the case.'

'Oh, so it's a *case* now, is it?' Dora gasped. 'That must mean Ellie's been officially reported as missing.'

The policeman dispensed an accusing look, which was duly ignored by Dora, who put her glass down on the sideboard.

Peeping in at the pairs of polished black boots rucking up Pillowell's Persian rugs, Caroline, careful to keep out of sight, followed the journey of a stain that had dried as dark as old blood. It drew her gaze under the sofas and low oak coffee table piled with books: places eluding the nozzle of the vacuum that were doomed to remain thick with grime.

'If we could return to the subject we discussed earlier.' The officer stabbed his biro into the notepad.

'Yes, of course.' Dora pursed her little mouth. 'Although, you must understand, I can't be entirely sure what's been taken – it's just that some of my smaller items of jewellery, the odd silver ornament, that kind of thing ... well, they're missing.'

She knows things are missing?

A coldness settled around Caroline's heart as she loitered in the umbrageous hallway. It was as if some other hand had reached inside her and clasped it. Gawping at Dora, at her crumb-speckled chest and lack of lipstick, Caroline tried to work out what this meant, but couldn't get beyond the idea that her aunt must have been caught on the hop by these two men in their proud-black uniforms and vaguely menacing air. Her mind, swirling with the dust motes in the shafts of sunshine, landed on the knickknacks she'd been stealthily procuring and secreting among the bulrushes. How could Dora know, when she'd been so careful only to take things she wouldn't miss; things buried under so much junk, they'd surely been forgotten?

'If you could be more specific – provide us with a list of what's been taken?' The scribe turned over a new leaf of his notebook as a gust of wind from the garden made the chandelier tinkle above their heads.

'I would, but I can't be sure ...' Dora floundered. 'Like I said earlier, it's more of a hunch.'

'A *hunch*.' The tone bordered on sardonic. 'We're going to need rather more than a hunch, Miss Muller.'

Caroline's mouth went dry. Frightened Dora was indeed on to her, she scrabbled for ways to get out of this, deciding, if challenged, she would lie. Lie at all costs.

'Yes, yes, of course you do ...' Dora fidgeted with her hair. 'And I realise you've far more important things with little Ellie missing. But if Dean Fry's been stealing from me, then I'm sorry, much as I like the lad, I can't simply turn a blind eye. It might be a precursor to more serious crimes, don't you think, officer?'

'Dean Fry?' The policeman echoed the name. 'Just to confirm, we're talking about Ellie's stepbrother here, are we?'

Dora nodded.

'And if I could double check why you suspect him, again?' He dipped his head, scribbled whatever he might need to refer to later.

'Because he mows my lawn. Because he keeps an eye on the place for me when I'm in London.'

'And how long have you been letting him look after your holiday cottage?'

'About two years ... since his family took over the pub.'

'And have you ever had reason to suspect him of stealing from you before?'

Dora took a moment. 'No,' she said simply. 'I don't think I have.'

'Doesn't that strike you as odd?' The other policeman. 'Why abuse your trust after all this time?'

'Surely that's obvious.' A haughty tip of the chin.

'Obvious, Miss Muller? How so?'

'He's got this wretched drug habit to feed, hasn't he?'

'A *drug habit*? Miss Muller, could you explain?' A shifting of boots. 'What kinds of drugs?'

'How would I know?' She flapped a hand like she did when drying her nail varnish. 'Cannabis, marijuana ... he smokes stuff all the time. You can smell it a mile off.'

'Okay.' The policeman looked interested. 'If you're able to provide a list of what's been taken, we could start by searching his home.'

'But he'd have sold them on by now, don't you think?'

'Not necessarily.'

'Look, there's something else I must tell you.' Dora, seemingly on the verge of some kind of confession, shuffled to the sideboard for a fortifying glug of wine. 'Even though I'm probably going to be in trouble for having the damn thing in the first place.' She pressed her lips together. 'It's my late father's dagger. It's vanished too. Rather more serious than trinkets, I fear. I know I should've reported it immediately.'

'What kind is it? Can you give us a description?' one of police officers asked.

'From the war. Silver. With a long, sharp blade.' Dora's eyes narrowed to slits.

The pair of officers swapped furtive looks. 'Yes, madam, that just about describes most daggers. What make is it? Does it have any distinguishing features?'

'It's an SA Honor Dagger. German. Ornate silver crossguards, brown leather grip, scabbard. Oh yes,' she looked uneasy, 'there's an eagle on it, and a swastika logo ... and *Alles Fur Deutschland* embossed along its blade. My father was horribly proud of it.' She dabbed her brow with her handkerchief again, the heat evidently getting to her. 'To be brutally honest, I didn't know what to do with it after he died.'

'Was your father a member of the German Army, then?'

'No, of course he wasn't.' Dora baulked, but Caroline knew that what remained of her aunt's Dutch accent could be mistaken for German, and wasn't surprised the policeman asked the question. 'He was Jewish. My parents were Jewish.'

A band of light jogged across the wallpaper and Dora stretched out to touch it. From the way she shivered, Caroline could tell it sparked unhappy memories, not that she knew what those memories were. All she and Joanna had been told was that these rolls of William Morris pattern were precious to Dora's father, and that they were just one of the countless possessions they escaped to England with.

'Me, m-my family,' Dora stammered the explanation she seemed keen to provide. 'We were from the Netherlands. My parents owned a hardware shop in the northeast town of Meppel.'

'So, how did he come by the dagger?'

'He used it to get us out of Nazi-occupied territory.' Dora, blunt; but something in her aunt's expression informed Caroline that although this wasn't a lie, it wasn't the whole truth either.

'Where d'you usually keep it?'

'Sorry, what did you say?' Dora didn't appear to have heard.

'I asked where you keep it – was it somewhere safe?' The questions kept coming.

'Hidden away at the bottom of my wardrobe. It was a shock to find it gone.'

'And you think Dean took this too?'

'Yes, of course he did. Who else could it be? As I said, he comes to do the garden, and I don't always lock the cottage if I go out.'

The police officers traded further glances, and it pleased Caroline to see they thought her aunt was as doolally as she did.

'You say you've a property in London, Miss Muller?' the senior of the duo asked, a mocking smirk tickling the edges of his mouth.

'That's right. In Bayswater.'

'And you leave that unlocked when you go out, do you?'

'Of course not,' Dora snapped. 'I'm not an idiot.'

'But you leave this cottage unlocked?'

'It's different here, this is the countryside; this is,' she cooed, 'my little idyll.'

'That's as may be, madam, but crime does go on here too. We've been receiving numerous complaints of petty theft in the village recently. If you've a mind, it's easy pickings in these parts, people thinking it safe to leave their premises unlocked. D'you think you'd be able to identify this dagger if we found it?'

'Of course,' Dora confirmed.

Fearful their conversation may be drawing to a close, and Dora was about to lead the policemen out, Caroline abandoned her eavesdropping to race back to the kitchen.

'Who's Dora talking to?' Joanna swallowed the last of her drink and wiped her mouth on the sleeve of her sweatshirt.

'The police.'

'Have they found Ellie?'

'I couldn't hear much,' Caroline lied, her mind racing to where she'd dumped Dora's knife, and the possibility the police were going to find it. 'You didn't hear anything, did you?'

'No. I've been in here.'

'Good.' Caroline, as relieved with this as she was to hear Dora blaming Dean Fry for nicking her stuff, grabbed her sister and tugged her into the hall. '*Shhh.*' She pressed a finger to her lips. 'Quick, come on; upstairs.'

And watching from the landing, feeling the vibrations of heavy boots along the hall, the sisters heard a brief exchange between the police and their aunt, before the kitchen door slammed shut.

The following morning, Joanna spied Gordon's car parked up beyond the trees. She knew something was different about this Monday even before she came downstairs. Dora smelled different. Like the honeysuckle around Pillowell's front door, except artificial. The horses felt it too: reluctant to come to her as they usually would on their feeding trip to the bottom of the garden.

Dora hadn't been so bothered about Joanna and Caroline eating every last scrap of their breakfast either, her eyes too busy working herself out in the little cracked vanity mirror that, excavated from the odds-and-sods drawer in the sitting room, now balanced in a nook above the sink. Gordon smelled funny too, of tobacco and the spice of his aftershave; it was something she had come to expect whenever she sat in his lap. In the same way she'd come to expect his impromptu visits. Afternoons spent sitting with

213

his elbows on the arms of Dora's leather armchair, drinking coffee and blowing smoke rings. He reminded Joanna of the colourful birds of paradise in a book of photographs her mother used to show her before she was old enough to look at them for herself. Flamboyant and dramatic, he lit up her mind, and was the only person, apart from her mother and Mrs Hooper, she was happy to let cuddle her close and stroke her hair.

'Oh, Jo, there you are.' Dora skimmed her eyes to her. 'Gordon's here – he's taking us to Cinderglade for the day. We're going to get Carrie's hair smartened up.'

'But what about Ellie? She's still missing.' Joanna buckled her brow. 'Shouldn't you be helping to look for her? Me and Carrie wanted to help, but they wouldn't let us.'

'Oh, don't worry, the police are on to it – they're combing the area, it said on the news.'

'*What*? With a giant comb?'

'No, silly.' Dora gave her niece an awkward squeeze. 'It means they're doing a thorough search; that she's going to turn up safe and sound.'

Safe and sound. How many times had Joanna heard people say that since Saturday afternoon? The hollow words were enough to turn her stomach, especially when she thought of those white-beamed torches searching late into the night. Where are you, Ellie? Why would you disappear on your birthday, when there was cake and candles, and all those presents to open? Asking her silent questions, she tried to imagine where her friend might be as she sent something of herself out across the breeze to find her.

'And besides,' Dora continued, 'Gordon's taking us, and you don't want to disappoint him, do you?'

Joanna watched her aunt blot her shocking red mouth with a tissue. An action that made her want to scream. Didn't she care what had happened to Ellie? Dora's selfishness was shameful, she was as nuts about Gordon as Caroline was about Dean. They should be out there with the rest of the village, looking for her missing friend, but it was like trying to talk to a madwoman – look at her; her brain was all warped. Love made you dangerous, it brought out the worst in you, and Joanna swore she was never going to let a man do this to her. She would apply herself to her music, be the best she could be – the piano was a far safer addiction than some silly man, and she was getting good at it, Mrs Hooper said so.

Trapped inside Gordon's BMW, they glided past the Boar's Head. Saw a large poster of Ellie taped to a window. Another nailed to a telegraph pole. Their friend's brown hair and dimpled smile overseeing her search. The word MISSING heaved in the breeze. The sisters also saw the blue flashing lights of patrol cars, the spill of journalists, cameramen, as well as a white Luton van emblazoned with GLOUCESTER-SHIRE NEWS. Further away, marching into the woods, a cavalcade of villagers armed with walking sticks and binoculars led by the Reverend Mortmain, his dog-collar visible beneath his walking clothes. They identified Ian as the car grazed alongside his face: grey, unshaven; close enough to touch. But there was no sign of Liz. No Dean.

'They must be off looking for Ellie,' Joanna said, her nose rubbing the glass.

'We should be too.' Caroline bounced her frustrated fists in her lap.

'It's not fair. I don't wanna go shopping.' Joanna drew a heart shape into the condensation she'd made.

'I don't want a bloody haircut,' Caroline said, and sunk into one of her sulks.

Hot in the back of the car, the sisters felt every bend in the windy road. They unstuck their legs from the leather upholstery and craned their necks to the last of the action through the rear windscreen, until all had dissolved into the enveloping frondescence.

'Out all night again, they were,' Dora informed a staunchly silent Gordon. 'It's been almost two days; they should've found her by now, surely. Tilly said they questioned Ian, Dean too, more than once – have they talked to you?'

'Of course they have,' Gordon snapped. 'I should think they've been *talking* to everyone.'

'I suppose.' Dora fidgeted in her seat. 'They've certainly been on to all the parents of Ellie's friends. Liz has apparently called everyone they know round here, and where they used to live. But there's no sign of her.'

Gordon didn't respond. Gripping the gearstick, his knuckles white as a snow-capped mountain range through the tautness of skin. Registering the unreadable pale of his gaze caught in the driving mirror, Caroline did her best to remove herself from his eyeline by squeezing against the passenger door.

'What's the matter with him?' she murmured.

'He's worried about Ellie.' Joanna dragged her mouth down in sympathy.

'He's worried about something.' Caroline knitted her dark brows together.

*

216

Despite the perceived urgency of Caroline's hair appointment, Gordon, although permitted to drive his sleek, black BMW at the national speed limit of sixty miles per hour, chose, as usual, to meander along at forty. The road, a relentless tunnel of green broken only by the periodic peppering of red pillar boxes, added to his despondency. The only evidence of the diamond-bright day going on beyond Witchwood was the sunshine that now and again splintered the car windscreen, making him blink. Needing to slow for a convoy of horses, he swung wide to avoid the mounds of droppings and their clip-clopping hooves and thought how his mother would have been out with a shovel if they'd ridden past Pludd Cottage. She was fanatical about her garden. He frowned, flexing his arm muscles that were still aching from the annual trim he gave her perimeter hedge on Friday.

Relieved to get away from the suffocating feel of the village for a few hours, he seized the opportunity to ferry Dora and her nieces into town. But as the road opened out to the spread of the Cotswold countryside under meringue-whipped clouds, he wondered if he should have stayed behind to help search for Ellie. It would have looked better if he had. Perhaps, had his mother not shared what she overheard Ian Fry calling him in the shop the other day – insults about what sort of man he thought Gordon was, and why he was still single with no family of his own – he might have felt able to.

Reflected in the wing mirror, Dora saw a backlog of cars and imagined the frustrated stream of drivers who had no opportunity to overtake along this twenty-mile stretch of zigzagging A-road. The truck behind them administered a long drone of its horn. Dora pulled down the visor to check her lipstick, saw the driver slap his forehead and make a series of obscene hand gestures in the vanity mirror.

'People are so aggressive.' Gordon, his onyx ring glinting in the sunshine.

About the exasperated lorry driver, or what might have happened to Ellie Fry? Dora didn't ask. Reluctant to spoil the rare opportunity of a day with him, she stared out through the passenger window at silver rivers cutting through ripening farmland, the layered rise of hills jostling the horizon.

Itching to be out there helping to find their friend, the girls mulled over the trouble they'd left behind in Witchwood and scratched the exposed stretch of shin between ankle sock and hem. Sensing their agitation – the sound of nails on skin grating her nerves – Dora reached behind her seat to smack their legs still.

'We're going to enjoy today if it kills us,' she announced, then asked Gordon: 'D'you mind if I put the radio on?'

The tail end of Betty Boo asking *Where are you, baby?* before Radio Two cut to the news, and the measured tone of the announcer plugged the space between them like foam. *Gloucestershire Police, continuing to search for missing ten-year-old Ellie Fry, are to deploy a specialist team of officers and sniffer dogs in what will be the second full day of searching the large area of woodland around her home . . .* Gordon switched it off.

No one talked again for a while. The underbelly of a buzzard diving for carrion between verge and tarmac. Its angel spread, wheeling away, made them gasp. Dora, mouth stale from her recent breakfast, hunted Gordon's glove box in the hope of finding a mint.

'What's this?' she quizzed. 'I didn't know you played the guitar.' And she tugged free a shiny-covered volume of *A Tune a Day*, squinting at the music she couldn't read.

'It was for Ellie,' Gordon said, snatching it back and stuffing it into the side pocket of the driver's door. 'Liz was teaching her to play.' Dora, alarmed by his use of the past tense, heard him swallow – a dry, wretched sound strangled in the back of his throat. 'I thought she might've liked it . . .' He ran out of steam as the missing Ellie Fry sat between them like another passenger.

'What d'you think's happened to her?' Dora watched a bumblebee bash itself repeatedly against the dashboard. She dropped her window and guided it to freedom. The amplified rush of wind carrying the smell of recently mown hay engulfed them. She closed it again, sealing them off from the outside, and felt Gordon's eyes leave the road for a split second and turn on her. The look was cold as he changed down a gear to accommodate the sharp bend into Cinderglade. Dora was relieved he didn't reply. Saved from further awkwardness by the sirens on the level crossing, they squeezed to a stop as the gates came down. Seconds later, the scream of metal on metal as the 10.23 from London whizzed through, as panic bounced like a rubber ball against the wall of Dora's stomach. Did Gordon know something – something about Ellie? Did it have something to do with the police finding one of her roller skates in the woods? These were questions Dora would return to time and again, but fearing Gordon's answer, she never dared ask him outright.

Present Day

'I took the day off to mark these.' Joanna points to a pile of essays. 'But I was kidding myself. I can't concentrate.'

Pauline Baxter – attractive, thirty something, a single mum since her husband of seventeen years ran off with their dentist – says nothing. When Pauline pops round for coffee, as she does from time to time, Joanna makes it obvious she has things she wants to get off her chest.

'All this with Carrie,' Joanna continues. 'It's making it impossible for me to put the necessary piano practice in too. I'm frighteningly behind. So much so, it's looking like I'm going to have to postpone the recitals I agreed to give in Germany this autumn.'

'That's a shame,' Pauline answers. 'But if it helps take the pressure off. Mike said things had been full-on – you went to sort out your sister's flat, didn't you?'

'That was more of a fact-finding mission. I needed to piece together what happened. To find out why she managed to kill herself while trying to stab that bloke.'

'And did you find out much?' Pauline sips her coffee.

'A bit. But it's all so complicated – and the more I unravel, the more confused I get.'

'Two heads, and all that,' her neighbour offers.

'I wouldn't know where to start.' Joanna plonks down on

a chair beside Pauline. 'But it's colouring my life. Whatever I think I uncover just creates new questions I don't have the answers to.'

Chin in her hands at the kitchen table, the dog at her feet, Joanna watches the world turn through the large casement windows of her beautiful Wheathampstead home.

'Death's so horribly final, isn't it?' she says, her voice flat. 'I know to even say that sounds stupid, but I think it's taken me till now to understand it fully.'

'You've lost enough loved ones to know, and you've had your own health troubles, you poor thing,' Pauline consoles. 'I'm lucky, the only person I've lost is my grandfather, and he was well into his nineties.'

Clouds bubble like sand castles behind the panes of glass. They lead Joanna back to that long ago, happy seaside holiday in Caswell Bay, and bring unexpected thoughts of her father bobbing beyond the collapsing breakers. He was blind without his specs but on the rare occasion he removed them, his face took on a vulnerability that still makes her anxious to know how he manages to see anything of heaven without them.

'Dad's been dead for nearly thirty-three years, but d'you know,' a weighted pause, 'it still feels like pressing a bruise to think of him. Then Mum, now Carrie.'

'You poor thing.' Pauline squeezes Joanna's arm.

'My problem is I feel so guilty.'

'Guilty?'

'Yes. Even before I saw Carrie's mental health nurse ... and she said some pretty alarming things.'

'Really?' Pauline wrinkles her nose. 'Like what?'

'About me lying to Carrie. When we were kids.

Apparently she was still going on about it – couldn't forgive me, the nurse said.'

'Bit extreme, isn't it? D'you remember what you lied about?'

'Dean.'

'Isn't that the bloke whose name she shouted in the supermarket?'

'Yep.' Joanna sighs. 'She was nuts about him … well, *obsessed* more like. And I told her he liked her. That he'd told me he was going to ask her out.'

'And that was a lie?'

'Yes. But this was real playground stuff. I was only nine, for God's sake – I didn't think she was going to take me seriously.'

Pauline gives Joanna a look.

'I said it to cheer her up. I was sick of her moping around. She was so grumpy, it was spoiling everything.' Joanna defends herself. 'But, the thing was, Dean already had a girlfriend, didn't he? And even if he hadn't, he was way too old for Carrie.'

'How old was he?'

'Eighteen. Carrie was thirteen.'

'And this is what your sister couldn't forgive you for?' Pauline asks.

Joanna nods. 'And get this – and this is more alarming – according to Carrie's nurse, me duping her into thinking Dean loved her when he didn't – yes, she actually used the word *duping* –' she slumps further into her chair – 'well, it drove her to do something terrible, apparently. Something she couldn't forgive herself for.'

'Really? D'you know what?'

A shake of the head. 'I knew Carrie could get fixated on things – I could give you loads of examples of that. *And* she had a memory like a bloody elephant, could be very unforgiving. I've never known anyone bear a grudge like her. But I didn't think for a minute this was her problem with me – I'd forgotten all about what I said.'

'I can see why you think so, it is rather over the top.' Pauline fiddles with her long dark hair. 'But remembering what I was like at that age, I can sort of identify a bit with your sister.'

Joanna looks surprised.

'There was this older boy I had a huge crush on,' Pauline confides. 'It lasted right through school, and beyond. Pathetic, I know, but it's powerful stuff, first love – it can really screw you up. Look at what happened to Romeo and Juliet.'

'*Romeo and Juliet?*'

A sharp laugh from Pauline. 'Perhaps not the best example.'

'Okay.'

'I still dream about him, my schoolgirl crush – even though he never wanted anything to do with me. *Or*,' Pauline pulls a face, 'perhaps *because* he wanted nothing to do with me. So, while I can understand where you're coming from, I can sort of understand your sister's predicament too.'

'Can you?' Joanna's eyebrows shoot up.

'Weren't you ever infatuated with someone as a teenager? Someone who didn't fancy you.'

'Not really. Too focused on the piano.' A fleeting smile. 'Mike was the first guy I was ever interested in. And then we got married.'

'Lucky you. You've never had your heart broken.' Pauline stares out through the windows at the bare cherry trees lining the bottom fence. 'Because I don't think you ever find that intensity of feeling again.'

'Oh, come on.' Joanna is disbelieving. 'Course you can – if Carrie'd gone on to have relationships when she was older, she'd have forgotten about Dean straight away. That was only puppy-love, all she needed was to experience the real thing, and she'd have seen that for herself.'

'It didn't work for me.'

'*No?*'

'No. If I'm honest, the memory of him has never really gone away – in fact, I'd go so far as to say that I've built him up into something more since Tony left me. He's like this fantasy man who would've given me this fantasy life. Mad, I know, but maybe that's what your sister did with this Dean too.'

Joanna isn't sure how to respond, so says nothing.

'Didn't she go on to have any relationships, then?' Pauline asks.

'Not as far as I know.'

'That's sad.'

'It is, isn't it. If only she'd told me what was bothering her, we might have been able to sort it out. I wasn't even aware she knew I'd made that up about Dean. I certainly didn't tell her, it never came up,' Joanna rambles. 'Although, I should have guessed it had nothing to do with the money Dora left her – accusing me of being resentful was just another excuse for her to have a go. Because we were never the same after we came home from Witchwood.' She picks at the tapestry of her thoughts. 'But then, what is odd –' she turns to

Pauline – 'is the scrapbook I found in her flat. Full of photos of me, cut from the papers, brochures, you name it . . . She'd been following my career from the off. Why would she go to all that trouble, if she hated me?'

'Because she was mixed up? She sounded mixed up.' Pauline suggests. 'Or maybe her mental health nurse got it wrong?'

'D'you see what I mean?' Joanna flung her head to the string of halogen ceiling bulbs. 'The more I find out, the more questions there are.'

'I do.' Pauline nods sympathetically. 'What did Mike say when you told him what the nurse said?'

'I didn't.' Joanna looks uneasy. 'You can see why – it takes some swallowing, and I'm not sure he's the stomach for it.'

Pauline rolls her well made-up eyes.

'But supposing I was the root of her problems, I shouldn't have dismissed her as a hopeless cause, should I? Because she wasn't hopeless, was she?' She looks at Pauline. 'She was just troubled and . . . and lost, really. And what sort of person does that make me?'

'I think you're being too hard on yourself. You were only a child.'

'I know, but—'

'And Mike says she was a handful.' Pauline tries to be helpful.

'Yes, maybe, but I still think Carrie deserved better, that's all I'm saying. I'm wondering whether I was right to listen to Mike.'

'Oh, Jo.' Pauline drains her coffee. 'Course you were. He was looking out for you. He thinks the world of you, you know that.'

Rootling her handbag for the postcard Caroline wrote but never sent, Joanna passes it to Pauline. Watches her neighbour's expression as she reads the frantic: *He's here. He's hunted me down. He wants to kill me. You've got to stop him. You've got to help me.*

'I shared that with Mike as soon as I came home, but he wasn't at all bothered by it.'

'Wasn't he?' Pauline certainly looks bothered.

'He dismissed it as a symptom of a deranged mind. He said, if things were that bad, then why didn't she just pick up the phone and tell me straight.'

'Yes, but he's not saying it to be unkind, Jo.' Pauline returns the card. 'It's because he's got family problems of his own. What with his mum on her own now, she's his priority, along with you and the boys – not your sister, who from what I can gather did nothing but push you two away.'

'I suppose.' Joanna stares into the whorls of wood of the tabletop. 'And it's not like he didn't try; he was far more patient than me, if I'm honest.'

'There you go then,' Pauline affirms. 'You can't blame him if he was sick of her moods, frustrated she never returned your messages, ignored the cards you sent for Christmas and birthdays.'

'You're right. Carrie never showed any interest in Freddie or Ethan either.'

'How about we stop all this introspection and blame, eh?' Pauline gets up to rinse her mug under the tap. 'It's not getting you anywhere. Now –' she twists to face her – 'you seem to think your sister was still hung up on Dean, so much so she hadn't forgiven you for what you said about him when you were kids.'

'Yes,' Joanna agrees.

'And,' Pauline pushes her logic into Joanna's eyes, 'the last thing she called out before she died was his name. I don't know about you, but, maybe … What's this Dean bloke doing with himself these days, then. You thought about that?'

'Yes, I was a bit curious. I did a quick search for him on the internet coming home on the train. But there didn't seem to be anything and I've not had the chance since.'

'Why not have a proper look now? You said yourself you're in no fit state to get any work done.'

Somewhat reluctantly, Joanna opens the lid of her laptop, activates the internet and keys *Dean Fry* into the search engine. She doesn't know what she expects to have changed, but again there's nothing much: a LinkedIn profile, and 192.com telling her it's found thirty-eight people in the UK with his name.

'He could be any one of them or none of them.' She points at the screen. 'There has to be an easier way of finding him.'

'Have you tried Facebook?' Pauline suggests. 'Everyone's on there nowadays, I've found loads of my old friends.'

'He's hardly a *friend*,' Joanna says bluntly. 'But, yes, I did, as it happens, it's the first place I looked. There were a few with that name, but none of them were him.'

'Oh, okay, shame that – you can usually find anyone on there.'

'Hang on, I've just thought of something.'

'What?'

'That poor bloke, the one Caroline tried to stab. Perhaps I could have a look for him on Facebook, because I've been thinking … and I know the police didn't want me talking to him, but it's been niggling me, I feel I need to say some-thing . . . apologise on Carrie's behalf . . . I don't know, what d'you think?'

'Yes, why not. If it'd make you feel better.' Pauline heads for the stairs. 'D'you mind if I nip to the bathroom?'

'Sure. You know where it is.' Joanna, only half listening, is already typing the name Kyle Norris into the search box. It brings up twelve people and she spools through their faces carefully, reading their potted histories, their places of residence: a New Zealander, a black guy from New York, a man in his mid-fifties surrounded by his family, a Chinese guy living in Prague, a teenager in a hoodie from Newcastle-upon-Tyne . . . Totally absorbed, she misses the chirruping of the telephone in the background and keeps scrolling through, until the head and shoulders photograph of a man in his late-twenties stops her dead.

No way. A hand flies to her mouth in disbelief. Doubting what her eyes are telling her, she hunches closer, double-clicking the image to make it fill the screen. Staring back is a face she knows. A face as it looked to her that summer with Dora in Witchwood.

The ringing of the telephone eventually stops. And spinning to the here and now she mouths '*Dean?*' into the swaying silence. Her shock, loud enough to wake the snoozing Buttons.

'Are you all right? Didn't you hear the phone?' Pauline is by her side, leaning into the screen. 'God, Jo. You look like you've seen a ghost.'

Summer 1990

Caroline yawned. A big indulgent yawn that ordinarily would not be tolerated at Pillowell Cottage. It came as the floorboards in Dora's room creaked under her weight. '*Uch.*' She squirmed, stretching towards the sunlight bleeding in from the east. A furtive check to make sure Joanna was still asleep had her reaching under the bed for Mrs Hooper's snow globe. She held it up to peer into the frozen wonderland beyond its perfect glass dome. A shake, and the swirl of snow settled over the storybook-perfect cottage with its family safely entombed in an everlasting winter.

She got out of bed to make room for the snow globe in her underwear drawer. Too big an object for the hole she'd dug in the bank, she was going to have to risk keeping it here. But she must hide the gold ring she pinched from the pub, and the brooch with the wine-red stone she took from the vestry at St Oswald's. She must do it today. And as she was awake early, she could slip out now and be back before either Dora or Joanna noticed she was missing. She was feeling particularly anxious since eavesdropping on her aunt's conversation with the police on Sunday; the net was closing in, and she needed to be careful – if anyone discovered it was her doing the stealing, it would let Dean Fry clean off the hook.

Reluctant as always to expose her bare body, even to her sister, Caroline whipped off her nightie and tugged on her dungarees, T-shirt and cardigan in two swift movements. Avoiding the mirror and the haircut she'd been given in town yesterday, she positioned the Alice band she didn't strictly need any more and pushed her feet into her jelly sandals, the ring and the brooch safely stowed away in a pocket.

Stars were dropping out now. A couple of lights had come on in the village, and Lillian told herself there was little point going to bed. She'd never drift off without taking one of her late husband's sleeping pills, and she was trying to wean herself off them. Anyway, Gordon would be getting up in less than an hour, expecting his breakfast, and the idea of going and lying down only to hear him wake up and steal his first sigh of the day, she didn't think she could bear it.

In the same way Gordon never needed sleeping tablets, he never needed an alarm clock either. Wired to be early, from having it beaten into him at his boarding school, he was up and out for his ramble through the woods or along the footpath to Slinghill every morning. Not that he ever took Laika, calling her an embarrassment because of her truncated legs, and moaning she couldn't keep up with him. What was an embarrassment, Lillian brought the slightly absurd image to mind, was him going about in his suit trousers fastened with a pair of his father's old cycle clips.

The clock on her mantelpiece – insistent, oppressive – she could envisage burying it, and the thing ticking away for years below ground. Lillian looked at a blur of wood pigeons through the window, or was it her reflection in the glass? Grey and tired, she judged, always harsh. She should sort herself out before Gordon came down, otherwise there would be questions. Questions he already knew the answers to but asked anyway, in the hope things had changed. She switched on TV-am, wanting the company of Anne Diamond and her co-host Nick Owen, and to forget for a moment or two the dire financial situation she was in; as reluctant to discuss it with her son as she was to think about it. Barely audible – she couldn't risk waking Gordon – the breakfast television presenters were refereeing a debate about new working-time directives between a woman economist and one of Thatcher's cabinet.

'We're trying to help small businesses,' Lillian imitated the woman's whine before the news cut in and showed a repeat of the police appeal made by Liz and Ian Fry the previous day. Grim and drawn, the trauma of their missing child had aged them overnight, and it was upsetting to see. 'Bring her home safe,' Liz's voice was breaking under the pressure of the insurmountable anguish. 'I need Ellie home.'

Lillian switched it off; the distressing images these news bulletins supplied were another reason she couldn't sleep. Poor Liz, she sighed, leaning down to stroke her dachshund's cinnamon-brown eyebrows. Supposing Ellie had come to harm, whoever did it was still out there. The thought was a terrifying one, and further soured her opinion of the place.

Gordon's up. The floorboards above her head groaned in protest. She yawned. *Wasn't it always the way?* Lillian wriggled in her chair and reckoned if she were to go to bed she'd sleep like a baby. Yawning again, she picked over Gordon's sudden decision to return to Italy tomorrow. Booking a flight for Wednesday when he was out in Cinderglade with Dora and the girls. She asked him what the rush was – he wasn't scheduled to go back until September. But he wouldn't answer. He'd been in a foul temper since Saturday, complaining he'd overdone it trimming the hedge the day before, but Lillian knew it had more to do with him not being invited to Ellie's party. Not that she said this, it didn't pay to push Gordon when he was in one of his moods. In her experience, it was better to stand well back, let whatever troubled him blow over.

Up on her feet, Lillian took the few necessary paces to her study to look at her favourite photograph of Ursula – the one she could now see so much of Joanna in. Along with Lillian's lover – a man whose darker side that others spoke of was never shown to her – Joanna was making life worth living too. A special child with such a gift for the piano, she was a joy to teach. Although, she wished Gordon wasn't quite so taken with her – worrying, the occasions she'd come home from organ practice, to find them so intimate. Of course, it was all perfectly innocent, Joanna was such a dear; who could resist? Not that people around here would see it like that. Gordon's fondness for Ellie got enough tongues wagging.

She stared into the photographed face of little Ursula, captured on the last family holiday before she died and Derek sent Gordon away to school. The memory was almost too much for Lillian as she looked at the merest circle of dust on her desk where the little snow globe used to be. The last thing Ursula gave her; it was her most treasured possession. Along with the garnet brooch her mother bequeathed to her that, pinned to the lapel of her best jacket, disappeared when she left it in the vestry with the discarded cassocks. She thought of Dora complaining of knickknacks disappearing from Pillowell, and the more serious issue of Dora's father's missing dagger. The idea there could be a thief in the village was deeply unsettling. This sort of thing didn't happen around here and, coupled with Lillian's fears of what the police might be about to discover in nearby woodland, had her heart jumping beneath her blouse.

A rattling from outside, startling, unexpected. Lillian jolted upright in her chair, fully alert.

What the hell was that?

Laika was on to it, springing from her bed and yapping wildly to be let outside. Ferreting the key from its vase and turning the lock, Lillian stepped on to her dew-wet lawn in time to see a darkened shape tearing away under the rose arch. Her lover wouldn't risk calling round while Gordon was here, would he? Surely he could wait, her son would be out of the country tomorrow.

The violent *thwop, thwop* of a police helicopter scooped low over the trees. Looking up to see the warming sun had swapped places with the moon, she appealed to the heavens for the safe return of little Ellie, before scurrying back inside her cottage, wanting the reassuring creak of floorboards as her son moved around upstairs.

'Where d'you get that?' Joanna's voice from the shadows, and Caroline jerked her head to it.

'It's Dora's.'

'She know you've got it?' Joanna sat up in bed and pushed back the covers.

'No.'

233

'You nicked it, then?' Joanna, at her elbow, extended a finger to touch the sparkly diamante hair clasp before Caroline could tuck it away. 'I'll tell.'

'No, you won't.'

'Yes, I will.' Joanna jutted out her chin, determined to have her say for once. 'Unless you show me what else you've taken.'

'I've not *taken* nothing.' Caroline touched the snow globe hidden in the drawer, its unyielding spherical shape hard under her cotton knickers. 'I'm going to put it back.'

'What? Like you're going to put that brooch back.'

Caroline glared at her.

'Don't look at me like that – it's red and about this big.' Joanna made a circle between finger and thumb.

'How d'you know about that?' Feeling around inside the pocket of her dungarees, Caroline satisfied herself the gold ring and brooch were still safe.

'Seen you.'

'Seen me what?'

'Playing with it.'

'You're naughty, you are.'

'You're the naughty one.' Joanna rubbed sleep from her eyes. 'But I might not tell if you show me what else you've got.'

Caroline said nothing and shut the drawer.

'What you hiding in there?' Joanna pointed.

'Nuffin.'

'Show me.' Joanna, her palm as flat as when she fed the horses.

Caroline handed her the snow globe.

'Cor, that's pretty. Look at the little family inside.'

234

'Lovely, isn't it?' Caroline said, unable to share how the little quartet reminded her of what life was like before the coastguard fished their father from the sea, turning four into three. And with the memory came a blaze of what she'd been that day – the sun on her face, the chime of an ice-cream van in her ears, running along the sand in her polka-dot swimsuit – and her mother, carefree and sandy-kneed, sculpting horses from the soft Welsh sand, eyes brimming with love ... There was no love in her mother's eyes now, she thought, gulping back tears, except perhaps for Joanna.

'Where d'you get it?' her sister wanted to know.

'Mrs Hooper's,' Caroline answered quickly.

'*Mrs Hooper's?*' Joanna's grin vanished. 'Oh, no, Carrie, you can't. Nicking from Dora's one thing, but Mrs Hooper? She's got nothing; you know that. You've got to give it back.' And she dropped the snow globe inside the drawer as if it burnt her fingers.

'Why do I? She's done loads for you, but nuffin for me. I'm keeping it, she won't notice.'

'She will, you've got to give it back.' Joanna, insistent, collected her towel and wash-ups. 'It's not right.'

'Will you shut up if I show you the other things I've taken?'

'Maybe.'

'Right then, after breakfast. I'll show you after breakfast.'

'No. I want to see them now.'

'They're not here, stupid. I've got a special place for them – down by the lake.'

'Promise?' Joanna creased her soft little brow.

'Promise.'

Present Day

Kyle Norris. The hairs on the back of Joanna's neck prickle against the collar of her shirt. K-y-l-e. Seated at the kitchen table, she hunts the letters for booby traps and warnings. Nothing; it sounds perfectly innocuous. But the similarities between Dean Fry and this man her sister attacked without provocation are startling. Even down to the wave in his light brown hair. This twenty-seven-year-old Kyle could be his twin – his twin nearly three decades ago, because Joanna knows Dean would be near fifty now.

Poor Caroline. This must have been what she thought that night in the mini-mart, and why she shouted out Dean's name – too irrational to understand he wouldn't look like this any more. Could it be that Caroline saw Kyle around and about in Bayswater before that night, and mistaken him for Dean? It's possible – the police said he'd moved to the area six months previously. And if so, could Dean be the threat her sister was going on about in the postcard she didn't send? But why on earth would she be scared of him, so scared she needed to carry a knife to protect herself?

Joanna would have liked to run it by Pauline, had she not needed to rush off to work. Weighing up what she does and doesn't know, Joanna shakes dog biscuits into a bowl for the ever-wagging Buttons. She thinks about the stuff her sister recorded in her notebooks – dreams, nightmares – that Joanna's been unscrambling. Dreams of Dean mutating from someone loving, into someone wanting to destroy her. It proves she never forgot him, but it wasn't her pining after her first love, as Joanna originally thought; it seems more likely now that she was terrified of him – terrified he'd come after her. Joanna's theory that Caroline couldn't let herself fall in love with anyone else because she was stuck aged thirteen and nurturing a crush on an older boy, wasn't what was going on in her sister's head at all. Caroline's life was on hold because of her fear of him, not a love for him. It makes perfect sense now. But what doesn't make sense is *why* she was frightened of him.

She double-clicks on Dean Fry's doppelgänger again. Studies the enlarged image. The similarities are breathtaking. In Caroline's unbalanced mind, this bloke just happened, unfortunately, to look exactly like someone she was afraid of for whatever reason. And to think she could have killed him. Joanna has got to explain to Kyle, it might make him feel better. It will certainly make her feel better.

With hours to go before she needs to fetch the boys from school, Joanna makes a fresh coffee and sits back down at the table. She gazes into the good-looking record producer's face – the accused, then swiftly acquitted Kyle Norris – then clicks on the icon to compose him a message. Happy with it, she presses send and hopes she hears something from him soon. Little point pretending she's marking – these papers on the significance of Benjamin Britten's chamber pieces will have to wait – her need to find Dean Fry is far more pressing as she now fully believes the mystery of her sister's state of mind and subsequent death are connected to him.

Despite her earlier trawl of the internet throwing up nothing new on Dean's whereabouts, she wants to have another look. But aside from a series of unsettling images of Drake's Pike and the hundred-acre section of dense and ancient woodland – which, as lush and green as it is in her memory, looks rather claustrophobic and sinister in the photographs the websites provide – there is little else. The village of Witchwood looks relatively unchanged, but she can't find anything about the Boar's Head. According to her searches, Witchwood's only pub is the Royal Oak, and the name of the landlord isn't one she knows.

Sipping her coffee, it dawns on her the only chance she has of finding Dean – which she must do if she wants answers – is through his parents. She scribbles down the number of the pub, taps the biro against her teeth. The brewery probably renamed it in an effort to stamp out its past, but the new owners might know where Liz and Ian moved to. It's a start, what else has she got?

'Erm, hello,' she begins, unsure what to say next. 'I don't know whether you'll be able to help, but I'm looking for a pub – the Boar's Head,' she says tentatively, her mobile pressed against her ear. 'It used to be in Witchwood.'

'Yeah, this used to be the Boar,' the man on the other end of the line clarifies. 'Changed it for some reason; donkey's years before we took it on.'

'Right.' Joanna, hopeful. 'You wouldn't happen to know Liz and Ian Fry, would you?'

'Who?'

'Liz and Ian Fry?' Joanna repeats. 'They used to run it when it was the Boar.'

'*Liz and Ian Fry*? Nah, sorry, love, never heard of 'em.'

'Really? Oh, well, it was a bit of a long shot.'

'Hang on a min – can you hang on?' the man asks.

'Course.' She nods frantically, hears the handset knock against the buttons on his shirt, a muffled muddle of voices in the background.

'Me wife's sayin' she knows someone you could try. That he might know where they've gone.' The man, re-joining her. 'He's been here for years.'

'Brilliant.' Joanna perks up. 'You don't happen to have his number, d'you?'

'Yep, just a tick.' More scrabbling, jumbled voices. Joanna holds her breath. 'Here you go ... got a pen?'

'Yes,' she says, jotting it down. 'And the name?'

'Petley. Frank Petley.'

Summer 1990

You'd hardly call it a path, just a scrape in the hip-high bracken and bramble, and a route through the woods the police and villagers obviously missed. Hot, the sisters slipped around inside their PVC sandals and barely exchanged a word. The pernicious breeze fidgeted with their hair as it gathered speed through the spooky, sun-starved interior that fell between the lofty trunks of trees. The police in DayGlo and dogs they had been anticipating were nowhere.

'I told you, no one comes this way.' Caroline was the first to speak. 'It's why I knew it was safe to hide the stuff.'

A dead deer stopped them in their tracks. Caught mid-leap on a snag of barbed wire. They clapped their hands near its ears to see if they twitched, but the smell should have told them, buffeting them sideways when they moved up close. Holding their noses, they were fascinated and repelled in equal measure. Portions of dead flesh moved as if still alive, and they couldn't tear their eyes away from the pulsating shroud of fat, white maggots. Death. This was what it looked like, they told themselves, as the buzz of bluebottles took off and landed around them. Disgust at the idea one could accidentally touch them was enough to have them sprinting away.

'Stop, stop,' Joanna yelled, out of puff. Slowing to a walk and replacing the stench of dead deer with the smell of the heat-packed ground, they tipped their heads to the ragged crowns of trees that were already rusted with autumn. Veering off to the left, weaving through slender birch saplings and more bracken, they were thrust into an unexpected clearing on their approach to the lake. Into the unnerving silence dropped the cold rippling song of a curlew, its ghostliness curling over them like smoke.

'Ellie brought us this way,' Joanna chirruped. 'We found that abandoned picnic over there, remember?' And she pointed beyond the reeds and scrub rustling in the wind, to the log under its canopy of weeping willow.

'I already knew about this place.' Caroline, excessively proud.

'When? You never told me.'

'You don't know everything I do.' A sly smile. 'I've got lots of secrets.'

Sudden squelching, the ground beneath them waterlogged, they ripped through rare marshmallow growing in secret pockets of warm, the sodden stretch of shoreline steaming through the gaps in their sandals. This was another country entirely: enigmatic, weather-beaten and eerie; a place that nosed out into Drake's Pike and its low-lying watery flatness. The girls loved it here, not that either voiced it – it seemed wrong to be enjoying themselves without Ellie chattering alongside.

Batting away midges, they reached the edge of the lake and smelled its slightly stagnant breath. Their eyes grazed the opposite shore, the distant rise of ripe green pastures dotted with sheep.

'What's that?' Joanna pointed at something in the rushes. 'C-Carrie! *Carrie!*' she shrieked, darting away – and with pigtails swinging, held her find above her head.

Recognising it, Caroline was beside her in an instant, and they stared, bewildered, at the muddy pink leather roller skate oscillating from its multi-coloured lace.

'It's Ellie's, isn't it?' Joanna's eyes like two blue pools.

'The police found the other one in the woods on Sunday.' Caroline was crying too. 'I heard them telling Dora about it.'

'*What?*' Joanna squawked, scrubbing away tears; whatever doubts she had dying in her mouth.

'I didn't want to frighten you,' Caroline replied to her sister's unasked question. 'I knew it looked bad – we both know there's no way she'd have left them behind. But I just kept hoping she'd turn up.'

A robin redbreast balanced on a rotten stump of fence post, an anguished song in its throat, seized Caroline's attention. She pointed it out to Joanna, and they waited until the bird wheeled away, their gazes trailing its flight across the winking, blinking sheet of sun-kissed water.

Then they saw her.

A dark shape out on the lake, beyond the spread of grasses and reeds.

Ellie Fry.

Floating on her back. Her half-submerged body bobbing stiff as driftwood, her eyes staring blindly at a ruinous sky. Her hands, balanced on the skin of the lake, looked as tender as the upturned heads of chrysanthemums. Saved from the greedy current by the noose of weeds snared about her neck – gilded in sunlight and transformed into silky blue-green threads – they had speared her to something below the waterline. Edging closer, to the lip of the shore, they leant out, saw between her legs, under her arms, the upsetting brown froth where dead water had gathered.

Ellie's pink roller skate: a pendulum between them in the swaying seconds neither could move. Equally reluctant to accept what their eyes showed them, the calmness held in the jaws of the unfolding horror made it difficult to breathe. Without speaking, they dropped the roller skate and lunged forward, ignoring the razor-sharp spines of rushes, to break through the lake's glassy sheen, the vividly cold water cutting their denim-clad legs off from the world at the knees. Shaking with shock, their limbs wouldn't work, and they cursed their arms for not being long enough. Quickly realising they were out of their depth, that Ellie was too far out and they couldn't reach her, Caroline, mind spinning, had a moment of clarity. She stepped free of the lake and dragged the longest stick she could find to the shore's edge. Working together, sloshing through chest-high water, they risked everything to reach their friend.

'We've got to do something.' Caroline, her eyes yanked wide in desperation. 'We're going to lose her to the current otherwise.' She gripped what little remained of Ellie's pink-and-white striped skater dress.

'Into the boat.' Joanna, teeth chattering wildly. 'Get her into the boat.'

Neither stopped to consider whether they had the strength to lift her. Wading through the secret peace below their waists – a dark green world knitted with the skeins of weeds – they hauled Ellie's surprisingly heavy body over the sides of the boat and rolled her over. She lay with her wet hair fallen back and her lips parted as if for a kiss, and the sight of her reminded them of Millais' pale, floating Ophelia on Dora's landing. The marbling on Ellie's skin was shocking, and with all suntan washed from her face, her only colour was a smattering of freckles across her nose.

Caroline closed the purplish lids over the eyes, but there was nothing she could do about the distressing way Ellie's lips were parted so trustingly. Both of them set about arranging her weed-slippery hair, tidying it with wet fingers, positioning what remained of her party dress to cover the worst of her cut and broken body. Wanting, without the need to communicate why, to make her as neat as they could; concerned how she would look when the others came to find her.

'Why's she so cold?' Joanna, exchanging fretful glances with her sister, didn't understand. 'Take your cardigan off, Carrie – we'll give it to her to make her warm.'

Caroline did. And the two of them covered Ellie with it. Tucking her in carefully, softly; worried about disturbing her while at the same time half expecting her to wake up, to laugh, and tell them it was all a silly joke.

Staring again at the shocking sight of that cold blue marbling on Ellie's legs and arms, they waited a moment, hands clasped behind their backs in a way that suggested they couldn't trust themselves not to keep touching her. Watched by the swans that knew to stay away: creatures who understood more than anyone what had gone on here, they drifted unperturbed as white-sailed galleons on the horizon. And shifting their attention to them for a moment, the girls felt their heart rates slow. Caroline told herself she wasn't crying, that it was only the breeze, always the breeze, and tilted her nose to the heavens that in the last few minutes had darkened into a weight of purple cloud. If the world turned, neither was aware of it; their breathing, muffled as a ghost's, seemed to test the emptiness. Kicking free of the water, Caroline turned to help Joanna out. Together they stood amid the occasional birdsong and the summer slap where lake met bank, the air brittle with thunder.

Did Ellie drown like their father drowned? Was it an accident? How did she get that horrible gash on her neck? Why did she take her skates off? Ellie never took her skates off. But more puzzling was the idea she could have come all the way down here to swim in her best party dress when she had presents and birthday cake waiting at home.

The silence that hovered between the sisters was worse than if they had cried. Nothing made sense. All they could be sure of was their sopping clothes and squelch of mud inside their sandals. A wood pigeon took flight; frightening as gunfire, and into the silent aftershock Joanna reached for Caroline's icy hand. This time she didn't shrug it off; both needed the warmth of the other. The stolen treasures forgotten, all that preoccupied them through the amplified dripping of their clothes and violent chattering of teeth was a shared recollection of Ellie from only days ago: full-stretch on roller skates, hair at half-mast, her arms and legs dusted with fine gold hairs that glinted in the sun, and the tinkle of her impulsive, joy-filled laugh – a sound that wouldn't play out again anywhere but inside their heads. Abandoning Ellie to this lonely stretch of marshland, the balls of mist clenching like fists over the water, it was a relief to return to the woods with its melancholy boughs, and the village they were familiar with.

Present Day

The house telephone rings almost as soon as Joanna returns her mobile to her handbag.

'Having fun?' Mike jokes. 'How's the marking going?'

'Okay,' she exhales and, noticing how prematurely dark the day has become, switches on the thread of halogen ceiling lights.

'I rang earlier – didn't you hear the phone?'

'Can't have done. Sorry.'

'You all right? You sound funny.'

'I'm struggling to concentrate, if I'm honest.' Sudden rain sprays the kitchen windows; she turns her back to it, strokes the dog with her slippered foot.

'Oh, you're not still fretting about your sister, are you? We know what happened to her, it was just unfortunate, nobody's to blame. There's no crime to investigate, is there?' His chirpiness is pinched into a question she can tell he doesn't want the answer to. 'For God's sake, Jo, you've got to let it go.'

The rhyming of *Jo* and *go* was something he used to tease her about when they were first together. Jo-Go is Mike's nickname for her when he's larking around, but he's not larking around today.

'I can't,' she says simply, placing her coffee mug in the sink.

Silence. And into it she hears him heave a sigh. Feels its perforated edge squeezed down the handset.

'I discovered something, Mike. It's really odd.' Joanna is the first to speak.

'Go on.'

'I don't know what to make of it really, but y'know that Kyle Norris bloke, the one—'

'Yes, I know.' Mike cuts her off, not wanting the upsetting details again.

'He's the double of that Dean Fry I told you about.'

'Dean Fry? *Dean* – what, the bloke your sister claimed was involved in the murder of your little friend, you mean?' Mike sounds interested. 'Huh, she really screwed his life up, didn't she?'

'Yes, him.'

'His double, you say?'

'Yes ... and because of it, I'm wondering ...'

'What?'

'I know nobody's to blame for Carrie's death, it's on CCTV, I'm not questioning that. But seeing this bloke's face, and the fact the lad in the shop said Carrie shouted out Dean's name. It was the very last word she said.' A pause. 'I know Dean had nothing directly to do with it, but if I could just speak to him, he might be able to ... I don't know ... give me some kind of pointer as to why she reacted the way she did.' Her doubts falling like stone petals between them.

'What pointer?'

'I don't know, do I? And I can hardly ask her. But whatever was going on in that head of hers, whatever she was obsessing about, it had something to do with Dean ...

maybe she was fearful he was going to hurt her like she saw him hurt Ellie Fry—'

'Claims he did, you mean,' Mike interrupts. 'He was never charged with anything, it was never proven, was it? Poor sod's probably still living with the stigma of her accusation. And anyway, you said you didn't know what happened, that you were too little to understand what he was supposed to have done to his stepsister?'

'I was, but I've a fair idea.' She rotates on her heels, looks out at the continuing rain. 'And I'm sure what happened to Carrie's all mixed up with Witchwood. Her nurse said she was going on about it the last few times she saw her.' Joanna focuses on the cherry trees that, like the espalier pear tree – its branches coaxed by Mike's careful fingers into a pretty fanned effect – is poised to burst into blossom.

'So, you think this Dean bloke can enlighten you, do you?' Joanna can tell Mike stops short of telling her she's as mad as her sister.

'Yes, just go with me on this, will you, Mike?' Joanna worries at a snag of skin on her nail. 'Perhaps if things had gone differently – if the two of us had stayed in touch ... I can't help it, I feel dreadful she was on her own for the last ten years.'

'Why? You've nothing to feel guilty about.'

'Don't I?' she says despondently.

'Carrie was the one who closed the door on you,' her husband reminds her. 'And anyway, you had us to think about – we're your family.'

Caroline was my family too, she thinks but doesn't share. 'Her nurse said that whatever was troubling her happened long before she ran out of her medication.'

'How would she know?'

'Carrie told her, pretty much.'

'Huh, your sister was the biggest storyteller going. You don't know what she was up to.'

'That's why I want to find out.'

'You went to London *to find out*.'

'Yes, and it's led me here. It's led me to Dean Fry. I can't let it go now. I've got to get to the truth.' The truth – or the little she thinks she's uncovered – swings between them. Cold as a stalactite which, narrower and narrower, is sharpening to a lethal point. 'If I find him, and ask him, I'll feel better then.'

'All right, but why not ring Mrs Hooper first? She's still living there, she might know something.'

'I don't want to involve her yet. And anyway, I've got his parents' address now. They're only in Cinderglade. I don't think Mrs Hooper's in touch with them any more, they left the village years ago; but I bet they'll know where Dean is. *Please*, Mike, let me, I'm so close now.'

'I can't go swanning off to Gloucestershire at the drop of a hat; I've got meetings back-to-back tomorrow.'

'I thought I could go,' she tentatively suggests. 'And you drive the boys over after work on Friday. I'll ring Pauline,' she adds quickly. 'She won't mind looking after Freddie and Ethan until you get home.'

'You're going now?' Mike sounds horrified.

'Why not? I'll take Buttons.' She swills her mug out under the tap, turns it upside down on the drainer. 'I thought I could see his parents on the way.'

'And if they tell you where Dean is? I don't want you confronting him without me.'

'No, don't worry, I wouldn't do that. But I can't come to much harm dropping in on Liz and Ian, can I?'

'Jo?'

'Look, it's only for one night. You'll be joining me before you know it.'

'You're not seriously thinking of staying in that old cottage of Dora's?'

'Pillowell, yes. Why not?'

'B-because,' he sputters, 'you've not been there for years.'

'I know, but the place is ours now, isn't it, and aren't you the teeniest bit curious?'

'Not really. God knows the state it's in.'

'Oh, come on, where's your sense of adventure?'

'You've changed your tune. You always maintained you were too frightened to go back there – that the memories were too awful.'

'Oh, it'll be all right,' she says, convincing herself that she isn't the least worried about returning to Witchwood on her own – the drive to discover what might have been going on in her sister's mind spurring her on. 'It's Valentine's weekend, I can cook us a romantic meal Saturday.'

'Yeah, right – on what, then? You don't even know if it's still got a cooker.'

'It'll have a cooker. And if not, we'll go out, or get a takeaway ... Come on, Mike, it'd be fun. If I go on ahead, it'll give me a chance to make it cosy, get some shopping in, see what's what. I'll take linen and stuff. Say yes, Mike, *please* ... The kids will love it.'

'You sure about this, Jo-Go?' Mike lowers his voice. 'Going on your own. Can't it wait until the weekend? We could go together then, as a family.'

'I'm fine, really,' she assures him, revealing nothing of her rumbling trepidation – she must do this, she must find Dean as soon as possible, even if it means going back to a place she thought she could never face again. 'I think Carrie had enough bad memories for the both of us, don't you? And isn't it about time I faced up to my demons?' Enough said – the events of that summer in Witchwood are a conversation these two have raked over many times. 'And actually, funny as this sounds,' she tells him, wanting to believe her words, 'now the cottage is ours, I'd rather like to get to know it again. You never know, it might be nice to have as a country retreat. It's only three hours or so from here.'

'If you're sure?'

'I'm sure.' She bites her lip.

'Just don't go disappearing off-piste, okay? Text me when you get there. Let me know you're safe.'

Summer 1990

As they burst into the muddle of Pillowell's kitchen – wet clothes, muddy legs – Dora's bulk blocked their way. She was comfortably propped against the Formica work surface, chopping onions for their evening meal, her bright blue eyes moistened by tears. Does she know? The sisters' first thought. How can she, they've told no one, they came straight back here. Joanna, who up to then had been calm, began to cry; her narrow body painfully heaving in air, her ribs pumping like little bellows.

'You are naughty girls,' Dora started, sputtering, an engine warming up. 'I've just been told that Gordon's going back to Italy tomorrow.' She directed her complaint to Caroline – for it was Caroline she held responsible. 'You were so rude to him when he took us to Cinderglade. So rude.'

Caroline turned away, painfully distracted; she was trying to put what they'd just found floating in the lake into some kind of order. But all she could focus on was the small metal sign hanging on a hook beside the cooker that read *Chicken Today, Feathers Tomorrow*; the letters a blur through her tears.

'We've found Ellie.' Joanna was the one to speak, holding her neck as if to squeeze the words free. 'She's ... she's ...' But they wouldn't come.

Caroline gripped Dora's hand, shiny with onion juice and still clutching the sharpened stump of a paring knife.

'Ellie,' she said, shaking it, wanting her aunt to understand the horror of what they'd seen. 'She's in the lake.'

'Can you get that?' Liz, on high alert for news of Ellie, was too anxious to answer the door in case of bad news. 'Ian?' she called through to her husband who, back after yet another search of the woods led by the indefatigable Reverend Mortmain, was finishing the bottle of Scotch he'd started at breakfast. 'It'll be Dean; he's probably forgotten his key.'

It could be true, she supposed, fear thumping in her chest; they had taken to locking up early since Ellie went missing. The flood of journalists, the fierce police presence, keeping their regulars away. Not that she was capable of opening for business, consumed by fears for her missing child.

The front doorbell trumpeted again.

'Ian?' she shouted, holding her breath for his answer. But nothing came.

Running through the darkened, empty bar, her heart fluttering like a trapped bird behind her ribs, she saw the distorted shapes of two black uniforms through the mottled glass of the pub door.

Liz and Ian were still sitting in their numbed silence when Dean, back from seeing Amy safely home, loped along the passageway and into the living room.

'Shit.' He jumped at the unexpected sight of his father and stepmother's silhouetted backs, indistinct in the orange glow of the electric fire that was needed since the temperatures dropped. 'You scared the life out of me. What's going on, what's the matter – why you sitting in the dark?' His fingers, agitated and fretful, twirled the curls at the nape of his neck.

'*Don't.*' Liz's voice, sharp from the shadows, prevented him from switching on the lamp. 'Just sit down; we've something we need to tell you.'

'Liz, you're frightening me – what the hell's the matter?'

'Sit down, son.' Ian now.

'*Dad?*' Dean tried his father.

'Do as Liz says. There's a good lad.'

And he did. Whipping off his leather jacket in the over-stuffy room, he pulled up a chair opposite them.

'Ellie's dead,' Liz announced with no preamble.

'*Ellie?* Ellie's dead?' Dean sprung to his feet.

'The police were here,' his stepmother's voice, still bereft of emotion.

'*Ellie?* What? What are you saying?' Dean threw his arms around in panic.

'The Jameson sisters found her.'

'*What?* Where was she?' Dean heard himself: shouting, hysterical. 'What are you saying? For God's sake, what are you telling me?'

'She's been murdered, son.' Ian, his cheeks soaked with tears. 'They found her floating in the lake.'

'*The lake?* What the hell was she doing in there?'

'We don't know, lad.' It's Ian who answers.

'Liz?' Dean reached out for her through the dark. '*Liz?*'

But Liz couldn't move, couldn't speak. Fighting for breath, the sound when it came was akin to the braying of a cow in nearby farmland. A raw, base, animal sound. A sound the men in her life were forced to listen to, there being nowhere to run and hide from it; nowhere to shelve their feelings and detach themselves as they usually might.

Present Day

Number twelve, a short step from where Joanna parks the Audi and her snoozing dog, is not like other houses in this street. The front garden is more or less wild and there are no pretty borders to turn the head of the passer-by. Seeing its rusty gate swinging open on her approach, her mood takes a dive. The lawn, nothing more than a thatch of nettles and knee-high grass, is littered with builder's rubble and splintered glass. Conscious of the twitching curtains of neighbours, she walks down the crumbling path to stand in the porch. A space she must share with dried-out paint tins, stiffened brushes and cracked wellington boots – things no one has bothered to clear out.

Poor Liz and Ian. This is a far cry from the pretty Tudor-fronted Boar's Head, she thinks, assessing the squat brown, pebble-dashed façade, the greying nets hanging unevenly behind smeary windows, still unsure why she's driven all this way, or what she hopes to gain. Then she reminds herself of the questions she wants answering – questions about Dean she's been rehearsing with Buttons since she decided to make the journey.

Above the incessant barking of dogs – an echoing, empty sound that reverberates around the Cinderglade estate – Joanna presses a finger to the buzzer, and is on the verge of changing her mind when Liz Fry appears, her mouth moving well before Joanna is in range of hearing it, and she knows she's come too far to turn back.

'Yes – who is it?' Liz comes at her in a sideways scuttle, her bones creaking like rigging.

'It's me, Liz – it's Joanna,' she tells the opening door.

Liz, in a jumper much too big, folds back the cuffs to use her hands. Her face blank as she looks over Joanna's shoulder, on to the street washed yellow in the failing afternoon.

'I said I'd be here about four,' Joanna prompts her. 'I've made good time.'

'Oh, darling.' A tilt of the head and Liz registers her at last, reaching out to cup Joanna's face in her hands. 'Is it really you?' Still disbelieving. 'What a beauty you grew up to be.'

Joanna blushes, plays with the buckle on her handbag.

'Come in, come in.' Liz beckons. 'Ian's out – we've the place to ourselves.'

In the spread of intervening years, Liz has become a woman of sixty-three and well-bedded into what was unidentifiable in her when younger. With virtually nothing of the woman Joanna remembers, the change is shocking, and when Liz turns to lead the way along the constricted hall, Joanna sees the matted hair on the back of her head, and how her signature peroxide-white hair has dulled to a battleship grey. Trying not to stare, Joanna's eyes can't help but be drawn to the roll of fat below her breasts, the grease spot on the seat of her skirt. This woman is a mess; the sorrow for her child has altered her beyond all recognition.

Joanna identifies Ellie's pink leather roller skates hanging from a peg with a rack of coats; automatically extends a hand to spin the little plastic wheels. But there isn't time for memories of the traumatic day when she and Caroline found one among the bulrushes before discovering Ellie in the lake, because Liz turns, her eyes communicating the same wide, expectant look Joanna's boys give when they are struggling to swallow something too big to understand. It scares Joanna; she hadn't expected this mother's grief to be so raw.

'You go through.' Liz's voice, rusty, could do with an oiling. But catching a whiff of the sweet decay of booze on her breath, Joanna decides she's lubricated enough. So, this is how she's survived, is it? Her gaze, unjudgemental, wanders over Liz again, doubting she's been properly sober for years.

The living space smells of stale cigarettes and whatever was cooked for their midday meal. Liz flicks a wrist at the sofa, forcing Joanna to sidestep the television set that dominates the room like a prattling relative.

'D'you mind if we switch it off?' Joanna asks, and is surprised at Liz's bovine compliance as she does so without question. Seated, Joanna absorbs the run-down décor, the mismatched furniture and nicotine-stained walls. Depressed further by the sight of Liz's once-white knickers, spread out to dry like flags on the clothes airer, she hunts for things she might recognise, then tells herself: how could she, she's never set foot in here before.

'It was the brewery what shoved us out, we didn't necessarily want to leave Witchwood ...' Liz's words, given as some kind of apology for the dilapidated state of her home, slip into one another as she reaches for a packet of

258

Embassy Regal. 'Said the pub was going belly-up, that they needed to rename it, get new people in right away. God, they were heartless – Ellie was barely in the ground.' She shakes a cigarette free, puts it between her lips and lights up. 'Never mind the hounding we got from the press.' She exhales, lowering her eyelids. 'Not that they spent money in the pub, mind you. That would've been too much to ask. Anyway, it got so we couldn't go out.' She nods as if reliving it again. Lifts the red-hot end of her cigarette to draw squiggles through the air. 'Our lives weren't our own,' she wheezes, 'punishment, I suppose, for not keeping Ellie safe.' Glazing over, she is lost in private thoughts.

They seem to bring plenty to occupy her. In the dangling minutes, the two of them sitting in silence. Joanna watches Liz readjust herself: ironing the grubby viscose skirt smooth with her palms, picking fluff off her jumper – an item of clothing Joanna wouldn't give Buttons to sleep on. Her movements are listless through the ever-thickening smoke screen. Joanna tries not to lean her weight too far into the sour-smelling sofa. She could do with something to drink after the drive, but isn't offered as much as a glass of water, let alone a tea or coffee – suspecting these aren't the sorts of beverages served in this house.

'It ruined our life, you know.' Liz, unexpectedly forthright from her armchair, as Joanna, on her feet, leans over the electric fire to peer at a framed photograph of Ellie on her roller skates. 'It nearly split me and Ian up.' Liz takes a protracted drag on her cigarette and coughs. 'I think we only stayed together because we couldn't afford not to.'

'I've never forgotten Ellie,' Joanna says as some kind of compensation, sitting down again. She'd already guessed that Liz and Ian kept to their sides of the house, that their love for one another had long expired – she knew it the moment she stepped beyond the garden gate. And what a strange house this is, with its faded tapestry announcement of *Home Sweet Home* hanging on a nail in the hall, because this is no place to return to. 'She was such a special little girl.'

'You got kids?' Liz asks, dropping ash on her skirt.

'Two. Boys.' Joanna touches her wedding ring, the large diamond Mike bought her on their tenth wedding anniversary.

'That's lovely.' Liz smiles: warm, kind; a chink of the woman Joanna once knew. 'You still playing the piano?'

'You remembered.' Joanna scoops up her smile, throws it back.

'Course. You were very talented. Mrs Hooper always said you'd go far.'

'Are you still in touch with Mrs Hooper?' Joanna resists telling Liz what a success she's made of things: the sell-out recitals she gives throughout Europe; the lucrative recording contract; her significance at the Royal College of Music. Acutely sensitive to this woman's loss of a child who never had the chance to fulfil her potential as Joanna has done.

'No. We don't have anything to do with anyone from there.' Liz coughs, mucus rattling in her throat. 'We try and visit Ellie's grave now and again, but when we do, we make sure never to see anybody.'

'Gordon's retired. Apparently he's not in Italy now, he lives in London.'

'*Ooo.*' A flimsy laugh. 'Ian never liked him. Didn't trust

him. Said he was a bit odd with you kids. Not that I saw any harm in him, I liked him – thought he was a real gentleman. Are you going to see her?'

'Mrs Hooper? Yes. I'm on my way to Witchwood now.'

'Going to be strange, isn't it. You ever been back?'

A shake of the head.

'You staying at Pillowell?'

A wry smile communicates Joanna's intention.

'Nice for you.'

'That's not what my husband, Mike, says.' Joanna pulls a face. 'He's worried it's not habitable. It's partly why I've come ahead: it'll give me the chance to see if it's doable. Mike and the boys are joining me tomorrow night.'

'You said on the phone you wanted to ask me something, something to do with Carrie?' Liz moistens her lips. 'We heard what happened, we're ever so sorry.'

'Thanks,' Joanna says. 'I've been trying to find out what went on – we lost touch, you see.'

'That's a shame, you seemed so close as kids. But I don't know how we can be of any help?' She blows out a snake of grey smoke, and into it, a series of hacking coughs.

'I'm looking for Dean,' Joanna says quickly. 'I thought you might know where he is.'

'*Dean?*' Liz, watery-eyed, loads the word with enough venom for Joanna to taste. 'What the hell d'you want him for?'

'I think he might have had something to do with Carrie's death – apparently she shouted his name out the night she died.'

'Christ.' Liz twists her face away.

'For some reason, I think Carrie was frightened of him.'

'Not surprised.' Liz returns her gaze to Joanna, takes another pull on her cigarette. 'Nasty bastard, especially to little girls. It's a wonder he didn't do anything to you ... and if Carrie was still frightened of him all these years on, perhaps he hurt her and she was too scared to say.' She blows smoke through her words. 'I know he did it. I know he killed my Ellie. I'm the one who watched him grow up – he was trouble from the off. I could never control him: drugs, thieving ... I'd have kicked the shit out soon as it was legal, but not Ian, *no*, he wanted to give him another chance, didn't he? Said Witchwood would be the making of him: a steady job, a stake in the pub.' The force of Liz's conviction makes her voice crack. 'Ian's still sentimental about him, insists on keeping stuff of his in case he turns up here one day. Turns up *here*? I'd skin the bastard alive.'

'I'm really sorry,' Joanna responds to the distress it causes Liz to talk about her stepson. 'I didn't mean to upset you.'

'It's not you, Jo,' Liz softens. 'It's just hearing his name again, so out of the blue. I can't bear to say it to myself, even though I live with his face in my head every day.'

'I'm sorry to keep on, Liz.' Joanna waits a moment before asking again. 'But if you had any idea where he might be, it might help me get to the bottom of this mess, I'm sure it would. It doesn't matter if it turns out to be nothing to do with him, I just have to know. I don't think I'll ever be able to rest otherwise—'

'It's the not knowing that does you in, isn't it?' Liz butts in, a remote look in her eyes. 'Like a maggot gnawing at your brain. You can't grieve properly, and the idea you may never know the truth is the hardest thing to bear. But, no,

I'm sorry, Jo – I've no idea where he is, and nor do I want to know.' A final pull on her cigarette, and she makes room in the crowded ashtray to screw it out.

More coughing, followed by silence. Far more awkward this time. It's as if her child's death has been steadily taking her with it, and Joanna wishes there had been some other way to find Dean Fry rather than churn all this up for Liz again. Her attention wanders to what can be seen of the kitchen, to the spilt smiles and unwashed crockery Liz and Ian have eaten their happiness from; a happiness neither would have tasted since Ellie was killed.

'But, I suppose, if you're set on finding him.' Liz stands up, unsteady inside her animal print slippers. Her lighter slides from her lap and she bends at the waist to pick it up. Joanna notices the joints in her fingers – how they are swollen like her ankles – and how the effort leaves her so breathless she is forced to sit back down. 'You could start in Weybridge. It's where he was from. Ian had a card, years back, no address or anything, just saying someone had been stupid enough to give him a job. He could still be there, I suppose; in the same way Ian could still be in touch with him, for all I know. He wouldn't tell me if he was, he knows how much I hate him.' Tightening her grip on the arms of the chair, Liz turns the bitten-down ends of her fingers white. 'But you'll take care, won't you? Make sure you take your husband with you if you see him. I wouldn't trust him not to hurt you too.'

'No, don't worry. I've promised Mike I won't go on my own. Weybridge, you say. That's in Surrey, isn't it?' Joanna asks. 'Well, it's a start, thanks, Liz. There can't be many with his name living in that neck of the woods.'

Liz, lost in thought for a moment, snaps back to her, saying, 'D'you wanna come and help me feed the chickens?'

'I should really go and check on Buttons,' Joanna says feebly.

'Oh, go on, your dog will be all right for a minute.' A sad smile. 'It'll be like old times.'

Joanna follows Liz outside, into what is left of the daylight, and they wander to a collection of ramshackle coops. The merriment from a nearby primary school playground floats over to them from beyond the nettle-filled lane at the bottom of the garden.

'We had a little girl go missing from here four years ago.' The laughter of children obviously triggering the memory. 'Freya Wilburn – her parents still live on the other side of town.' Liz rolls her cuffs higher up her arms. 'You might have heard about it, it was all over the papers.'

The child's name is strangely familiar, but because Joanna can't be sure where from, she shakes her head. 'No, I don't think I did.'

'Awful time. Huge police search – not that they found her, poor little thing.'

Joanna says nothing, thinking of Ellie; she suspects Liz is too.

'They did house-to-house searches, everyone was under suspicion – bit like it was in Witchwood after Ellie died. Although, the police were more thorough about Freya and hauled us all in to give statements; necessary, I know, but it was a horrible time. They called Ian in twice. *Yes!*' Liz raises her eyebrows. 'Alleging there were discrepancies in his statement, that he wasn't where he said he was – which was ridiculous, as I'd told them he was with me. Ian wasn't the only one, of course, but he felt as if he was being victimised, I can tell you.'

'I bet,' Joanna says, wondering why she's being told all this. 'Must've been upsetting.'

'Same they did with him when our Ellie was killed. Interviewing him over and over ... but I told Ian at the time,' Liz continues, 'it was textbook stuff – because they always suspect family members rather than strangers, don't they.' It isn't a question, and Joanna is grateful she doesn't have to answer. 'Anyway, they soon, quite rightly, lost interest in him when they arrested that son of his. Until the idiots let him go. They really screwed up there.' Liz grimaces. 'Might have helped if the autopsy had been more use. But it was so vague, it couldn't even tell us when she died ... and with her being in the lake like that ... any evidence was washed away ...' Her eyes full of tears. 'The police took statements, checked out alibis, but no one could be entirely sure who was where. The investigation was a bloody shambles from start to finish.'

'Did they ever find who took Freya?' Joanna is far more comfortable talking about an anonymous child than Ellie.

'No.' Liz rubs her nose on her sleeve. 'They had someone in custody for a while, but it didn't come to anything; like everyone else they questioned, it turned out he had a watertight alibi. Honestly,' she lifts her eyes to Joanna's, 'it was like living through it all again, except –' she inhales deeply – 'at least we were able to bury our daughter, poor Freya's parents didn't even have that awful closure – they don't know where she is.'

Joanna watches Liz take a handful of grain from a bucket, scatter it for the chickens flapping at her ankles.

'Freya would be twelve now.' Liz stares down at her slippers. 'It makes me think of everything we missed out on with Ellie. She'd be your age, wouldn't she? She could've had little ones like them playing in there.' Liz swings out an arm, points beyond the unruly laurel. 'I, *we*—' She breaks off. 'We could've had grandchildren. If that *bastard* hadn't destroyed everything.' Liz spits out the expletive for the umpteenth time. 'Hang on a minute, I've just remembered ... there's stuff Ian's been holding on to for him. Come on.' Liz encourages Joanna inside the house again. 'If you're so hell-bent on finding him, well, you can give it back to him, can't you?'

The rustle of plastic bags and newspapers as Liz rootles through the cupboard under the stairs. 'I know it's in here somewhere ... Ian keeps it in here ...' Her voice muffled by its darkened caverns. 'Hang on a tick, there it is, I can see it ... it's just ... let me ...' Liz, straining from the effort it takes to pull whatever it is she's looking for free.

Hovering in the passageway, Joanna sees Liz's slacked-stringed guitar on the bend in the stairs and is stirred by a fluctuating image of Ellie. Sitting cross-legged, the guitar that was almost as big as her in her lap, plucking the chords of 'Yellow Bird', getting on Caroline's nerves. Joanna summons Ellie's singing until a choking pain squeezes its fist around her heart and she is forced to fold the memory away.

'Here you go.' Eventually tugging out a small, old-fashioned suitcase, Liz gives a glimmer of a smile as she wipes away decades of cobwebs. 'Give the bastard this when you find him; it's about time he had it back.'

'What's in it?' Joanna asks.

'Keepsakes of his dead mother's. He should've taken them

266

with him when he left Witchwood, except he just cleared off, quick as you like. It's got nothing to do with me, I've never gone near the damn thing.' Liz raises a hand. 'Like I said, it was Ian – he insisted we hold on to it, treating it like some bloody shrine.' Joanna listens to the bitterness in Liz's voice. 'I've been living in that woman's shadow all my married life, and if Ian hadn't been so precious about it, I'd have chucked the blasted thing out years ago.'

'Won't Ian mind you giving it to me?' Joanna wants to double-check.

'He's not here to mind, is he?'

'But supposing I don't find Dean – do you want me to bring it back?' Joanna considers the suitcase Liz hands her, decides it's the sort of thing that ladies of a certain age own; Mike's mother has one she uses when she goes into hospital.

'No. Throw the damn thing away. No one's going to miss it, trust me.' Liz is vehement.

Joanna gives it a shake, feels whatever's inside it slide around, ignorant of the danger she has put herself in by accepting it.

Summer 1990

Rain: sluicing down windowpanes, flooding out gardens, turning roads into fast-flowing rivers. 'That's summer done with, then,' those who have congregated beneath the dripping awning outside the Petley's shop grumbled. Their sarcasm worn in thick layers beneath the iron-weight of weather needed to be shared with the hiss of tyres on asphalt and the drenched piles of grass cuttings the council left to rot on verges around the village.

Caroline and Joanna, dressed in the matching yellow cagoules Dora was forced to buy when the weather broke, thought the hunchbacked storm-clouds hanging over them looked close enough to touch. With summer well and truly over – abruptly, angrily – Witchwood had been cast into a gloomy darkness, but not simply by the weather. The sister's playground had mutated into a shadowy underworld of sopping vegetation, and the woods, with its brooding malevolence, wasn't a setting they felt safe in any more. Heading to the shop on an errand for their great-aunt – Joanna on Ellie's old roller skates, Caroline in a mood – they descended with the final bow into the village. Rain crackled against the synthetic material of their hoods and spiked their cheeks. Viewing the world through a tunnel of yellow plastic, they saw the first bright blackberries they'd watched ripen from green to red to black.

The weather hadn't let up for days. It whispered against the eaves of their bedroom, keeping them awake. On and on, the plump, rural kind; it annoyed Caroline in the same way it annoyed her to see Joanna so proficient on her skates. She was getting as good as Ellie.

Lillian Hooper saw the sisters drift past; the discord in their pairing screaming at her even from this distance. She heard about the dreadful goings-on, but as always, was keeping out of village affairs, even if recent events were unprecedented. Such awfulness, it could drag her down if she let it; sad enough that in a day or two her little protégé would be going back to her London life. Silly to expect the sisters to stay in touch – Lillian doubted Joanna would give her a second thought after Dora waved them off from Gloucester station, but she hoped she would continue with her music.

Peering out from a downstairs window on a morning as dark as the dusk, she listened to the rising wind garnering the leaves in a rush of excitement. Determined to drown it out on the piano, she sat down to play; the counterpoint of Bach mimicking her heartbeat. The house felt empty without Gordon, but she wouldn't go so far as to say she missed him. Pulling up at the end of the first Goldberg variation, reluctant to launch into the others, her mind tiptoed to the flaky relationship between her and her son. Cross with herself for missing the opportunity to talk to him when she caught him looking at a photograph of Ursula the evening before he left. Slipping an arm around his waist, thinking he might like to talk now his father wasn't around to ridicule.

But he stiffened and backed away, not knowing how to yield to it. Ursula's death still hurt. And why wouldn't it? It still hurt her. The death of a child wasn't something you could ever get over, it was something you just had to find a way to live alongside, and all Lillian hoped was that her son's sudden decision to return to Tuscany didn't have anything to do with what had happened to Ellie Fry.

She was aware Gordon gave a statement to the police, that he said he'd been with her all day Saturday, the two of them trimming the beech hedge around her garden. And what choice was there, but to give him an alibi? She could hardly admit to not coming home until mid-afternoon herself, and finding his car missing from the drive. It would have meant disclosing where she'd been all morning, and, more importantly, who it was she'd been with. It wasn't Gordon's fault he'd mixed up the days, and Lillian couldn't imagine it would matter either way if in actual fact it had been the previous day, the Friday, when he'd been wielding his father's electric shears.

Head down in her piano stool, rummaging through years' worth of sheet music, nothing suited her mood. And what was her mood? Now life, with Gordon gone, and her husband buried, could go back to normal. What was normal? She prodded the word. How could things ever be normal, with the stain of that poor, defenceless child's murder polluting the landscape?

Closing the lid over her music, she stood looking out through the windows at her precious garden, pressed her organist's fingers against her lips for the earthy smell that wasn't there. Her vegetable patch – the rows of lettuces in their loamy beds, the blush of tomatoes in their pots against

270

the south-facing wall – was rotten from the rain. Even the sprays of beautiful yellow roses she spent the season nurturing into a perfect arch were tinged with brown and decaying on their thorny stems.

'I don't know how you can bear it.' Caroline took a sidelong snipe at her roller-skating sister. 'It's like wearing a dead man's shoes.'

'Leave me alone.' Joanna, reddening, saw Frank Petley in his washed-to-beige shop coat, watching them. 'Just shove off – you're always being horrible to me.'

Frank didn't speak, didn't move; but his eyes, sharp as daggers, were busy from the shadows. And, finished gobbling down Caroline, he turned his attention to Joanna.

'Be like that then, see if I care,' Caroline shouted before running ahead. Disregarding Dora's instruction to *stay together*, she dipped inside the shop in time to catch the whiplash of conversation going on at the till.

Liz tipped the mug of tea and round of buttered toast Ian made her into the sink and sat down on a hard kitchen chair. With heavy thoughts and no radio to distract her, she poured a generous shot of Smirnoff from the litre bottle she'd taken from the bar. Her fourth this morning and because she was no longer bothering with ice and lemon, it was as easy as running the tap. Gulping it down in one, she stared at a crack in the glaze of the mug and, thinking it was a hair, dropped her fingers inside to try and tease it out. She gave up, her gaze drifting out through the open kitchen door with its shabby fly screen and into the soggy garden beyond. There was an unexpected beauty in the coloured plastic strands that, made to dance by the wind, frolicked in a way her daughter's hair used to do when free of its bunches.

It seemed to Liz as if the roof of the world had been bolted down over the tops of the trees. Lost to the overhanging mist, everything waterlogged, the wooden half-barrels of pansies she planted with Ellie in the spring were ruined. She picked up her guitar, strummed a few chords into the light leaking into the kitchen. Automatically, absentmindedly, forgetting for a moment her child had gone, Liz sang the song she'd been teaching her '... *yellow bird, up high in banana tree ...*' and caught Ellie's sweet little voice from somewhere behind her. Jerking her head to it, expecting to find her daughter standing there, it was Ian she saw. His bald head, shiny with rainwater, bobbing in through the fly screen.

'You seen the damage?' he complained, dripping water on to the tiles. Seeing the half-empty vodka bottle on the draining board, there was no need to ask if Liz had eaten the breakfast he'd made her.

She saw his expression slide. At his wits' end, and Liz could tell he was blaming himself for not being able to help her; that the ripe, new grief she was dragging around had aged her beyond recognition.

'I've never seen anything like it,' he told her, but she wasn't really listening. 'Feathers, blood – you know the fucking thing's nearly killed the lot?'

Already forgotten, the news she'd been given first thing: her precious poultry massacred in the night by Mr Fox. With a limp shake of her head, Liz propped the guitar against the fridge.

272

'I'm glad Ellie's not here to see it.' A scrape of her chair, and she stood up. Unsteady on her feet, she knew Ian had seen it, in the same way she knew that the change in her was frightening him. But with nothing beyond the life of her now dead daughter, she couldn't help it, she didn't have the will to care. Engulfed in memories: of Ellie learning to swap her baby sounds for the vocabulary she gave her, until they too became her words; how she began walking, falling, bumping against the world she had stared into shape from her cradle. And to survive all that, only to be taken before her journey had properly begun – it surpassed cruelty. It was as if Ellie's whole life, small as it was, had been nothing more than a countdown to now – her fate poised like a dagger over her from the moment of her birth.

Without looking at her husband, Liz shuffled to where she kept her rubber boots by the door, stuffed her bare feet down inside them. A brief look at Ellie's little red ones, lined up perfectly neat next to hers in a way she'd been taught. Liz bit down hard on her knuckles.

'It took them all, then, did it?' she asked, welling up with hot, painful tears.

'Oh, love, I'm so sorry.' Ian gathered her in his arms, pressed his heartbeat to hers. Liz resisted the urge to pull away; hating to be touched, hating everything that forced her to acknowledge she was alive and her daughter wasn't. She gritted her teeth, aware of little more than the wind bubbling like a pan of hot water over his shoulder.

'It left a few chickens, most of the geese; didn't touch the cockerel.' Ian stroked her hair in a way he'd once done to Ellie's. 'Don't concern yourself, love. Me and Dean will see to it.'

'*Dean?*' she screeched and tried to pull away. 'You keep that bastard away from me, d'you hear?'

Ian, close to tears himself, held on to her; forced her to listen to what he had to say. 'He didn't do anything, Lizzy ... Come on, darling; you know he loved Ellie as much as we did.'

'Do I?'

Ripping away from him, she charged into the dripping garden with no idea which direction to go in. Aiming automatically for her chicken coops, vodka fogging her senses, she stopped in time, realising she couldn't cope with the carnage, and so veered off in the opposite direction: drawn by the *whoosh, whoosh* sound of plastic wheels on wet tarmac coming from the front of the pub.

A sound that made her insides flip over.

Her child was back.

'Ellie?' she croaked, as Ellie was always her first thought. 'Ellie, is that you, sweetheart?' A swell of hope as cold rain slid down inside her collar. She rushed into the road without looking. Only to find this wasn't her Ellie. This was Joanna Jameson on a pair of her daughter's old skates.

'Wow,' Liz mouthed, trying to appear normal, loath to frighten the child. 'You're getting good on those.' Her grief, a knot of thorns beneath her breastbone, made it hard to breathe.

Joanna skated towards her and, without a word, slipped her soft little hand into Liz's and saw both her newly bitten nails and how the pearly buttons on her pea-green cardigan – a needle-defying creation of bobbles and loops – had been done up all wrong.

Neither spoke. Until eventually Liz dipped her head to

smell Joanna's hair. Eyes closed, breathing deeply, befuddled by sorrow.

'Like new-baked bread,' she whispered, her heart breaking. 'Ever since you were a baby.'

Unaware of the villagers that stepped out of their houses to mill about the waterlogged green; villagers who watched the spectacle from afar, afraid to come too close, fearing this woman's heartache could be contagious.

'Dreadful weather, isn't it?'

'Awful.' A well-muscled woman who was a regular of Frank and Tilly Petley's rubbed her arms through crinkly waterproofs.

'It's not let up since they found Ellie,' another said.

'They're dredging Drake's Pike, you know.'

'Are they? Whatever for?'

'The murder weapon. Apparently it's a knife of some kind.'

'Dear me, that's horrendous,' one of them gasped, shoulder-deep in the freezer wrestling with a leg of lamb. 'Poor Liz and Ian.'

'Investigations are getting nowhere fast.' A sigh. 'I heard they had Ian in for questioning again, poor bugger. As if he weren't suffering enough.'

'It's what they do with family, though, isn't it? They always suspect them closest to home.'

'But they can't think it's him, surely? The man doted on her.'

'Course they don't, they're just doing their job.'

'A job that's being made near on impossible. You know they're saying the pathologist can't confirm when Ellie died?'

'Why not? She went missing on her birthday, didn't she?'

'Yes, but with her not being found until Tuesday, they can't be sure.'

'Aren't there tests they can do?'

'Yes, but they're being hampered by the fact she'd been submerged in cold water.'

'A right Miss Marple, you are. How come you know so much about it?'

'She reads them crime novels, don't she?' The woman in the crinkly waterproofs threw her theory into the ring.

'I do, as a matter of fact, and yes, I've learnt a lot.' The voice indignant. 'And I know the lake would have cooled her body down … preserved her, I suppose. So, what I'm saying is there's no way of telling if she was killed hours before she went into the water or immediately.'

'This is terrible.'

'Not for the murderer,' someone said gloomily. 'I'd say it's pretty lucky for them.'

'How d'you mean?'

'Think about it – the murderer … well, everyone … they've all got alibis now, haven't they?'

'You're right. What's the point of asking people where they were, if they can't pinpoint a time?'

'Didn't stop them questioning my Jim – they made him account for every minute between Saturday morning and Tuesday.' A groan from her listeners. 'Which as you can imagine was near-on impossible.'

'They had Frank in, too,' Tilly volunteered. 'Course, I could vouch for him when he was in the shop, but he went off with his camera sometime Saturday morning, taking pictures of the woods like he does.' A shrug.

'Is Frank a suspect then?'

'Don't be ridiculous.' Tilly, outraged.

'Took Dean down the station too.'

'Yeah? Well, he's a different kettle of fish altogether.'

'Big trouble, him,' someone else piped up.

'Bound to've had something to do with it.'

'Didn't Liz say that Dora's niece – you know, the older one – saw Ellie and Dean fighting?'

'Yes, the morning of her birthday. They're saying he was the last person to see Ellie alive.'

Another unified groan.

'Says in the books I read, the last person to see them alive is the murderer.'

'It doesn't bear thinking about ... a monster like him living among us.'

'I admit it doesn't look good for the lad, but you can't act like judge and jury.' A single voice of reason. 'Dean might not have done anything wrong.'

'*Anything wrong?* He's been trouble since he got here. Drugs ... riding around on his bike all hours. And don't forget what the girl said she saw,' Tilly is keen to remind them. 'She said Dean was being really violent with Ellie, and that he made her cry.'

'She said she saw him go off after Ellie on his motorbike too, I heard,' another added.

'Down to Drake's Pike.'

A united shiver.

'Yes, all right, but I'm just saying, we shouldn't jump to conclusions. The police should get on to that Gordon Hooper, too. I always thought how weird he was with Ellie.'

'You're right – playing with her like that at his father's funeral?'

'Shocking.'

'*And* he scarpered back to Italy pretty sharpish, didn't he? Why would you do that if you weren't guilty of something?'

'Lillian told me he's a bit screwed up – that Derek refused to let Gordon grieve for his little sister, then sent him away to that horrible school.'

'They've got excuses for everything nowadays.' Another, her eyes sour as apple pips.

'Gordon was getting rather attached to Dora's niece too, I heard.'

'Which one?'

'The younger one.'

'Oooh, I don't like the sound of that. Such a sweet little thing.'

At the ring of the shop bell, they sprang apart and swivelled on their heels to receive it.

'Oh, hello, poppet.' Tilly Petley was the one to greet her, and Caroline could see even she'd been forced to cover up on account of the unexpected chill. 'How're you feeling? It must have been the most terrible shock finding Ellie like that.'

'I'm okay, I suppose.' Caroline rustled inside her cagoule, reluctant to move away from the shelf of women's magazines.

'You're such a brave girl. Your sister too, is she all right? She was with you, wasn't she?' another asked tentatively.

'Yes, she's okay. We're both doing as well as can be expected.' Caroline doled out the platitudes she'd heard Dora giving their mother, Imogen, on the telephone the night before.

'Your auntie's not still letting you out on your own, is she?' A tweed-bottomed pensioner juddered for dramatic effect. 'I've told my Shirley she's not to let her two out unaccompanied.'

'You're right, Phyllis,' another nodded. 'There's a child killer on the loose, it's not safe for you littluns. I'm not letting mine out of my sight.'

'You told the police about those dreadful things you saw Dean doing to Ellie?' Tilly asked, brimming with gentle concern.

Caroline shook her head and chewed on a fingernail; she'd been hoping the claims she made about Dean out of anger and spite would have been forgotten by now. 'They've been too busy looking for Ellie.'

'I think you should make a proper statement, tell them exactly what you saw. It might help with the investigation.' Tilly pushed a little more.

'What does your auntie say?' someone else asked.

'I haven't told her yet.' Finding herself the focus of attention in the same way she'd been in the pub when she first dropped the bombshell about Dean, buoyed Caroline along. She liked being listened to and taken seriously; it made the dwindling idea Dean needed punishing for the hurt he caused her grow a fresh set of wings.

'I think Tilly's right,' another chirruped. 'You've got to tell the police, love. Even if Liz and Ian have told them what you saw, they're going to need to hear it direct from you, rather than second-hand. And the sooner the better.'

'Look,' Tilly proposed, sensing Caroline's reluctance, 'if you don't want to talk to the police – and I can understand it would be daunting talking to strangers – the vicar's a kind man, and you like him, don't you? Why not tell him what happened? He could talk to the police on your behalf, then.'

'Good idea. He'll know what to do,' someone else agreed.

'Oh, he's marvellous, isn't he? Involved from the off – he's led all the police searches.' The voice was venerating. 'He's definitely got the ear of the police, they'll be sure to listen to him.'

'You'll tell him what you told Liz and Ian about what Dean did to Ellie, won't you, love?' Tilly, seemingly the keenest of them all to push Caroline in this particular direction.

'Yes, if you think I should?' Being made to feel this important gave Caroline all the impetus she needed.

'Eh-up.' Frank Petley, unexpectedly among them, fiddled with the protruding snout of his Canon zoom-lens that hung from a strap around his neck. 'What's goin' on 'ere, then?' he demanded in his pungent East Riding accent.

At the sight of the shopkeeper slipping between such words as *police* and *vicar*, Caroline broke through the surface of her thoughts. This man, she realised, was going to want to know what she saw Dean doing too, but she had a more pressing engagement and couldn't waste any more time. It was what these women wanted, she had their permission; Dora would have to go without her chocolate fix. And in her dash to get away, nearly toppling a stack of three-for-two toilet tissue, she stepped outside just as Liz Fry's cockerel crowed its warning.

Then it was Liz she was looking at. Sitting beside Joanna on the kerb in the rain. The change in her was frightening; she used to look like the women in films, but now she was shrinking inside her clothes, her pretty face ravaged by grief.

'Liz, Liz ... come on, love, you can't sit there.' Tilly, following on behind. 'This one's been such a brave girl,

280

haven't you, love?' she said, and pressed a Curly Wurly as some kind of incentive into Caroline's damp hand. 'You get your sister safely back to Pillowell, then go and tell the vicar everything you saw Dean doing to Ellie – *okay*?' she murmured into Caroline's hair. 'Say we sent you, and that he's got to go to the police.' Then, returning her attention to Liz, 'Come on, pet,' she fussed, gathering her in her arms. 'Let's get you in the dry, shall we?'

'That Caroline kid's here to see you.' Amy, pivoting in socked feet on the threshold of the rectory's spacious living room, waited for her father to look up from his *Telegraph*. He didn't, and she needed to tell him again. 'Dad?' A grunt from behind the photographed face of Margaret Thatcher, strangled in a noose of pearls. 'That Caroline girl's here.'

'Who?' Timothy Mortmain lowered his newspaper to peer at his daughter over the rims of his reading glasses.

'Dora Muller's niece; the older one.'

'What does she want?' A clunk as he slotted his incisors into the grooves they'd made on the stem of his pipe down the years.

'How do I know?' She glared at him, at the way he sucked on his pipe as if it was a dummy. If anyone else had done that it would be amusing; but nothing her father did was amusing – she hated him too much for that.

'Did you invite her in? Please tell me you didn't leave her on the doorstep.' He squeezed his criticism through his teeth.

'I told her to come in, but she won't budge. The creepy cow.'

'*Amy!*' the vicar snapped his automatic rebuke, knowing

his daughter's insult was mild when comparing it to the expletives he applied to his parishioners behind their backs. Leisurely folding his paper and removing his glasses, he dropped them and his pipe on to the shelf-wide arms of his chair that, littered with everything from biros to TV remote controls, resembled the flight deck of a jumbo jet.

A noise from above. The dull bump of wheels rolling from rug to floorboards, then back to rug again. Amy and her father tilted their heads to it.

'Mum's woken up,' Amy said. 'I'll go and see if she wants to come down for something to eat.' And she dived from the room, taking the stairs two at a time.

Cecilia Mortmain was washed almost curd-yellow in this strange light. She knew she was still beautiful from the way people looked at her in admiration whenever she was well enough to go out. Not that she craved praise, certainly not in the way her husband did. Although, whenever she gave it, digging deep for fresh adjectives to describe the potency of his sermon, or a new poem he'd written, he made her feel as if the receipt of compliments were somehow beneath him.

She could never get it right and wasn't sure she cared either way any more. As a girl, and full of romantic notions of what a marriage should be, she believed for love to survive you needed to live your life through each other and keep nothing back for yourself. This would have been fine, had her husband been as open as she was, but Timothy could be so secretive, increasingly so since her diagnosis, and his moods made him a difficult man to penetrate and be close to. It mostly stemmed, Cecilia was certain, from his growing disenchantment with God. Something that was glaring in his poetry. But in giving way to a general malcontent, it oozed from his pores and was increasingly hard for him to disguise. She realised over time, their love would only last if she too shut aspects of herself off from him – for him to be ultimately less important – otherwise it was all too painful, and his rejections too hard to bear.

'You all right, Mum?' Amy was beside her; such a darling girl. 'Need a hand with anything?'

'No, I'm fine. Just come and chat with me, tell me about your morning.' Cecilia patted the bed, wanting her daughter to sit. 'The rain's stopped at last,' she said, trying to sound perky. 'Who was that at the door?'

'Dora Muller's niece,' Amy said flatly. 'The older one. She's come to see Dad.'

'Is it about Ellie?' Cecilia asked.

'Dunno, she wouldn't talk to me.'

'You don't like her, do you?'

Amy smiled. Her mother didn't miss a trick. 'Not much. I don't trust her. She was always following Dean around like a lovesick puppy. It was pathetic.' Amy listened to the meanness of her words and was surprised by them.

'Don't be too hard on her, sweetheart.' Cecilia heard it too. 'She's had a rotten time. Did you hear what her mother tried to do to herself?'

Amy nodded, ashamed. And avoiding her mother's searching gaze, stepped up to the window.

'Wonder what they're talking about?' Cecilia rolled alongside to look down on Timothy and Caroline, who stood facing each other on the vicarage's wet front lawn. 'She's got a lot to say.'

*

283

'I told Liz and Ian, and the women in the shop. They was the ones who said I had to come and tell you – that you'd tell the police what I saw.' Caroline stared at the hairy dunes inside the vicar's ears and shifted nervously from foot to foot.

'This is the first I've heard of it. Why've you waited until now?'

'I haven't waited till now – I told Liz and Ian on Ellie's birthday.' This wasn't going well; Timothy Mortmain wasn't nearly as gullible as other villagers. 'But then with everyone trying to find her, they must've forgotten about it.'

Mortmain didn't answer, his eyes busy working her out from beneath his black flap of hair.

'But now Ellie's been found.' Trapped by what she'd set in motion, but too embarrassed and overwhelmed, Caroline couldn't go back on it now. 'They said they need you to tell the police 'cos it could be important.'

'*Dean*, you say?' Timothy Mortmain, throwing his head heavenward, was given an unwitting glimpse of his wife and Amy looking down from the upstairs window. He prayed they couldn't lip read. 'Being rough with Ellie, then chasing after her on his motorbike? But that doesn't sound like him – whatever else he is, he's not a bully.'

'I know what I saw.' Caroline persisted with the lie that was too late to recant. 'He was shaking her, hitting her. He looked really scary and angry, he made her cry, and everything!' Her voice was loud enough for the vicar to throw an arm around her shoulders and steer her towards the gate, out of any possible earshot. 'Ellie tried to skate away as fast as she could, but he went after her on his bike ... He chased her into the woods. I saw him.' Losing herself to the part in the same way she did on Ellie's birthday, it wasn't hard to adopt a suitable face to show she was on the brink of tears; she needn't dig deep, not when the pain of Dean's duplicity continued to float so close to the surface.

Timothy unravelled the implications of what this child was telling him ... They rushed at him like bullets he couldn't duck away from. 'And you say you want me to drive you to the station, so you can talk to the detectives in charge?' He glowered at her. 'Gracious me, child; can't your aunt take you?'

'No, she can't,' Caroline said as she arranged the vicar's smattering of moles into some kind of order. 'I can't tell Dora, she wouldn't understand – she knows nothing about the terrible things men do.'

'And you think I do?'

'Course you do,' she sniffed, eyes dry. 'You're a man. *And* you're the vicar – they'll take notice of you.'

The Reverend Mortmain was no longer listening. His mind a honeycomb of possibilities ... *Dean? Dean?* Would it be such a bad thing if the druggy bastard was put away? It would solve a lot of problems if he took the blame for Ellie's death. Amy, for one, never mind his own sordid little secret. Taking a moment to assess what Caroline might or might not have seen, he had to concede the girl could be telling the truth; and if not, who cared? Plenty around here, himself included, would be happy to see the back of Dean Fry.

Present Day

Back in the car, her hair smelling of cigarette smoke, Joanna checks her mobile for messages before driving away. She sees she has one through Facebook. From Kyle Norris. It's short, concise, but what he has to say lifts her spirits: *Are you in London? I'd be happy to meet up, would make me feel better to have the chance to talk it through with you too;* and as a P.S. he gave Joanna his number.

She presses the number into her phone before reversing out of the parking space along Liz and Ian's street and driving away. Out on the main road, heading towards Witchwood, she activates the call, her heart thumping.

'*Hi* . . . hello . . . *hello*. Is that Kyle. Kyle Norris?'

'Hi, yeah, that's me.'

'Oh, this is, um . . . it's Joanna Peters calling. You messaged me, I'm Caroline Jameson's sister.'

'Hi, Joanna.' He sounds nice, it immediately puts her at ease. 'Thanks for calling me. Are you in London, then?'

'I'm afraid I'm not.'

'Oh, shame,' he says. 'It would've been nice to meet up.'

'Are you okay for us to talk on the phone – I'm not interrupting anything, am I?'

'No. Cool. Great,' Kyle assures. 'Look, I'm so sorry about what happened to your sister, it must be awful.'

'Thank you, Kyle, but it must have been pretty awful for you too. It's why I wanted to speak to you ... I want to explain.'

'Just wrong place, wrong time,' he chips in lightly.

'That's the thing, Kyle, it wasn't as straightforward as that. Me and my sister, we've not been in touch with each other for years ... I don't want to bore you with all that, but I need to try and explain her state of mind to you. She was suffering from mental health problems, and although she was having treatment for it, she'd sort of been neglectful of it lately. And the thing is, Kyle, seeing your photo on your Facebook page, I'm afraid, looking like you do – and you're a nice-looking guy, I don't mean it that way.' A jittery laugh. 'I think, in her state of mind, I can see how she would have mistaken you for someone she was, for whatever reason, very frightened of.'

'Wow, *really*?' A beat. 'Well, they do say we've all got a double, don't they?' Kyle sounds philosophical. 'It was obvious she had some sort of problem with me from her reaction. So, that's what it was? Wow. Weird things happen, I suppose.'

'Yes, and I'm really sorry you got caught up in it all. I didn't want you to think my family and I thought you were in any way to blame. You were just unfortunate, looking like you do ... and I wanted to find out if you were okay? Are you okay?'

'Yeah, I'm doing all right. I've been offered counselling and stuff, but I'm not really into all that ... I feel bad about your sister, I wish I could have done something, you know, saved her.'

'Oh, I'm sure you would have if it had been possible. But,

well … after everything that happened, it's really good of you to say these things.' What a lovely guy, she thinks. 'I'm so glad we had the chance to talk.'

'Me too,' he tells her. 'But are you all right?'

'Yes, thank you, I'm getting on with things. You have to, don't you?'

'Well, please accept my condolences, and um … we'll keep in touch, yeah? Maybe when you're next in London, we could meet up?'

'That'd be nice, yes. Yes, we'll do that.'

'Okay, bye for now then.' Kyle, drawing their conversation to a close.

'Yes, bye then. Look after yourself, won't you?'

'You too,' he says, ending the call.

Joanna had forgotten how this far-flung part of Gloucestershire, butting up to Wales, felt about as removed as it could be from the golden glamour of the Cotswolds. Leaving behind the gentle sweep of vast agricultural fields, she and the panting Buttons – daft as a puppy and strapped into the front seat like a proper passenger – follow a signpost for Witchwood, when the road suddenly dips, snaking down into a tight tunnel of trees. Unsettled and tense since deciding to make this trip, her sense of foreboding intensifies on her approach to the village; she had hoped things would be all right, but now she's here, she isn't so sure. Was this a good idea? Should she have waited for Mike? This is one spooky place. Joanna, responding to the darkening atmosphere with an adult's perspective from the driving seat of her Audi, has none of the excitement she experienced when seeing it for the first time as a nine-year-old. The lane

is only just wide enough for the car, and overgrown shrubbery scrapes against its sides. High and tangled, the verges
are still cloaked in winter, although there is some evidence
of spring: with snowdrops on the wane, clusters of daffodils
bob among the stiffened briar and scrub; but it does nothing
to lift her deepening unease.

A bend in the road, and there it is. Looking just as it did
all those years ago, except without the jungle of greenery
remembered as a child – Witchwood's giant custodians of
beech and oak are now bare. She switches off the stereo,
cuts Eric Coates' 'Bird Songs at Eventide' mid-surge, and
takes a sharp right turn. The clicking indicator loud in
the silence, as the generous bouquet of roses and box of
chocolates bought for Mrs Hooper slam against the side
of the passenger footwell. Gritting her teeth, fearing they'll
be damaged, she passes the pub, slows to look through to
the beer garden, and sees a family kicking a ball through a
carpet of last year's leaves. She hears their collective laughter, the squeals of joy from toddlers who teeter about on
new-found legs. But she can't bear to go near it, it's still too
sad, too raw, even with its newish sign depicting a huge oak
tree and the names of different licensees above the door.

She then sees Frank Petley, fixing a poster to the inside of
his shop window. Slightly stooped and wearing what could
be the same worn-out shop coat, his hair, although almost
white, is styled in the same greasy way. The sight of him
makes her toes curl inside her leather boots. Speaking to
him on the phone to ask for Liz and Ian's number was one
thing, but actually seeing him, *yuk*; the man always gave
her the creeps. She drives on past the shop, even though it's
highly unlikely Frank Petley would recognise her – she was

only little when last here – Joanna's still wary, and took care to give her name as Mrs Peters when she rang him.

She pulls up at the kerb, engine running, to stretch down to save the roses from further damage. A sharp rapping on the passenger-side window. A faceless black shape pressed against it. The dog collar gives him away.

'Reverend.' She leans over Buttons, drops the window to greet him. Older and greyer, he's as fit as he ever was.

'Oh, it's Joanna, isn't it? I recognise you from your CD covers. Lillian said you were coming – how marvellous to see you again.' Timothy Mortmain, ignoring the inquisitive snout of her chocolate Labrador.

Joanna swings her legs out of the car and fastens her coat against the chilly wind.

'I was so terribly sorry ... ' The vicar pauses. 'To hear what happened to your sister. It must have been terrible for you. I know what an upsetting ordeal it was for Kyle,' he says, then immediately covers his mouth as if wanting to push the words back in.

'*Upsetting for Kyle?*' Joanna frowns as she tugs her curls into a ponytail. 'What? You know him?'

'*Oh.* Oh, my dear – I thought Lillian had told you?' he flounders, steps away.

'Told me what? No, she hasn't. She hasn't told me anything.'

'I ... erm ... I think you best speak to her.' And he's gone. Surprisingly agile for a man of his age, it is with a sinister tinkle of the bell that he disappears inside the shop.

Summer 1990

Caroline was sticking to her story and didn't care who she told. Not the cliché of a man with scribbling hand and greasy raincoat who came to write a feature for the *Cinderglade Echo,* or the nice lady family liaison officer and the young male police constable that have called round to go over her initial statement.

'I saw him. In his motorbike shed. He was being really nasty to her,' she said, enjoying the sound of her own voice as she worked at the hole in the sleeve of her cardigan. 'And so angry, I'd never seen him that angry. He really hated Ellie, you know.'

Thrilled by the attention, the nods of interest from her audience, she happily spiced them with details about how aggressive Dean would get with drinkers at the pub, how scary it was when he hid in the woods puffing on his wacky baccy.

'I told you not to go in there.' Dora, unable to contain herself. Cross with Caroline on so many levels, she blamed Gordon's rapid vanishing act on her niece's behaviour, and now, having to contend with yet another interruption to her afternoon indulgences; it was too much. 'I told you it was dangerous.' Dora meant both the pub and the woods, although she knew the truth of it was that she didn't warn anything of the sort – glad to be shot of her charges, she couldn't have cared less what Joanna and Caroline got up to. Only since Ellie's murder had she started questioning their safety, but not rigorously enough to stop them wandering off to play wherever they liked.

The sharpness of Dora's rebuke did nothing to alter the course Caroline was determined to travel.

'They were always fighting. But the morning of Ellie's birthday was the worst.' Caroline, eyes glinting, adjusted her Alice band and combed out her fringe with her spoiled finger-ends. Unperturbed by Dora's noises from the sidelines, she was showing off to the rather good-looking police officer in the same way she did with the stone-faced hack. She would deal with her aunt later; ensuring he wrote everything down was far more important.

'Dean is such a bully. He hit Ellie when she wouldn't get off his motorbike, yelling, "You scratch my bike with those skates, you little bitch, and I'll kill you".' Caroline screwed her face up. 'And when Ellie went off on her new roller skates, crying, he got on his motorbike and went after her.'

Dora didn't recognise her niece: self-confident and brazen; where was the shy, woebegone child she collected from Gloucester train station six weeks ago? Was the trauma of finding Ellie's body having this awful effect on her – and was her need to invent things perhaps her way of blocking out the reality? There was talk of counselling, Dora remembered, but they seemed to have dropped that idea now. She wished Imogen was here to sort her child out. Dora didn't know what to do; all she could think was how out of her depth she was – how little she knew about bringing up children.

'Come, come, child – that's enough now.' Dora tossed the officials a look of despair. 'She does have the most vivid imagination – don't you, Carrie, dear?'

Putting these accusations of Caroline's aside, it didn't sound as if things were going too well for Dean. The rumour was that the police already had him in their sights, and had questioned him several times already. Reading only this morning in the *Echo* how Ellie had been raped and suffered a fatal knife attack before her body was pushed into the lake, and now detectives were engaged in a finger-tip search of the area for the murder weapon. Dora's mind spun again to her father's dagger, still missing from its hidey hole at the bottom of her wardrobe ... the traces of dried blood embedded in the silver cross-guards ... the fact she'd reported it stolen. She hoped the police weren't about to find the wretched thing in Dean's possession.

'Shut up,' Caroline said to Dora fiercely, pirouetting on her toes. 'This has nothing to do with you. You weren't there.'

'But Carrie, dear ... *please*,' Dora said feebly. 'Whatever would your mother say?'

'She'd want me to tell the truth, so I am.'

Dora disliked doubting her niece, she wanted to trust her own flesh and blood over the say-so of some long-haired dreamer, but the child didn't make it easy – look at her, the little madam, there was more of Imogen in her than Dora first appreciated. All she could hope was that the police investigated this crime thoroughly; that they didn't leap to conclusions by putting too much emphasis on what Caroline said she saw. She cheered a little when the liaison officer sneaked a look at her watch, and the uniformed constable stifled a yawn; they didn't seem to totally believe her either. Dora just had to trust the rest of the village had the brains to follow suit, but suspected they'd only taken Caroline's assertions this far because Timothy Mortmain had got behind it.

Dora envisaged the vicar rubbing his hands together in delight. Timothy hated his daughter hanging out with Dean, and if Caroline's story could be proven, then it could be the answer to his prayers – as what jury wouldn't find Dean guilty of murdering Ellie if there was a witness claiming he'd been mistreating her shortly before she disappeared? And besides, Dean was just their sort of man: a history of drug abuse, a whiff of petty theft – it would be easy to pin the blame on him, and a way to be rid of him once and for all.

God help the boy, Dora sighed, hoping that, along with the dagger, Dean had the sense to sell the trifling baubles she reported missing; things she wished she'd kept her mouth shut about now. Because stealing a few baubles from a silly old spinster who had too much stuff to begin with, didn't mean he had it in him to kill a child. Dean wasn't a bad lad; why people were so quick to hate, to presume the worst, she didn't know.

'You have to lock him up.' Dora had tuned into her niece again. 'He's dangerous to little girls.' Confident in her assumption, Caroline threw the recently acquired vocabulary into the room. 'You have to lock him up before he hurts someone else.'

Dora dragged a hand across the striations on her forehead; grooves she swore weren't there a month ago. Yes, she accepted Caroline may well have heard Dean shouting at Ellie now and again – her brother, Lion, used to shout at her all the time – but the rest of her allegation about Dean hitting Ellie and making her cry, then almost running her down on his motorbike ... Dora decided, in the tapering moments of this conversation, was preposterous.

Dora needed to set the police straight, Liz too – hearing how she'd swallowed Caroline's story hook line and sinker. Enlighten them on the warped personality they were dealing with. But she knew it was going to take rather a lot more. Even if the police didn't pursue this, what future was there for Dean in Witchwood now? The lad was undoubtedly as ruined at home as he was in the village – true or false, Caroline had probably blackened his reputation forever. The only chance he had to fully clear his name was if they got on and caught the murderer, but even then, now Caroline had planted the seed, there would still be no way for him to prove he hadn't been maltreating his stepsister.

Cecilia used to be so industrious, now she had all the time in the world. And living within the smallness of things, confined by her illness on days she couldn't go out, she had come to realise just how precious her memories were, how precious life was. Reduced to the essence of herself, an essence that was unconnected to her failing body, helped to process the pain – a word she never understood the meaning of until seven years ago. A pain so severe, it transcended everything, so that only the extremities of her existence were identifiable to her any more. It was why Amy was so important. Amy was her legacy – she was what she was leaving behind.

She watched her daughter in the reflection of her mirror and heeded the pulsating rain. Amy was brushing Cecilia's hair. Cecilia hadn't the strength to lift her arms today and was enjoying the ritual, the way her hair crackled with static, its fine flyaway strands rising up to follow the brush.

Amy, oddly unforthcoming, looked, now Cecilia had noticed her properly, as if she'd been crying.

'What's the matter, love?' she asked eventually.

'They've arrested Dean for Ellie's murder.' Amy dropped the brush to her side. 'They found a dagger that belongs to Dora Muller in his motorbike shed. It's got traces of blood on it, so they've sent it away for forensic examination … They're saying Dean stole it, that he used it to kill Ellie.' Cecilia saw the awful turn of events was almost too much for her daughter, and that she needed to sit down. 'But he can't have, anyone could have put it in there,' Amy continued from a dainty balloon-backed chair, 'and, anyway, Dean's fingerprints aren't on it, they tested it, said it's been wiped clean.'

Cecilia didn't respond right away. She let the horror of it settle over them as she looked beyond her reflection at the room behind her. A lovely space her daughter had helped to fill with beautiful things, all of which held special meaning; when life was still a country for her to explore, and she was able to use her limbs and her nervous system wasn't shot through with painful spasms, these were things she'd taken for granted.

'*Wiped clean*, you say?' Cecilia spoke at last. 'But why would it be wiped clean if whoever'd been handling it wasn't guilty of something?'

'I don't know.' Amy wrenched her eyes wide.

'I'd say that was *more* incriminating.' Cecilia knew she must tread carefully, but she also knew her daughter needed to hear the truth. 'Your father says the older Jameson girl saw Dean being pretty aggressive with Ellie the morning of her birthday.'

'Well, that's just rubbish, that is.'

'Is it?' Cecilia turned her head to the window, watched veins of lightning zigzag between the clouds.

'Course it is, it's a pack of lies,' Amy asserted from her chair. 'She also said she saw him go after Ellie on his bike, but he didn't.' Then, dropping her voice and sounding less confident, 'You didn't see him, did you, Mum?'

'I don't see everything, love. I saw Ellie, but then I went for a lie-down.'

'Yes, you did, didn't you?' Amy picked at the hairs on the brush. 'But anyway, there wouldn't have been time – I only left him for ten minutes max.'

'I don't know, sweetheart. All I know is that the police are taking the girl's claims very seriously. She's the only witness they've got.'

'Yeah, but you can't believe what she's saying.' Amy, on her feet.

'But it's not about what I believe, is it?' Cecilia sighed. 'You just want to hope the police don't go finding Ellie's blood on that knife he stole.'

Her daughter staggered backwards, threw her arms in the air. 'He didn't steal that knife! And you know Dean wouldn't hurt a fly – how can you even say that?'

'It didn't magic itself there, did it, love? And you don't know that about Dean, not absolutely.' Cecilia looked uneasy. 'I'm not sure any of us know the harm our men are capable of.'

Amy placed the brush on the dressing table. 'I found this in Dad's room.' She tugged the Polaroid of Ellie Fry in pink legwarmers from the back pocket of her jeans. 'In his desk ... I wasn't snooping, I was looking for stamps,' she explained hurriedly. 'What the hell's he doing with that?'

Cecilia knew her husband was a man in crisis, but she didn't think for a moment it was this kind of crisis. What was Timothy doing with a photograph of Ellie Fry? Was this the photograph she saw him looking at the afternoon the children ran out of the church in such obvious distress?

Cecilia turned it around in her ineffectual hands, corner to stiffened corner, the sharpness almost puncturing her flesh ... She saw him, didn't she? She saw Timothy go into the woods not long before Ellie that Saturday morning. Is that why they didn't go to the party? Not because Timothy was too late back, but because he knew there wasn't going to be one? And she found she preferred the pain of the physical to the dark thought that was crawling into her head uninvited. The thought her husband could be a child killer.

Present Day

Lofty trunks of trees loom like spectres in the drag of dusk. Joanna senses them shift when she cuts the engine. These invisible spirits are all she has to invite her back to this place she knew as a child, and it takes her a moment before she feels brave enough to get out of the car. Grateful to have the dog for company, she strokes his ears and gathers the roses, chocolates and handbag, deciding to come back for her other stuff when she's established the cottage is habitable.

Mike will be with her this time tomorrow, she's only got to get through one night on her own. Digging out the keys, she unhooks the side gate and navigates the path with its rain-filled potholes. Instantly identifying the terrace: a crumbling affair of cracked paving slabs plundered by thistles where she, Caroline and Dora occasionally ate *alfresco* meals. The abandoned wrought iron chairs with their mouldy cushions are so unchanged she could almost imagine the three of them had just stepped away for a moment.

Encouraging the dog to wander the garden, it surprises Joanna how small everything looks. In less than a few strides she's reached the fence where the horses used to come for apples. Could they still be here? The thought is ridiculous. She scans the spread of darkening horizon.

Those creatures would be long gone. It will be night soon, and remembering how it draped everything in a tangible blackness, an infinitesimal tremor runs the length of her. She wonders if it's the same nowadays, or whether the sprawl Cinderglade has become in the intervening years now pollutes the night-time dark. The world beyond the village's barricade of trees doesn't feel closer, but neither does she recall the rumble of the M5 that is clearly evident now. Everything changes, she thinks a little gloomily, watching phantoms of her and her dead sister, the spilt light of childhood in their eyes as they canter across the lawn on their hobby horses.

Unlocking the back door, she flicks on the overhanging bulb. Mrs Hooper did say the electricity was connected, but it still comes as a relief to see she'd been right. Strange to be back, she inhales Pillowell's stale, unlived-in smell, blinking against the brightness. A white dust, thick enough to draw your name in, hangs over everything, but it's not as bad as she anticipated. Aside from the mottled brown marks on the walls above the sink, the hammocks of cobwebs quivering in the rush of air, the place looks pretty sound, and although obviously in need of love, it is at least warm.

Placing the Belgian truffles on a work surface littered with the bodies of desiccated insects, she brushes them aside and strains low into a cupboard under the sink for something to soak the roses in. The white petals, to her disappointment, are already fringed with brown, and she doubts they'll last much beyond tomorrow. She retrieves a grimy jug; the tap creaks when she untwists it, spewing a draught of brown water that takes a few minutes to run clear. Investigating further, she finds the cutlery weighting the drawers is corroded; likewise, the array of cooking utensils suspended from rusted hooks. And a quick poke inside the fridge displays a jar of pickled gherkins, a saucer of something furred in blue, bulbs of wizened onions, which makes her close it again.

'Hey, Buttons,' she calls to the dog. 'Fancy a shot of penicillin?'

Moving to the cooker, turning a dial to the corresponding hob, she is reassured by the building heat as she opens up cupboards, empty but for three rusty tins of minestrone soup and mismatched crockery. Exploring the hall, with its musty smell and lumpy rugs, she finds the radiators are warm to the touch as she leans into the sitting room. With its bare walls and minimal furniture, it looks sad, but they could fill it with the stuff in the London flat after it's sold; it wouldn't take much to restore Pillowell to its cluttered beauty. Brightening when she spots a neat stack of wood by the hearth, she decides she'll light a fire tomorrow, make it cosy for when her family arrives. Kind of Tilly to see to things here, suspecting Mrs Hooper told her she was coming and she went the extra mile. Joanna toys with the idea of dropping into the shop to thank her until the thought of seeing Frank Petley bumps up against her and she changes her mind. The bloke was disturbing enough to her nine-year-old self, she doubts the effect would be any less so now she's thirty-seven.

'Come on, boy – let's go fetch the rest of our stuff.' She claps her hands at Buttons who, nose to floor, doing a room by room, insists on giving their temporary quarters the once-over first. Watching him, she falls in love with him all over again. 'I don't know who you're trying to kid,' she jokes. 'Pretending you're some kind of guard dog.' A jerky laugh that makes him look up at her. 'You'd lick a burglar to death.'

It takes three trips to empty the car. Black bin bags of linen and towels, bags of groceries, a box of cleaning products, her holdall, the dog's bed. She leaves the suitcase Liz gave her in the boot. Satisfied the fridge is clean enough, she fills it with the foodstuffs bought on the way, loading the fruit and vegetables for the weekend into Dora's old vegetable rack. Seeing it has slipped down, she repositions the little kitchen sign – *Chicken Today, Feathers Tomorrow* – to its nail behind the taps, and smiles into a thinning memory of her and Caroline reading it aloud and giggling. Joanna carries her sister's remembered laugh, along with the bumper bags of linen, through the glow upstairs, stopping halfway to slide an arm over the cobweb-covered *Ophelia*.

She makes up the beds – Freddie and Ethan are to have her and Caroline's old room, her and Mike, Dora's. The carpet and curtains smell damp, but the overall impression isn't too bad. The duvets and pillows she brought from home, with their pretty cotton covers, are fresh, and the boys, much as she and Caroline had done, will think it's a great adventure. The latch on the window is stiff and rust comes off on her hands, but prising it open, a fresh breeze travels the room. With it another memory: netted in shadows that never cut her free, she turns to see the spirit of her younger self, staring out at the thrashing rain on her final afternoon in Witchwood. A time when she feared the sun would never shine again after the death of her summertime friend.

Shunted back to the present, Joanna believes those last few days in Witchwood were the saddest in her life. And touching the windowsill, avoiding a toxic spray of mushrooms sprouting from the wall, she picked around the peeling paintwork, her mind spinning to Caroline again. What the hell was the vicar going on about? Referring to Kyle Norris by his first name, as if he knew him. Joanna's mind, working overtime, scrapes around for something, anything, that allows her to sew the truth together.

Head buzzing, Joanna needs a glass of wine to relax her, help her sleep. 'Bugger,' she says, back in the over-bright kitchen, realising the most important provisions have been left in the boot. 'Another trip to the car it is, then,' she informs Buttons who, reading her mind, is waiting and wagging by the back door. 'Come on, boy.'

The screech of a barn owl, amplified against the cloth of night. It spooks her. Grabbing a bottle of Shiraz from the net in the boot, she snatches up the torch Mike keeps in here for emergencies. Stabbing the beam into the flickering undergrowth, her frantic searching triggers a long-buried memory of torchlight around Witchwood: fierce shafts of white, poking the crevasses of the woods as villagers, piloted by the vicar, searched all night long for Ellie Fry.

What was that? Human or animal, Joanna doesn't know, and Buttons, soppy as he is, misses it. But something definitely scurried into the trees. She swallows, hears the ancient creep of Drake's Pike's undercurrent in her ears, and waits for confirmation; for whatever it was to show itself again.

But nothing does. And breathing into the dangling moments of eerie calm, what the torchlight claims next makes her jolt in horror. A scattering of spent cigarette ends littering the back gate. Bending to examine them, she's surprised how dry and fresh they are. Someone's been here, watching her moving around inside the cottage – the assumption, a shocking one, has her pulse bouncing wildly in her wrists.

Rushing inside and locking the door against her fears, she excavates a wine glass from Dora's old sideboard, noticing the tremor in her hand as she wipes dust from its insides with the tail of her scarf. Untwisting the cap and pouring a generous amount, she gulps it down to steady herself, and wishes she hadn't come back here, sensing she isn't welcome. Mike, she thinks, her heart rate slowing; she'll feel better if she talks to him. Pulling herself together, telling herself the cigarette butts were probably there before she arrived, she takes another fortifying mouthful of Shiraz and retrieves her Samsung Galaxy from the pocket of the coat she hasn't bothered to remove.

It's dead.

Not the battery, she's plenty of that, the problem is the lack of internet or mobile signal. She shakes it through the air, switches it on and off, all to no avail. Maybe – the thought a desperate one – Witchwood is one of those rural blackspots she's heard about. Just her luck. It's okay. Determined to stay calm, she hastens to the twilit hall, reaches for the brown shiny-shelled telephone that's familiar from childhood. She lifts the receiver to her ear. Nothing. The silence communicating the line has been disconnected.

Now what? She promised to call, Mike will be worried. In the unravelling seconds, it dawns on her with a cold clarity that she is totally cut off from the world and, apart from her Labrador, utterly alone. Mrs Hooper will have a phone. But the idea shrivels before it properly forms – there's no way she's setting foot out there again tonight. Trailing her billowing unease through Pillowell's downstairs rooms, drawing curtains and dropping blinds over the blackened window panes, she shuts out the eyes she fears are peering in from outside. No one would hear her scream if she was in trouble. Her trepidation: a bolting horse she can't rein in, as she feels the pinch of danger.

Summer 1990

A break in the rain and Dora took Joanna – back from her piano lesson – out into the dripping garden to feed the horses. The invitation wasn't extended to Caroline, and it spoke volumes. Caroline stomped upstairs, making the most of every tread; knowing she was being impossible, not that the realisation stopped her from doing it. She had lost the ability to be reasonable since she caught Dean and Amy smooching. And ambushed by the weather that hadn't let up since they found Ellie's body, trapped within the oppressive interior of her aunt's holiday home only frustrated her further.

Pillowell Cottage, with its treasures and dainty-legged furniture, had seemed idyllic at first, but on closer inspection, it revealed woodworm-riddled skirting boards, blooms of mushrooms behind the bath, dripping taps and draughty windows. The grubbiness and dust, decay and rot, was rather like life, she thought despondently – it looked all shiny from far away, until you started delving into what was really going on. Witchwood was the same, in that it was a place that began by answering her prayers, but since Dean's betrayal, it had spiralled into a nightmare.

Watching the dramatic sunset from the bedroom window, it surprised her how the dull afternoon had suddenly ripened into a glorious evening. Not that it tempered her mood to see the sky – a crumpled piece of silk – turn from blue to yellow to pink. '... *When other helpers fail and comforts flee; help of the helpless, O abide with me ...*' Fortified by the line of a favourite hymn from school assembly, she strode across the landing, bold as the bullfinch seen outside the kitchen window, and into Dora's bedroom, determined to do some damage. Marching up to the dressing table, spying her aunt's favourite lipstick in its expensive gold case, she untwisted it until it was fully extended and pressed it forcefully against her mouth. So hard it snapped clean off. Seeing its ugly artificial pinkness, she squashed it into the carpet with the toe of her sandal and proceeded to walk around the room, dragging the ravaged stump over the backs of furniture and Dora's bedcovers. Delighting in seeing the candy pink on the frilly white pillow cases, she scrawled JO in baby-big letters on the floral headboard. Serves her aunt right for not believing her about Dean, she thought as she tilted her head to the call of the telephone.

Chirruping from the hall, sunny as a canary. Caroline dashed downstairs to answer it. Brown and shiny as a cockroach she found behind the toilet on her first morning there, the phone, a leftover from the seventies, was congested with grime. Caroline, careful not to let the handset make contact with her face, heard a male voice introduce itself as Detective Sergeant Scott Gallagher.

'Is Dora Muller there, please?'

'Sorry, she's not in at the moment, but this is her great-niece speaking – can I help?' Impressed with how grown-up she sounded, the detective's reluctance to share whatever he was calling for surprised her.

'When will she be back?'

'Not sure.' Caroline didn't tell him Dora was only in the garden. 'But you can tell me what it's about, can't you?'

'No, sorry, miss; if you could ask her to call me back on—' DS Gallagher began to reel off a number Caroline wasn't ready for.

'Is it about the dagger Dean Fry stole from my aunt's cottage?' She cut him off. 'Did you find Ellie's blood on it?' The question, callous, as she appreciated the blobs of alarming pink lipstick that, stuck to the sole of her jelly sandal, she'd trailed down the stairs, along the hall. 'That was my great-grandfather's dagger; I've a right to know if Dean used it to kill Ellie,' she insisted, recalling the conversation between Dora and members of DS Gallagher's team.

'Well, um . . .'

She could tell she'd flummoxed him, that he toyed with whether to share what he'd called about.

'It's okay,' she assured. 'I know all about it. We knew Dean took it, like he took all those other things that belonged to my family.'

'It is about the dagger, yes,' Gallagher relented. 'If you could please ask your aunt to call me the moment she comes back.'

'I knew it, I knew it!' Caroline, joyous, noticed stubborn traces of Dora's lipstick on her hand and wiped it against the plush velvet cloth covering the telephone table. 'He really is a very bad person, isn't he? I hope you're going to punish him for all the horrible things he's done.'

'You've got to talk to the police, tell them that bitch lied.' Amy, waiting by the front door, was ready to waylay her father as soon as he put his key into the lock. 'They'll listen to you.'

'What are you talking about?' Timothy Mortmain, standing in the subfusc of the rectory's hall, looked tired.

'*Dean*,' she shouted. 'Tell them that Caroline girl retracted her story, that she changed her mind.'

'But she hasn't changed her mind,' he said mildly.

'Who cares, you know she's lying; you're the only one who can get him out.'

'I don't know anything of the sort, and anyway, I can't go interfering with police procedures.' Timothy flourished a white cotton handkerchief from a pocket and polished the tip of his nose. 'This is a murder investigation, for goodness' sake; Dean's not been done for speeding.'

'You interfered with police *procedure* on that cow's say-so.' Amy flapped her arms through the air. 'You've made the biggest mistake of your life siding with that vicious little bitch ... Dean's got a record, you know – they're bound to use everything they can against him. The tabloids are already having a field day – they've already got hold of his name somehow, and according to them he as good as did it. What happened to *innocent until proven guilty*? He doesn't stand a chance – his name's mud whether he's guilty or not. For *god's sake*, Dad, you've got to do something – the police are going to throw the book at him.'

'And if they do, there's nothing you or I can do about it. Now, if you would please let me pass, I've had a busy day.' He tried squeezing between Amy and wall, but she blocked his way with a kind of baulked ferocity.

'What's she got on you? What does she know?' She challenged him in a way she never had before. 'It must be something pretty big – how else has she got leverage? There's no other possible reason why you would take the word of a thirteen-year-old. Why can't you see that she's invented these things about Dean being violent with Ellie because she's obsessed with him?'

'I haven't a clue what you're talking about.' The vicar groaned as Cecilia's cats, slinking down through their shadows on the stairs, circled his calves. 'Now, come on, stop this silliness.'

'Dean doesn't stand a chance.' Amy's expression was one of grim determination; she was not letting her father dismiss her as he usually would. 'They're going to lock him up for something he didn't do – he's had a shit time of it. That step-mother of his, you may think she's all sweetness and light, but since she got together with Ian she's been desperate to get shot of Dean. Can't you see what you're doing, Dad? *Please*. You're playing into their hands.'

'Look, Amy, I'm sorry about Dean, really I am – but justice must run its course, I can't be seen to interfere.' Mortmain, unmoved, pressed his soft vicar's hands together.

'*Justice*,' she shrieked. 'You make me sick. I'm never going to forgive you for this – you've no idea the damage you're doing. Don't you care? You're supposed to be a man of God; you're supposed to be a bloody Christian. You can't let them do this to an innocent person just to save your own neck.'

'*Save my own neck*?' The reverend looked uneasy for the first time during their exchange. 'What are you talking about?'

'Dean takes the blame, they lock him away . . . the police won't come after you then, will they?'

'*What*?' Mortmain wrung his hands. '*Come after me*? I had nothing to do with Ellie's death.'

'*No?* Then how d'you explain this?' Amy handed him the same Polaroid of Ellie she showed her mother. 'Mum said she saw you heading off to the lake just before Ellie, the day she went missing.'

'This is absurd.' His turn to shout, kicking his wife's cats away. 'Where d'you find this? You've no business going through my private things.'

'You admit it then?' Amy, pleased to have provoked him.

'I admit nothing.' He gave her a black look. 'Your mother has an overactive imagination, and not enough to occupy her mind.'

'I think Mum knows exactly what she saw, and you know it too.' Amy stuck to her argument and refused to be side-tracked by the unfair accusation made about her mother. 'It makes sense to me. Why you were so keen to lead those searches, for one. Why you convinced the police you were the best man for the job, saying you knew the woods like the back of your hand. I heard you tell them, so don't bother denying it,' she said, watching him shake his head. 'I reckon you deliberately took them the wrong way. It's not that vast out there, and you and your parishioners were out looking for two solid days. What other reason could there be for you not finding her? I'll tell you, shall I?' she persisted, denying her father the opportunity to speak. 'You didn't find her because you knew exactly where she was.'

Present Day

In the morning Joanna props open the windows with Dora's old paperbacks, lets the fresh air fill the cottage. Tired after a fitful night sleep, she yawns and stares out on to the vaporous, wet sunlight. She hasn't the energy for a good long yomp so once outside, she lets Buttons off the lead to exercise himself.

When her dog bounds away into the bare-branched wood, Joanna is alone. The smell of mulch and damp decay that hangs in the emptiness unnerves her. A violent flapping, high in the treetops. It has her spinning to what looks like a peregrine falcon; its dark shape wheeling above her. Mike would know, would probably give her the Latin name for it too. She smiles, thinking of their conversation only minutes before. Calling him from the shop phone to explain the lack of mobile reception and the disconnected telephone at Pillowell, she was grateful to see no sign of Frank Petley, and refrained from mentioning the cigarette ends she hoped she'd imagined, but were still by the gate this morning, as Mike shared his plans to be with her by eight o'clock tonight.

Accompanied by an unfolding thought of finding Ellie Fry's grave, Joanna pinpoints the direction of the church-yard by what can be seen of St Oswald's spire. Swathed in the hush of the woods and carrying the spray of roses, she walks the length of Dead End Lane. She suspects, had she not been so enthralled by Witchwood as a child, if she'd been just that little bit older, as Caroline was, then she too would have been aware of the dangers lurking beneath the idyll, because there is something undoubtedly unsettling about this place. The wind is oddly human, an ancient language licking through trees made bald with cold. Aware of the involuntary rise and fall of her ribcage beneath her thick winter layers, Joanna visualises medieval huntsmen with bow and arrow, the Tudor horse and hound, deep in the sun-starved heart of a forest that dates back to the Magna Carta. She shivers, not from the cold, but because of the yawning barrenness spreading around her. She quickens her pace, tries to keep her imagination in check; it's bound to feel weird in this grey winter stillness. No wonder Dora was only a fair-weather visitor, she thinks, tightening her scarf.

The little wrought-iron gate leading into the churchyard squeaks its complaint as she pushes it wide. The rectory, with its majestic cedars, is as imposing as ever, but its buttery façade isn't half as glamorous as it was in her memory, and the fat-rooted wisteria, now gnarled and brown and devoid of foliage, snakes across its frontage like arthritic fingers. She remembers the vicar's wife who used to look down from its upstairs windows and is about to check if she's still there, when something shimmers within the tombstones. A nebulous shape she tries to compute, to categorise, but to focus on anything beyond the irregularity of darkened trunks multiplying off into the distance is impossible. Her breathing light, she waits. *Nothing*, the wind tells her. *It's nothing.* Probably Buttons meandering along the track, but checking the lane there's no sign of him.

To the cold accompaniment of a crow, Joanna finds Ellie Fry's curved headstone, her eyes prickling with tears as she reads the smallness of life recorded in those ten short years. Tugging a single white rose from the spray bought for Mrs Hooper, she places it at its base. All the graves in this cold corner of St Oswald's are set among trees. Ellie's is a Japanese cherry, but there's everything in here: vast spreading oaks, rowans, cascading weeping willows, a magnificent copper beech or two, but only Ellie's tree is decorated with toys, hanging from the branches in an attempt to cheer. 'Ellie's Special Place', Liz said they call it; as if to give it a name saves them from having to say where she is. Not that it looks special to Joanna. The cherry tree is quite bedraggled on such a wintery day. What it needs is a good hard pruning to make it ready for spring, and someone should take down the grimy Tiggers and Eeyores pinned to its bark. So old, they've almost dissolved into the featureless moss, and the only splashes of colour come from the tawdry ASDA labels sprouting from their backs. Surely Ellie would have been too old for them. Joanna reaches out with a gloved finger to press the tummy of one. She's sure she wouldn't miss them.

From the lengthening shadows, it must be time to head to Mrs Hooper's, and she calls for her dog. Joanna hears the piano long before she sees the cottage with its grey stiletto of chimney smoke, and checks the lane for the umpteenth time. But with no sign of Buttons, her eyes wander to the abundance of catkins dripping like coloured water from the otherwise naked hedgerow. Nature's jewels, she's always thought of them as, and a sign the dense belt of hazel and willow will soon be in leaf and shielding Pludd Cottage from the world again.

Buttons joins her as she steps on to Mrs Hooper's lawn. With boots instantly saturated by the recent rain, she lifts the little fox knocker that is easily reachable now she's fully grown, but the door is already open and, pushing it wide on to the warm, smoky smell of burning wood, she tells Buttons to wait as she steps into the familiar hall, calling as she goes.

'I'd forgotten how lovely it was to sit and hear you play.' Joanna, perched on a couch she remembers from childhood, sips sherry from a dainty glass. 'You certainly are as good as you ever were.' Extending her compliment, she watches her dog lying spread-eagled before the roaring hearth. 'D'you still teach?'

Mrs Hooper, in a polo neck as reddy-gold as her hair had been when Joanna was last inside this cottage, swivels on her piano stool. 'The odd pupil, but no one as special as you, m'dear,' she says. 'You're a natural, and to play with such unique passion ... ' She makes a whooshing sound of admiration. 'That's a true gift.'

'It was you who gave me the head start – I might never have looked at a piano.'

'But your facility for *feeling*,' Mrs Hooper stresses. 'That can't be taught, Jo – you play the way you do because you've felt things. It wasn't all Caroline, you know? You channelled yourself into your music.'

'I'm sorry I never came to see you.' Joanna, bubbling with emotion, gets up to hide her face. 'It wasn't that I

315

forgot you.' She moves to the shelf of photographs. 'That summer ...' An awkward pause. 'It was such a precious time for me, but after Ellie ...' The words die in her mouth.

'I understand, luvvie,' Mrs Hooper assures.

'I took two of your curlers.' Joanna picks up a framed snapshot of little Laika captured in a perpetual summer garden. 'Hid them in the ottoman in my mother's bedroom.' She kisses the photograph of the little sausage dog she had loved and set it back down. 'And whenever Mum was rowing with Carrie, which was nearly all the time, I'd get them out to smell them so I could have you close again.'

She sets down her glass and goes to sit beside Mrs Hooper; strokes the hands that loved her.

'I called in on Liz Fry yesterday.'

'Did you?' Mrs Hooper pulls back her hands. 'That must have been a nice surprise for her. However did you find her?'

'Easy. I rang the pub.' Joanna neglects to fill her in on the exchange she needed to have with Frank Petley first. 'Ian wasn't there, he was at work.'

'Good. I never liked that man. He used to say terrible things about Gordon.' Mrs Hooper tugs down her jumper. 'How was she, the dear? I've not seen her since they left, which wasn't long after Ellie's funeral.'

'Greatly changed, but I was only a kid when I last saw her. Whereas you,' she looks up, 'you haven't changed a bit.'

'Thank you, dear.' Mrs Hooper rubs her arms and shivers. 'But it's all so horribly sad. If only they'd caught the person who did it. It's a horrible term, but it might have helped if there'd been some kind of *closure*.'

'Liz is convinced it was Dean. Even now.' Joanna, sombre,

shifts her gaze to the comforting fireside. 'When I was little, I used to think it was the bloke who owns the shop.'

'Frank Petley?' Mrs Hooper is shocked. 'You can't be serious.'

Joanna wrinkles her nose.

'Why would you think that?'

'Because he was creepy. Because he was always watching us girls.'

'Did you ever tell anyone?'

'No – but his wife knew; I'm sure of it.'

'Why d'you say that?'

'Because she was the one pushing Carrie to tell the police she'd seen Dean mistreating Ellie. Tilly was keener than most for the focus to be on Dean – they weren't looking at her husband then, were they?' she says dryly.

'There were lots in this village who were happy to pin the blame on Dean Fry for one reason or another.' Mrs Hooper is about to include herself in the count, but changes her mind.

'Oh, I'm just being silly.' Joanna flaps her hand. 'I was only nine – what would I know?'

'You shouldn't have underestimated yourself, children are most perceptive ... your sister certainly was—' Again, about to say more, Mrs Hooper scrunches her lips.

'Do you remember Ellie's funeral?' Joanna looks out at the amorphous grey day going on beyond Pludd Cottage's windows.

'That was terrible.' Mrs Hooper grips her knees with a grave intensity. 'Terrible for you youngsters ... especially after you'd found her like that.'

'It was about as bad as it can get,' Joanna says. 'I don't

317

think a day's gone by when I haven't thought of Ellie.' An image of Freddie and Ethan swim out to meet her, their faces distorted as though looking at them from underwater.

'It certainly destroyed the little community that was here, so much suspicion – it's never really gone away.'

'Really? That's awful. I remember the way the village rallied round, searching for Ellie into the night.'

'Doubt they'd let you do that now,' Mrs Hooper says tersely. 'Probably destroyed any evidence that might have helped the police catch who did it.'

'How did Liz and Ian cope, d'you think?' Joanna's mind wanders back to number twelve on that rundown Cinderglade estate.

'Not sure they did,' Mrs Hooper asserts. 'Liz was a wreck … No one could reach her, and then, of course, she started hitting the bottle.'

'I think she's still drinking now.'

They fall into a brooding silence.

'I saw the vicar when I drove into the village yesterday,' Joanna announces.

'Have much to say to you, did he?'

'Yes, I was coming to that.'

'*Oh.*' Mrs Hooper knits her fingers in her lap.

'He mentioned Kyle Norris.' Joanna blinks at her. 'Said something about how upsetting it had been for Kyle. It was like he knew him, or something.'

'And did he say anything else?'

'Only that he thought you'd already told me. *So*, told me what, exactly?' She hands the question over.

'I did tell him – in light of what's happened – that I'd have to tell you.' Mrs Hooper seems reluctant.

'Tell me what? You're making me nervous.'

'Okay.' Mrs Hooper rubs her arms and stares at the peacock-patterned carpet. 'Kyle is Amy's son. He's the reverend's grandson.'

'Amy's son?' Joanna repeats, trying to straighten the revelation out in her mind.

'Yes, Amy's son. And that's not all.'

'Go on,' Joanna pushes.

Mrs Hooper takes her time, tweaks the arrangement of roses Joanna brought and found a vase for. 'His father is, um ... his father's Dean Fry,' she says eventually.

'*What!*' Joanna's hands fly to her face. 'I don't believe this ... I can't take it in. He can't be. But, yes,' she gasps. 'I suppose, seeing his photograph, it's obvious. He's the spitting image of him. This is incredible ... this is just ... s-so ... *incredible*.' She pauses, darts a look at Mrs Hooper. 'But Kyle didn't say anything to me when we spoke on the phone yesterday.'

'You spoke to Kyle?'

'Yes, I found him on Facebook ... I felt terrible about what had happened, Carrie could've killed him.' Joanna takes a breath. 'And he was such a nice person, really understanding.'

'The thing is, Jo, he wouldn't have said anything. Kyle doesn't know Dean's his father – he doesn't even know who Dean Fry is.'

'What d'you mean, he doesn't know who he is? How the hell did Amy keep that a secret?'

'You knew about Amy's mother, Cecilia, passing away a month or so after Ellie died, didn't you?'

'No, I didn't. Oh, she died, did she?' Joanna summons

up the beautiful, pale-haired lady who used to look down from her high rectory window. 'That's sad.'

'Amy was heartbroken. She was ever so close to her mother. And to top it all, she found herself five months pregnant.'

'Poor Amy.' Joanna stares at the red-hot logs collapsing in the grate.

'Yes, it was a dreadful time,' Mrs Hooper continues, 'and so, with her mother gone, and Dean banished from the village – something she partly blamed her father for – there was nothing for her in Witchwood, so she went to live with her aunt in Cheltenham, Cecilia's sister. The reverend put it about that Amy had gone away to college there.'

'Did she ever come back?' Joanna wants to know.

'No, never. With the awful associations she had with the place, you can understand it.'

'What, and nobody questioned her sudden disappearance?'

'It was a plausible enough reason for her going, and by then, not many of the old villagers were left. There was a kind of mass exodus in the wake of Ellie's murder – I'd have gone too, if I'd been able to afford it.'

'D'you know what happened to Amy?' Joanna asks.

'Yes, things worked out all right for her in the end. While resigning herself to motherhood in Cheltenham, she happened to bump into her old boyfriend, Philip Norris. D'you remember him?' Joanna shakes her head. 'No, probably a bit before your time here. Anyway, he was a junior doctor at the hospital, and when he'd fully qualified, the three of them – he adopted little Kyle after he and Amy got married – moved to Cumbria.'

'How come you know all this?'

'Timothy told me. We've been friends for years. I first got to know him in his old diocese, long before I came here.' Mrs Hooper skims her eyes to Joanna. 'And, of course, I played the organ at St Oswald's. We became especially close after Cecilia was first diagnosed, and he was very kind to me when my Derek was ill.'

Mrs Hooper's rather lengthy explanation puzzles Joanna, but she doesn't comment, asking instead, 'Do you know if Amy and this Philip guy ever told Kyle who his real father was?'

'No, luvvie. They didn't.'

'So, Kyle thinks Philip Norris is his father, then?'

'Yes.' Mrs Hooper fidgets with her skirt. 'Amy was determined to keep it a secret, made Timothy swear never to tell. I'm the only one who knows.'

'Isn't that a bit unfair on Kyle? Not knowing he's adopted. Not knowing who his real father is.'

'I'm sure Amy had her reasons. It's what she wanted,' Mrs Hooper answers. 'And I'm sure Philip's been a wonderful father to him, given him everything he needed.'

'But don't you think it's strange that Kyle should be in that mini-mart with Carrie that night? Because in a roundabout way, there's actually a connection here, isn't there?'

'It is a strange coincidence, isn't it?' Mrs Hooper, thoughtful from beneath her waves of snow-white hair.

'I'll say. So how long have you known it was Amy's son who was involved that night?'

'Not long. Timothy took ages to tell me. I'd been home from my sister's for at least a month.'

'So.' Joanna stitches together everything she's been told.

'Dean's got a son he knows nothing about, and Ian and Liz have a grandson.' She rolls her eyes at the injustices.

'No, they know nothing about Kyle, they know nothing of his existence. I'm only telling you because of what happened with Carrie.' Mrs Hooper indicates to Joanna's empty glass. 'Would you like a top-up?'

'No, thanks, I'm fine. You won't know it,' Joanna begins, 'but Carrie shouted out Dean's name in the shop the night she died.'

'Really? How odd for her to be thinking of him after all this time.' Mrs Hooper frowns. 'But I suppose, if you say Kyle looks just like Dean did, that's probably why. I've never seen the boy; Timothy's only met him a handful of times, and that was when he was a little lad, long before they moved up north. He's in touch with Amy, of course, but only the occasional phone call; there's no love lost there, as I've said.'

'That's a shame,' Joanna says, before bringing the conversation back to her sister. 'The thing is, from what I've been able to piece together so far, Carrie, for some reason, was convinced Dean had come for her – it's why I wanted to talk to Liz. I need to find him, to ask him if he knows anything.'

'Why would Dean know anything?'

'Because something went on between them that made her think she needed to protect herself from him. And look—' Joanna dives for her handbag, retrieves the dog-eared postcard. 'I found this. Carrie meant to send it to me.'

Mrs Hooper holds it aloft, peers at it through her reading glasses. 'But you said she was getting her life together, that she was under the care of a mental health nurse at the hospital?' Another frown. 'This is so, so ... *frantic*.'

'Yes, her nurse said she'd been doing really well.' Joanna steers clear of the other things Sue Fisher told her. 'But then I think Carrie must have seen Dean – or Kyle, and thought it was Dean, because we now know they look so alike. But anyway, it's what stopped her from going out.'

'And in so doing, she stopped taking her medication?' Mrs Hooper joins the dots. 'But why would Carrie think Dean was after her? That's absurd.'

'That's what I need to find out – I don't know. It's why I've got to find him. I'm not blaming him for anything; I just want to hear his side of things so I can understand why Carrie was so preoccupied with him.'

'D'you think, and this is just an idea ...' Mrs Hooper pauses. 'That what preoccupied your sister were the tales she told about him?'

'*What*?' Joanna pulls her mouth into a disbelieving O. '*Tales?* Are you saying she made those things up about Dean? That they were lies?'

'If Carrie was convinced he'd come after her, it was probably because she was guilt-ridden – that she thought she deserved to be punished for blackening his name.'

'I've not thought of it like that.'

'That's because you trusted her, like certain villagers and the police trusted her.'

'I did, yes. Same as she did me,' Joanna mumbles, thinking of the part she played and her own mendacities where Caroline was concerned.

'You what, luvvie?'

'Nothing.' Joanna, fearful of opening up that can of worms. 'It's funny, but Mike always said Carrie had real trouble distinguishing fact from fiction.'

'Did you never question her story?'

'No, I didn't. But I suppose I was too young to know what was really going on, wasn't I?'

'You were, and you were such a trusting little girl.' Mrs Hooper smiles for a moment. 'You know Dora had her doubts, don't you?'

'No. Did you?'

Mrs Hooper pulls a face.

'I feel sorry for Dean.' Joanna leans down to stroke the prostrate Buttons. 'He wasn't that bad, was he?'

'No, I don't suppose so; just your typical teenager,' Mrs Hooper says softly. 'Although, leaving school without proper qualifications didn't help; drifting from one low-paid job to another, petty crime, drugs ... Until Liz and Ian brought him to Witchwood and gave him a say-so in the running of the pub.'

'He got Carrie the job there. I was really envious at the time, but I suppose it was the worst thing for her.'

'How so?'

'She was so needy, craving attention – Dean's attention. She was a troubled kid, a troubled adult – and Mum doing what she did didn't help her either.'

'You lived through it too,' Mrs Hooper reminds her. 'And you didn't tell lies.'

'I suppose,' Joanna says, mindful of the contrary. 'But it was different for me, though, wasn't it?'

'Was it? how?'

'I didn't have a massive crush on Dean Fry, and Mum didn't blame me for Dad's accident.'

Mrs Hooper says nothing.

'The trauma of us finding Ellie like that can't have done

Carrie any favours either. D'you think that's why she was incapable of forging relationships or holding down a proper job?'

'It could have been.'

'Thank God for Dora. Who knows where Carrie would've ended up without the flat and the money she left her.'

They take a moment to think about where it was that Caroline did end up.

'It was you that Dora was fond of,' Mrs Hooper says at last. 'She left everything to Carrie because she was ashamed for doubting her about Dean.'

'Even so, I'm grateful.'

'You're a good girl, Jo.' Mrs Hooper returns the postcard she's been holding. 'There are those who would've resented her for that alone.'

'Oh, hang on, I've got something that belongs to you.' Returning the postcard of *Ophelia* to her bag, Joanna passes Mrs Hooper the snow globe.

A gasp. 'Ursula bought me this,' she says, cradling it in her hands. 'The Christmas before she died – I never thought I'd see it again. Wherever did you find it?'

'In Carrie's flat,' Joanna explains.

'Poor Dean, he took the blame for so much. I knew it wasn't him stealing from villagers. I knew it was your sister.' A faint squeak from the piano stool as Mrs Hooper adjusts herself. 'Lots of things went missing that summer you girls were here. Small things, things you might just as well have mislaid yourself . . . I had a brooch disappear from a jacket at church after I'd seen Carrie looking at that book of Victorian photographs. It was my mother's, a beautiful garnet, and the finest thing I owned. Well, the only thing, really, by that point – we'd had to sell off everything else of value.'

'A garnet, you say?' Joanna, remembering the brooch she found in London, the one she pinned to her own coat.

'Yes, that's right.'

'I think I may have found that too. I thought it was Dora's.'

'Good grief, Carrie pinched that as well?' Mrs Hooper drops a lozenge of a sigh. 'She probably took Dora's dagger, I often thought it ... put it in Dean's motorbike shed for the police to find ... ooof.' She exhales through her teeth.

'Why would she do that?'

'For the same reason she lied about what she saw him doing to Ellie. To cause mischief.'

'It certainly caused that.' Joanna grimaces.

'The police thought it was the murder weapon, it's why they held him in custody for so long.'

'Must've been frightening for him. Were his fingerprints on it? Because they'd have been better off checking it for Carrie's.' Joanna, remembering how she burst in on her sister moments after she'd found the dagger in Dora's wardrobe.

'I think the police were more interested with the traces of blood it had on it, and anyway, I heard it had been wiped of any fingerprints.'

'*No fingerprints* – bit suspicious, isn't it? Someone must have handled it.' Joanna takes a minute to consider the gravity of their discussion, then asks, 'How did you know Carrie took your snow globe?'

'I didn't, not to start with.' Mrs Hooper holds her precious, newly returned memento up to the light. 'It dawned on me later, when I realised it disappeared the morning

I was giving you a lesson, and Carrie was the only other person here.'

'Why didn't you tell the police? I mean, if you were so sure Dean wasn't the one doing the thieving.'

'Because it was convenient for me not to,' Mrs Hooper admits, her eyes moist with tears. 'I'm not proud of it, but now you're a mother too, I'm hoping you'll understand.'

'Understand?' Joanna, puzzled. 'I'm sorry, I don't think I do.'

'With the police focused on Dean,' she lowers her voice to a whisper even though they are the only ones here. 'they weren't concerned with Gordon, were they?'

A shake of her head, still no clearer. 'Gordon? Why would they be concerned with him?' Joanna gets up to prod the fire with a poker.

'Because of Ellie, and Gordon's fondness for her. Because of the aspersions Ian Fry was casting.'

'But Gordon and Ellie were sweet. She loved him. It wasn't anything more than that, surely?' Joanna throws on a chunk of hazel.

Mrs Hooper gives her a withering look. 'That's not how the village saw it. How Ian Fry saw it. Ellie reminded Gordon so much of Ursula, you see; you too, when you arrived that summer. He was so little when Ursula died, he missed her terribly, he still does; I don't think he's ever got over the shock.' She rubs her nose. 'There were those who made noises about his affections for you, but then you went back to London and the rumours stopped, so that was okay.'

Joanna sits down on the couch again, looks out on the frostbitten garden, at the tables and feeders baffled with birds.

'I had no idea about any of that,' she says finally. 'But if I've learnt anything in life, it's that people do have a tendency to judge others by their own sordid standards.'

'Don't they just. And small communities like this are the worst.'

'I'm sorry to bring it up again, but I can't stop thinking about it.'

'What's that?' Mrs Hooper looks at her.

'About Carrie making up those things about Dean – because, if she did, they were pretty terrible lies. To accuse him of ill-treating Ellie like that, then saying he chased off after her ... with what ended up happening ...' Joanna pulls up short. 'Yes, the police acquitted him of murder, but they couldn't clear him of being abusive to Ellie, could they? And that's ultimately why his family kicked him out ... why the whole village turned against him. And knowing you'd caused all that by telling lies – it must've been a terrible burden for Carrie to live with.' Joanna looks pensive. 'No wonder Dean was still on her mind.'

'Carrie certainly didn't do the boy any favours, but what happened to him wasn't all her fault. It was the narrow-mindedness of the village and the wretched gossipmongers who did for him. But,' Mrs Hooper says, 'he got out of Witchwood, didn't he? I doubt the boy's life's been totally blighted.'

'We can hope that's been the case, but we don't know for sure, do we?' Joanna tucks a stray curl behind an ear. 'I suppose that's what that Jeffrey bloke at the rescue centre was on about. He said – and I know he meant Carrie – that people volunteer out of some need to redress the wrongs they've done.' Joanna shares her thoughts although not all of them. Not the part she believes she played in her sister's cold-hearted defamation of Dean, something that had nothing to do with making mischief as Mrs Hooper supposes, but everything to do with revenge.

'I think you're going to have to accept that whatever was going on in your sister's mind, be it through illness or guilt, you're not going to solve it – I'd just let it go. I've had a bad feeling from the moment you told me you were going to do some digging around,' Mrs Hooper warns. 'I know what happened to Carrie was an accident, but it still came from her fixation with Dean and the trauma of Ellie's death. So please leave it alone, Jo – nothing good will come of it, trust me.'

Present Day

Out in the wet lane, the lullaby coo of a woodpigeon drops into the torpid afternoon. Calling to her dog, Joanna chews over her conversation with Mrs Hooper as she follows the bow in the tarmac on the final approach to Pillowell Cottage. Despite the fervent warning she's been given, she decides to stick to her original plan and go to Weybridge on Monday to find Dean. She's got to talk to him, it's the only way she'll ever have any peace. Perhaps it will help him too. Because if Caroline did tell lies about him, however Mrs Hooper would like to dampen them down, they probably ruined his life.

Hang on a minute. What are those? Her concentration shifts to a set of muddy grooves on Pillowell's boggy grass verge. Tyre marks. Fresh. They weren't there when she left the cottage this morning.

Mike? Her first thought, and indomitably her only thought.

Is he here already – did he manage to slip away from work early? But where are the boys? Why can't she hear them playing?

Her heart soaring, then plummeting. She scans the lane, the driveway. The only vehicle is her Audi and no sign of Mike's SUV. So why is the gate swinging? She swears she didn't leave it like that.

Brisk along the garden path, fishing for keys but there's no need – the kitchen door is already open. Testing the handle and feeling its rattle, the lock, when she examines it, is slack to the door frame. Has it always been like this? Maybe she did it when she went out earlier, the thing's flimsy enough. She prods the rotten wood, the exposed screws, tells herself how little it would take to dislodge it.

'Mike?' she calls through her escalating anxiety, pressing the heel of her hand to the metal casing in an attempt to reconnect the lock to the door frame. But with nothing to fix it against, it wobbles loose again.

'Freddie, love? Ethan?' she pleads with the perpetual gloaming of the hallway, up the stairs.

But nobody's here. The cottage is empty. Buttons is going barmy: nose to the floor, sniffing, tail wagging; he's not imagining things. And neither is she. She follows her dog into the drab front room and watches a surge of spring sunshine slap the walls papered dark with rambling straw-berries and thieving thrushes. Flaking at the corners and faded into gridlines where paintings used to hang. Her eyes are drawn upwards, to the dish of damp where rainwater collects under the missing tiles.

Someone's been in here. Minutes ago. She can smell their cigarette smoke. What did they want? There's precious little to steal. Apart from essential pieces of furniture, there's nothing of value in the cottage any more. Her mind scurries to the spent fag butts she saw by the gate last night, and panic flaps inside her: a butterfly caught in a jar.

Her thoughts are chasing themselves like snapping dogs. Is she in danger . . . should she phone the police? She would if there was something to call them on. She supposes she could run back to Mrs Hooper's and telephone from there. But that would mean worrying Mrs Hooper. And anyway, whoever they were – village kids, most probably, using it as a den, the place has been empty for years – they've gone now, and Mike will be here in a few hours. It would be silly to make a fuss.

With a sudden need to rid the cottage of its musty atmosphere and dank root smell, Joanna casts the French doors wide on their corroded hinges, breathes in the ramshackle garden. The chandelier tinkles overhead and she watches the wind nudge a bank of beech trees, making the brown of their leaves rustle like paper. Fortifying the doors again, she returns to the kitchen to pour herself a large glass of Chablis from the fridge. She'll have the white wine as it's lunchtime, deciding to save the red for when Mike arrives. She swallows a large mouthful to steady her nerves. *I've been requiring rather a lot of ameliorating since arriving in Witchwood*, she thinks, downing more.

First things first, she must fix the door. A quick hunt, and she locates a screwdriver in a box of rusted tools in the cupboard in the hall. It's fiddly and takes her a while, but it's not a bad job; it will hold until Mike comes and can take a look. The wine takes the edge off her anxieties a little, but she knows she must plug the unnerving silence if she's to keep her imagination in check. With no radio or television, Joanna decides one of Dora's old LPs will have to do. Dusting off the record player, she raises the lid and drops the stylus into the first groove of Beethoven's 'Violin Concerto' waiting ready on the turntable. A memory of Dora heaves into view. Not of here, but a time they met for lunch in Bayswater, a year or so before she died. Their conversation unusually candid and emotional. Her great-aunt's hand in its soft leather glove, gripping Joanna's sleeve as she openly evaluated the lives she might have lived, mourned the men she might have married, the houses she might have inhabited, the children she might have filled them with, that for reasons unknown never materialised. It was a sadness, Joanna thought, not unsympathetically, that Dora had especially honed. Her lack of family provided her with a legitimate excuse to compensate for her loss by pandering to her every whim.

The sweet surge of strings along with another gulp of Chablis allows Joanna to forget how acutely alone she is. Increasing the volume, she is suddenly hungry, and sets a pan of water to boil on the cooker. Turning the hob down, she drops in two eggs and watches them knock together in the bubbling water. Slicing a couple of rounds from a loaf with a rust-speckled bread knife, she is buttering them and feeding half to the dog when a goldfinch flies down at the glass to peck at its reflection. She stands up to eat, in a way she would never allow her boys to do, and it doesn't take long to finish her soft-boiled eggs. Wiping their innards clean with the last of the crust, she turns the empty shells upside down in their egg cups. A trick she learnt when little that's become a habit now she is all grown up. Anxiously checking her wristwatch, guessing how far away Mike and her boys might be, Joanna tries not to dwell on the chilling fact she is completely cut off from civilisation, without mobile or landline, and busies herself with preparing what will be, after precisely three hours in a medium-hot oven, a tasty meal for her family. But a squeeze of apprehension as the tail of afternoon light gutters into a second night has her returning to the fridge every now and again to top up her wine glass.

She lights the fire and is pleased with how it instantly improves the feel of the place. Homely and snug, she relaxes a little. But before getting too comfortable, and while there is still a sliver of light in the sky, she nips to the car for the Bonios she promised Buttons. Unlocking the Audi and opening the boot, she reaches inside and sees the suitcase Liz gave her to pass on to Dean. Curiosity gets the better of her, and she brings it, and the dog biscuits, inside the cottage.

After securing the lock on the kitchen door as best she can, she carries the aroma of simmering casserole back into the living room along with her wine and the old-fashioned suitcase. Opting for the elegant chaise longue – an object of fascination to her as a child – she kicks off her boots and snuggles down on the raspberry-pink upholstery that, although a tad faded, is otherwise in mint condition.

Against the backdrop of Beethoven and a somniferous fire, wine at her elbow, Joanna drags the suitcase into her lap and releases the antiquated spring clips. The lid bounces open, emitting a puff of sweet mustiness and revealing a treasure trove of someone else's memories. The first things she uncovers are a pair of cute little Staffordshire china dogs, then a mother-of-pearl hairbrush and mirror set – not unlike the ones that once adorned her own mother's dressing table in Camden. A pocket-sized Bible bound in soft white leather, a tapestry-cased manicure set, and a parcel of tissue paper, yellowed and brittle with age. It crackles in her hands, and unfurling it reveals a beautiful green silk blouse with little half-moon sweat marks under the arms. Sifting through the remaining items, Joanna lands on something bulky and buried deep in the lining. She pushes a hand inside and tugs out an old red-and-white striped Kwik Save carrier bag. Interesting, she thinks, taking a sip of wine before unravelling the hefty stack of photographs it contains. The first section is the Polaroids from the Wall of Shame at the pub. The misbehaving punters Caroline said Dean liked to photograph. A small smile of remembrance curves her lips as she skims through drunken antics frozen in time, until it is she who freezes.

A Polaroid of Ellie.

Almost identical to the one she remembers them finding in the *Book of the Dead*.

Laced into roller skates, in bright pink legwarmers, absorbed in her own little world, Ellie is clearly unaware she's being photographed. Another of her summertime friend slides under Joanna's fingers, then another, and another, until she reaches the last of the Polaroids and moves on to a seemingly random bundle of regular five-by-seven prints. Again, of Ellie, mostly taken from within heavy foliage, they are over-intimate, intrusive and have a disturbing voyeuristic feel. Joanna can tell Ellie is totally oblivious of the camera in all of them, and that her private space has been violated. Several photographs slip to the floor. Among them, another two Polaroids. Reaching sideways to retrieve them, Joanna finds she is looking at a picture of Caroline aged thirteen. Snapped only days before the two of them were despatched back to London, going by the wet weather gear and her sister's newly cut fringe. In it, Caroline appears to be as ignorant of the photographer as Ellie was in hers.

She thinks again of the Polaroid they found of Ellie days before she was killed. Are these photographs linked? Both are of little girls, both – albeit years apart – suffered violent deaths?

The next few are of Joanna: podgy, pretty, taken throughout her two-month stay with Dora that summer; pictures she knows she didn't pose for. There are others of Joanna, Caroline and Ellie together. Knapsacks strapped to their backs, journeying through the woods and playing by the water. The stretch of lake where Ellie's body was found.

This is a sinister collection. She shudders. A collection of little girls. Innocent in their singularity, and why they would have raised no alarm in whoever was paid to develop the regular prints. But together they project quite a different mood. Something about them reminds her of a collection of butterflies she saw as a little girl on a school trip to the Natural History Museum. An experience that was deeply affecting. Those beautiful creatures, taken against their will, and pinned to board, put under glass. She thought then, what kind of mind would want to steal such innocence and keep it for their own private pleasure? Sickened, she feels the same way now about these.

The photographs that follow upset her further. Pretty little girls in thin summer clothes, visitors to Witchwood with their families, snapped without their consent. Stolen. Joanna speeds through, half-recognising children from the village, all little girls, and again unaware of the prying camera lens.

A chill settles over her. What do they mean? Did Dean take them? There's another of Caroline in her yellow cagoule and rubber boots, this time being spied on from above. Then finally, four or five Polaroids of a child who is curiously familiar, not that Joanna can immediately recall where from. Pigtails of light brown hair, her eyes clear as a swimming pool, playing with a skipping rope. Then she remembers. Gasps. Caroline's scrapbook. The headlines and articles her sister had, for whatever reason, cut from the tabloids. Police appeals for a missing eight-year-old girl believed to have been abducted from her home in Cinderglade. Freya. Freya what? Joanna can't remember. But she can remember Liz telling her about it when they fed the chickens in her garden. She hadn't made the connection at the time, but she's making it now. With a grave sense of foreboding as Yehudi Menuhin brings things to a close, Joanna folds the Polaroids and photographs away in their carrier bag. She notices a tremble in her hands and, tainted by what she's seen, places the open suitcase on the floor beside her.

Time passes. No sound other than the faint ticking of flames in the hearth, the odd whimper from the dreaming Buttons, his head heavy on her feet. She loses herself completely in the mystery of who killed Ellie Fry. Something that up to now has been an amorphous shape floating on the edge of her vision; a permanent reminder of the injustices in life, as her killer was never caught. But finding these photographs, the shape is becoming a tangible thing, and her fear that she may just have solved the mystery is picking up speed as she hands herself over to the tug of sleep.

Blackness. Joanna wakes with a jolt to it. Opening her eyes, she blinks, blind and disorientated, conscious of her breath bouncing back to her against the fabric of night. Her mouth is stale from sleep and she can't move; her limbs beneath her fleece and jeans too stiff with cold. She must have been asleep for hours, as the room is chilly and the fire's gone out. But Buttons is busy, gnawing on his toy bone; the hard yellow rubber glowing in the dark is easily as long as a man's humerus and just as heavy.

She is struggling to orientate herself when the dark is abruptly exchanged for the glare of car headlamps. Bursting in on her: startling, dazzling; saturating the room from floor to ceiling. Then the unmistakable thud of a car door.

Mike. At last. Joanna hurriedly gathers herself, switches on a lamp, and casts Pillowell in a warm pink glow.

A quick check of her face in Dora's oval mirror in the hall, and she skips through to the kitchen in her socks, Buttons trotting alongside with his jolly yellow bone.

'Hang on, love – I'm coming,' she calls.

The back door crashes open: violent, splitting the silence.

'Boys!' She flings her arms wide to embrace her family, but her joy is throttled in her throat.

This isn't Mike. Or Freddie. Or Ethan. The person blocking her way is someone else entirely. She gapes in shocked disbelief at his round, bare face; the flat of his eye, unreadable beneath the rainbow-coloured beany hat. Older and decidedly heavier, but she recognises him – and seeing him through adult eyes, his malevolence, his menace, she knows she's in trouble.

'I think you've got something that belongs to me.' He barges inside, slamming the door with such force it makes the glass rattle. 'And I want it back.' His demand, as he leans his weight against the only means of escape, trapping her inside.

Summer 1990

The village woke to the tolling of church bells through the perpetual drizzle. On and on, the noise was enough for Liz – who'd begun biting her nails after the police called with news that Ellie had been found by the Jameson sisters – to clamp her hands to her ears. And in the bleakness of dawn – a time when most will die and most are born – she sat amid shadows as indelible as ink stains, looked truth in the eye and squinted. These bells were for her child, her child who got up on her birthday, full of life and love and light, but never went to bed again.

Liz twisted round to look at her own bed, a place that, however exhausted, she couldn't return to either. Despite the copious amount of alcohol she needed to get her through the day, to lie down alongside her husband was out of the question. The vast white cotton sheet was a barren wasteland over which she hadn't the strength to traverse. If she did sleep, it was only for snatched half hours, upright in her wingback armchair. Swaddled in its padded embrace, it was a place where less than a decade ago, she had nursed her precious daughter through the slow turn of night-time hours.

Liz watched the involuntary rise and fall of her husband's body beneath the duvet. How was it that he could sleep when her mind wouldn't leave her alone? As persistent as the rain, it offered up a dizzying array of alternatives: if she hadn't done this or hadn't done that, then her child would still be here and in less than three hours Ellie's coffin wouldn't be lowered into the hole made ready for it in St Oswald's sheep-scattered churchyard.

Later, perched on the unmade bed, Liz touched the various black items she'd fished from her wardrobe, unable to decide what to wear. Then she began to cry. 'What does it matter?' she wailed, loud enough for Ian to step out of the shower to check on her. 'What would Ellie care?'

Frightened of his wife's grief, Ian dipped back inside the en-suite and waited for her to calm down. At a loss to know what to do, shaky and jumpy, he nicked himself shaving, once, then several times more. He swore as he blotted his cheeks with toilet paper and unsteady hands, and thought, staring into his face, if this was what a man going to his execution would look like, and supposed it was. He thought of his beautiful wife, drastically altered in the space of a few short weeks and, although only yards away in the adjacent bedroom, felt as removed from her as he did from the dark side of the moon.

Liz's drinking was gathering pace. He noticed the new four-litre bottle of Smirnoff he replaced on the optic the day before yesterday was already a quarter empty, and not because they'd been busy. Apart from the hordes of journalists, who ordered bugger all, people were staying away; it was another thing he worried about – they would lose the pub if things didn't pick up soon. Not that he could get Liz to take an interest – her world had stopped turning, and his inability to pull her back was a drastic failure.

'How's Liz?' someone asked as they paid for the only round of drinks he served all night. 'Not good,' he said, his already grooved forehead furrowing deeper. Wandering round in a daze himself since it happened, with nothing to look forward to and profits sliding, Ian knew things would never be right again.

Joanna and Caroline dressed in silence. They were remembering the day of their father's funeral. Their parents' bed, heaped with coats, and them refusing to go downstairs to show their faces.

So many flowers, such blazing sunshine – it was all wrong. It should have been a day like today, they thought, peering out through the skylight at the rain. A day like this would have been far more fitting.

The vicar, deliberately averting his gaze from Dora and her nieces, talked of the abrupt slide from summer to autumn as a metaphor for Ian and Liz's lives. No mention was made of Dean who, released without charge and driven back to Witchwood in a patrol car less than twenty minutes ago, floated restless in the wings, his guitar a wreath slung around his neck. Caroline pictured the dagger that had since been returned to Dora on condition she got it registered and kept it somewhere safe. The police had dismissed it as the murder weapon, because although the blood on it had been identified as human, it was more than fifty years old, and therefore wasn't a match to Ellie Fry's.

'. . . their life with Ellie –' Reverend Mortmain projected his poetry to the rear of the crowded church – 'was a sap-filled wood in spring, and now,' he paused to roll his eyes over the funeral-goers, accusing beneath his thick black brows, 'to have her taken from them in such a violent, evil way, has become as withered and friable as an autumn leaf . . .'

'Quite the poet, isn't he?' Dora whispered almost admiringly, looking at the sisters, rigid as stones either side of her soft circumference.

Identifying the veneration in the voice emanating from under that high wedge of black hair made the tearful Caroline want to give her aunt a Chinese burn. Was she going after the vicar now Gordon was out of the way? She was an old woman, for God's sake, it was disgusting. And she wasn't even upset: look at her, make-up still intact – all that made her cry was Beethoven and her soppy Richard Clayderman records. The contempt Caroline had for her aunt's fickleness hardened around her heart like the rind of a cheese. There was no way she would forget Dean, or ever let another man touch her. It didn't matter that he'd been horrible and broken his promise by choosing Amy over her; if she couldn't have him, she wouldn't have anyone. What would be the point? She'd never find a man like him as long as she lived.

Caroline made her silent vow as she rootled the shadowy pockets of the church for the object of her obsession. She knew Dean was in here somewhere, she'd seen him skulk inside: careful, not letting his family see him, tugging down his cuffs, nervous as a bridegroom. Her bridegroom. She sighed, the sound loud enough for Joanna to lean forward in her seat and feed her a look that made her snap back her neck.

*

The Reverend Mortmain, apostolic behind his spectacles, invited the congregation to drop their heads in prayer. Dora closed her eyes obediently, aware of her nieces shifting beside her, their eyes red from crying while hers remained strangely dry. If she concentrated on her sadness for Gordon she might be able to summon tears; might, if the reality hadn't been that he was nothing more than a stupid fantasy. Misreading the frequency of his visits as a sign he was interested in her, when they weren't about her at all. But then Gordon was a hard man to fathom, a hard man to touch. She thought it was because he was hiding something precious, like a pearl in a shell, but now she knows there was nothing. He was empty. An empty shell.

In Loving Memory, Dora read the Order of Service, the black on white under the banner of a simple gold cross. She supposed it was because she hardly knew Ellie that she couldn't rally the necessary emotion. But what was the matter with her? It didn't get worse than the death of a child. Responsive to the darkening mood echoed in the weather, she tried to let the occasion move her – Lillian's organ-playing was stirring enough.

These supposed cold, unfeeling traits of hers were what Caroline accused her of during the argument that unravelled after the policeman and the family liaison officer left. Remembering this made Dora think of the Cinderglade incident too: the reason, she assumed, for Gordon's sudden departure to Italy. Dora won't ever forgive her niece for that, any more than she would for tramping lipstick all through the cottage. The little sod, blaming Joanna – Dora wasn't stupid. She could envisage Caroline's sour-faced temper just because she didn't invite her to feed the horses.

But she'd better watch it. Dora adjusted herself. The little minx might start making up stories about her next.

She listened to the rain buffeting St Oswald's roof, spilling along the guttering, down the drainpipes, enclosing her further into the hush. Would it ever stop? On many levels, this was the worst summer she'd experienced here. But it wasn't only the weather that had ultimately made her decide. She made the call before coming out; she was going to pay to have Pillowell refurbished, rent it out as a holiday let. Tilly and Frank Petley were talking about setting up a cleaning company – let them do it, the Saturday changeover, clean linen, that kind of thing. Dora couldn't imagine she'd want to visit the place again. All she hoped was that possible holidaymakers wouldn't be put off by recent events; that the journalists camped out on the village green wouldn't be littering the place for too much longer, and this little nook in the woods would be allowed to return to its sleepy self.

'I never got to hold her, they just took her away,' Liz cried out from her position beside the tiny white coffin.

The congregation responded as one and lurched upright in their pews as Dean – perhaps taking advantage of eyes being elsewhere – stepped out of the shadows. Unshaven and sporting a nasty set of purple half-moons beneath his eyes, he looked oddly unfamiliar in an ill-fitting black suit that obviously didn't belong to him. At the sight of him, a gasp went up from the churchgoers, and he hovered on the edges of the transept, catching no one's eye except his father's. With a reproachful look from beneath his dripping curls, he began to pluck the opening chords to 'Yellow Bird' into the confused silence.

A burst of action and Ian Fry leapt to his feet. A muted scuffle ensued, and Dean shot off down the aisle, guitar sighing as it banged against his thighs. Ian hesitated before re-joining his wife, wanting to ensure his son had gone. But without her husband's big, brawny torso to shield her from the unwelcome scrutiny of the congregation, Liz was exposed to the murmuring and muttering of those who'd come to pay tribute to her dead child.

'I pity them,' Caroline heard people whispering behind her.

'Look at her, poor thing – such a devoted mother.'

'She's aged terribly.'

'And Ian, such a happy-go-lucky chap – he loved Ellie to bits.'

Gradually, now the rain had eased, the flock of mourners tiptoed into the murky daylight. Edging forwards, necks extended, they emerged one by one from the gloom. Careful to keep their high heels and polished leather uppers on the gravelled path, no one dared venture on to the sodden grass where the stone-faced angels outnumbered their congregation.

At the sound of raised voices, Caroline turned to see it was Ellie's grief-weary parents who now blocked the arch of the church doorway.

'You – you're still here?' Liz flew at Dean: a wild animal, flailing and clawing and screaming. 'You bastard. You bastard. The cops might not think you did it, but I know ... *I know* you killed my baby. You were abusing her all along, weren't you? I know you were, and Carrie saw you, and I saw the bruises ... the bruises you gave her ... Clear off, go on, clear the hell outta here ... I swear, if I ever lay eyes on you again, I'll kill you.'

It was someone else who eventually prised Liz off her stepson. Ian didn't move, didn't speak; he simply turned from his boy to put an arm around his wife's juddering shoulders. Calming, soothing, the gesture required no words, and Dean read it perfectly. His father's loyalty displayed in the tenderness of his act, as the sky, serious now, dropped solemn rain. Umbrellas bounced open. One. Two. The third, a huge black dome, was ceremoniously held up to shield the blighted couple.

The mourners, no doubt with their own warm-skinned children to go home to, whispered Dean's assumed guilt behind their black cotton gloves. It mattered little that the eighteen-year-old had been released without charge after a two-night stint in police custody, or that the supposed murder weapon he'd been accused of stealing from Dora Muller was nothing of the sort. The fact remained that Caroline Jameson said she'd seen him bullying Ellie the morning she went missing, and then him charging off after her on his motorbike. It was all the proof they needed.

Shunned by everyone, Dean shrugged and walked away. Intending to pack what he could carry in the panniers on his motorbike and leave before his father and stepmother came home. But Amy Mortmain – her hair lifted by the ululation of the wind and flapping like a big, black sail – ripped through the congregation after him, a tide of tutting disapproval in her wake.

'*Please*,' she begged when at last Dean turned to her. 'Please don't leave me here.'

'I have to,' he said gently.

Amy, up on tiptoes, touched the tender-looking skin beneath his eyes. 'Take me with you,' she pleaded, close to his lips. Then taking his hand, she pressed his palm against her tummy. 'Don't leave me alone with this.' Her voice breaking. 'Please, not in this place.' She flung her head around in desperation, aware of her father's black shape on her periphery. 'When they get whoever did it, they'll know it wasn't you ... Don't go, please don't go.'

It was all too much for Dean, now unsteady on his feet and fighting back tears. An upsurge of dread rippled through the onlookers – was he about to change his mind? No, they exhaled their relief, what followed extinguished any fear of that.

'Your mother needs you.' Dean broke off, then kissed and returned Amy's hand, obviously understanding nothing of what his girlfriend had tried to communicate. 'She needs you here. If I take you with me, you'll only end up hating me too.' He looked around, addressed the mill of mourners: 'Just like this lot do ... every single one of them ... Happy to believe the vicious lies of a spiteful thirteen-year-old kid. I never stood a chance.'

Present Day

'What the hell d'you think you're doing? You can't just barge in here. Get out.' Joanna, blunted by sleep, tries to reason with her intruder; tries harder to keep the terror hammering in her chest out of her demand.

'Oh, you'd like me to leave, would you?' a face she remembers from childhood mocks: a face scored with crows' feet and a lifetime of cigarettes and booze. 'Well, first off, I'd like my suitcase.'

'Look, my husband's going to be back any minute, and he's not going to take—' She stops talking, watches a stomach-churning smile curve his mouth.

'Liar,' he growls from beneath a set of eyebrows wet with sweat. 'You're here on your own. I've been watching you.'

Stepping closer: invidious, intimidating; the sheer brutality held in his eyes is enough to force her back down the gloomy passageway, into the sitting room.

'Now, where is it?' he asks through the frantic barking of Buttons, without raising his voice.

Joanna shakes her head. The gesture is futile; he's already seen the suitcase lying open on the floor.

'Been having a good old nose, have you?' Rustling inside his bulky blue anorak, his stony sarcasm makes her flinch. 'Find anything interesting?'

She can't speak, the room is suddenly too small to stand up in, too small to think.

'A little bird told me you'd been sniffing around.' His cadence – calm, controlled – makes his presence all the more lethal. 'You really shouldn't go poking around in other people's lives. You really shouldn't.' He peels back his lips, forms another noxious smile that is as menacing as the increasing wind hustling the walls of the cottage. 'If you knew what was good for you, you'd have stayed outta this. Sticking your oar in – you don't know what you've done, do you?' He cocks his head, ugly in the pinkish lamplight.

'You took those photos, didn't you?'

'Just give them to me, please.'

His composure makes her shrink away, but doesn't stop her asking, 'Why did you take them, let alone keep them?'

''Cos I couldn't bear to throw them away,' he laughs.

'Your trophies, are they?' Her repulsion emboldening her. 'They're little girls ... What sort of person takes photos of little girls?' The challenge comes in spite of herself; in spite of pushing her spine to the flaking wallpaper to stop herself from shaking.

'I like little girls,' he leers, close to her.

'You've got some of me in there, why have you kept them?' She flaps a frightened arm at his suitcase; the stuff he wants back.

His eyes narrowed, angled at the floor, measuring what he's going to do next.

'You wanna watch your mouth.' His breath, rancid, crawling, condensing to a cloud. Joanna ducks away, but too quick, too strong, he seizes her wrists.

'It was you, wasn't it?' She winces under his grip. Seeing

it clearly – the savagery made identifiable by truth. And yet still the words keep coming. She really shouldn't rile him, it wouldn't take much to push him over the edge.

'You did it. You killed her ... you killed Ellie.' Joanna's heart: a bouncing jackrabbit. And she sees the black bruises, curved as finger ends, on her friend's arms as plainly as if she'd been standing beside her now.

'Shut your mouth.' He shakes her. Fierce. His stubble dangerously close to her face. The spurt of movement releases a waft of stale cigarettes, the reek of unwashed armpits. The smell grapples for room alongside their tall shadows that have bent in half against the wall.

'She was only a little girl – what did she ever do to you?' Stupid to challenge him, but she can't stem the flow, she wants answers. 'Why hurt Ellie?'

'Because she was gonna tell her mother.'

'Tell her mother what? What were you doing to her?'

The look he gives answers her question.

'But why her?' Nausea rising. 'Why Ellie?'

'Because she was there. It was easy.'

'What about that Freya girl, you've got pictures of her – did you kill her too?' Joanna, remembering the contents of her sister's scrapbook, the conversation with Liz.

'You know nothing about it. *Meddling* ... you stupid bitch.' He steps closer, the sourness on his breath buffeting her cheek. 'You and your fucking sister ... It had to be you two who found her, didn't it.'

It isn't a question, and Joanna doesn't answer.

Mike – where the hell are you? Hardly daring to breathe, Joanna makes her voiceless and desperate plea to a god she has never totally believed in.

350

'You haven't got a clue what it's been like for me, have you?' he accuses. 'Living your perfect little life. Well, just so you know, mine's been in ruins ever since.' He loosens his grip a fraction but pinned to the wall by his broad body, there's no escaping him, nowhere to go. 'But it would've been a whole lot worse for me if she'd opened her fucking gob and told everyone. Oh, yeah, *poor little Ellie* – poor little slut, more like. Coming on to me *all the time*. And when I took her up on it, threatening to tell.'

The monster wants me to feel sorry for him; look at him – he actually believes his twisted, pathetic reasons justify the evilness of his crime. Joanna keeps her thoughts to herself and tries not to make any sudden moves. Her chest tightening, her mouth dry, a portion of her brain constricts in panic. There is something terrifyingly calculating about him, something calm and deadly – he's insane, and she knows he is going to strike, she sees the brutality building behind his eyes.

'Yeah, it was me. I killed Ellie.' He spits his confession. A confession Joanna wasn't ready for. 'I don't think I even meant to kill her, but, well ... ' Another smile that makes the blood slow in her veins, 'once I'd done it ... ' He tapers off.

What's he saying? Snatching back her arm, Joanna gawps at him, wishing she could close the lid over the truth she doesn't believe she consciously sought.

'Happy now?' A callous laugh. His spittle on her ear, in her hair. ''Cos you know I can't let you go now, don't you?' A gravelly whisper. 'Not now you know. That would be beyond stupid, wouldn't it?'

He strikes her hard across the face, and she folds to the

floor. *He's going to kill me*, her thoughts in the ringing aftershock, catching his satisfied, almost gleeful look. Blood trickles down her face as she gropes for something, anything, to use as a weapon when he lunges for her again. This time she's ready for it and grabs his ankle. Stumbling forward, fumbling for the bevelled sideboard to save his fall, the lamp crashes to the floor, extinguishing their shadows. With blood in her mouth, she uses the seconds he needs to correct himself to crawl towards the light haemorrhaging from the hall.

'Come here, you bitch.'

Close on her heels, he dives for her, dragging her towards him by her socked feet. She thrashes to get free, but his arms are strong, practised in the art of pinning and confining. And in the struggle, things are knocked over and crash to the lumpy rugs, splintering against the wooden boards beneath. Clumsy, messy, he wrestles her to the ground, holds her wrists above her head with one hand and straddles her. A drop of sweat lands on her neck. Then her lip. Tasting salt, along with her blood, the world spins and stops. She cowers, primed for him to strike again. Buttons is barking. Weaving between them: the pink patina of his gums, his puppy-white teeth circling their heads; ineffectual as a toddler. On her periphery, his foot swings out to boot her dog aside. A sickening crack and Buttons yelps and falls away. She rams her knees into her attacker's crotch – for Buttons, for her – and as he scrabbles to his feet, leaning down to strike her again, she smashes her heel into his head and a dart of pain shoots from foot to groin.

Vulnerable without her boots, her thoughts solidifying

with a bizarre regret for removing them as she tears away on all fours. The elastic of her ponytail has worked down to within a smidge of her hair's end, but she crashes on through her confusion, aiming for the searing white light of the kitchen. His booming voice inches away, as strands of hair float about her face, stinging her eyes, and she scrambles the length of the hall before he catches her. Stretched out, he snatches hold of her damaged foot and squeezes. She screams in agony and in her effort to get upright, loses her sock and the floor slips beneath her. With an almighty thud, she's down. Down on the slippery linoleum with him mad-eyed and close to her face.

She doesn't smell the dinner burning. Her nose is clotted with blood and she must open her mouth to breathe. Pressing an agitated hand to her churning insides, she watches him on his hands and knees, sickened by the way he drags a heavy arm across his wide, wet brow, panting as if he's just finished running a race.

They stop moving.

They watch one another: the killer and the prey.

Has he had enough – is he going to let her go?

Listening to the silence, all she can hear is her own heartbeat.

The cold is moving in. Spilling into the cottage through the gap in the doorway, filling up the rooms, its icy breath creeping under her clothes. Conscious of a chronic numbness spreading over her, Joanna holds him steady in her sights: her eyes big and pleading, it's the lack of pity she finds reflected in his that makes her shiver. She isn't going to get out of here, this is it. This is the end.

His boots. Brutish black, steel toe-capped workman's boots. Joanna registers them in a flash of horrific clarity. One well-placed kick will kill her.

Rolling to the right, up on her knees, with a single movement she spreads her strong pianist fingers and clasps the dog's yellow bone. Heavy at the end of her arm, she dodges the boots, the clumsy fists that pummel the white puff of her breath, and swings it wide to clobber Ellie's killer hard on the side of his head. The force is enough to knock him sideways, and he wheels away to tend to himself, an animal sound bubbling in his throat.

This is her chance. And hoping her dog has the sense to follow, she breaks into the night. Straggling thoughts of her husband, her children, how they might never find her, how she might never see them again, she staggers out into the quivering blackness.

Summer 1990

Joanna stared out at the weather through the bedroom window and fiddled with a loose-fitting milk tooth. She pressed her cheek to the cool of the windowpane, as rain thrashed the roof and the wind shook out the trees against the glass. Nothing was visible beyond the patio with its table and chairs and sodden cushions. As with the rest of the village, Pillowell's garden had been nibbled away by the sallow light. Hard to imagine only days ago they were basking in a hot, high sun, but that, along with so many things, had been snuffed out since Ellie, and she doubted it would ever shine again.

Watching a row of silver birch being blown inside out, the metallic backs of their leaves close enough to touch, Joanna didn't think she could be any sadder until she dredged up what Caroline said she saw Dean doing to Ellie. One thing bothered her, though: Joanna, more than most, knew how much her sister liked inventing stories, liked an audience if she could get one. But not about this? Caroline had never said things like this before, this was serious; it had got Dean into big trouble and made everyone turn against him so badly he was forced to leave Witchwood. To leave Amy.

Joanna's mind twisted to the little bruises she saw on Ellie's upper arms in the boat the afternoon they talked about pain – or Ellie's horror of it. The bruises Ellie hadn't wanted them to see. Did Dean give her them? She supposed if Caroline said he hurt Ellie, then he must have done. The police seemed to think so, for a little while anyway; why else did they lock him up for two whole nights? But then they let him go, and this was where it got confusing – maybe he was cleverer than he looked at hiding what he'd done. Didn't her teachers tell her that bullies were clever, that they could disguise their nasty side from those they didn't want to see it by only hurting you in invisible places; like Ellie was hurt in invisible places?

But Joanna knew she, too, was far from perfect. What about the lie she told Caroline about Dean wanting her to be his girlfriend? She should have kept her mouth shut, even if her intentions were good and she wanted to make her sister happy. She should come clean, tell her it wasn't Dean's fault. He wasn't the one who tricked her, it was Joanna, and she was sorry. If she had kept her mouth shut, it's possible Caroline would simply have carried on loving Dean from afar, expecting nothing; never building her hopes up for something that wasn't ever going to happen. Joanna knows her lie made her sister's discovery of him and Amy all the more crushing; it would have seemed to Caroline – believing it was her that Dean wanted – like the ultimate betrayal.

She watched the rain, anxious that all traces of Ellie would be washed away. She didn't know much, but she knew Ellie's death wasn't an accident like her daddy's was – reading in the *Cinderglade Echo* words like *raped* and *stabbed* and *left for dead* ... before the newspaper was whipped out of reach, to the accompanying cry of: 'You're too young; it's far too awful for little eyes.'

'But I'm almost the same age as Ellie,' she'd tried to reason. 'And no one stopped those awful things happening to her because she was too young.'

With temperatures dipping to record summer lows and the rain showing no signs of stopping, Dora had to concede to firing up the boiler. What it meant was a continuous supply of piping-hot water and, taking advantage, in a chin-deep bath of bubbles, the fear Caroline had about the lies she'd told to the police, to the newspaper, to Liz and others in the village – lies that meant Dean had been driven out of Witchwood forever – burned in her mouth. She positioned a flannel at the nape of her neck to make a pillow and eased her head back against the rim of the bath. Loops of vapour coiled over the water. Scribbles in the steam, she thought, breathing through them, trying to decipher what the scribbles meant. Probably a list of her wrongdoings, she thought miserably. Her wrongdoings were polluting both her dreams and her daylight hours; they were making her as unrecognisable to herself as a visitant from another planet. But had she been so very wrong? Dean did say he wanted to be her boyfriend, he'd told Joanna. Was it really her fault she'd built her world around his promise, that she'd pinned her life on a belief she was going to be close to him? To then have it thrown in her face by him taking up with that Amy cow. Dean had to take some responsibility for the part he played, for what she'd been driven to do.

Woken early by the insistent drum of rain, Caroline was already packed for the London train the following morning. With the rest of the day to herself, knowing the unlikelihood of ever coming back here, she had planned to say a proper farewell to Witchwood and collect her steals from the lakeside. But, too afraid to go down to Drake's Pike, the snow globe, the gold ring she took from the pub, and the red-stoned brooch she found in St Oswald's were all she was going to be able to take home; it was a shame, but the other trinkets would have to stay here.

The translucency of her skin, so alabaster-white, always had the facility to frighten her. But locked inside Dora's bathroom seeing its blue-veined intersection mapped across her body frightened her more. She traced it, searching, but couldn't find a clear route out of the mess she'd got herself into because there simply wasn't one. She knew what she had done to Dean was wrong, and how much worse she'd made things for him with his family, with the villagers, but despite being sorry about this, what plagued her too was a billowing unease about the Polaroid of Ellie. The one she found at the pub and deliberately planted between the last plate and hardback cover of the *Book of the Dead* for her to find that day. It was wicked of Caroline to want to show Ellie that the world she lived in was as nasty as hers and Joanna's, and that no one, no matter how special they were, or how much their family loved them, could get off that lightly. Regretting it now, it was horrible of her to taunt and scare their friend that way, because now their friend was dead.

While thinking of her badness it was as if a cold moth landed lightly on her heart. And, despite the hot water she was immersed in, where its icy dorsal tufts touched, she was left with goose bumps. There would be consequences, she told herself; she would be made to pay for what she had done. It mattered little that by this time tomorrow she and Joanna would be on a train heading back to London. Caroline knew she would never be allowed to forget what she did to Dean, to Ellie, regardless of the distance she put between herself and Witchwood, or however long she lived. One day she would be punished. One day she would pay. It was all she deserved.

Present Day

Out under a fretwork of stars, Joanna, eyes wild, rotates on the spot, and for a few frantic seconds her legs don't seem to want to work. Teeth chattering and feverish, the night slaps its clammy skin to hers and holds her upright. She fumbles for the exterior wall of the cottage and gropes her way along, the brown-stemmed rose bushes by the gate ripping her jeans as she pushes herself into the luminous black lane. Blood mixes with her tears. She has no idea which way to go. She swings her head in panic, tastes the lake's breath drifting towards her through the trees.

She risks a quick look over her shoulder. Sees Ellie's killer. His unwieldy silhouette gaining on her through the dark. She's blind in her left eye and the evil air sharpens in her throat as she springs headlong into the brushwood, the icy wet mulch of last year's leaves sliding beneath her feet. One soaked sock on, one sock missing, the pain is severe, but her fear drives her on. Fresh blood from the cut above her eye trickles down her face, but she doesn't stop, won't stop. Branches and twigs snap against her – scratching, wounding – but still she crashes on, hurling her terror against the frozen rime of night. But there is no one to hear her. No one to save her.

Tarmac under her feet. It hurts to run. Her breathing

ragged, her heartbeat banging in her ears. There is a flicker of hope in the squares of ochre light in the distance. Beacons through the dark. Pludd Cottage. Mrs Hooper. Her hope curdles to dread. She can't lead the monster there and put her in danger.

Breath on her shoulder. She is knocked to the ground. Lies dazed and sprawled full-length on the lane. His big black shape is above her. Everything hurts, but it's the cold that strikes her. A small spot where her cheek meets the icy asphalt. Head down. She mustn't provoke him. Her eyes roll to the left, to Mrs Hooper's gate, as if by some miracle there might be someone there to rescue her. She squints, lifts her head an inch or two and wriggles forward on her belly. Someone is shouting. Buttons is barking.

Then the sound of a car. Headlamps swing with the bend in the road. And like the fox and the rabbit, she crawls instinctively towards the cones of light. A screech of brakes. The big dark car stops just in time. Up on her knees, she slams her hands down on the hot bonnet.

The next thing she knows she is screaming.

'Help me. Help me.'

The driver: ghost-white and open-mouthed behind the wheel.

'Help me.' She thumps the bonnet. 'For God's sake … stop him. *Stop him!*'

The driver's door of the BMW opens and a tall, grey-haired man slips out. Bewildered and silent, his sizeable onyx ring winks in the indeterminate light.

'Stop him,' she bawls at the driver again. 'He killed Ellie … he killed Ellie.' Her eyes wide with fear. 'And now … now … he wants to kill me.'

The following morning

Joanna wakes up. Freddie and Ethan are watching her with red-rimmed eyes. Mike is here too, gripping the metal bar at the foot of the bed, his expression fretful. The room is as warm as a bakery. The air sluggish. She turns her head to the large window, looks out at the day. A day she didn't think she would see. She stares at bruised black clouds gliding above the hospital car park. Thinks again of the previous night and lifts an arm to brush hair from her clammy forehead. Pain shoots from shoulder to wrist. She'd forgotten for a moment the extent of her injuries and how much they hurt.

'Careful, Jo,' Mike responds to her whimper, and reaches over the starched sheet that feels as rough as toast against her bandaged ribs. 'Remember, you've an IV tube attached to you.' And he gently helps to reposition her arm at her side.

Tears, hot and painful, roll over her cheeks. Mike looks desperate, then turns to the creak of the opening door.

Mrs Hooper, buttoned into a thick winter coat, dithers with her stick and a bunch of chrysanthemums on the threshold.

'Come in. Come in,' Mike encourages quietly, his relief clearly visible. 'Jo's awake, it's all right.'

Mike and Mrs Hooper stand opposite each other in the

cream-walled side room, holding hands as if caught in a still moment during a dance. They talk for a minute, but things turn quiet when they run out of things to say. Joanna's eyes flutter and close ... the scattered fag butts, the violence of those brutish black boots flickering behind her eyelids.

'Is it okay if Mrs Hooper stays with you for a bit?' Mike whispers near her head, and she opens her eyes in time to see him tug on his jacket. He looks shattered, Freddie and Ethan too. 'The boys are a bit restless.' His voice low. 'I'll take them to the canteen, get them some breakfast. We won't be long.'

Mrs Hooper answers for her. Joanna can't unstick her tongue in time. 'Yes, yes,' she tells him, dropping the flowers into the hand basin and scanning around for something to put them in. 'Off you go, poor loves; you've been here all night.' She steps up to Joanna, plants a gentle kiss above the bloodied butterfly stitch on her brow. 'The three of them have been here all night,' she repeats for Joanna's benefit, supporting herself with her stick and frowning her concern. 'I'll stay with Jo until you get back. Go on. Take your time. She's safe with me.' A forced smile to reassure.

When Joanna's family leave, Mrs Hooper props her stick against the wall and pulls up a chair. Sitting beside the bed, she cautiously strokes the exposed skin on Joanna's forearm between the tubing and the welts and grazes. Behind her back the clamour of a hectic hospital ward, and the rise and fall of unknown voices. Together they listen, neither knowing what to say.

'Would you like some water?' Mrs Hooper gestures to a clear plastic beaker on the bedside cabinet.

Joanna nods that she would and waits for Mrs Hooper to

guide the straw to her damaged lips before lifting her head. She drinks the tepid liquid, holding it in her mouth for a long time before swallowing. Swallowing is agony, and her discomfort is reflected in Mrs Hooper's strained expression.

'. . . be out tomorrow.' Joanna begins halfway through a sentence, it is all she can manage.

'I think they're going to want to hold on to you for a while longer than that, luvvie. You've had concussion. They'll want to run tests, keep you under observation. And you don't want to rush things, that was a nasty blow you had to the head . . . never mind the broken ribs.' Mrs Hooper heaves down air. 'It's a good job Gordon turned up when he did.'

Joanna pushes the straw away with her tongue, drops her head back on her pillow.

'He's admitted it. Admitted to killing Ellie.' Mrs Hooper replaces the beaker on the bedside cabinet with a clunk. 'They've charged him.'

A grunt from Joanna as she tries and fails to shift to a more comfortable position.

'It's quite something to get your head around,' Mrs Hooper shares her thoughts. 'Him keeping it quiet all these years . . . Twenty-eight years he got away with it.'

'But why Ellie?' Joanna croaks. 'She was such a lovely little girl.'

'Think there was rather more going on there than any of us knew . . . or want to know.'

'But his own child? Sweet little Ellie,' Joanna again. 'How could he kill his own child?'

'Oh, no, luvvie.' Mrs Hooper is keen to set her straight. 'Ellie wasn't his. Ellie wasn't Ian's – Ian was her stepfather.'

Autumn 1990

Mid-October. The chill had tightened its hold on Witch-wood, and the blackberries in the hedgerows, plump and ripe only a week or so ago, had already rotted and grown their mildew coats in readiness for winter.

Standing outside in the cold drizzle, Liz, minus a coat and still in her slippers, didn't budge. She propped her elbows on the roof of the car and pulled on her sixth ciga-rette of the morning. Exhaled thin grey streams of smoke. Soon they would be in Cinderglade: in a dull little house, with dull little rooms, on a rundown estate where everyone was a stranger. No pub. No business. No nothing. Just her and Ian. Liz had hardly spoken to him since Ellie's funeral, she didn't know where to begin, so she watched him instead. Today he was taking his frustration out on a set of muscled removal men the brewery arranged for them along with the haulage truck that blocked the lane. Liz wondered if they were dawdling deliberately, to pro-voke her husband: a man they could tell from his frenetic hand gestures and gruffness was struggling to keep a lid on his anger.

With lips shiny from his own spit, Ian gave a little rub of his hands and glanced behind him. 'Careful with that, you idiots,' he barked, aggressive, surly; close on their heels as they transported a heavy oak table to the open-doored truck. 'Do I have to do every flamin' thing myself?'

The men swapped looks Ian was too slow to see. But Liz did, choosing to turn away in case they caught her eye; she was no one's ally. Her cigarette finished, she dropped it to the kerb, screwed it out with the heel of her slipper. Was she going to be able to put up with him? Her doubts folding in on themselves. Wouldn't she be better off starting again on her own? She'd wanted to share her misgivings about Ian with Mrs Hooper when she called round to say farewell to her the previous evening. So caring, so kind, it would have been easy to be unburdened of what she carried in her heart. Thoughts of Mrs Hooper's beautiful organist's hands had Liz assessing her own – the bitten nails, a habit she'd been cured of for years. Not that her hands were ever her best feature, but they were completely ruined now. The skin on her palms was rough and mannish, the knuckles broadened from years of mopping out and washing up; her wedding band couldn't be removed even if she'd wanted to.

'You've got the address?' Liz heard Ian shout. 'Right. See you there, then. We'll probably get there before you do,' he added, before ducking away to retrieve something from just inside the Boar's main door.

Liz opened the passenger side to wait in the car. Damp-haired and despondent, she stared out through the rain-mottled windscreen at the wind shaking what remained of summer from the trees. Her socks were wet from where rain had seeped through the lining of her slippers, and her feet were freezing – it was all she was conscious of; the fact she was about to leave a place she'd once been so happy in left her surprisingly numb and disconnected.

'Fucking brewery.' The door behind her clunked open. It jolted Liz out of her introspection. 'They're such bastards,' Ian growled and slid whatever he'd gone back to fetch from the pub on to the back seats of his Volvo. 'Could have given us a bit more time. It wouldn't have killed them.' He slammed the door shut again.

Liz flinched when he swung his burly, belligerent self into the driver's seat.

'All they're fucking concerned about is money,' he continued to rant as he turned the ignition. 'Business would've picked up soon enough ... once the fuss died down.'

Fuss? Died down? That's my darling Ellie you're talking about. His callousness banged inside her head, but she didn't challenge him. From his blotchy face and sweating brow, it was obvious he was spoiling for a fight. A fight she didn't have the energy to give him. Instead, she swivelled to see what he'd put on the back seat.

'What's that?' She jabbed her thumb at an old-fashioned suitcase.

'Nothing much.'

'Give it to the removal men, then – they can take it on the lorry, can't they?'

'No, they can't. I need to keep hold of it.'

'Why, what's so special about it? Why can't it go with the rest of our things?'

'I don't want it getting lost.'

'Getting lost? For God's sake, Ian, we're only going to Cinderglade.' She looked sideways at him. 'You wouldn't let me bring my guitar separately, and that could easily get broken. What's in it?' She gestured to the suitcase again.

'Just stuff.'

367

'What *stuff*? Must be pretty important stuff if you're afraid to let it out of your sight.'

'Look. It's stuff of Dean's, all right.'

'*Stuff of Dean's*,' Liz shrieked, smacked her hands against the dashboard. 'Why d'you want to keep anything that belongs to that bastard? If I ever clap eyes on him again ... I swear ... I swear ... '

'Calm down, love.' Ian spoke in his reasonable voice – the one that had the facility to rile her even more. 'It's just stuff of his mum's.'

'Oh, yeah, the wonderful Maggie ... I wondered when she was going to rear her head again. The perfect wife ... the wife and mother I'll never live up to.' Her face crumpled and she burst into tears.

'Love ... *love*.' Ian placed a consoling hand on her sleeve: to soothe, to temper; but Liz could tell he didn't mean it and shrugged it off. 'Be reasonable, eh? The boy left in such a hurry. He meant to take it with him ... He did. You know how much he loved his mum.'

'Don't. I. Just.' Liz spat out her bitterness. 'But I still don't know why *you* have to be so bloody precious about it.'

Present Day

'But it suited the vicar to have Dean out of the way too, didn't it?' Wearing a poppy-red bruise on her temple and a butterfly stitch on her brow, Joanna watches fast-moving clouds obscure then expose the sun through Pludd Cottage's windows.

'It's true he didn't like him,' Mrs Hooper agrees.

'*Didn't like him*?' Joanna blurts. 'I know I was only a kid, but even I could tell he hated him.'

'There was more to it than that. It was complicated.'

'Was the *complicated* how Carrie persuaded him to talk to the police on her behalf about Dean?' Joanna asks this through the continuous drone of a headache: one of the many leftovers she's living with after her terrible ordeal just over a week ago.

'I think Tilly Petley was the driving force there; you said yourself she was keen to shift police focus away from her husband.'

'Maybe.' Joanna doesn't sound sure. 'But reading Carrie's notebooks in hospital – scribbles, most of it nonsense – she kept making references to a dreadful secret the vicar was hiding.' She lifts her eyes to Mrs Hooper's. 'You wouldn't know anything about that, would you?'

'*Me* – why would I know anything?'

'Because you said you and the vicar have been friends for years. From what you told me about Amy when I was last here, he obviously confides in you.'

'Okay, okay. I suppose it's safe to tell you.' Joanna watches a blush travel up from Mrs Hooper's neck. 'The person it would have hurt's no longer alive.' She inhales deeply, as if about to dive into a swimming pool. 'Carrie may well have seen us together; Timothy and I weren't always as discreet as we should have been.'

'Seen you together! *What* – you and the vicar?' Joanna presses her damaged knuckles to her lips.

Mrs Hooper looks uncomfortable. 'We managed to keep it a secret for years.'

'You're telling me it's still going on?' Joanna looks away, her incredulity muffled by her fists.

'We don't have furtive meetings in the woods any more – we're both too old for blankets and picnics, but yes, we keep one another company,' Mrs Hooper whispers, even though Gordon, Mike, Freddie and Ethan are still out on a walk, and they've the place to themselves.

'That was you, was it? Yes.' Joanna answers her own question and drops her injured hands to her sides. 'It makes sense now. Us kids ... we found one of your abandoned picnics down by the lake. I should have guessed it was you, Carrie obviously did. There were chocolate brownies, weren't there? We ate them in the boat ... you used to give us them when we came round.' A brief smile into the memory. 'I can't pretend I'm not shocked.' She skims her gaze to Mrs Hooper again. 'Honestly, though, I'd never have put the two of you together in a million years.'

'I know Timothy's a bit of an acquired taste.' Mrs Hooper

fiddles with the cuffs of her blouse. 'But he's been good to me. I was at my lowest when we started seeing each other, worn down from providing round-the-clock care for Derek. And, of course, he had troubles of his own at home.' She bunches her shoulders. 'I'm not proud of it.'

'No, I don't suppose you are.' Joanna is having difficulty picturing Mrs Hooper as the scarlet woman. 'Did his wife ever find out?'

'I don't think so,' Mrs Hooper answers.

'You hope she didn't. But whether she did or not, it was pretty mean of you to be carrying on with her husband when she was … was … stuck in that wheelchair.' Joanna runs out of steam.

'I'm not making excuses, but –' Mrs Hooper seems to want to explain – 'I think Timothy was a symptom of what living in a place like this did to me. Looking out, day after day, on nothing but greenery. You could forget you were human.'

'I can understand that much, I suppose. Coming back to Witchwood as I have as an adult, there's nothing here, is there? You can't even get the internet, for goodness' sake.' A sigh. 'So,' Joanna, wanting to move things on, 'that's how Carrie got the vicar to take her to the police station, is it? By threatening to expose the pair of you.'

There isn't the time to answer.

Their heads dart to the opening door and the bubbling chatter of Joanna's children.

'Oh, you're back – did you have fun?' Joanna cuddles Freddie and Ethan with as much gusto as her battered body allows. 'Your dad given you a towelling?' she asks the wagging Buttons, ruffling his damp head. 'We don't want you bringing mud into Mrs Hooper's cottage.'

371

'I'm boiling the kettle,' Gordon announces, and bends to remove his cycle clips. 'Anyone for tea?' Lean as ever inside his usual shirt, tie and suit trousers. His full head of steel-grey hair gives him a distinguished look. 'Great,' he says to a show of hands, and pitches from the room.

'You all right, Jo?' Mike asks, giving her a kiss. Keeping Gordon company in the kitchen since they arrived that morning – peeling vegetables, stirring the gravy – he looks scruffy by comparison in jeans and Sunday stubble. ''Cos, you're looking a bit pink – isn't she?' He twists his question to Mrs Hooper.

'I'm fine,' Joanna smiles. 'It's probably the fire – lovely as it is, I'm a bit over-warm.'

'You're not running a temperature again, are you?' Mike tests her forehead with his hand. 'Isn't it time to take your painkillers?'

Joanna checks her watch and unbuckles her handbag to dig through its rattling innards. Unscrewing the lid of prescribed co-codamol and tipping the recommended dose into her palm, she puts the bolus in her mouth and swallows with a sip of the tea Gordon's just made her. Tasting the bitterness on the back of her tongue, she wishes the distress of nine days ago, along with her week-long stint in Gloucester Infirmary, could be as easily numbed.

'Thanks for that delicious lunch, Gordon,' Joanna says. Then, determined to banish her recent trauma, along with the news Mrs Hooper's just divulged, she swivels her attention to her fair-haired sons. Back from their yomp through the woods, they sit rosy-cheeked on Mrs Hooper's peacock-patterned carpet, Buttons spread between them, totally absorbed with an old Monopoly set someone fetched from the loft.

'Glad you enjoyed it.' Gordon draws on the last of his gold-tipped cigarette before extinguishing it in an ashtray. 'You must come again.' As elegant as ever, he folds his violin-making hands in his lap.

'It's a real treat not to have to cook – not that I'm in any fit state.' Joanna continues with her gratitude. And with the cup of tea balancing on the arm of the couch, her bruised legs and bandaged foot tucked under her, she scans the front page of the Sunday paper Mike brought in from the car.

'No, you're not in any fit state. You're to take it easy, Jo – d'you hear? It's going to take a long time to get over what that brute did to you.' Mrs Hooper fiddles with the garnet brooch Joanna returned to her, which is now pinned to the collar of her blouse. 'You were lucky to get out of there alive, you poor love. What a thing to happen.'

'Gave as good as you got, though, didn't you, Jo-Go.' Mike, proud from his position by the fire.

'What I can't get over,' Mrs Hooper shares her amazement with the room, 'is how your search for Dean Fry ended up solving Ellie's murder. But I have to say, I always had a bad feeling about you digging around in the past – and now I know why.'

'I never liked Ian.' Gordon, from his armchair. 'And the cheek of the man, calling *me* a pervert.'

A resigned ripple of agreement from the grown-ups. Freddie and Ethan, heads bowed, throwing dice, counting out pretend money, don't look up.

'I always said he was a nasty piece of work. He was vile to Gordon,' Mrs Hooper adds for the benefit of her Sunday guests, then turns to her son. 'He was only like that to you to deflect any blame and suspicion from himself. It's clear as day now, love.' Her cup clatters noisily into its saucer.

'All I can say is, thank God Gordon arrived when he did. He meant to kill me, you know.' A glance at her sons; Joanna is thankful they aren't listening. 'I reckon he'd been watching the cottage from the moment I arrived. Liz must've told him I'd come here when she said she'd given me the suitcase. He knew I'd be alone until Mike arrived later Friday night.'

'Only in conversation, though,' Mrs Hooper says. 'I'm sure Liz didn't have the first idea what he was up to.'

'Oh, no.' Joanna shook her head. 'She can't possibly have known what Ian was hiding in that suitcase, or how desperate he'd be to get it back. I was working it out in hospital – that suitcase was the key to everything. And while he had it safely stashed away, he was in control. No wonder he went off his head when he realised it was, for the *first time*,' she stresses, 'out of his control, and that someone else had it. And he wasn't able to contain what he'd been holding in for the last twenty-eight years. It didn't matter that he'd have to kill someone else, *me* –' aware of her children sitting close by, Joanna drops her voice – 'all that mattered to him was getting his suitcase back and being in control again.'

'Bit irrational, isn't it?' Mrs Hooper frowns.

'Yes. But what d'you expect? The man's a murderer. Imagine the sort of twisted mind he'd have. But, I tell you,' a tentative touch of her temple, 'I wish I'd never taken the damn thing.'

'I was going to ask why Liz gave it to you.' Gordon throws one knee over the other. 'If it was so easy to get rid of, then surely it could've been lost years ago?'

'I suppose. Except it wasn't hers to get rid of, was it? Ian told her it belonged to Dean, making out it contained precious things belonging to Dean's mother, and he was keeping it for him,' Joanna explains. 'The only reason Liz gave it to me was because I said I was going to find him.'

'Fair enough. But Ian took a hell of a risk keeping hold of those photographs, anyone could have found them.' Mike shares his thoughts and sits down next to Joanna on the couch.

'It was only the two of them living there, and Liz had no reason to question what Ian had told her. Liz wanted nothing to do with anything belonging to Dean or his dead mother. As far as she was concerned, they were just keepsakes he forgot to take with him in his rush to get out of Witchwood.'

'He did leave in rather a hurry, didn't he?' Mrs Hooper chips in.

'Thinking about it, Liz was only able to give me the suitcase because Ian was at work. I was the one who prompted her to it. It was buried under a heap of junk and took her an age to dig out. She told me she'd wanted to sling it years ago, but couldn't because Ian was so precious about it – and we all know why now.' Joanna pauses into the weight of the revelation. 'My fault for looking inside the damn thing.' She hugs herself. 'Talk about curiosity killing the cat – it nearly killed me.' Another glance at her sons.

'But then we'd never have known what he'd done, would we?' Gordon defends Joanna's recriminations before they have the chance to properly form.

'And how were you supposed to know what was in there? You thought it was all perfectly innocent,' Mrs Hooper adds.

'I did, yes.' Joanna squeezes out a smile. 'But after I'd seen those photographs of his . . . and then him confessing what he'd done –' she sucks in air through her teeth – 'there was no way he was going to let me go.'

'But how can he have got away with it for all these years?' Mike quizzes. 'He'd have been the first person they'd have suspected, wouldn't he?'

'You're right, and it's not like the police didn't have him in for questioning enough times,' Mrs Hooper says. 'He can't have had an alibi, can he?'

'Liz told me there was some confusion about when Ellie actually died.' Joanna shares what she discovered a week or so before. 'Everyone knew she went missing early on the Saturday, but because me and Carrie didn't find her until the Tuesday, it was difficult to pinpoint the exact time.'

'More to do with her being found in fresh water, I should think. It must have been like keeping her in cold storage. Sad thing is,' Gordon pulls a face, 'there may well be ways to test the body temperature more accurately now, but not back then.'

'Talk about a muddied timeline – must've made it near on impossible for the cops to establish exactly where anyone was.' Mike rubs a hand over his stubble.

'And with all the evidence washed away.' Mrs Hooper, eyes downcast.

'It's why the police kept on at Dean,' Joanna says. 'With so little to go on, Carrie's claim about seeing him being rough to Ellie would have seemed pivotal.'

The room goes quiet, its occupants lost in private thought.

'I dread to think what would have happened to you,

Jo, if I hadn't phoned Gordon to say you were here.' Mrs Hooper is the first to speak. 'You were so keen to see her, weren't you, love? You drove from London as soon as you could.'

Gordon nods through the mellow glow of firelight.

'I'm so grateful.' Joanna tries not to cry. It hurts too much to cry.

'Anyway, like I said, he was a nasty bugger,' Mrs Hooper pipes up again. 'And to think he was happy to let the whole village blame his own son for Ellie's death.'

'Happy for the police, too,' Gordon adds. 'It was only by the skin of his teeth Dean was released.'

Another chorus of agreement.

'Liz as well, don't forget. Living as man and wife, lying to her all those years, letting her believe her stepson had done it. What kind of man does that?'

'A monster,' Gordon says gloomily.

'And all to protect his own scrawny arse,' Joanna affirms, before remembering her boys are within earshot. She flicks her eyes to Freddie and Ethan again, relieved to see them still engrossed in their game of Monopoly.

Lamplight leaches into what remains of the day as they sit on mismatched armchairs and sofas. To stop himself from dozing off, Mike gets up to rekindle the fire from a basket of hazel sticks.

'Freddie.' Joanna gets her son's attention. 'Be a darling, offer the chocolates round.'

'Oh, just the one. Thank you, dear.' Mrs Hooper plucks one and bites it clean in half.

Joanna takes a coffee cream herself, closes her eyes as it dissolves on her tongue.

'Gordon?' A slightly flushed Lillian jabs a finger in the direction of her study. 'Wasn't there something you wanted to show Joanna?'

'What? Now?' Gordon, dithering, looks unsure.

'Yes, now. I think we've all waited long enough, don't you?'

'Righty-o.' Gordon slips to his feet in one easy movement, as lithe as he ever was. 'Be back in a jiffy.'

Joanna pulls her eyes away from the *Sunday Times*. She doesn't turn the page, so doesn't see the photograph of Dean Fry as he looks today; doesn't read the article that would have provided further clarity to their conversation . . .

After nearly twenty-eight years, Dean Fry has broken his silence and spoken publicly for the first time about the murder of his stepsister, Ellie Fry. Raped and stabbed, Ellie disappeared on her 10th birthday, and her body was found three days later floating in a lake in woodland near her home in Witchwood, Gloucestershire. Dean Fry – 46, married with two daughters, a successful businessman now living in Weybridge – was 18 at the time. He talks openly about the case that made the headlines in August 1990, revealing his shock and revulsion at his father Ian Fry's confession of sexually abusing his stepdaughter, Ellie, and killing her because she threatened to tell.

Dean shares his own memories of the fretful nights he was held in police custody, and although eventually released without charge, how frightening it was to be accused of her murder. A tearful Dean says he's never forgotten Ellie, and talks of the shame and sorrow he still feels about being driven out of Witchwood.

'The little reputation I had,' he says, 'was destroyed overnight. I became someone the vengeful, angry community could vent their fury at and punish because they couldn't get their hands on the real killer.' Learning it was, in fact, his own father who killed Ellie – a father who was happy to stand by and watch his own son take the blame – is something Dean doubts he'll ever recover from. Ian Fry is also currently being questioned by police about Freya Wilburn, an eight-year-old girl who went missing from her home in Cinderglade, Gloucestershire, in 2014.

'What are you two up to?' Joanna gives a cautious smile at Lillian through the trembling firelight. 'D'you know, Mike?' she asks her husband, who has moved to the window to watch a blue tit wrestling with a fringe of crust on the bird table.

'No idea.' He picks up and puts down the conkers that have been lined up along the windowsill.

'Hang on. Only one moment more, he'll be back presently. I've been bursting to tell you.' Mrs Hooper licks chocolate from her fingers. 'He told me when you were in hospital last week, when he was worried you wouldn't pull through – but swore me to secrecy.'

What Gordon passes Joanna is a small pink envelope. Taking it, she turns it over in her hands. The letters of Mrs Hooper's address that begin their lives as neat and round, mutate into smudged, erratic shapes before reaching the opposite side.

'Open it,' Gordon encourages. 'It's a letter your mother sent me just before you and Carrie came to Witchwood that summer.'

'My mother?' Joanna doesn't understand. 'Why would my mother write to you?'

'We were friends. Good friends. Once upon a time. Read it, *please*. It'll explain everything.' And he sits beside her, in the gap Mike left behind on the couch.

'We came to Witchwood because ... because ...' Joanna looks up at him. 'I'm not sure I want to be reminded of all that again.'

'It's okay,' he reassures. 'I'm here.'

The letter is thin at the folds from where it's been read and reread. Joanna holds her breath as she scans her mother's words; words that begin with *Dear Gordon*, and snaking from left to right unsettle her. *I'm frightened ...* she reads:

... my children will be orphans after I've done this terrible thing, but I can't go on, I have to make the blackness stop. I know you'll understand, the shame I carry is too heavy, the lies I told a good man, a man who died loving me and the daughters he believed were both his own, is too much to bear. I'm only telling you this because my intention is to die today, but if I don't succeed, you must swear never to breathe a word of what I'm telling you to anyone. Joanna must not know that you are her real father, and that I lied to her, until I'm safely gone from this world.

Love, Imogen.

'Is it a horrible shock?' Gordon's expression is congested with concern.

Joanna can't speak.

'D'you understand what it means?'

'Well, I-I ... yes ... I suppose,' she answers eventually, her hands shaking.

'I didn't know how to tell you. Sworn to secrecy, I couldn't even risk telling Mum.'

'But my mother's been dead for two years.' Joanna, searching him with fresh eyes, still can't fathom it.

'I know, but it's taken me this long to pluck up the courage.' Gordon's hands, balanced on his knees, look as vulnerable as the heads of flowers. 'It was when I thought I'd lost you ... seeing you lying there, in that hospital bed ...' The feebleness of his explanation fizzles out.

'I can't take this in.' Her bruised face flushes. 'You said something at Carrie's funeral,' she says to Mrs Hooper. 'About that summer Mum came to stay with Dora before I was born. How friendly Gordon and Mum were. Was it then?' she asks, turning to Gordon. 'Did you two have an affair?'

Gordon bows his head and stares at his shoes. 'I didn't want to upset you; it hasn't, has it? I know it's a lot to take in, but I hope in time, you might be pleased.'

'I don't know what I am.' Joanna is thinking how adultery seems to be the overriding theme in this household. 'What you and my mother did, it obviously caused her a huge amount of stress and unhappiness ... read the letter, it's all in there.' She flaps the pink sheet of paper at him. 'She's so riddled with guilt, she thought killing herself was the only way out. Why didn't she just tell me? At least when

I got older. This *swearing you to secrecy* nonsense – that's her all over; so bloody selfish. What harm would it have done? The father I thought was mine had died.'

'I don't know what to say.' Gordon, still hanging his head.

'I bet you wish you'd not said anything now,' Mike says to lighten things. 'Come on, Jo-Go – it's a lot to take in, but it's not so bad. There's no need to get upset, not really.'

'I'm sorry, love,' Mrs Hooper addresses her son. 'But I'm on Jo's side with this. I'm an old woman – think of the years I've missed out on having my granddaughter.' Mrs Hooper passes Joanna a tissue. 'Try not to stress yourself, Jo. You've been through so much already.'

Mike puts an arm around his wife in an attempt to rally her. 'Yeah, but none of it's really Gordon's fault, is it? Not if Imogen made him promise.'

Joanna dabs the tender skin under her eyes. 'Yes, okay, but what am I supposed to do with the memories of a man I thought was my dad?' She drops her voice, gives way to further tears.

'Your mother wanted nothing to do with me beyond that summer.' Gordon squeezes his thin knees. 'But when she sent me that letter, telling me I had a daughter, and then actually *meeting* you ... ' He pauses, struggling to supress his own emotion. 'It was the hardest thing not to tell you.'

'Carrie used to think you were creepy.' Joanna blinks through wet lashes. 'The way you used to follow us around as kids.'

A tight laugh. 'Did she? I suppose it could have looked like that. But if I followed you around it was only to keep an eye on you. Bit overprotective, I know,' he admits, almost an apology. 'Probably because of what happened to my sister.'

The room goes quiet. Gordon, awkward, looks at his shoes again. The only sound is the crackling flames in the hearth.

Mike exhales into the general bewilderment. 'Well, that's quite something to get your head around, isn't it, boys?'

Abandoning their game, Freddie and Ethan spin their heads to him. Open-mouthed, the concern clouding their young faces isn't about what's been going on, neither have fully grasped that. Their worry is for their mother, who has suddenly turned a deathly pale.

'What's wrong with Mummy?' Freddie, up on his feet, Ethan close on his heels, whispers his fear at his father's elbow. 'She isn't going to have to go back to the hospital, is she?'

Lost in thought, Joanna doesn't hear her child. 'It's like I've been hit by a train ... *another train*. Honestly, I don't know what I'm supposed to do with all this.' She leans back and shuts her eyes.

'It's quite a shock,' Mike says, his arms around his sons. 'But we've had worse, haven't we, Jo?'

Joanna opens her eyes to him, gives the suggestion of a smile. 'Certainly been a pretty eventful few months. I didn't think there could be any more surprises.'

Meanwhile in Bayswater . . .

'They say that, don't they?' Kyle Norris murmurs to himself as he stands outside the 24-Seven store along Queensway. 'About always returning to the scene of the crime.' A little chuckle. 'Talk about a stroke of luck – or a stroke of the knife, more like.'

He assesses his reflection in the shop window. Sweeps a hand through his Jim Morrison-style hair. Took a bit of cultivating to look just like his dad did in 1990, but worth the trouble, though. He grins at himself. It had been great fun tormenting her, especially with her falling for it hook line and sinker. Mad bitch. All he wanted to do was shake her up a bit, he didn't think she'd react as violently as she did, but the first time she set eyes on him, the way it put the shits up her – it's what gave him the idea. She was in a state already, even before he did anything; the shabby bag of laundry was putty in his hands.

So, he thinks, stepping aside to allow a mother pushing a buggy inside the shop, *she* was traumatised by what happened in her childhood, was she? Should've had his fucking childhood then. Brought up by that bastard, passing himself off as his dad. And the way he treated his mum – because she'd have had a far better time of things if she'd been able to be with the man she loved, the father of her child. And it was all that bitch's fault. *Poor Caroline*. She was the reason why his real dad wasn't in his life. Those lies she told, trashing his reputation so badly he was kicked out of his home, from the village where he lived . . . Kyle found all this out when he traced his real father last year – discovering it by accident, not that it came as much of a surprise; Kyle always knew he wasn't anything to do with that bastard Philip Norris – and when Dean filled him in on what that Caroline had done, the shit she caused, well, she couldn't be allowed to get away with it, could she?

And finding himself living just around the corner from her, boy, that was a fluke and a half . . . or as he likes to think of it: an omen. It couldn't have been easier, the woman was already a shambles, it took bugger all to push her over the edge. Talk about a crunchy nut cornflake . . . Thinking, what? That his dad, Dean, hadn't aged a day since 1990, and had come back to get her? But she wasn't so crazy in other ways, was she? She knew exactly what she'd done, and it was her own guilt that made her scared. And after their initial encounter, it was simple. Bit of psychological torture, as long as she noticed him – which he made damn sure she did, at every possible opportunity. Kyle enjoyed stalking her through the park, around Bayswater, to the hospital and back. Even the odd silent phone call in the early hours just to put the boot well and truly in. Seeing photographs of his real dad and how he used to look in those days, it was easy for Kyle to model himself on him when he looks so like him anyway. Wearing rock band T-shirts and a nice-fitting pair of Levi's was no problem.

Driven by a desire to make that woman's life as shit as his has been, the very worst Kyle thought he could do by hanging around, turning up unexpectedly and taunting her, was to make her totally lose the plot. He didn't even know the fat cow was going to be out on that particular night, he'd not seen her for weeks – so that was a bonus. He'd only popped in there for a pint of milk. And there she was. A trolley full of sweets and chocolates. He couldn't resist terrorising her some more, could he? A cold night, too. He had his leather bike jacket on, and he supposes it just about tipped the scales. She must have thought he was Dean and that Dean was coming to get her. The knife was a bit of a shock, though, not that it took Kyle much to guide it in the right direction. And, as it turns out, being caught on CCTV did him a favour. He was hailed as the victim ... to the various witnesses, the police, it was him being attacked by some random nutter. Something even her own sister believes. Yeah, a nice touch, that.

'Ho-hum. What goes around, comes around, don't they say?' Kyle continues to talk to himself, as he steps into the 24-Seven store. 'I think I'll just grab myself a pint of milk.'